CW08541196

DON'T
TALK

DON'T TALK

A JAN MASON STORY

IAN RIDLEY

60 Verulam Road
St Albans
Herts
AL3 4DH
www.v-books.co.uk

Twitter: @VBooks10
Facebook: vbooks10
Instagram: vbookspublishing

Cover design by Steve Leard
Cover image by Alex Ridley
Typeset by seagulls.net

ISBN: 978-1-7396396-1-7

For Vikki.

Though lovers be lost, love shall not.

A woman is like a tea bag.
You never know how strong she is
until you put her in hot water.

Eleanor Roosevelt

SUNDAY

1

THE DOCUMENT was staring at her, daring her to sign. And it was so tempting. Especially at this time of night. And with the bottle of red in its drained state. She lifted it from the coffee table and raised it to her eye level, closing one and focussing with the other to gauge whether she might just squeeze one more glass out of it. Hard to tell with its dregs slooshing from side to side. Maybe. She shouldn't make a decision just now. Not like this. But she'd been putting it off for a month and had to decide by Friday. After a day off walking in Hyde Park she'd reasoned that perhaps a few drinks would help speed up the process. If a clear head hadn't worked, maybe *in vino veritas* would be a better strategy.

Let's weigh up those pros and cons again, Jan thought. First and foremost, the money they were offering. A year's salary. Not bad. Particularly as she was now the highest paid news reporter on the paper. Or, get her, Chief Reporter at Large. She'd be able to pay off what was left of the mortgage on this flat with half of it. Then she'd quite literally have something concrete to show for her career. A two-bedroomed flat in Maida Vale. Not bad. She'd bought when the area was still relatively cheap and could make a good profit if she fell on hard times.

It would also allow her to take some time to rethink her life and what she was going to do with it now. People did that when they got to their fifties, right? She could travel to all those places she'd fantasised about for years: Machu Picchu, the Iguazu Falls,

Ayer's Rock. And Wakefield. Yes, she could see more of her mother. Suddenly the mellowness of her mood was punctured. Seeing more of her mother. Should that be a pro or a con, she wondered, and smiled.

Maybe after a month or two's jet-setting, she could set herself up as freelance. She still had a good name in the business. A big name, even. Reporter of the Year in the British Newspaper Awards when she'd been one step ahead of the police in catching the man who had burned five people to death with a flamethrower at the Central London Mosque just after the London Olympics.

The London Olympics. My God. A whole decade ago, she thought. Really? A melancholy came over her to which only *Who Knows Where the Time Goes* by Sandy Denny would do justice and she called it up on her Spotify. It had been a while, she had to admit as the haunting song came through her Sonos speaker, since the words BY JAN MASON had had all the other media scrambling to follow up what was written beneath it. The game had changed even more, too. Much more being tied down to a desk, rewriting. More "churnalism", fewer staff. She'd continued to be professional, turning a few decent tales, about a philandering politician or a human interest special on a missing child, but nothing that had made quite the same impact as that inspired and painstaking work to track down the ex-squaddie now serving life for murdering those innocent Muslims. Nothing where she'd been the one breaking the news, setting the agenda.

She'd had a good run, she told herself. She'd known the best days of what was once called Fleet Street, loved the cut and thrust, savoured the sounds and smells of the newsroom that were gone for good. She'd done her best to fight the good fight for the ethics and values of print against the wild west of the internet – ink versus link, as she'd seen it called in the crime thriller set in the world of newspapers that she was reading, *Betty Boo* by Claudia Pineiro. But she'd seen, felt, her combativeness wane. She'd embraced the new technology, could see its value in the divulgence of fingertip information, as well as supplying instant songs and dating website faces to be rejected, but she still had no love for its exclusion of the human touch.

And how much longer could she keep up her side of the battle against the news editor Ivan Vickers, known amongst the reporters as TGV – That Gobshite Vickers? He hated her elevated status on the paper that was deserved no longer, he reckoned. Too big for her boots that should be a lot smaller these days. That was the word that came back to her anyway. Then there was the fact that the editor with whom Jan had come up through the ranks, and who had given her the current role, was gone, to be replaced by a bright young thing from the group's London evening paper. And once a new editor came in with a mandate to make changes, anything could happen. Vickers was clearly biding his time, awaiting his moment to strike.

So it was best, Jan reckoned, to get her retaliation in first. To go on her terms rather than be beaten by Vickers and suffer a humiliating exit. If she didn't take voluntary redundancy this time around, it would probably be compulsory next time. And she'd be first in line as a high-earner when youngsters who did what they were told and were more tech-savvy came so much cheaper. The terms wouldn't be this good again. And while freelancing was a rough old world, with too many ex-staffers chasing too little work, she would have the reputation and financial cushion to soften the landing. Given her status, she might even secure a column somewhere.

Let's not forget finally having time to sustain a relationship, she then considered. She might actually meet someone in person, on a holiday or at a social event, rather than all this desperate faffing around online. Even doing that, it had been a while since she'd found someone she liked and then none that had lasted more than a couple of evening dinners and regretted nights together.

She looked back – what, sixteen, seventeen years? – to the needy, needs-must relationship that she'd had with Frank Phillips, a police contact she'd used too literally, as positively stable.

'I have no fear of time,' sang Sandy, to a "yeah right" before Jan stopped the music. In the background, the soundless TV picture was flashing out the opening titles of the BBC News. She leant forward from the sofa and commanded volume from the remote. The lead story was about a vote in Westminster that would be taking place tomorrow. New immigration bill. She recognised the far right figure on screen offering a soundbite in the taster headlines about the country needing to look after its own. How come Peter Carew looked so distinguished but sounded so crass? *The people's politician, my arse,* she thought. She was more concerned about what a weak lead this was, though. Even for a Sunday night, leading on some Westminster vote that was going to happen tomorrow, however important the issue, was dull stuff. Couldn't anybody find a story any more? A proper one. *News is people*, she always remembered from her training. A juicy murder that resonated with the public, maybe. A series of them, perhaps.

She signed the document that had gone from staring to winking at her and she would hand it in to Human Resources when she started her late shift tomorrow. It would be day one of a new life. But first tonight, Sunday-bored, she'd finish the bottle. Definitely one last glass left in there.

MONDAY

2

FRANK would look back and remember in detail the exact words the guy spoke that night. They would return to him insistently like an earworm from a catchy pop song, well beyond the sleepless hours that would torment him through that coming night. And just when he thought he'd heard everything in this room, or rooms like it, and knew how to handle it all.

'I might have been in what you people call blackout... I may need to go to the police... I think I might have killed her.'

The meeting of Alcoholics Anonymous had proceeded like any other here before *he* had arrived. The crypt of the church was its usual dingy self, at its centre a candlelit circle of plastic chairs ready to embrace a set of souls in need of shelter from their solitary storms.

Frank stirred the one spoonful of sugar that was the legacy of his lingering craving for sweetness into his cracked mug of tea and took his seat. He always liked the one nearest a door, just in case. His police training had taught him to look for an exit in the event of emergency. He'd always done that anyway, needing an escape route as all his failed past relationships had confirmed. It had all been very messy with Jan during that once-upon-a-time of his drinking when they'd been ports in a storm for each other and it had left him with a legacy in his sobriety of being a bolter when it came to getting close to women.

The new guy in the group, Sean, wiry and wary, was already seated, next to his friend Aesha. Neighbours in South London,

Frank had discovered last week, the one in his late twenties, the other early twenties. This was just Sean's second week since quitting the drink after nervously communicating his desire, even need, to stop at his first meeting this time last week. Recognising him despite the dimness, Frank shot him a smile as he settled into the unyielding chair and Sean smiled weakly back.

'How you doing this week?' Frank asked.

'Fine,' he replied. 'Yeah, fine thanks.'

'You do know the letters of fine stands for fearful, insecure, neurotic and exhausted,' Frank said.

Aesha, more at ease as someone who had been coming to the meeting for a few months, placed her hand on Sean's knee and laughed loudly. 'Then, I for one am genuinely fine,' she said.

'OK, me too,' said Sean, a jittery tone to his voice, clearly grateful to be given permission to say how he really felt.

'Welcome to our club,' Frank replied. 'I've been coming for fifteen years and I still feel like that some days.'

'Wow. Fifteen years,' Sean said with the awe of the newcomer, before a thought came to him. 'And you still have bad times like the rest of us?'

'It will get better,' Frank replied. 'But you won't become completely immune to all the feelings that brought you here. If you do stick around, though, you'll learn ways to cope with the bad days without the need to get pissed.'

Sean half-smiled again, just as the meeting's secretary Roberto, a city trader known in the meetings as Italian Bob, banged an empty tin on the coffee table in front of him to signal the 7.30pm start time.

'Welcome everybody to the Monday night meeting of the Blandford Road group of Alcoholics Anonymous,' he said. 'My name is Bob and I am an alcoholic.'

'Hi Bob,' the meeting chorused.

In a mature, authoritative voice, Bob read the preamble, about AA being a fellowship of men and women who share their experience, strength and hope in an attempt to solve their common problem and help others to recover from alcoholism. The only requirement for AA membership, he added, was a desire to stop drinking.

He then called upon Erroll, a stalwart of the group in his early forties, to read the Twelve Steps before handing over to the woman sitting next to him who was tonight's "chair", the speaker who was to address the gathering.

'My name is Jennifer and I am an alcoholic,' she announced.

'Hi Jennifer,' came the customary reassuring and welcoming unison from the other five people in the room. Tonight was a quiet meeting. It was a cold, rainy and forbidding November night outside and the traffic for a televised Premier League football match a mile or so away at Chelsea had deterred a few.

Jennifer summed up her drinking – 'I drank too much, too often, for too long,' – before delivering the detail that newcomers always needed so they could check themselves out and identify with the other people here. Or decide they weren't as bad as these people. That detail told of secret stashes, amounts consumed; whether it was beer, wine or spirits.

Twenty minutes in, she'd switched from her drunkalogue to the change that her two years of abstinence had brought about, describing her improvement as a mother of two young kids, when the somnolent, safe and serene atmosphere was suddenly interrupted. The handle of the main door clanked and the heavy portal creaked.

All heads turned to see a man pause in the threshold to take in the scene. Almost reluctantly, but knowing it needed to be done, he closed the door behind him and took a few steps towards the centre of the room. He waited again, as if having second thoughts.

'Come in. We don't bite,' said Italian Bob, adding quickly, 'Any more.' The room laughed to ease their own tension and offer encouragement to the man to take the half a dozen or so more paces to the circle and one of the half dozen vacant chairs in the circle.

It was a man. They could make that out at least as he moved slowly towards the candlelight. Perhaps in his mid to late thirties, maybe even forty. Drink ages people. A few strands of hair escaped from a hoodie he was wearing under a black puffer jacket and his dark facial hair was somewhere between heavy stubble and unkempt beard. He had on black jeans and, incongruously, expensive suede boots. Frank would remember those later. When you sit at an AA meeting, looking down at the floor deep in thought as people tell their stories, you tend to notice their shoes.

The man stood still for a moment before Frank rose from his seat and walked over to him.

'Can I get you a tea?' Frank whispered and the man nodded, looking down the whole time. Frank guided him towards the hatch of the crypt's kitchen, where he retreated from the pool of light, as if a wild animal confronted by fire, and Jennifer finished up her talk. About how she realised these days that she was good enough, as a person and in her job, and no longer needed to be the perfectionist who always fell short, and then into a bottle as a result.

'I need to be real and not ideal,' she said, to nods of recognition.

Frank returned with the mug-carrying man behind him, still hanging his head in what Frank surmised was shame, and sat him down. The guy was clearly agitated. He sipped the tea with hands shaking around the mug. To Frank, he looked to be in that state of internal conflict of everyone in their early days in AA went through – wanting to flee but knowing he needed to stay.

Bob the secretary thanked Jennifer for her talk, picked up on several statements that had resonated with him and opened the meeting for "sharing". One by one they spoke, at varying stages and ages of recovery and articulacy, telling of their day and the state of their lives currently. The good and the bad, the gratitude, the fear, the anger, the shame and the joy.

After a while, there was just one person left who hadn't spoken. The silence in the room endured for a minute or so, its tension heightened by the dimness, before the secretary became the one who felt the responsibility to fill it the most keenly.

'Would you like to tell us your name?' Bob asked.

The man looked up, then around, now aware that he was the one being spoken to. He shook his head.

'Anything at all you'd like to share with us?' There was another pause before Bob added: 'This is a safe place.'

The man drew in a deep breath and began.

'I don't know where to start,' he said, his voice well-spoken but trembling. 'I think I need to stop drinking.' His eyes darted around the room. Nodding heads urged him on.

'She keeps on at me about my drinking. Or used to keep on. I'm not sure what comes, or came, first. Me drinking and her on my case or her on my case and me drinking.'

Sean laughed nervously but quickly stopped when the man fell abruptly silent. Sean could feel, if barely see, a glare piercing the half-light.

'She took up with another man,' the guy added after a moment. 'I got very drunk. I might have been in what you people call blackout, I think... I may need to go to the police. Or not. I don't know.'

There was a long pause. His audience, rapt and silent, had by now been taken hostage by his story.

'Either way, whatever came first,' he continued slowly. 'I think I might have killed her.'

He looked around the room again. This time there were no nods. All he could make out was the whites of a series of stunned eyes.

'Or maybe I'm just going mad,' he added.

Having shocked them verbally, the man now stunned them physically by rising quickly from his seat and rushing for the door. The swift clank of the handle and the squealing of its hinges contrasted with the slower, tortuous noises of his entry.

His copper's instincts kicking in after the initial surprise, Frank leapt up to follow him and ran through the open door, up the steps from the crypt and into the darkness of the West London street.

There was no sign of the man, however. Stalled by his astonishment, Frank had taken those few seconds too long to react. He scanned the pavements for a second, up towards Fulham Road and down towards the King's Road. Empty. He heard a roar from Stamford Bridge in the distance, before finally descending back into the meeting.

The numbed silence of the room that Frank had left was now a chatter of voices on his return, wondering what the hell had just happened. They stopped when he appeared.

'Nothing. He's disappeared,' said Frank.

'Well, there's still five minutes left of the meeting,' said Bob, a tremor in his voice, trying to restore protocol to a meeting unlike any that any one of them had ever attended before, no matter the length of their sobriety. 'Shall we sit down?'

Once they had gradually retaken their seats, Bob asked if anybody had anything else they wanted to share.

'Plenty,' said Frank. 'But maybe after we've wound up the meeting, eh?'

Bob nodded and passed an empty mug around the room for donations towards rent, tea and coffee. The men jangled the change in their pockets to find a pound coin. The women reached down into their handbags for their purses. All seemed to be moving in slow motion, the reverberations of the stranger's words still hanging in the air.

Once the mug had been returned to the table in front of him, Bob wrapped up the meeting.

'One final thing,' he said. 'Can I remind everyone of the importance of what this says.' He held up, in the light of a candle, a yellow card bearing a slogan in black capital letters. It had been sitting on the table in front of him, facing the meeting, throughout the last hour. It read:

WHO YOU SEE HERE
WHAT YOU HEAR HERE
WHEN YOU LEAVE HERE
LET IT STAY HERE

3

JAN swiped left after left on her dating app to pass the time. It had been a while since she'd swiped right. The last time she did, she'd engaged the guy in a conversation only for him to back off pretty quickly once he found out she was a journalist. Mind you, he'd only just beaten her to it. She was ready to terminate the conversation at the next boast about how much he made as a city trader.

Waiting for Mr. Right was not an option for Jan, mainly because she was old enough and wise enough to know there was no such person. She'd worked that out, what, at least fifteen years ago after realising that she and Frank had been ships in the night rather than the soulmates she'd hoped for. She stayed on the dating app for the reason many people seemed to believe in a God, a tinge of faith that grew with age. Just in case there was something in it.

'Nothing decent on the menu tonight?' came a voice behind her. Jan hastily shut off her phone and turned to see Sarah Joyce, the deputy news editor, behind her, buttoning her coat and ready to leave for the evening to go home to her lovely young bloke who worked as a fitness instructor and their sweet toddler of a son.

'Don't worry, I won't tell,' said Sarah and smiled. Jan, busted, couldn't help smiling back. She got on well with Sarah, who had been at the paper just six months and was a breath of youthful fresh air.

'So, keep your voice down then,' said Jan, whispering. 'I don't want him knowing.' Her eyes darted towards Ivan Vickers some ten yards away. The news editor was like Jan only in not having anyone to go home to, so often stayed on late. But she didn't want him knowing anything about her private life, even if there wasn't much of one. Any knowledge was power over her.

'So, did you hand in the redundancy papers?' Sarah asked, her voice now lowered.

'Um. No. There was nobody in HR when I went and I didn't want to just leave it on a desk.'

'Right. Well, you know I wish you wouldn't, don't you?'

'I know. But I've thought it through now,' said Jan. 'Worked it all out last night. I'll put it in tomorrow.'

'Great shame, Jan. They don't make reporters like you any more.'

Jan thanked her and Sarah departed, leaving Jan to go back to the waiting game that she often played at this time of an evening on the news desk, scrolling through the websites. In the old days, she would have been impatient for the first editions to drop. These days, she was just killing time until 10pm when the national newspaper sites started carrying the stories that would lead the printed versions tomorrow. Stories the executives insisted they had to release tonight to satisfy the rolling news lust that they were sure was out there – beyond TV and radio stations waiting to follow it all up, that was. Waiting for the arrival of stories that might possibly be worth filching was soulless, hack work but it had to be done.

The trademark Vickers bark interrupted the lull that always descended at this time of day. The paper's first edition had been put to bed, most reporters had left their desks in the news room – or their work stations in the hub, in modern parlance – leaving just a few duty staff seeing out time on their shifts, as Jan and some sub-editors were doing now. Once, there would have been change after change to editions with late-breaking stories but cost-cutting meant fewer staff and fewer page changes. Besides, the website could monitor anything beyond midnight. The major vote going on in the House of Commons on the bill to tighten immigration laws was being handled by the politics guys in the Westminster press room. Only Sport, down the end of the editorial floor, was still busy here with anything live. She could see a few blokes with their feet up on the desks watching the Chelsea game.

'Anything?' Vickers demanded.

'Nothing yet,' Jan replied.

To the younger reporters, Vickers remained a fearsome, snarling figure; a man who made daily life a dance on burning coals and who had a habit of ruining evening plans by sending those he wanted to punish out on wild goose chases. Some years back, after a young female reporter whom he'd fancied had told him that she was going to the theatre with her boyfriend that night, he'd promptly sent her to doorstep a couple whose young daughter had been murdered in Lowestoft.

He'd had to give up pulling stunts like that on Jan after the Mosque murders story. It had been brilliant, old-fashioned legwork, hitting the streets, using all her contacts inside Scotland Yard, following leads. Going where the story led her. She'd also given the editor, and even the paper's proprietor, a memorable moment in their lives at that Park Lane hotel as they basked in the glory of their dominant mid-market tabloid winning News-paper Front Page and Website of the Year.

And, transcending peer envy, she'd also earned the grat-itude of all the traditionalists in the profession who still believed in the time-honoured skills of cultivating contacts and chasing tales, rather than tails. Amid the daily grind of "content-providing" from press releases and stories robbed and recycled from other media outlets, she'd struck a blow for journalism, indeed. This at a time when the old Leveson report, phone-hacking and more rabid political posturing against the written press had seen a sharp decline in trust – and sales – of newspapers. The big pay rise and the promotion had also been gratifying, she couldn't deny that.

As a result of her spell without a jaw-dropper of a tale though, Jan knew from conversations over drinks with other reporters, and Sarah, that Vickers was sensing a chink in her armour. Time had told her that with his practiced nose of a print industry predator, he could smell vulnerability. She'd overheard him in the pub telling Sarah that he hated big-time reporters. Not as pliant as the youngsters. Jan knew he wanted her taken down a peg or two. He'd even quietly told Sarah to suggest to Jan that she'd be doing herself a favour by taking the redundancy package.

'Worth a couple of calls to see if anything's happening?' Vickers enquired reasonably enough but with a passive-aggressive subtext, as opposed to the more usual aggressive-aggressive that he felt at liberty to use on the less favoured. Once upon a time, when she was still a rookie Yorkshire lass come up to the smoke to try her luck, and still to anyone junior to her currently, it would have been: 'Well, make some fucking calls then.'

She picked up her mobile and hit the button for the Metropolitan Police press office. Danielle, the junior only to be expected on the other end of the phone at this time of night, picked up.

'Hi Jan,' she said. 'What's happening?'

'Thought you might tell me.'

'Very quiet,' said Danielle. 'We like cold, damp nights with football on the telly keeping everyone indoors.'

'Come on Danielle. Must be something going on. Please tell me there is. Unlike you, I hate quiet nights.'

'You know you'll get something via the wires or a press release when there's anything you need to know.'

Jan's hackles rose. Danielle would be aware that she was meant to show civility to such a senior reporter from an influential newspaper but Jan sensed less respect in her tone than Jan's track record deserved. Or perhaps it was Jan's paranoia as the fear of becoming yesterday's hero was insinuating itself into her more and more. This redundancy must be preying on her mind more than she'd realised.

'Danielle. That is the sort of standard reply you give others. This is Janet Mason you're talking to. Darling of the Met? Remember?' She hoped Danielle did, or at least that somebody had related the legend.

'You know we can't be too cosy these days, Jan, be fair. Not since Leveson. Give me a break.'

'Well, I'll be very nice about you to your boss if you find anything decent,' Jan said.

There was a pause on the end of the phone as Danielle pondered.

'There might be something.' she said.

'Yes, go on…'

'No real details but there has been a call-out to a possible serious crime at an address in Chelsea.'

Jan's ears pricked up. She looked up from her doodle and across at Vickers.

'OK…'

'A neighbour phoned in having heard what she thought might have been a scream. An old lady. Uniform found a young-ish woman dead in a ground floor flat.'

'Dead as in murdered?'

'We're not sure yet. But could be.'

"Could be" was good enough for Jan but it was the "address in Chelsea" part that made her sit up. The paper would always cover murder, like any other media outlet, but there were murders and murders. As distasteful as it might sound, there was no getting away from it: her Middle England readers were by and large more interested in high-end, aspirational rather than council estate. In any human interest news event, the first question on the editorial floor of a mid-market tabloid was always "How much is the house worth?" If the victim was attractive, so much the better. A weariness of such cynicism these days was part of her redundancy considerations but then again, anyone's death triggered her instincts to tell their story.

Jan got the address from Danielle and cut short the call. Her mobile pinged again straight away. Someone had swiped right on her dating profile. She ignored it, muttering "not now".

Then came the ringtone. Her brother Robert's name and face appeared on her screen. She was in two minds about answering but work, more specifically the lure of a tale, won out. Easily. Anyway, he was probably only ringing for a catch-up, as they did once a week, about this time of night, often on a boring Monday night. Unless it was about Mum. But she couldn't deal with that now. She would ring him tomorrow night. She hit the "decline" icon.

'Got to go,' she said to Vickers, closing her laptop, stuffing it into her voluminous blush pink leather shoulder bag – hard to lose, easy for people to remember her – and walked over to a stand to retrieve her prized Burberry raincoat. But not too eagerly so as not to overexcite him.

'What you got?' he asked.

'Not sure yet. I'll let you know if it turns into anything.'

'What about the desk? I've not got a duty reporter now?'

'I'm sure there's people you can ring if anything breaks,' she said as she put on her coat. 'People whose lives you can ruin like you used to do mine.'

'You can't just piss off, Jan.'

'Oh I think I can. My title is still Chief Reporter At Large,' she replied as she disappeared towards the lift in the centre of the glassy Thamesside building's atrium.

Something had kicked in – old instincts, adrenalin – and the scent of a story was in her nostrils. It might be nothing, but then, she told herself, no ticket, no lottery win. If she was going to go down, albeit with a sizeable redundancy payment as consolation, she was at least going to be remembered as going down with guns blazing.

4

THE DRINKS, Frank said in an attempt to ease the tension as silence descended again, would be on him. He was aware of the bad-old-days irony of the phrase and it elicited weak smiles from the other five.

Usually, they were all out of the crypt within 10 minutes, having counted the money, tidied away the books and leaflets, put the chairs back where they'd found them and completed the washing-up. Tonight, though, the six AA members there who'd started and finished a meeting shocked to its core by the bombshell delivered by the mystery man, had not felt able even to begin those tasks after Italian Bob had closed the meeting. They'd been split between those who sat shaking heads, lost in thought, and those who chattered in their nervousness, seeking to make sense of the episode and torn between what they should do next. Now all were pensively quiet again.

Frank's suggestion of coffee in that little cafe on the King's Road that stayed open till 11 received a mixed reception. Jennifer and Erroll felt compelled to go straight home to their partners and young children. Both were motivated by what followed a shock, be that bad medical news, sadness or danger: the lure of loved ones and the sanctuary of home. The other four who were single wanted company too, reluctant to return to the aloneness of their flats. So Bob, Aesha and Sean agreed to the cafe with Frank once the mundane tasks of closing up were completed and Bob had locked up.

Together, the four walked the couple of hundred yards to the cafe in lonely thoughts as yet unspoken but bubbling intensely beneath the surface. Collars and hoods were turned up against the damp and chill. Once inside, they took a table in the corner, as far as possible from the two other people finishing up their drinks. There was a difficult discussion to be had and subconsciously they all knew that privacy was preferable.

Frank went to the counter to order from Enzo and they exchanged the usual warm greetings, the two of them well known to each other after all these years, each valuing the other's small but meaningful contribution to their lives, one to his till, the other to his sobriety.

Frank liked Enzo's. He had come to know in his years of not drinking that it was in coffee bars like this all over the country, almost as much as in the meetings themselves, that drunks got sober. In the rooms of AA, there were boundaries and ground rules that worked well. You didn't interrupt people when they were speaking or give them advice unless asked after the meeting. You certainly didn't judge them or point out where they were going wrong, as often happened in pubs where the later in the evening, and the more the drink that had been consumed, the less people listened to each other and simply conducted their own monologues. In coffee bars, you could be more expansive after meetings, share dialogue rather than simply say your piece.

Frank stood at the counter waiting for the drinks he'd ordered and looked across at his three companions. Bob wanted a latte. A tea for Aesha, a single mum raising a baby over the bridge in Battersea and who was determined to make the most of her babysitter. And a Sprite for her friend Sean. He needed the sugar, he'd said, offering a brief smile. He looked edgy but Frank just put it down to the nervousness of the newcomer, the fizzy drink an example of the craving of the newly dry. Frank bought a mineral water for himself.

Aesha had it particularly tough out of all of them, Frank reckoned. He'd seen it before. When the disgrace of actually owning up to the alcoholism was almost more shameful than being an active alcoholic. That could be glossed over and covered up most of the time. But it was the knowledge of a drink problem, amongst a strict family and wider community, even if it was being solved, that so often upset them.

An old joke he liked came to Frank's mind, about two people standing over a grave at a funeral.

'What did he die of?' asked the first.

'The demon drink,' said the second.

'Did he not go to AA?'

'Oh no. He was never that bad.'

Frank set the drinks down on the table before the silent three. 'So,' he ventured. 'What does everyone think about what just happened back there and more importantly what are we going to do about it?'

'I thought we weren't supposed to discuss anything we saw or heard,' Sean said. He had a point, as the glance between Frank and Bob, the two with the longest clean time among the four of them, confirmed.

'I think we'd be less than human if we didn't want to process what we heard with safe people,' said Bob.

'What about that yellow card? You know, about not passing on what we'd seen and heard in the meeting?' Aesha asked.

'Well,' said Frank. 'I think it means that it's a complete no-no talking about anyone or anything that goes on at a meeting with outsiders and the general public but we have to be able to discuss issues and feelings raised at meetings among ourselves if we are to help each other.'

'OK…' said Sean, intoning it with scepticism the way the young did. He was twitchy. Frank put it down again to the doubts of someone out of his comfort zone, who had been to only his second meeting and was still learning the ropes, the nuances of this organisation.

'I think,' added Bob. 'We also have a duty as citizens. If a crime has been committed, we have to examine our consciences, to check it out with others. And to decide what to do.'

'Is a meeting not like the confessional box for a priest, though?' Aesha wondered.

'That is precisely it,' said Frank. 'That's what we have to decide. I mean, I for one have never been in this position before. But the overriding consideration here is that if we think this is something that has some truth behind it, we have to consider the wider implications. About catching a murderer.'

'You're speaking like a copper now, Frank,' Bob said.

'You police?' Sean asked, a snap in his voice.

'I work in counter-terrorism,' Frank replied quickly.

'Oh right.' Sean began to tap the floor with his foot and to fidget with the drinks can.

'You have a problem with the police, Sean?'

'No. Well, maybe. I haven't always found them, shall we say, helpful.'

'Want to tell me more?'

Sean shook his head and took a glug of his Sprite.

'That bloke. He gave me the creeps,' he said. 'I've seen and heard people like him before.'

Frank started to smile.

Sean noticed. 'Sorry, this ain't funny,' he said. He rocked forward and back in his chair.

'Of course it's not. It wasn't funny in the meeting either when the bloke shared about someone being on his case and you laughed. I get that it was nervousness. I was just trying to identify with you. I've seen and heard plenty at AA like that too...'

Frank was about to try and explain himself better but Sean was spooked. 'Coppers and murder confessions. This is doing my head in,' he said. 'I'm out of here.' He leapt up with a screech of the chair on the tiled floor and made a dash for the door.

Frank chased after him, catching the door as it was closing behind him. When he reached the street, however, it was full of blue and white scarves lamenting loudly the manager's team choice and a striker who couldn't have hit a cow's arse with a banjo. Chelsea had obviously lost and Sean had been swallowed up in the sea of their angry supporters.

Aesha followed not far behind Bob and the two stood in the threshold.

'Let him go,' she said. 'I'll catch him up. We get the same bus home.' She smiled at Frank and headed out into the tide of replica Chelsea shirts poking out from beneath unzipped quilted jackets.

Frank nodded and returned to the table.

'Shit, shit, shit,' he said.

'You're not having a good night catching people, are you, Frank P?' said Bob. 'Hope you're better than this in your job. For all our sakes.'

Frank couldn't help but laugh, if not loudly, nor long.

'He's obviously got stuff going on with him,' Bob added. 'Nothing we can do about that for now. Maybe when he comes back to a meeting…'

'If he comes back,' said Frank. 'I've put him off. Some induction to AA this is.'

'You don't have that power to put him off,' said Bob. 'We obviously touched a nerve and he's got things to work out on his own.'

'I should never have talked about what I do.'

'It was me that mentioned you sounding like a copper. Apologies.'

'Guess he would have found out sooner or later anyway.'

'We're bound to come from all types of backgrounds,' said Bob. 'That's the nature of this illness. It's a great leveller, that's for sure.

Anyway, if we've driven him away, the booze will drive him back. Maybe he's just looking for a reason to go out and drink again.'

Frank nodded, though he wasn't so sure. Once he might have been. These days he was more at peace with himself, certainly a different man from the detective who would have been well stuck into a bottle of scotch by now after a hard day at the Yard and on the streets of the capital. Possibly in those days in tandem with Jan. He'd liked it that when they'd reconnected during that Regent's Park episode that had worked out so well for them both ten years ago they seemed more settled in their respective lives.

Not that he felt settled tonight. The meeting, what the stranger said, and Sean's reaction and exit had thrown everything into turmoil within him. A growing anxiety was gnawing at him and he was in rare conflict with himself. It was a three-sided conflict too: between law enforcement officer, AA member and citizen.

'So what do we do?' Frank said.

'About Sean?'

'No, the bloke who came into the meeting half way through.'

There was a moment of silence.

'What do you think we should do? What can we do?' Bob asked. 'I mean, let's go over again what actually there is in this? He said he was in blackout... He said he didn't know what he'd done.'

'Bob, he talked about having killed someone.'

'He said he *may* have done. He also said he might be going mad. To be honest, he didn't make a lot of sense. And you know what drunks are like when they're still drinking. Do you reckon he'd been on the sauce? He didn't sound too much as if he had, but then he didn't say much, did he? You got closer to him than anyone. Did he smell like he had been?'

'I thought I picked up a whiff of something but it wasn't overwhelming,' said Frank, adding after a pause: 'What do you mean, "You know what drunks are like?"'

'Unreliable. Liars. Attention-seekers. You don't remember?'

He smiled at Frank, who smiled back as if memories were coming to him.

'Well, even if it's all messy and sketchy, we ought to take it to the police. Just in case there is anything in it,' said Frank.

'Take what to them exactly?' Bob wondered. 'A confidential share, which we don't know whether to believe or not, about a crime that we don't know has been committed? I mean, they don't even investigate burglaries these days. Crimes that actually have been committed. And then there's the hazy description of a bloke in a darkened room. A bloke who didn't give his name.'

'Why do you think he didn't say his name? I mean, it's a safe space.'

'Is it? That's what we're debating, isn't it?' Bob said. 'Anyway, would you give your name if you'd killed someone?'

Frank looked anxious and took a long swig of his bottle of water.

'Fair point,' he said. 'So you do think he might have killed someone?'

'How can I know? I'm just trying to look at it from all angles,' Bob replied. 'Anyway. It's already with the police. You. You just have to decide what to do with it. No pressure.'

5

POLICE TAPE had already sealed off Charmouth Square in the expensive backstreets of Chelsea when Jan arrived. She showed her press card to the Constable, who nodded, and walked the twenty yards to where the arc lights had already been set up outside the entrance to an elegant two-storey, red-brick townhouse that had long since been divided into apartments. Already it looked promising. A two-bed flat around here would set you back a minimum of two to three million quid. There was definitely the smell of money in this story.

When she reached the building, she could see that up the three front steps and beneath an arch, the front door was open, showing the hallway. Beyond that, she glimpsed another open door, leading into a ground floor flat. Inscribed into the white paint of the arch was the name of the block: Lyme Mansions. Great word, mansion. That would stir interest in the shires. Now she just needed someone to talk details.

And suddenly there it was, or there she was, and Jan felt a surge of excitement at the alignment of the story stars. Out of the flat walked a figure with whom Jan shared history and a bond, even if she hadn't seen her for a while. DS Deena Campbell stopped at the top of the steps to take off her blue latex gloves.

Jan's mobile rang with yet another 121 call that she'd been ignoring. She cursed it and quickly turned off her phone.

'Deena,' Jan called out.

The young woman – now, what, late twenties? – turned to the direction of the voice.

'Jeepers. Jan?'

'How the heck are you doing?'

'OK. Yes, good thanks. Wow. It's been a while.'

They stood there for a moment in the chill of the night looking each other up and down, the arc lights illuminating them as if shining light on the memories of working together. Jan smiled and Deena returned it before recalling they had had some run-ins too, then reassuming the poker face of a police officer confronted by a journalist.

'Heard you got a move into plain clothes,' said Jan.

'Yes. Took a couple of years after Regent's Park but I got there.'

'Well deserved. You were always a bright and brave one.'

'Thank you. Moved up from DC to DS as well a couple of years ago.'

'Nice work,' Jan replied, offering another smile.

There was a brief silence.

'How you been doing?' Deena asked.

'Ah, you know. My game changes almost week by week now. I'm hanging in there. Just for now. Thinking about taking redundancy.'

'No?'

'Yeah, well. You know…'

The two stood looking at each other for a moment, shaking their heads. Deena recalled how Jan had used her, and her naivety as a PC, to get information early in the Regent's Park Mosque murderer story. They'd made up, though, to the point where they'd worked together to trap the guy.

'How's Rashid?' Jan asked, recalling the young man who had worked in the Mosque's bookshop and with whom Deena had hit it off.

But the question just reminded Deena that the only reason she had got the call to be here was because she was the only single person on the team.

'OK. We speak now and then but… You know. He moved to Manchester. Took work in a mosque up there.'

'Ah, right.'

'And your lovely mum and dad?'

'Yeah, OK. Better since between us we managed to stop Grandad being deported back to Jamaica.' An anger came to her voice. 'After sixty years in South London.'

'Oh God. So shocking all of that.'

'So what you doing here?' Deena asked.

'Er…' Jan replied. She got a pen and a notebook out of her bag and held them up.

'Oh yes, of course.'

Deena stood there for a moment, embarrassed. It dawned on her that, no matter their shared history, formative experience was reminding her that she was a copper, Jan a journalist and it was growing ever harder to make the twain meet.

'So what can you tell me?'

'We've been this way before, haven't we Jan?'

Jan smiled at the memories: Deena spilling beans, getting a rollicking from a superior for it, them nailing the villain together and Jan telling Frank Phillips that Deena was detective material so that he would pass it on to the relevant powers.

'Look Jan. You know how it is.' Deena sounded sheepish, her debt to Jan coming to her mind too.

'No, I don't. How is it?'

'I can't tell you anything right now. My DCI would have me back handing out "Have You Seen" leaflets on the street.'

'And who is your DCI?'

'Dave Hanley. Been on his team a month.'

'Jesus. I've got a news editor like him.'

'Then you'll know...' Deena suddenly realised she was already saying too much.

Jan did know. And immediately there was a reminder.

'The famous Jan Mason,' boomed a voice from a few yards away at the top of the steps to Lyme Mansions. 'Well, once famous. We are fucking honoured, are we not Campbell?'

'Yes guv.'

'The right answer is "no we're not". Still using the old methods then, Jan? Trying to get info out of the underlings.'

Jan shot a glance at Deena, who was scowling at the insult.

'You keeping well Dave?' Jan inquired. There had been bad blood between the two of them years ago after she'd solved a case before he did but she was hoping that the residue of her standing with the Met would earn her some respect from him at least. Even if the chance of that was somewhere between plump and obese.

'Great, yeah. Love being disturbed when I'm watching the football. I was enjoying it as well, what with Chelsea losing. I hate Chelsea.'

Jan wondered to herself if there was anything that Hanley didn't hate.

She started fishing. 'I'm sure it's worth it, though, Dave. Nice juicy murder case to get stuck into.'

'Yeah, well. We're still establishing the circumstances. Some posh girl dead in a ground floor flat but that's about it. Don't even know if it's foul play yet.'

'Really? So why you and a murder team here then?'

'That's enough for now, OK? And none of that was on the record, right?'

'You can't do that, Dave. Say something then tell me it's off the record afterwards.'

'I can do what I fucking well like. You print anything tonight and that's you and me finished.'

'I didn't know we were even started…'

'Don't get clever with me.'

'Fact remains Dave. You've just told me the victim is female, posh and lives on the ground floor. A bit of checking and I have a story.'

'Not if it's a suicide you don't.'

'Could well still be big news, depending on who it is.'

She stared hard at Hanley, who looked away. A sure sign that the body in the flat was a somebody.

'Anyway, I don't really need you,' she added. 'I have plenty of other contacts inside the Met. I've got this far without your help haven't I?'

Hanley looked across at Deena, who was trying to conceal an involuntary smirk but had failed as her DCI made eye contact.

'You think something's funny?' he barked at her and she shook her head quickly.

'Don't take it out on Deena, Dave,' said Jan. 'She wasn't there when I got to that knife killer before you did, was she? Actually, you wouldn't want that to happen again, would you? Wouldn't you rather have me inside the tent…?'

Anger contorted Hanley's face but he knew he'd been outflanked.

'OK, OK. I'll work with you but I don't want the woman's name out there tonight, all right?'

'I'm assuming the relatives are being informed as we speak so there must be another reason why not.'

Hanley looked across at Deena again.

'Something's going on with this one,' he said. 'I've been told from higher up to keep this one under wraps for now.'

'You'll give me the beat first thing in the morning then?'

'We'll see.'

'Not good enough Dave.'

'All right then sure. But don't write anything tonight, right?'

'I have a demanding news editor…'

'Just give us twelve hours and I'll know more OK? You can do your checking for background and we'll let you have first dibs with quotes tomorrow before any press releases. Call me at 10.30am.'

Jan looked at him intently for a moment then finally nodded agreement.

'But don't mess me around Dave, OK? You still on the same number?'

'Yes.'

He stared at her again, his face betraying a subdued rage, while pointing to Deena.

'And don't go pumping her for info, OK.' He turned to Jan. 'I know you two ladies have some history, so don't go putting her in a difficult fucking position.'

Ladies. Jan hated that. Sure, patronising, sign of a bloke who hated working with women. Not worth riling him too much this soon into it, though. Jan nodded.

She turned to go and took her mobile out of her bag, switching it on again and finding the news desk number in her "favourites".

'Sorry Ivan. Bit of a false alarm. It's actually looking a bit like a suicide and nobody well known at this stage. I'll check again in the morning.'

Vickers was annoyed at the other end, hoping for a late-break-ing exclusive but Jan was successfully keeping the buzz out of her voice that Hanley's comment had aroused. About somebody higher up trying to keep this under wraps. While trying, and of course failing, to intimidate her and get her to back off, he'd instead just confirmed that something significant was going on.

'I know Ivan,' she added. 'I like a bit of drama last-knockings too. But let's hold off for now, shall we? Nobody else has got anything and we'll know more first thing. I'll get in early tomor-row. Best things are worth waiting for.'

After ending the call and tucking her phone back in her bag, she didn't hear another ping of a text from 121 informing her that she had a message. Her mind was too focused on getting straight back home and looking up who lived in that flat.

TUESDAY

6

FRANK barely slept. At times, the fifteen years of his sobriety felt like just fifteen minutes without a drink as he dozed, woke, tossed, turned and in his agitation got up twice to make tea. Like a newcomer doing anything not to take that first drink. He wasn't sure about the second mug of tea. It would probably mean that he'd be needing to piss every few hours. It was the curse of men walking the eggshells of their early fifties.

Being at peace with yourself, he reflected in his less anxious moments, was hard won over years but could be lost in minutes. And it was a condition of the recovering addict that their brain could tell them that if they felt good, the feeling was going to last just a few hours. If they felt bad, it was going to last forever. Fortunately, he now knew that if he just hung in there without taking a drink, things would change. This too shall pass, and all that. But then, as a poster he kept in his small office had it: Lord grant me patience – but hurry.

There was nothing like conflict within to disturb the equilibrium. And this one was at the heart of the professional and personal for him. He had managed to avoid stepping into the messy morass so far but now his feet were firmly planted in it. The words of Italian Bob last night played on a loop in his brain. Where were the boundaries between his job as a copper of long standing – a detective for seventeen years and, for the last twelve, the Met's Deputy Head of Counter Terrorism – along with his responsibility as a citizen? And then his duty to confidentiality and anonymity, the basic traditions at the heart of AA? Surely his training and sense of public duty trumped all else? But what was the "all else"? Just tread carefully for now, eh Frank?

He sat in the kitchen drinking more tea when he heard the alarm go off in his bedroom at its regular 6.30am setting. There was no need for it, given his wakeful night but he had left it on out of habit. He showered and dressed and took his regular half hour walk from his Pimlico flat to New Scotland Yard, as it was still called despite the move a few years back from the old Broadway building to Victoria Embankment, nearer the seat of government.

He picked up his coffee at the Starbucks outside Westminster tube station and headed for his office, up on the sixth floor. It was only 8am but already people were at their desks. Preoccupied by what he knew he had to do before he could deal with the official business of the day, his face clearly betrayed his anxiety as he walked through the department.

'Cheer up Frank,' said young Tom. Promising kid. Ambitious. Cocky too.

Frank stopped. 'What?'

'It may never happen.'

'Well, let's hope not,' Frank replied sharply. 'That's what we're all supposed to be here working for.'

As he strode on, he missed the raised eyebrows among his team that would later, once he was in his office, find voice as: "Who rattled his cage?" He was too busy wondering about the impact this might have on the job. He wouldn't lose rank if people knew he was a recovering alcoholic – would he? – but would they view and treat him differently?

Once installed at his desk, Frank logged on to the Met's system and then the intranet, which afforded access only to those few, like him, with the high enough level of access to all the crime activity being logged by other departments. These were supposed to be the days of joined-up policing, after all. His logging-in wouldn't lead to any questions being asked as he did it regularly, checking to see if any crime might be terror-related, or involved people they were watching. To decide if there were jigsaw pieces that fitted together. There were more than 500 on the go currently, to varying degrees of intensity. No-one would know that he had an ulterior motive.

He went through the usual catalogue of drinking and drug-fuelled crimes, fights and affrays. There were two stabbings involving rival teenage gangs in South London. These knife crimes had become so prevalent that only a death would make it on to the regional news, though not often the national these days, unless there was some kind of human interest back story.

Then there was the dead body of a woman in her thirties. Foul play suspected. Awaiting forensic report. In Chelsea.

Frank felt butterflies build in his stomach. He clicked on the case and saw the details, such as they were at this stage. Woman, aged thirty-eight. Blonde. Name of Camilla Carew. (Sounded posh. Sounded familiar). Lived on her own but had an ex-boy-friend they were keen to speak to. Investigating Officer: Dave Hanley. Him.

Frank got up from his desk and walked to the window, gazing down on to the river, as he often did involuntarily when he needed to think. He loved that view across to the London Eye and the other attractions on the South Bank, had welcomed the move, not least because his promotion into counter-terrorism, some eight years ago now, meant that he would get an office with a river view. If you're going to ponder and stare into the distance, he'd tell people if they ever caught him in this pose, make what-ever's in that distance interesting.

OK Frank. Let's revisit it, he told himself, anxiety level rising again. It could, of course, be nothing, he tried to tell himself first.

Just a coincidence that a bloke had walked into an AA room and spilled his guts about possibly having killed a woman, and then a dead woman had turned up in a flat a few streets away. As Bob had said last night, they'd both heard enough drunks talking about blackouts, heard enough telling of tall tales to get attention and sympathy. And many of them he'd never seen again.

Come on Frank, who you kidding?, he said to himself. He knew he'd had people put under surveillance on less of a link than that.

He did not relish speaking to Hanley but knew he would have to. It was always an uneasy call speaking to a former colleague who resented your promotion when you had outstripped him in the force. But then, surely Hanley realised, he was better off investigating murders rather than second-guessing terrorists? Hanley was as old school as the backgrounds of some recent Prime Ministers, though his was an East End comprehensive. His talk-tough, nail-them manner, his contacts and a nose for sniffing out the guilty was better suited to the streets than the strategy of offices.

Hanley picked up quickly enough. 'Counter-terrorism. What have I done to deserve this?' he asked Frank, suspicion immediately in his voice.

'Just a check call really,' Frank replied. 'This case you're listed on. Seeing if it might impact us.'

'Impact you? Fucking hell. You've picked up some new language up there, haven't you?' Hanley replied from his own office vantage point, looking upriver from the Met's Homicide and Serious Crime Command on Putney Bridge Road.

'The woman found dead you're waiting for forensics on…'

'The one in Chelsea?'

'Is there another one?'

'Don't get fucking smart with me. You're phoning me remember. Presumably because you want something.'

Frank paused. He knew he needed to keep Hanley onside.

'Yes her.'

'Working on things. Mobilised the team overnight. Still putting it together.'

'So can you tell me the pieces you're putting together?'

'Can you tell me why you're interested?'

'You know better than that Dave.'

'Well, I do seem to be getting interest from higher up on this one. If there's anything I need to know about this case…'

'If you do, you will be told.'

'Don't think you're taking it off me.'

'No question of that at this stage. Just need a bit of prelim info. Those pieces you're putting together…?'

'Camilla Carew. Thirty-eight years old. Her Daddy's rich and so is she.'

'And her Daddy is?'

'Peter Carew.'

Of course. Frank thought he'd recognised the name Carew.

'The politician?'

'The very same.'

'We're pretty sure she was strangled,' Hanley continued. 'She had some marks around the neck but there is no obvious murder weapon lying around. The flat's still being searched.'

'Suspects?'

'Looking for her ex. Quick checks last night showed up some domestics and the neighbour who called it in reckoned she might have seen him leaving. Bloke called James Bexington.'

'OK. Anything else?'

'Well, as you've just told me Frank, if there's something you need to know, you will be told.'

Frank didn't want to arouse any suspicion in a man for whom suspicion was a way of life and who might start checking with Frank's colleagues if he sounded too interested this early on.

'Fair enough. I'll be back in touch if there's anything more I need.'

Frank closed down the call. He thought about the names. Camilla Carew. James Bexington. They needed checks both on the system and Google. Peter Carew would certainly be on the system. He also thought about his AA sponsor, his mentor in sobriety. Perhaps he could ring him too, for some guidance.

Another old friend came to mind. Someone who might also have had their interest stirred by a case like this. He knew Jan was still around as he'd seen her byline online plenty, if not on anything major in recent years. He'd need to be careful about what he said, though. And how he said it. He wondered whether she might be a way for him to direct some attention towards this stranger without doing it directly himself.

Frank called up Google and typed in the name of James Bexington, concentrating on the images. He increased the size of the pictures and craned his head forward to stare at the guy. Maybe. He couldn't be sure. The hoodie, the candlelight. His instincts were right about one thing, though. Over at the murder team's office at Putney Bridge, Dave Hanley was wondering not just why he'd just had a call from counter-terrorism, but why it had come from such a senior figure. And why that senior figure had not asked to be kept informed.

7

ARMED with her double espresso bought from the coffee cart in the building's atrium, Jan settled in at her desk. The first sip poured fuel on her smouldering fire. She knew she had a good story already. Or at least part of one. She'd gone home to her flat in Maida Vale last night, logged into the paper's database, which included the electoral roll, and realised she was sitting on something hot and exclusive to start the day with. A story to make the rest of the media sit up and take notice, and to bring a bundle of hits to the website. To stir her paper's Middle England demographic.

There were two people living on the ground floor of Lyme Mansions in Charmouth Square, Chelsea, in flats one and two. One was an older woman, aged seventy-eight. Nancy Preston. Clearly, from her conversation with Hanley, the deceased wasn't her. It had to be the other one. Wow. Camilla Carew. London socialite. Bit of a name in the diary columns. More than that, though, daughter of Peter Carew, the leader of the far-right political party UK First and an interview waiting to happen on TV rolling news and radio stations. As she recalled from the Sunday night TV news and the Westminster immigration debate and vote last night, which featured a Prime Minister tight with Carew saying that it was time to pull up the drawbridge. More wow.

The triumph of the Regent's Park story had given her the freedom she wanted to get out back on the road, the print edition having increased circulation for a while on the back of her reporting, but she had come to see the value of the website these days. Quite apart from having been forced to. While it may be difficult to get ahead of competitors in the era of rolling news, if you did have an exclusive, you had an immediate outlet for it rather than having to wait nervously for up to twenty-four hours hoping that nobody else got a whiff of it.

It was what she didn't have, though, that bugged her for now. She needed that heads-up Hanley had promised her. She was pretty sure this was no suicide, with which Hanley sought initially to divert her. He and Deena wouldn't have been called out if it was. But how was Camilla killed? When? Had they found a murder weapon? She needed detail. Detail made the story. And quotes. Hanley had promised her quotes.

She looked across at the big digital clock on the news room wall. Another fifteen minutes until the appointed time that Hanley had told her to call. She just wanted to be sure she was still ahead on this story, though, and rang Danielle from the press office on her mobile.

'Christ, Jan. I was on lates last night. I haven't had my coffee yet.'

'Have I still got this to myself?' Jan asked.

'For now,' Danielle replied. 'There's going to be a press conference at midday. I'm guessing you've found out who the victim is by now?'

'Yes.'

'So you'll know this is a sensitive one. I've already had Imran on to me with a mild bollocking. Hanley rang him early this morning ranting about you rocking up at the crime scene. If it hadn't been you I'd told, and some other reporter, it would have been a major bollocking.'

Jan laughed. She knew the head of media Imran Prasanna was a fan of hers. Which meant that she could be useful to him.

'Anything else you can tell me?'

'Jan…'

'No. That's fine. Thanks Danielle.'

'What's this about redundancies on the news desk there by the way?'

'Voluntary,' said Jan quickly, before ending the call with "speak later".

She looked down towards the signed document in her bag, then up at the clock again. Ten minutes till it was time to call Hanley. Out of habit, she did a quick scroll of new faces on her dating app. No one worth swiping right for yet again. Her phone rang.

Robert again. Unusual time for him to be ringing. She decided she'd better pick up.

'Hello bruv? How's Edinburgh, wifey and kiddies?'

'For fuck's sake, Jan. You know how I hate those words. Where have you been?'

Jan sat up. When Robert swore, she knew she needed to pay attention.

'Working. What else?'

'I rang you last night. Left a message.'

'Shit. Yes. I saw your call but I was on a job. And I forgot to pick up the message.'

'Mum's had a fall.'

Jan was suddenly, momentarily silenced. She knew her mother was frail, and this call from Robert was not unexpected. At times she balked at the £1,000 a week care fees being forked out from the sale of their mother's house to keep her there but this was still her mother, her 81-year-old mother who deserved the best care possible.

'That's shocking. What happened?'

'She misplaced her hand on her walking frame and tripped. She's got a broken ankle. They had to call an ambulance. Get it set properly at A and E. She's back at the care home now and in bed but it's shaken her. Staff say she's been delirious and doesn't know where she is. When she's conscious, that is.'

'But she'll be all right, yeah?'

'Bloody hell, Jan…'

'What?'

'This you saying you're not going up there?'

'Do I need to?'

'I can't go for a few days. Not until the weekend. Gemma's working long hours just now and I have to do the school runs and the cooking.'

'Well, I'm in the middle of something important.'

'You're always in the middle of something important.'

There was another silence, a stand-off. Both knew that Elsie was their responsibility. Both thought the other should be taking it. Robert had always been the closer. Mum had always loved him better. She'd been cruel to Jan, verbally and even physically. They clashed. Too similar in personality, people said. But then Jan had also said some nasty things to and about her, Robert always reminded her. When, he added, she took her head out of all the books she read and hid herself in. Jan's guilt kept telling her that she should be going more. But Robert was so much better with her. He'd smoothed everything out that time when she hit a care assistant with her stick. Elsie, with the vascular dementia taking over, had thought that the assistant was a twelve-year-old Jan.

'Come on Robert,' said Jan. 'What can I do? She's being taken care of, isn't she? She's in good hands.'

'She is. But she'd probably welcome a familiar face. Family.'

'OK. OK. But I can't go up to Wakefield today. I've got this thing on… Maybe tomorrow eh?'

'Yeah. Maybe tomorrow Jan. Maybe tomorrow.'

Robert ended the call without a goodbye. It was designed to crank up her guilt and it worked. But there was work to be done. All the time she'd been on the phone to Robert, she'd been keeping an eye on the clock.

She rang Hanley.

'Oh right, yes, I did, didn't I?' he said, after Jan reminded him that he'd promised her more information last night.

'Well?' she asked, piqued by his tone, one that betrayed an amusement at him being one up on her. In control.

'Sorry. Still a bit of a blackout on this one. My chief's still not sanctioned any info going out.'

'But you said last night…'

'And now it's this morning. Life moves on. Nothing I can do.'

'I'm told there's a press conference at midday.'

'Is there? Could be.'

'You know what, Dave?'

'What?'

'Big mistake. Huge,' she replied, feeling that cheering sense of one-upwomanship made famous by Julia Roberts in *Pretty Woman*. 'You've just ensured that you get nothing from me on this inquiry.'

'Like that's gonna be a big loss,' Hanley said.

'Well, plenty in the Met have enjoyed my help down the years. And I already have the basis for a story that will be going out in the next half hour. I know who the victim is. And whose daughter she is.'

There was a silence at the other end of the phone.

'I think you'll get to a point where you'll be begging for my help, Hanley,' Jan added.

'Begging for anything from you, darling? Do fuck off.'

Jan had heard enough and slammed her mobile down on her desk.

'Fucking snake,' she exclaimed.

'Problem?' Vickers inquired from his desk ten yards away.

He had been following the phone call and was enjoying seeing Jan discomforted.

She picked up her mobile again, unlocked it and brought up another number. It rang just a couple of times before her call was answered.

'Go to the toilet now,' Jan barked down the line.

She shut off her phone and made her way out to a terrace at the back of the news room that looked out onto the river. There was one benefit of working for a paper whose owner listed lucrative porn channels in his portfolio. He could afford a picturesque location, in this case between Southwark and Tower bridges, for his offices. Word was that his daughter, who was chief executive, had insisted on the location, rather than some suburban industrial estate, if she was going to run the business.

Though mid-morning, the newspaper day was barely dawning. The smokers were already nicotined up before getting into work, enough to be able to take them through to the 11 o'clock cigarette, and so, for now, Jan had the terrace to herself.

Her mobile buzzed with a text. 'OK. In the ladies now.'

Jan called back and Deena picked up the phone.

'Better make this quick Jan. He's very edgy this morning. What's going on?'

'He's shafted me. How do you work with him?'

'I don't. I work for him. He's made that clear.'

'You were there last night when he told me he'd give me a beat on this story. He's backtracked.'

'I can't tell you anything Jan, you know that.'

'Old times…'

'Look Jan, I'll always be grateful to you for my break. But you can't expect to keep trading on that. Anyway, rules have tightened up even more since then about dealing with the press.'

There was a pause.

'No, you're right Deena. It's not fair of me. But one thing's not changed. Coppers still need journos. And the other way round.'

Jan could hear Deena sigh on the other end. There was a pause.

'Listen,' Jan added. 'I know who the dead woman is.'

'You do?'

'Yes. Camilla Carew. Didn't take much digging. At least tell me that it's definitely murder.'

'OK, OK. Yes, it's a murder.'

'Suspects?'

'It'll be coming out in the press conference Jan. There's a bloke we want to interview. Hanley wants to be in control of this. Not it controlling him.'

'Jesus. Deena. Come on. Who? Give me a steer. It's only an hour ahead of the presser.'

'In which case you can wait. You get it and put it on your website and he'll know it came from me. And he wants to get one over on you. Says he's not getting shown up by Jan Mason like plain clothes did on the Mosque murders.'

Jan smiled to herself. She liked the thought of having irked Hanley.

'I'll put him off the scent,' Jan said. 'I'll text him and say I've been going through the electoral roll and have spoken to people in the other flats.'

There was another pause. Deena was thinking.

'It'll get it out there quicker anyway,' Jan added. 'And once I'm on it, you know I'll stay ahead of it. And share anything I get with you.'

'Fat lot of good it'll do me. He'll take all the credit for it.'

'Deena… Come on, you're better than that. This is about bringing a killer to justice. Not about outflanking Hanley. That's just a bonus for both of us.'

Deena laughed. 'All right,' she said. 'The bloke we want to speak to is a recent boyfriend.'

'James Bexington?' Jan asked.

'You know him?'

'Just came up on Google images when I keyed in Camilla's name. How was she killed?'

'Looking like an asphyxiation. Forensics about to confirm, we think.'

'Can I use that?'

Jan could hear a door being opened in the ladies toilet and a voice saying: "All right Deena?" Clearly Deena did not want to look suspicious by shutting down the call immediately so instead she said to Jan:

'Mum. It's not even lunchtime. I don't know what I want for supper.'

'Sure,' said Jan. 'Got it.'

'All right, all right. Chicken will be fine. Again.'

The call ended and Jan rushed from the terrace back to the laptop she insisted on using rather than office computers. With those, it was far too easy for people to gain access and see what she was looking at. And what she was writing.

She googled Camilla Carew and James Bexington together. Pictures of them attending society functions and summer sporting events showed them to be an attractive couple. Well connected. He was described as an antiques dealer, with a shop in Lots Road.

The path of true love did not run smoothly with these two, however, and there were gossip column pieces about their on-off relationship. Off latterly, it seemed. Tucked in amongst it all was a tale carried by the nationals about six months ago of police being called to a domestic at her Chelsea flat by a neighbour who'd heard a loud argument.

There was, though, an innocent – well semi-plausible – explanation of her broken wrist, it seemed. 'It was, I'm afraid, a – what can we call it – rather passionate encounter that got out of hand,' Camilla was quoted as saying. Hmm, Jan thought.

She got up from her work station and walked across to Vickers.

'Right Ivan,' she said. 'I've got a seriously good tale for you.'

She had him at seriously and he looked up from his screen.

'When you go into the Editor's conference in half an hour, you can tell him that we have a murder in Chelsea. And the victim was strangled and is a posh bird. None other than Camilla Carew.

'What the daughter of...'

Jan was ahead of him, and again with this story, of the game. The position she most liked to be in.

'The very same,' she said. 'This is why I didn't want to jump the gun last night with some sketchy story that was going to make half a dozen paragraphs. Today we have a real exclusive. They're announcing this at a midday press conference but I've got the inside track. And the name of a suspect they want to interview.'

It was all the sweetest music to Vickers' ears.

'Thank fucking Christ,' he said. 'I'm sick of all this politics, the-right-say-this, the-left-say-this shit. Something human interest at last.'

'I'll do five hundred words for the website now and then I'm going out to do some digging, OK?'

'We might need you in the office to update as the day goes on. Take in quotes from the Dad and all their toff mates.'

'Ivan, you're getting back into your old ways again, aren't you?' she reminded him. If Jan Mason, Chief Reporter at Large, for a while longer at least, wanted to go out on the road, she was going to go out on the road.

'Fair enough,' he replied, put back in his box. Besides, this was the sort of story he lived for and wasn't going to bite this hand feeding him. 'Fucking hell. We can call him the Chelsea Choker.'

Vickers wasn't going to wait for the morning editorial conference. He tore off towards the Editor's office, keen to get his brownie points immediately.

Jan returned to her laptop and began writing…

POLICE are hunting for the ex-boyfriend of London socialite Camilla Carew after the UK First leader's daughter was found strangled to death at her Chelsea flat last night.

Ms. Carew, 38, had been involved in a turbulent relationship with playboy antiques dealer James Bexington for 18 months until it came to an unhappy end recently, according to reports, following a domestic incident between the two earlier this year.

It is a relationship known to have angered Ms Carew's father, Peter Carew, who was among the leaders of the successful Leave campaign in the 2016 Brexit vote and has been pressurising the government on stricter immigration controls.

After that, a bit of background on the domestic and the pair's colourful and chequered relationship – to use two journalistic adjectives that covered a multitude of sins in readers' imaginations without being libellous. And some more on Carew. She pressed "send" to Vickers's inbox, copying in the website editor.

She reckoned she deserved another coffee before the expedition she had in mind. She would text Hanley when she got there.

8

WESTMINSTER was late-morning quiet. The office workers were installed at their desks and the politicians' staffs and
researchers, the few who used this cafe in preference to one of
the chains, had made it into Parliament and Portcullis House
ahead of their bosses who had been voting last night. It was why
Frank had chosen this backstreet sandwich bar. He could meet
Eddie in a quiet corner well away from some of the most highly
attuned eavesdropping ears in the country.

And there he was, already in situ when Frank dived quickly
through the door to get out of the cold. It was Frank's turn to
get the teas. Actually it always was. If Eddie was coming in
from over the river, the least Frank could do was pay. And AA
members mostly seemed to be tea-drinkers rather than coffee
consumers. Perhaps it was because it came instantly rather
than all that faffing about with machines. Drinkers liked their
drinks best when they came quickly. Many things changed
but not that.

'So what's the problem?' Eddie inquired as soon as Frank sat
down. 'Which one of the only three there are? Sex, including
relationships, money or work?'

Frank smiled, though it was a weak one given what was going
on. Eddie always began their meetings with the same questions.
It was a good tactic. Making sure his sponsee cut straight to
the issue, without bullshit and dancing around the subject. And

if there was any time left, Eddie could then tell Frank what a shambles his beloved Chelsea were this season.

It was what Frank liked about Eddie and why he had asked him to be his AA mentor those five years ago. Eddie's honesty, his twenty-six years of sobriety, and the fact they had something in common, even if they were opposite sides of the same coin, combined to form the attraction.

Eddie had been a low-level criminal back in the nineties, a wheelman, until he crashed a getaway car when drunk. In his prison cell, he finally wised up that it was a sign he needed to stop drinking. It had worked but he found that when he did get sober in order to keep his job, he no longer wanted to be a driver for lowlifes. He'd thought that getting himself out of that scene might be tough but fortunately for him, word had got round and they let him go to get on with a different life. After all, no robber wants a driver likely to get drunk. Now he worked afternoons at a homeless shelter in South London and did a bit of cabbying a few nights a week. Ironic, he used to say, that he'd ended up taking a flat in Wandsworth near the nick though that was the only link with his old life.

'You know, I think I might shock you finally,' said Frank, who had never yet shared anything with Eddie that Eddie didn't seem to have done and felt, and done and felt it worse. 'I can't work out a link with sex, money or work.'

'They'll be at the root of it somewhere,' said Eddie, but he certainly sounded more intrigued than usual. 'Go on.'

Frank outlined the story from last night of the mystery man, hooded and bearded, who had walked into the meeting. He told Eddie of the bloke talking about his blackout. And then what he had seen on the police computer this morning and his conversation with Hanley. He realised he was divulging sensitive and confidential information. And to a former criminal. But this was Eddie. And the relationship between him and Eddie, sponsee and sponsor, was as close to keeping a secret as he could get.

He paused, waiting for Eddie to say something. He wasn't quite expecting the response that came back.

'Heard a story at a meeting once from a bloke who woke up one morning, got showered and dressed and went outside to get in his car to go to work. Found a dead body between the garage door and his bonnet.'

'Holy shit,' said Frank. 'What happened?'

'He'd been ratarsed, remembered a bump as he turned into his drive after a night on the piss after work but didn't think much of it. Thought he'd just bounced the car driving too fast. Turns out he'd hit this bloke out walking his dog. Bloke grabbed on to the bonnet and got trapped against the garage door. Dog was dead too.'

'And he didn't even notice?'

'Nope. Had the radio on loud. Neighbours heard a bit of a shout and a noisy radio but just thought it was him coming home pissed as normal and nobody bothered.'

'So what happened?'

'He was mortified. He rang the police. Turned himself in. Went to prison for six years for manslaughter. Got sober and devoted himself to AA and working for charity.'

'You're saying I should tell what I know, Eddie? Make a formal report?'

Once, comfortable in his sobriety, Frank would have trusted his instincts. He would have analysed any situation calmly, balanced up the arguments, run it past Eddie and maybe shared at a meeting or spent a quiet half hour in meditation in Westminster Abbey. Answers would come.

That was for things like whether he should move flats or ask a woman out though. Not a situation like this. Where his personal and professional lives seemed about to collide so sharply, of which he'd had no previous experience. Today he found himself trapped in a fog of anxiety and uncertainty as he had in that state of early sobriety, when it really had been touch and go whether he would drink again, a day at a time. An hour at a time.

Now he had enough clean time to realise that he needn't drink again. But it was about so much more than simply not drinking. It was about having a balance, a peace of mind. A sense of spiritual wellbeing. He just wasn't feeling any of that. He hated being catapulted back into those edgy early days. Back then, he'd wanted instant answers, to be told what to do, because he didn't trust his own judgment. He'd just about held down his job as a detective, partly because he could lose himself in the drinking culture that existed in the force then. With sobriety, down the years, he'd come to believe in himself a bit more, even like himself. Hence the progression of his career. Now, though, he had regressed, to the person desperate for guidance from outside himself.

'No,' Eddie said. 'I'm not saying you should spill what you heard in an AA meeting. Not yet anyway. Just hold your horses.'

'But delays in police investigations can be fatal,' Frank replied. 'If they don't catch someone in that first forty-eight hours, the trail can go cold.'

'So it is about work, then?' Eddie asked. A weak smile came to Frank's face.

'Let's just think it through, shall we?' Eddie went on, pausing to take a sip of tea from his mug. 'First, this Hanley seems to have more info than you. They've got the dead body and they're looking for the boyfriend already.'

'Yes, and…'

'What can you tell them they don't already know? Was that definitely this James…?'

'Bexington?'

'Yeah him. Was he the one that came into the meeting last night?'

'Could well have been but…'

'Exactly, you don't know yet. You said yourself, it was a candlelit meeting and the room was half dark. He was wearing a hoodie and had facial hair. Could have been anybody.'

Frank thought about it. Eddie was right.

'In fact, you might even look a bit of an arse if you go to Hanley with this.'

'How come?'

'Well, not only does it show that you don't abide by a code of ethics, he has power over you then. He knows you go to AA.'

Frank thought about it, as he had during his tortured night. Was it a valid worry that might affect his role and ability to do his job or just feeble self-protection?

'I think everyone knows I used to drink but don't now,' he said.

'But do they know you're in AA? And if they do, or do now, Chelsea meetings will be having a sudden influx of cops who are there for the wrong reasons.'

Frank thought about it. If he did name the meeting, he could risk undercover cops and reporters turning up at the next one. And Eddie was right. That may not have been Bexington at all last night. The Google pictures showed a clean-shaven man. Was it worth jeopardising his working relationships on such thin "evidence"? He might be wasting his own and police time.

'So what you do reckon I should do?' Frank asked.

'Like I say, put your foot on the ball,' said Eddie. 'Wish Chelsea had last night. Headless fucking chickens…'

9

HANLEY stood back from the whiteboard and contemplated its currently thin display – just a 1:1,250 metre map of Chelsea with a pin in Charmouth Square and pictures Blu-Tacked around it of Camilla Carew, Peter Carew and James Bexington. Beneath that, crime scene pictures of the victim sprawled on the living room floor of her flat. A close-up showed her blonde hair swept back to reveal a red weal on her neck.

'OK,' he said addressing his five-strong audience and taking a Sharpie to the board to write two words, 'We are calling this Operation Camilla. Thanks for the middle of the night start. I thought we should have a catch-up now I've got the prelim forensics.

'When the pathologist got there just after us at 9pm, rigor mortis was just setting in around the eyes and the mouth, meaning she'd been dead at most two hours. Definitely strangled, but with something smooth rather than rough like a rope.'

'What, like a scarf, sir?' Deena inquired.

'Or maybe a fucking mobile charging lead. Course it could be a scarf, Campbell but in the absence of one, we don't know, do we? Which is why we need to find something. I want everything in that flat that could have strangled her bagged up, right?'

'Being done, guv,' a voice piped up.

'Good, well done, Terry,' Hanley was in the process of telling DI Sykes, cockney and blue-eyed boy, when his mobile pinged with a message.

Thanks for nothing, it said. *Luckily, I've still got better contacts than you have.*

'What's she on about?' he wondered to himself.

'Seen this guv?' came a voice across the floor of the office. 'Jan Mason's named the victim and the prime suspect.'

Hanley wandered across to a computer screen and saw Jan's story displayed. He scanned it quickly.

'Bitch,' he shouted.

'Careful guv,' said another on the team, DS Darren Dillon. 'Equality and diversity.' Deena couldn't quite suppress a giggle. It was enough for Hanley to round on her.

'This your doing? You're tight with her.'

Suddenly in the spotlight, with all eyes trained on her, Deena froze. She didn't want to lie and she didn't want to be confronting Jan again for having let her down. She was mightily relieved when Hanley's mobile pinged again with another text and his attention was diverted back to his screen.

And before you go accusing anyone on your team, it read, *I have friends in high places.*

Hanley looked up from his phone at the faces of his team, three of whom looked concerned, including Deena, and two of whom were struggling not to smirk.

'OK,' he said. 'Nothing we can do about it now. It's out there. We just have to use the rest of the media to our advantage. And freeze her out.'

'Is that wise, sir?' Deena asked.

'Don't push your luck, DS Campbell.'

'Given her record and influence, I just thought it might be better having her onside…'

'Unlike Chelsea's forward line last night,' said Sykes. 'Born offside that lot.'

'Matter in hand, Terry,' said Hanley. He thought for a moment. 'OK. If we do work with her, we make sure it's on our terms. She's giving us info. We give her the bare minimum. Right?'

They all nodded, including Deena even if just a little less enthusiastically. She couldn't afford to look out of place.

'Right, let's get back to work then,' said Hanley. 'First off, there is CCTV from the hallway and Terry's looked at the hours before the murder. Two men seen coming and going to Camilla's flat yesterday. Her father Peter Carew came for half an hour in mid-afternoon. Plainly visible. Then a bloke in a hoodie, puffer jacket and black jeans at 7.35pm. He left ten minutes later in a hurry. No clear picture of the face. Looks like he might well have been aware of the cameras.'

'Quite a few pictures on Google images show Bexington wearing those sort of clothes,' said Terry. 'Ageing teenager by the look of it.'

'I want him found soonest,' added Hanley. 'No answer at his address in Kensington when I went with Campbell last night and all quiet at his work. Antiques place by Chelsea Harbour. Terry, you and Darren get on it. Find him and get a search warrant for his flat. Ask around the neighbours.'

Sykes nodded. 'On it.'

'He can't be the only bloke in her life. Him and her father. Find out who else she knew and how closely. Stay on top of the fingerprints in the place.'

'Women too, guv? Could have been a woman,' said DC Rachel Thomas.

'Equality and diversity guv,' said Dillon, and Sykes laughed. Hanley smiled.

'Fair point, Thomas. Find out more about her women friends as well. You Campbell. She's an only child but check on any other family.'

'What about the neighbour who called it in?' DC Sanjay Chaudri asked.

'Old biddy. Heard a shout, then a silence. Saw someone storming out. As per the CCTV. Could have been Bexington but she couldn't say for sure. Got a bit worried and rang 999. What was her name, Campbell?'

'Nancy Preston. Aged seventy-eight.'

'Yeah. Seemed she might be going a bit Lady Gaga to me.'

'Other flats guv?' said Sanjay.

'Two upstairs but no-one home. One a young family away on half-term, other empty. Anyway, obviously we also need to establish motive and very quickly. Likely to be down to sex or money or both.'

'Does sex include love?' Rachel asked.

'It doesn't always have to,' Terry piped up with a smirk.

'Yeah, that too,' said Hanley, quickly continuing. 'So as well as finding other significant people around her and speaking to them, we need to find out more about her personal circumstances. Sanjay, check out her finances and what happens to them now. She's likely to have had plenty of dosh if she's Peter Carew's daughter.

'And remember. Because she is his daughter, we will have resources on this one. Use the researchers, use the analysts. Get them on profiling, mapping, anything. CCTV and public transport cameras. Check the streets around for ANPR and council cameras, though it's Kensington and Chelsea so there won't be so many. Darren, I'm putting you in charge of the HOLMES suite.'

Darren nodded. He liked being seen as the techie one. 'Thanks guv,' he said.

'Make sure the guys in there keep the computer files up to date. And we make sure we input everything we get to them. Everything about this case will be in computer files, so keep yourselves abreast of it all. Above all, let me know everything. By everything, I mean every cough and spit. Call me old-fashioned but I like a whiteboard. And I like everything on it. There's not enough on there for me at the moment.'

The double doors leading on to the office floor suddenly swung open and all heads turned. Chief Superintendent Jackie Donovan, Senior Investigating Officer to Hanley's IO, had presence and commanded attention. Deena always enjoyed seeing how men, particularly Hanley, jumped to it when Donovan appeared. Just behind came the Met's media chief, Imran Prasanna, along with another figure everyone in the room recognised. His face betrayed little emotion. He could often be that way on television, inscrutable between the bouts of bonhomie.

'DCI Hanley,' Donovan said. 'This is Peter Carew. The deceased's father.'

'Yes, I'm aware. Good to meet you Mr Carew.'

So deferential was Hanley's tone and manner that Deena and Imran flashed each other a look that involved raised eyebrows.

'I'm very sorry for your loss sir. This is shocking.'

'Yes, well. I want that bastard Bexington arrested and charged with her murder.'

'You seem very certain he's done this, sir.'

'Gold digger. Wrong 'un. Mark my words.'

Carew's eye was drawn to the whiteboard, with its picture of him and Bexington.

'I'm pleased to see he's got prime position up there,' he said, pointing. 'But why am I on it?'

'Just people we need to speak to at this stage. To gather information. Build up background. Nothing more sir,' Hanley replied. 'No rush in your case. When you feel up to it. Today must be very difficult for you. We appreciate that.'

'Yes. I do have a couple of meetings this afternoon. Tomorrow OK?'

'Thank you sir,' said Hanley. Deena and Imran again

swopped looks. 'We don't have a custody suite or interview facilities here so it will be at Hammersmith police station.'

'Custody suite? Police station? Is all that really necessary?'

'We have to do things properly sir. I'm sure you understand.'

Carew looked tetchy. Donovan changed the subject.

'I see somebody's jumped the gun in the press,' she said.

'Afraid so ma'am. Very sorry.'

'You have a leaky team here?'

'Absolutely not. Loyal as the day is long. I'm afraid the reporter concerned is well connected.'

'She is indeed,' Donovan replied. 'So you ready?'

'Yes ma'am,' he replied, with just a little less reverence than he had shown for Carew.

*

Imran opened up proceedings, the media packing the ground floor conference room. Unlike the bun fights and shouting matches of movies and dramas, this was real life and the media conference would be a structured, organised event which he, and Donovan, would control. It was the secret, the strategy. Stay on top of the story and the media. Lead, don't follow. Don't let anything run away from you. Which was why Hanley was already feeling uncomfortable after Jan's morning holding story, though he guessed he should have expected it from her.

'Thank you ladies and gentlemen for attending today,' said Imran. 'You'll all know Chief Superintendent Jackie Donovan. Also present is DCI Dave Hanley, who is the Investigating Officer on this case. We're going to hear a statement from CS Donovan, after which we will take questions, from TV first as I know you're live. CS Donovan…'

There was a rush of photographers' shutters being clicked as all trained their attention on Donovan. She cut a formidable figure, her black trouser suit well cut, her white blouse crisp. A greying bob framed her 55-year-old face, her game face. It told of battles won down the years. Her voice brooked no argument, as Hanley had regularly discovered to his cost.

'Thank you Imran...' she began. She fixed her gaze on the camera directly in front of her at the back of the room. Her media training had taught her that simple technique. The BBC always got the best spot and she knew this would make the most-watched news programmes in Britain, the BBC One pm, Six and Ten o'clock bulletins.

'To begin with,' Donovan continued. 'I would like to offer our sincere condolences to Mr Peter Carew following the death of his daughter Ms Camilla Carew, which I imagine by now you are all aware of from a very recent report. We are deeply sorry for his loss.'

She looked across at Carew, who returned a weak smile, designed to convey pain as well as polite thanks for the sympathy. The shutters clicked on him feverishly.

'The sequence of events is this,' Donovan went on. 'At 7.45pm last night, police were called by a neighbour to Flat Two, Lyme Mansions, Charmouth Square, Chelsea. The neighbour heard a loud scream and the sound of the front door of the building being slammed shut as one person exited the block.

'Upon arrival, two uniformed police officers gained entry to the flat and discovered the dead body of Ms Camilla Carew, aged thirty-eight. Foul play was suspected and our Homicide and Serious Crime Command immediately alerted. A Major Investigation Team was quickly assigned to the case. We are now anxious to interview a Mr James Bexington, aged thirty-nine who is known to have been in a relationship with Ms Carew until recently. A relationship that was known to include examples of domestic conflict. Officers have been to Mr Bexington's private and business addresses but there was no sign of him.'

She held up a picture for the cameras of a smiling Camilla Carew and James Bexington at some art gallery opening, a picture that all the bulletins would be carrying full screen later and one that had already been on Jan's paper's website, dragged from the files. In it, Bexington was seen in all his glory, his face tanned, a shock of black hair and a twinkle in his eye. A golden couple. They wouldn't be the first, though, to look it for press cameras.

'This picture was taken several months ago,' Donovan continued. 'We will also be releasing the CCTV image of a figure in a hoodie and dark jeans and puffer jacket. We hope members of the public will be vigilant and if they spot Mr Bexington, ring 999. We are unsure currently if he is dangerous but we would advise members of the public not to approach him but instead to make contact with us. Thank you.'

The cameras clicked again as the press officer thanked Jackie Donovan for the statement and then invited questions, first pointing to the BBC reporter in the front row. It was obvious immediately from whom, in common with everyone else there, she wanted answers. This was politics and human interest rolled into one. Stories came little juicier.

'Mr Carew. Can you tell us please your feelings today?'

Peter Carew put his head in his hands. The motor drives on the cameras whirred noisily again. He looked up.

'Today,' he began hesitantly, the room now silent and almost holding its breath, 'is the saddest day of my life. I have lost my beloved daughter, a kind, gentle and loving young woman. She did not deserve what this apology for a human being has done to her.'

'So you believe you know who killed her?' came the follow-up question.

'Of course,' Carew replied. 'Who else can it be but James Bexington? You heard the police. They want him caught as soon as possible.'

Jackie Donovan intervened.

'Ladies and gentleman. We are keeping an open mind at this stage. All we are saying is that we would like to interview Mr Bexington, as the person who has been closest to Ms Carew, apart from her father that is. Perhaps you would like to address any more questions to Detective Chief Inspector Hanley.'

Imran pointed to the ITN correspondent.

'DCI Hanley,' he said. 'Can you tell us what you found at the scene?'

Hanley cleared his throat. He hated this part of the job, resented divulging information that should be for police ears only. He had never been one of those coppers who liked a pint with a press contact. Saw them as poncers, rather than givers. 'You only know what we tell you,' he used to say to the likes of Jan Mason, reckoning they did more harm than good. In this case, though, he knew he needed their help. Track down Bexington and this could all be wrapped up in 24 hours.

'Well, we found Ms Carew on the floor of her living room, having been strangled.'

Carew gave a deep and loud intake of breath. He'd already been told this detail earlier by Donovan but hearing it out loud in public seemed to hit home more painfully. The photographers trained their lenses on him again.

'Can you tell us what she was strangled with, Detective Chief Inspector?' came the one follow-up question that the correspondent was allowed.

'Not at this stage, no.' said Hanley. 'We are continuing to examine Ms Carew's flat forensically for fingerprints, the object she was strangled with and any clues to the perpetrator.'

Imran pointed to Sky News.

'And James Bexington is your only suspect?'

'As CS Donovan has said, we are obviously keen to interview him but all avenues of inquiry are open to us. We will go where the evidence takes us.'

'Any ideas as to where he might be?'

'We have already made a start this morning on locating him and will be speaking to people who knew him. Obviously we have alerted all ports, railway stations and airports to be on the look-out for him.'

The next part stuck in his throat.

'Any help you people can give us, we will obviously be grateful.'

Donovan looked across at him. It was the "you people" that betrayed him and his disdain for the room. And it hadn't gone unnoticed.

Imran opened up the questioning to the newspapers and all the angles were exhausted. The backgrounds of father and daughter, the relationship between Carew and Bexington, were questioned in detail. When Carew began to mop his forehead with a handkerchief, Donovan could see that enough was enough. She shot Imran a glance and he brought proceedings to a close.

None present, either in police or media, could have known at this point the difference to the last 45 minutes that information Jan was about to discover elsewhere would have made to everything.

10

PRESS conferences were for other people. The best strategy, Jan always reckoned, was to be somewhere else while they were going on. That way, while other papers dined on scraps tossed from the top table, you could be feasting on your own meal.

She'd watched the conference on the BBC news channel on her mobile, taking particular notice of Carew. Around half of the country would never have voted for him and what he stood for, and of the half who entertained it, probably at least half of them didn't trust him. Neither did Jan. Hanley? Well, he was a bit of an arse, actually a lot of an arse, but she knew she would be wise not to underestimate his weasel cunning. Donovan was a different box of biscuits; smart and savvy. She and Jackie had always got on reasonably well in their occasional dealings – a mutual respect coming from being career women well used to dealing with men who underestimated them – but there were healthy boundaries between them.

Jan shut off her phone and from a distance on a bench in the middle of Charmouth Square, not wishing to be noticed in the media pack even if it was slimmer now with most still at the press conference, watched the scene unfold in front of her. Though access to the square had been opened up again, police tape still cordoned off a sizeable area around Lyme Mansions and two uniformed officers stood guard. Even with her nous, there was no way she was getting into the building. A forensics van was still parked in front. The body would have been removed by now but they would still be fine-tooth combing the place.

She would have liked to have read her book but didn't dare get too engrossed in it in case she missed what she was waiting for. And so, for almost an hour, keeping one eye on the building, she perused her phone. Twitter, Facebook, the news feeds, were all leading on Bexington being the prime suspect and a massive manhunt being launched. She posted a link on Twitter to her piece on the website. Very soon there were the usual replies – about her paper being a lying rag – as well as a few hundred retweets and more than a thousand likes. She also picked up a load of new followers to take her tally over the 91,000 mark. Maybe she would hit 100K as this story unfolded.

Pleased, she checked the dating app for some light relief. Still more drips than the leaky shower head at her flat. (She put calling a plumber on her to-do list). She texted Robert to see if there was any update from the care home.

Why don't you ring them for yourself? he texted back. She couldn't tell if its intent was tetchy but she got the message. She didn't reply. She didn't want to ring the care home in case the call stretched out. Not now. Something might happen. She would ring later. Yes, later.

She also re-read her text to Hanley and was pleased with it. It didn't say directly that her information hadn't come from within Hanley's team, but it implied it could have come from one of her high-ranking contacts. It also carried a threat that if Hanley continued to mess with her, she'd be talking to those high-ranking contacts as well.

Then, as she'd hoped, a figure finally emerged from the building.

The woman was small, old, stooped but well dressed, a camel coloured coat protecting against the chill. She carried what looked like an expensive handbag over her arm and exchanged words with the two police officers, shaking her head as if still disbelieving what had happened here last night, before heading in the direction of Fulham Road. Jan followed at a distance, watching the old lady plant her walking stick firmly with each step, then enter a little Italian restaurant.

From across the street, Jan could see her take a table by the window in a conservatory at the front. Jan made her way inside, asking the maître d' for a table next to her, even though it was early afternoon, the lunchtime rush at an end, and the restaurant was two thirds empty.

'I do like your conservatory,' Jan said by way of explanation to Riccardo. She liked to get everybody's name and had done so immediately. They didn't teach such things at journalism school but they should, she always said. It showed an interest in another person, one more used to showing it to others and thus grateful, and got them on your side.

By now, the *Evening Standard* had hit the streets and Jan noticed a copy on a table next to the maître d's lectern. A picture of Bexington's face, beneath the headline **HUNT ON FOR CAREW DAUGHTER KILLER** stared up at her.

'Mind if I read this?' Jan asked.

'Be my guest,' he said.

Riccardo showed Jan to her table and she smiled at the old woman as she took her seat. The woman wanted to look out onto the street, so Jan decided to sit with her back to the window, enabling her to make eye contact with the woman.

Jan began reading the front page story, which was a digest of the press conference and her own website piece this morning, and noticed the woman glance across at the paper. Jan quickly followed the turn at the foot of the story inside to page three so that the woman would now see the front page. Jan, pretending to read, noticed her staring at it intently. Was that a moistness in her eyes that Jan detected?

The woman shivered a little, tut-tutted, and Jan looked over the paper at her.

'Shocking, isn't it?' Jan said.

'Too terrible for words.' She looked down.

'Not far from here as well.'

'Yes. As I know to my cost.'

'Really? Has it affected you then?'

'You could say that.'

There was a short pause that experience told Jan not to fill.

'I live in the flat opposite,' the woman added, vindicating Jan's absence of response. 'And I was very fond of that young girl.'

Jan noticed a small tear trickle from the woman's eye. She was tempted to offer a tissue but the woman was already reaching for one from her handbag.

'Sadly, she never had much luck with young men,' she continued, dabbing the tear.

It was clear to Jan that the woman wanted to talk. The job had taught her that so often those touched by loss have much to talk about and are keen to find a good listener. Sometimes she had to endure the antagonism of those who decried the media for apparently intruding but the bereaved often wanted their and the loved one's story told. Jan took her chance.

'You knew this man the police are looking for?'

'I wouldn't say I knew him well, but I am familiar with him.'

'Ah,' said Jan. She had her start but didn't want to press too soon and spook the woman. Best to keep things informal for now. There would surely be more, much more, if she stayed patient.

'Very nice little place this,' said Jan.

'Yes, I come here regularly. Riccardo keeps this table for me after the rush. It saves me cooking in the evening.'

'It's nice to see a woman comfortable eating out on her own.'

'Took me a while after my Roland died. Don't have much choice really.'

'I know. When you live alone and the alternatives are cooking or starving, you have to, don't you?'

They both laughed.

'Would you like to join me perhaps, dear,' said the old lady.

Bingo, Jan thought.

'Well, if you're sure? That would be lovely.'

'Please…' The woman gestured to the seat opposite her. Jan quickly took the chance.

'I'm Jan Mason.'

'Nancy Preston,' said the woman offering her hand and Jan shook it.

'Delighted,' said Jan. 'I feel like I know that name?'

'Perhaps dear,' she said. 'I used to be in things.'

'In things?'

'Plays. TV dramas.'

'Of course. Your face is familiar too.'

'I was blessed in many ways,' Nancy said. 'I was not quite leading lady material but I had my admirers, shall we say?'

'I'm sure you did. I can certainly see why.'

'Fortunately, I had an interesting enough face to be in regular work as a character actress.' The woman, from the stiff-upper-lip generation, had now managed to compose herself, Jan noted.

'How fascinating.'

'Of course, nobody really remembers your name but you see the odd flicker of recognition in people. And what do you do, Jan Mason?'

Jan quickly assessed the situation. Sometimes it was best to keep quiet about being a journalist, even if these days not obeying ground rules about identifying yourself could lead to trouble. Now, she thought, she might just risk it with Nancy. The old girl was old school, from the days when the press was not viewed quite as sceptically, even detested, as now.

'I'm a journalist,' said Jan.

'Always liked the press,' said Nancy. 'Especially when they gave me good reviews. In the days when they carried reviews.'

Jan was relieved that her instincts had proved correct and she'd taken the risk.

'You could have a drink with press people in the old days too. Roly and I became friends with some of them. Weekends away, that kind of thing. Roland was in Emergency Ward Ten for years. Do you remember that?'

'Slightly before my time but I've heard of it,' Jan replied.

'And who do you work for?'

There was more relief when Nancy said: 'Ooh, that's my paper. I like that one,' after Jan had told her who employed her. 'I thought your name rang a bell.'

'You know,' Nancy continued. 'This is a very fortuitous meeting, isn't it?'

'How do you mean?' Jan asked.

'Well, you work for a national newspaper. I live in the same block of flats as Camilla Carew.'

Jan looked a little sheepish. But only a little.

'It's almost as if you might have been watching and waiting for someone to leave, then followed them and engaged them in conversation.'

This woman must be nearing her eighties, Jan thought, but clearly very little got past her. Which was a good thing, Jan decided, if she was going to be a source of reliable information.

'Well…'

There was a tense moment as Nancy looked Jan straight in the eyes. Then she reached across the table and touched Jan's hand.

'It's all right dear. I admire initiative.'

Jan smiled at her. 'And I admire such shrewdness and honesty,' she said.

'It's also rather nice to have company and somebody interested in what I might have to say. That police officer last night didn't particularly seem to be. All he was interested in was James Bexington and I have a strong suspicion that there's rather more to it than that. I mean, I even rang the station this morning and the woman on reception said somebody would ring back but nobody has.'

'Really?'

'Really,' said Nancy. 'But if I'm to talk to you, first things first. I know how these things work.'

'You do? How is that?'

'You will be on expenses, I'm sure. So you're going to buy us a nice bottle of white, order us the seafood linguine and the panna cotta and then we're going to go back to my flat to talk about Camilla, her father, James and her lovers over coffee.'

'Were there many lovers?' Jan asked.

'Later, dear. Later,' said Nancy and summoned Riccardo.

Jan smiled at the woman. She liked her a lot already. But the smile was suddenly interrupted as her mobile pinged with a text.

Can we talk? it said.

11

SURE, said the text that came back within a minute of him sending it. *Where and when?*

But Frank was having second thoughts about speaking to Jan. Actually, third, fourth and fifth thoughts. His sponsor may have told him to just sit with what was happening with him and wait for answers to come but he was finding that hard. This peace and serenity stuff was all very well until it involved the murder of a woman and knowing the man, or at least something about the man, who may well have committed that murder.

He didn't feel in imminent danger of taking a drink. Length of sobriety may not have given him any immunity but it did mean that he had accumulated some experience and insight into himself ready for a crisis like this. Except that while there had been plenty of difficult and dangerous professional crises, there had never been one so personal. And he wasn't complacent enough to think that experience and wisdom would be enough to keep him off the booze. Didn't it say in the book of Alcoholics Anonymous – the Big Book – that there would come a time when he'd have no mental defence against a drink? Eddie always said to add "yet" to the end of a sentence when he was tempted into statements of certainty about sobriety. He didn't feel in imminent danger of taking a drink – yet.

He put his phone down and even though he'd been the one instigating the text conversation, he decided not to reply. At least not for now. There was so much still to consider. Going to his old flame, one he may have still carried a torch for, even though their relationship was in the bad old days, may have paid dividends in the Regent's Park case but that had been about the need to catch a potential terrorist, and had fitted with his job. This was personal. But it was also professional, wasn't it? Where was the boundary?

He'd watched the Camilla Carew press conference, hanging on every word, noting every gesture. Donovan was her usual smart self but Hanley gave off an aggressive, unapproachable air at odds with what they were asking of the public. What to make of Peter Carew? He was clearly seeking to walk that line between grief and stoicism, to show himself to be human, though with the dignity of a leader, but it felt to Frank more the behaviour of a man too used to the public eye and concerned by how he was coming across, rather than that of a bereaved father.

There was a knock at Frank's open door and he looked up to see Tom Smithson.

'A word, boss?'

'Sure,' Frank replied and Tom walked in.

'We've just been talking after watching this media conference about Carew's daughter…'

Frank was suddenly very interested but made sure not to communicate that to Smithson. He was loyal and bright, as well as young and ambitious, but too fond of talking about people behind their backs. He would probably go far.

'And?' Frank replied.

'Well, as you'll probably remember from a few weeks back, we've been watching Peter Carew closely since a meeting he had with some far-right nutters.'

Yes, he had remembered since he'd found out that Camilla was the daughter.

'Which far-right nutters do you mean?' Frank asked. 'The ones in football shirts who go on Saturday morning marches through Luton shouting their heads off? Or those who go on TV and radio in suits trying not to shoot their mouths off but usually failing?'

'First lot. The tattoo brigade. Ones useful to him as a bit of muscle that him and his suits can hide behind,' said Tom. 'Anyway, Carew went to his daughter's flat yesterday late afternoon.'

'Right. Do we know what for?'

'No. The guy scouting him didn't worry too much as he knew that was where the daughter lived. Presumed it was a just a family visit. He stayed about half an hour, then went back to his own home down in Surrey.'

'OK. Have you told Hanley's team this?'

'Not yet.'

'Well don't. Let them come to us. Given Carew's profile they might well check with us if there's anything they need to know.'

There was a pause. Smithson was not about to leave just yet.

'There is something else, sir,' he said.

Frank was about to check his phone but looked up again.

'Go on…'

'Camilla Carew has been seeing a Labour Party aide for a while. It's why she and Bexington have been at odds.'

'I see… You know this how?

'The aide is known to us.'

'And he is?'

'Gavin Wilson.'

Frank shook his head. 'Enlighten me…'

'Special Advisor to Saleem Singh.'

'Shadow Home Secretary?'

'The same one.'

'And remind me why we're interested in this Gavin Wilson?'

'We're monitoring. Lightly so far. It came to our attention that he had a meeting about a month ago with a Palestinian liberation group known to have lobbed something more than stones into Israel.'

'So she's been slumming it with some bloke from the left. Probably upsetting the dumped Bexington and Daddy at the same time.'

'Looks a bit like it, doesn't it?'

'OK, thanks Tom.'

Smithson turned to go but before he could depart, Frank called his name and he turned.

'Nice work,' he said.

Indeed, it was nice work but what to do with it? What to do in this whole situation? Frank considered his options, pondered his next step, for about the hundredth time since hearing of Camilla Carew's death.

OK, one more time Frank, he told himself... He could speak to Hanley about the stranger who came to the AA meeting last night. But it was to betray the code of the fellowship – important to him and who he was these days, even if that code wasn't legally binding. And he had been there, after all, in a personal capacity not a professional one. As people had been telling him, and despite today's events, it still might have been a coincidence, last night's two events unconnected. Or the bloke might have been a fantasist. Anyway, he couldn't be sure it was Bexington. Though, to be honest, the photos that were shown on the TV at the media conference did show a bloke about the same age and build as the one who came to the meeting...

But what about what Tom had just told him? They should be sharing that with Hanley. Though again, if Hanley was doing his job, he'd be finding out about Gavin Wilson and this sort of stuff without any help. And if he or Tom Smithson poked noses in, Hanley was going to be pissed off about the interference. Best not to get involved with him at this stage as it might lead to complications. He certainly didn't want Hanley on his personal case. He had taken enough of a risk ringing him this morning. Actually, that in itself would surely mean that Hanley would be coming back to counter-terrorism soon enough. He would put him on to Tom.

All avenues led back to the idea that he needed to speak to someone else, someone independent, about the agony this was causing him. Somebody neither in AA nor the police. Jan had sprung to mind. She might even know something about this whole episode that he didn't. About Bexington. These days, they were far different people to that detective and reporter in their mid-thirties, more than fifteen years ago, who would swap information and buy each other drinks. And avoid lonely nights.

In addition, during the Mosque murders case, he'd told her he'd quit drinking and was in AA. Since then, they'd shared the odd drink – mineral water in his case, red wine in hers – without it leading to anything more. He'd fed her the odd story, when he in turn needed her cunning in return. Nothing major. So it wouldn't have been too much of a shock to her, him texting, would it?

He finally texted Jan back. *Tonight? Butcher's Arms, 7?*

He waited for a reply and went over to the window again to gaze out on to the winding, no longer dirty, old river that divided the country's capital city into North and South. One thing was still troubling him, something he felt ought to be known publicly, even if he wasn't going to disclose anything else for now. And Jan could help with that. The man who had walked into the AA room last night wore a hoodie, looked rough and had facial hair. The pictures the Met were putting out of Bexington showed him as handsome and clean-shaven.

12

THERE were more reporters and TV crews, now back from the press conference, congregated at the police cordon when Jan and Nancy returned to Charmouth Square. Both were fortified by a long lunch full of laughter at all the theatrical and newspaper anecdotes they had shared indiscreetly, though Jan noted a sadness on Nancy's face whenever the laughing subsided. They'd walked back from Fulham Road arm in arm, Jan coming to like this fascinating woman, whom she was starting to see as more than just a potential source or contact. She liked, too, that Nancy seemed to like her.

Seeing the throng of journos, Jan gripped Nancy's arm at the entrance to the square and the two of them stopped. Most of them would have recognised Jan and she really didn't want them to know that she was on to something.

'Something wrong, dear?' Nancy asked.

'Is there another way into your flat, Nancy? I don't really want to walk through that lot.'

'Me neither. There's an alley at the back of these buildings. And a gate leading into our communal back garden and to my kitchen door. We can go that way.'

At the entrance to the alley, Nancy introduced Jan as "my friend" to the young constable stationed on his own. He smiled. He had met Nancy during the last eighteen hours and, like everyone else still working around the crime scene, taken an instant shine to her, even if the detectives hadn't. Nancy unlocked the back gate and they walked through a neat, small garden, half lawn, half patio, bordered by shrubs.

The kitchen, the flat indeed, was bigger than it looked from the outside. Nancy took Jan's coat and hung it on a hook by the back door, drew the kitchen curtains as darkness approached, and led Jan through to the high-ceilinged living room, where she settled her into a comfortable sofa and went off to make coffee.

Jan checked her phone and picked up the second text from Frank she had missed on the walk back from the restaurant.

Sounds like a plan. See you then, she texted back as she waited for Nancy to return from the kitchen with the coffee. She gazed around the living room that was a remnant from a bygone era but a bygone era of quality. Antique chairs surrounded the Sanderson sofa on which she was installed, in front of which sat a mahogany coffee table. An opulent rug, of cornflower blue and pale yellow, was framed by intricate parquet flooring.

'Here we go dear,' Nancy announced on entering the room with a tray, interrupting Jan scrolling through her phone. She set the tray of silver coffee pot and china cups down on the table in front of Jan, who was enjoying the comfort of the sofa, and settled into one of the deep, aged armchairs as Jan poured the coffee.

'Lovely flat, Nancy,' said Jan.

'Thank you dear.'

Jan waited for Nancy, her face telling of courage, to speak next. She did not have to wait long.

'Well, I have to say that a lunch like that deserves something in return. Not that I was ever that easy a gal. Go on then. Fire away.'

'Mind if I use this?' Jan asked, pointing to her phone.

'You need to make a call?'

Jan smiled. 'No. I can record our conversation on this.'

'Ooh. Well, I'd better put my best RADA voice on then, hadn't I?'

Jan set the phone to record and carefully placed it on the table. She also took a digital micro recorder from her bag and set it up.

'And what's that one for?' Nancy asked.

'Back-up. Always use two machines to record an interview. Just in case one doesn't work.'

'Very professional. My Roly would have admired that. As do I.'

'First, can you tell me what you told that police officer last night?'

'The grumpy little man? Tommy Handley was it?'

'I think that's an old comedian. Dave Hanley, you mean.'

'Do I? Anyway, it was a bit late and I struggled, to be honest. I think I was still in shock and didn't tell him half the things I wanted to. I was only with him for ten minutes or so. I did tell him that Peter Carew came round in the afternoon. Late afternoon…'

'He came round here a lot?' Nancy looked away, pensive.

'Now and then. Not that often, come to think of it. Not that I always notice. I do like to sit in the window and gaze out on the square in the afternoons. I like the sunsets and the gathering darkness at this time of year. But I do miss things, I have to confess. At my age, you know. As I told that Hanley chap.'

'I'm not sure I believe that Nancy,' said Jan, smiling. 'Anyway, sorry, I interrupted you. Please go on.'

'Peter Carew is not a good man. I don't like his politics for a start. Roland always used to say that men like him drone on about patriotism then run for the hills when the nation needs them. He said that Carew would have been sporting a pencil moustache and selling nylons and rubber johnnies on the streets of London rather than enlisting during the War.

'Well, he saw me in the window and I waved to him but he seemed very pre-occupied. And angry, I thought. Just stood there for a moment looking towards me before pulling his coat collar up over his scarf and making off. Bit rude I thought. But then, that sort of sums him up. Is that awful of me, dear? I mean, the man has just …'

Nancy paused, scowling slightly, and gazed towards a sideboard bearing a gallery of framed photographs. A couple of theatrical promo head shots of her and a man who must have been her husband stood next to a black-and-white one of the two them with a small child holding their hands. Jan followed her gaze.

'… Has just lost his daughter,' Nancy went on. From her right eye, a tear fell. She quickly wiped it away. 'Nobody would wish that on anyone, would they?'

Jan rose from the sofa and went to sit on the arm of Nancy's chair so that she could put an arm around her. She reassured her that no, it was not awful and of course nobody should have to suffer that.

'No parent should have to bury a child,' said Nancy. And she looked up at Jan, an ache of loss in her eyes. Jan knew again to say nothing to fill a pregnant beat of silence.

'We had to with Daisy,' Nancy continued, nodding her head towards the picture on the sideboard. 'She was six years old. It was a burst appendix. Doesn't happen these days, of course, but children died from such things back then without the swiftest diagnosis and attention. We didn't know what was happening…'

Her voice trailed off and, as a trickle of tears followed the lone one already shed, she reached for the lace handkerchief tucked into the sleeve of her silk blouse.

'Nancy, I am so, so sorry,' said Jan, now kneeling in front of her to look her in the face.

'Oh, don't mind me dear,' Nancy said sharply, dabbing the tears, seeking to pull herself together. 'It's a long time since I've got like this. I suppose Camilla has brought all this back. I'll be all right. Where were we?'

'Actually, Nancy. I just need the loo…'

'Of course dear. Down the hall. Second on the left.'

Jan excused herself, saying she wouldn't be a minute. Once inside the elegant bathroom, she texted Frank.

Better make that 8, it said.

When she returned to the living room, Nancy had composed herself and she smiled as Jan sat down again.

'Sorry about the waterworks,' said Nancy.

'Absolutely no need to apologise,' Jan replied. 'So what happened later? When did it all happen? A couple of hours after Carew left?'

'A little bit longer than that. I made myself a light supper. Just some tea, toast and boiled eggs, and I listened to The Archers at 7. I left the radio on for Front Row, as they were reviewing a play that has just come on in the West End. I'd been in it years ago and I wanted to hear what they had to say about it.

'Anyway, after that item, I turned it off and settled down with a good book. An Agatha Christie. The Hollow. Ingenious. Do you like her?'

'The doyenne,' Jan replied.

'Yes, isn't she? Well, I'd been reading for about ten minutes when I heard the front door to the building slam and footsteps march quickly across the hall. They echo on that floor, you know.'

'And then?'

'Well nothing for a few minutes. Then I heard a scream. Or maybe a shout. Certainly a loud noise.'

'A man or a woman's voice, Nancy?'

'A man I think. Yes. It was quite deep. A man, I'm sure.'

'What next?'

'Well, I heard the front door slam again and I went to the curtain. I saw a figure walking quickly off down the street. Again, a man. I'm sure. After that, I went over to Camilla's flat and knocked on the door but there was no response. I called her name a few times but there was no answer. She had to be in because I was sure I hadn't heard anybody come or go between Peter Carew leaving and this man arriving.'

'Were you worried at this point?'

'I was. Very worried. I wanted to speak to somebody but there are two flats upstairs, over the two floors, and one is empty and the other has a young family in it and they are away.'

'I see. So what did you do, Nancy?'

'I went back into my flat and had a little drop of brandy and rang the police. And I thought about the man I saw.'

'Did you get a good look at him?'

'Not really at his face. He was wearing some sort of dark padded jacket. And he had a hood up. Slightly lighter colour than the jacket.'

'A hoodie. Worn under the jacket?'

'Could be dear. I've heard that word hoodie. Yes, possibly.'

'And you told the police all this?'

'I did, yes.'

'And that it was James Bexington?'

'I didn't say that. That Hanley fellow put the name to me and I said it could have been James. He did wear those kind of clothes a lot. Camilla once joked to me that he needed to grow up.'

'Do you think James would murder Camilla?'

A look of pain swept across Nancy's face again. Her voice faltered.

'Murder is such a brutal word, isn't it?'

'I'm so sorry...'

'No dear. That's what it was, isn't it? James and Camilla had their moments.'

'Like the time the police were called and she had a broken wrist?'

'Yes, that.'

'Was it you who called the police?'

'Yes. I heard the shouting and I was worried for her. She told me later that she'd grabbed him and he had pushed her away. She placed her hand down to break her fall and broke the wrist that way. It was six of one…'

'That's not what was in the papers,' said Jan.

Nancy shrugged her shoulders.

'And he was desperately upset when she ended the relationship. Couldn't get over her, it seemed. There was a night when he came round a few weeks ago and I heard him at the front door shouting into the intercom at her. I went to the window and saw him. Camilla wouldn't let him in though. But I don't see why he would be the only one the police would be interested in.'

'How do you mean?' Jan asked.

'Well, there were other men who've come and gone lately.'

'You told Hanley that?'

'I didn't dear, no. He didn't ask. I think by this point he thought I was a bit vague. I was in shock, and tired, and he seemed keen to be on his way. And things do come back to you, don't they?'

She smiled sadly at Jan, who smiled back sympathetically.

'Other men, you said Nancy?'

'There was a newish boyfriend. And her ex-husband, who was here a couple of days ago.'

Jan's heart began pounding. Hanley had started the investigation by putting his eggs in the Bexington basket. Nancy's information could put a new slant on things. And, for now, she had it to herself.

'Can you tell me about those men, please Nancy?'

'Certainly, yes. Let me see now… Her ex-husband is Simon. Simon Dewlish. I know he turned up out of the blue. I thought he was living in America. Then there was this other man who's been here quite a few times recently. I did see her kissing him goodbye yesterday morning on the doorstep. I heard her call him Gavin.'

'Nancy,' Jan said.

'Yes, dear?'

'I wonder if I might have another coffee.'

'Of course,' Nancy replied and got up to go to the kitchen.

While she was there, Jan texted Frank. *Better make it 9.*

13

THERE was a meeting every night in the crypt of St Leonard's Church in Blandford Road and Jan's text delaying their catch-up had made up Frank's mind to go back there tonight. On arrival, he saw there were at least twenty people here, more than double the usual number and three times last night's. Italian Bob was among them, and Erroll and Jennifer from last night, but neither Aesha nor Sean. There were some Frank didn't recognise at all and his defences and suspicions, even paranoia, rose. It seemed news had already spread about the mystery man from last night but surely not to "outsiders"?

People talked about how they'd been shaken by news of the murder just a few streets away from this meeting. But nobody mentioned what had clearly been discussed in private phone calls: that a bloke had come into last night's meeting and given some sort of incoherent confession to having killed someone in blackout. And it couldn't just be coincidence that a woman had been strangled near here the very same evening, could it? You often heard people talking in AA meetings about there being no coincidences, just an alignment of stars.

Maybe, Frank thought, he was taking the anonymity and confidentiality of the AA rooms too seriously. But then again, by the sounds of the sharing, to allay his suspicions about some of the people in the room, nobody seemed to have spoken to anybody official about last night and it was being kept within the immediate circle of AA people. That was certainly within the spirit of the "**LET IT STAY HERE**" edict. People had to be able to talk about something so disturbing with somebody they could trust, sharing for their mental, spiritual and emotional health, rather than bottling things up. That's why they were here in the first place, wasn't it? Anyway, he himself had spoken to his sponsor Eddie about it, so he was in no position to judge others.

At the end, Frank made a quick exit without talking to anyone, just nodding to Bob on his way out. Bob raised eyebrows in acknowledgement and reply at their shared experience. Frank walked up to Fulham Road, texting for an Uber as he did so. It arrived within five minutes and fifteen minutes later, he was sitting nursing a Coca-Cola in a semi-private corner of the Butcher's Arms. The pub was at the back of the old Paddington Green police station, where once terrorist suspects were held but had now been closed down. It was an old haunt for both of them. Frank had worked at the Green for a while and Jan's flat was nearby. In the old days, it had often been somewhere to end a working day together.

Jan arrived at around ten past nine. She looked tired and rushed but she liked being in that state. It showed she was busy; on to something.

Frank stood to greet her, planting a kiss on each cheek.

'Looking good, Jan,' he said. He could still be charming when he wanted to be. 'Still a red wine?' he asked. 'I wasn't sure, as it's been a little while.'

'Sometimes we need stability in a fast-paced changing world,' Jan said with a smile.

Frank returned it and went to buy her drink. He was long past the stage where ordering alcoholic drinks for people in pubs gave him palpitations but he was always careful not to spill a drop over him. He didn't like the smell lingering on him. He was hyper-sensitive to its scent.

'So. You busy?' he offered as a conversation starter, depositing the drink in front of her and then sitting opposite.

'Just a bit,' she said.

From Nancy's flat, she'd headed up to a coffee shop off Sloane Square where she knew she could work. There, she'd googled Camilla Carew and looked more deeply into her background, deeper than Bexington. Nancy had told her plenty but here was the confirmation and detail: Simon Dewlish, Camilla's ex-husband, had been a City trader who had gone to New York to try his luck. They'd divorced four years ago.

Then, googling images, she had found pictures of Camilla from a few weeks ago at a Labour Party fundraiser at Islington Town Hall standing alongside a man. Jan clicked on the picture. It came from a story in the *Evening Standard* Londoners' Diary. The caption to the picture described the man as Labour Party special adviser Gavin Wilson and a friend of Camilla's. More than that, it seemed.

Jan had rung in to tell Vickers what she had. Naturally he'd loved it, heading straight after the call to the Editor to tell him they had an exclusive. (Jan just knew he would be using "they" rather than "Jan" in his conversation). It would be front page material, for sure. Vickers had even told her what he envisaged for the splash headline.

CHELSEA CHOKER MURDER: LOVE TANGLE TRIO LINKED

She had sweated over the intro for a while, wanted to get it all in there to tease people to read to the bottom of the front page then to follow the turn to page 3.

THE MURDERED daughter of UK First leader Peter Carew was involved in a love tangle with THREE men in the days before her death, including a key Labour Party figure, it emerged last night.

Society girl Camilla Carew was visited by ex-husband Simon Dewlish just days ago according to a neighbour, who also recalled the Labour aide Gavin Wilson at the flat on the morning of her death.

Police are now sure to want to interview both of these two men as well as Ms Carew's former lover, James Bexington, who is the subject of a manhunt.

That ought to grab them by their bits so that their minds followed, she thought, and the piece flowed easily enough after that. All other decent media outlets – along with the police – would by now have dug into background and probably linked the names of Dewlish and Wilson with Camilla too. But they wouldn't have the detail she had, and the recent contact. And they didn't have the hitherto ignored Nancy.

Jan quoted her at length, finding the nuggets amid the chat in what was the worst part of the job – transcribing long recordings of interviews. Since her experience told her this was going to be one needed quickly, she had made discreet shorthand notes of the best bits as Nancy went along, still able to nod along and mostly retain Nancy's gaze, rather than look side-tracked.

Once filed, and after checking in with Vickers, she had recommended that the night's duty reporter in the office also do a backgrounder on Nancy, with the potential for pictures from her acting days, along with her husband Roland, who would have been known to many of the paper's older readers.

All that done, she had sat in satisfaction in the back of a cab watching her Twitter following shoot past 95,000 as she headed for the rendezvous with Frank. She'd agreed to the request for a meeting readily. She knew it meant he probably had something to share with her. And the Butcher's was on her way home. She was long over any of those painful old times there with him.

'Working on anything I might know about?' Frank asked, pretending not to know.

'The Chelsea Choker.'

'That what you're calling it?'

'Rather good don't you think?'

Jan knew it was, even if it was Vickers who'd thought of it. So good that it would stick in the minds of the public, and the other papers would be forced to use it, however pissed off they might be that her paper had got there first. She expected at least a half-smile of appreciation out of Frank but instead it was just a shake of the head. Something was eating him. Best take it easy for now.

'Why do you always ask me to meet you here after something gruesome?' Jan asked.

'What do you mean?'

'Der...? The Butcher's Arms? Remember we came here a lot back in the day...

'Yes.' Frank took a sip of his Coke. 'So?'

'And during the bloodbath that week after the Olympics?'

'Oh yes. Right.'

Frank was preoccupied, distracted. Their relationship of old may have been messy and random but when they'd reconnected in 2012, she'd found herself admiring and being surprised by Frank's new air of clarity, and how much more in control he was after giving up the drink. And in the odd meeting for coffee around Westminster on a couple of stories since, he had been as equally composed. Now the surprise she felt was about his edginess.

'What's up Frank?' she enquired.

'What do you mean?'

'Look, you ask for a meeting. I get here and you're in some kind of shell. You're normally so, what, urbane but now you're...

a bit scruffy, to be honest. And you're drinking Coke not mineral water. You're restless, anxious.'

Frank nodded slowly.

'You've always been perceptive, Jan. Perceptive and complicated. Perceptive, complicated and difficult.'

'Why thank you,' she said.

'Do you know a song called Don't Talk?' Frank asked.

'Already don't like the title. No journalist would.'

'Who's it by?'

'A band called 10,000 Maniacs. Lead singer called Natalie Merchant. Great song. Great voice.'

'I do like the band name. Probably worked with that many in newspapers down the years.'

He smiled at her.

'Been going through my head a lot lately. Have a listen. It's about drinking and how it affects people around drinkers.'

'Does this mean you've got nothing to say?' Jan asked.

'You first. Tell me about this Chelsea murder.'

'Why would you be interested in that? Nothing to do with counter-terrorism.'

Frank looked her in the eye, saying nothing, his face expressionless.

'Or is it?' she asked.

'I saw your story online this morning and guessed you'd be working on this today. What can you tell me?'

'Same old Jan-Frank rules?'

'Same rules Jan. You keep me in the loop with what you find out and are writing, and I'll give you what I can in return. Point you in the right direction.'

Jan looked at him and nodded. Even if sometimes there was a tortuous game to be played, involving a grown-up version of you show me yours first, she knew he was trustworthy, with nothing emotionally between them to complicate things. She ran through her satisfying day's work. She told him about Nancy, Carew coming to the house, the ex-husband visiting a few days earlier, of Gavin Wilson and James Bexington. Most of the time Frank's face showed no reaction.

'But I'm sure you knew all that already, given your internal contacts.'

'Some. Not all. So thank you.'

'Now, what have you got for me?'

Frank looked at her, almost pleadingly.

'OK. Usual deep background. No revealing of sources, no using my name in anything?'

Jan was surprised at him. There must be something different to this one for him to feel he had to emphasise the obvious. 'Of course. You know how I work. How our agreement works.'

'Right.' He paused and Jan was on tenterhooks. 'Bexington....'

'Yes, what about him?'

'All these pictures of him. I think you need to revise what you're putting out. He may well have a beard nowadays.'

There was a silence and Jan stared at him.

'That's it? That's fucking it? A beard.'

'More than stubble. Unkempt. Bit wispy.'

'Oh, and unkempt and wispy makes it a better story?'

'It'll give you something to start tomorrow with. And it's an exclusive.'

'Bloke grows beard. Some exclusive.'

Frank drained his Coke and got up to leave.

'Best I can do for now, Jan.'

'I can't believe you got me here to tell me a bloke might have a beard.'

'Christ, Jan. It's important. Can't you see that? He's the prime suspect and he may well have changed his appearance. You can get mock-ups out there tomorrow ahead of Hanley.'

'You're in touch with Hanley on this? So why haven't you told him?'

Frank said nothing in reply. Instead he turned and left.

Jan took a long sip of her wine. She checked her watch. She had fifteen minutes to get home until News at Ten. Her exclusive with Nancy's information would be up on the paper's website at 10pm and she wanted to see TV scramble to catch up; always a pleasure for a print journo.

She checked her phone. Somebody had swiped right on her profile. He looked decent, for a change. Salt and pepper hair framing an interesting, rather than handsome face. Late forties, maybe fifty. Worked in entertainment PR. Had his own West End agency. "OK," she thought, "why not?" It had been a while. She didn't have to go on a date with him straight away. Maybe just a phone call first. See how he sounded. Take it from there. One to think about overnight.

She'd also missed a text from Robert. *The home tell me you haven't phoned them, Jan. Come on. Play fair. FFS. Your turn. I mean it.* Bugger it. She knew he was right. She should have been the one to check on Elsie, maybe even go up there to visit. Robert was clearly getting tough, trying to call her bluff. She'd banked many times in the past on him giving in and going but there was a bit of "no more Mr nice guy" about that text.

She swilled the last swig of wine around her mouth, got to her feet and walked home. She searched for Don't Talk on Spotify and added it to her playlist, in amongst the Joni Mitchell and Sheffield bands, ABC and Pulp, that she loved. She contemplated men on dating apps, her mother, and Frank. Mostly Frank, or rather what he'd had to say.

Her disappointment, even anger, with him had subsided. She'd read the paper's astrologist saying recently that reason kicks in after ninety seconds of being angry, if you can just hold it together for that long. She could actually make something of

Bexington's beard for sure, now she thought about it. Though it wasn't some amazing counter-terrorism story she'd been half-expecting, it did have a telling bearing on the case. And she was a wizard at making bricks with very little straw. "Is this the new face of a murderer?" began to take shape in her mind for the website early tomorrow.

She thought again about how Frank had been tonight. This didn't seem entirely professional to him. He was jittery, which suggested something more personal. Was there really a counter-terrorism element to this story? Why did he consider it so important to tell her about Bexington's beard? And, more significantly, how did he know?

WEDNESDAY

14

DEENA was reading Jan's story about the various men in Camilla Carew's life when Hanley burst through the double doors and on to the office floor. She hastily closed the newspaper, folded it and slipped it into a drawer. She needn't have.

'I take it you lot have read this shit,' he said, holding up Jan's paper, with its "Love Tangle Trio" headline, before throwing it on to the floor in disgust. He looked dishevelled, his clean white shirt already crumpled and his tie askew, even though it was only 9am. 'How the fuck does she have all this and we don't?'

Deena imagined that that was the very question CS Donovan had just asked him, and why he was looking so stressed, and why he was passing on that stress. He wasn't going to endure it alone. There was a tense silence among the other five of them in the team. She would have said something, about how she'd thought they should talk again to the old woman in the flat opposite Camilla's though he'd told her to concentrate on Bexington, but as the new girl she felt on uncertain ground.

Terry, the most senior and certain of his status, spoke up. 'Well, it's obviously come from the old biddy in the flat across the hall,' he said. 'And to be honest guv, it doesn't look like shit.'

'Fucking genius. Thank you Terry,' said Hanley, keen to be getting on with his deflecting tactics. 'I know where it's come from but at least you've got the balls to say something. It's too quiet round here. You lot need to get stuck in to this. I want to know why we haven't got the detail about Bexington, Dewlish, Wilson and Carew like Jan fucking Mason has.'

'I told you about Dewlish and Wilson yesterday guv... when I was looking into people associated with them?' said Rachel. 'Working with the researchers? Dewlish the ex-husband. Wilson an acquaintance.'

'Yeah. Maybe. But not about the ex being over here and visiting her. Or Wilson being more than an acquaintance. They don't tend to stay the night and kiss on the doorstep, do they?' Hanley barked back.

He looked around the room. Suddenly the items on the top of everybody's desks had assumed a huge importance to them.

'And Campbell. You were with me when we spoke to this Nancy Preston.'

'Yes sir,' said Deena. Despite Hanley's little speech praising Terry for speaking up, the blue-touchpaper potential involved in going back over Hanley having led the questioning of the old lady, and wanting to get over to Bexington's quickly, was explosive. She decided to take it from him for now. There would be other battles worth fighting harder.

'Right,' Hanley raged on. 'This case is running away from us. We need to raise our game today. Everybody knows the importance of the first forty-eight hours. We're thirty-six in already. I want something, some big development, by tonight at the very least.'

He turned to the whiteboard, on which 10 x 8 headshots of Dewlish and Wilson had been added to the head and shoulders picture of Camilla, the one of her lying dead on the floor of her flat and the images of Peter Carew and James Bexington.

'It looks like we made a mistake just concentrating on Bexington yesterday,' Hanley went on. 'Even if he remains our priority.'

Looks were exchanged, their timing calculated to ensure their guvnor didn't see them. Looks that suggested the word "we" should have been "I" instead.

'So let's go over where we've got to. Terry? Where are we with Bexington?

'Well, me and Darren got the warrant, guv. Same as you the night before – no answer at his flat. Had to break the lock. Had a quick going over before getting forensics in. Nothing obvious there. No phone. Plenty of scarves and clothes like on the CCTV in the hallway at Charmouth Square but we need DNA from him. Neighbours said they hadn't seen him for a couple of days and that looked about right.'

'No sightings?'

'Nothing concrete. Few people phoning in. Bradford, Plymouth. Other unlikely places. Nothing more than cranks and attention-seekers by the sound of it.'

'Well, check them out. Get him found. His picture's been all over the media. He can't have left the country. His passport would have rung alarm bells.'

He turned to Rachel. 'So where's Dewlish?'

'I'll check with Heathrow and the hotels. See when he flew in and where he might be registered. He's got a sister who might know where he's staying.'

'Get Imran to put out a story to the press that we want to speak to him. That might flush him out.'

'Yes guv.'

'What about Wilson?'

'Well, it was yesterday afternoon by the time I got to the researchers about Camilla. That's when I told you about him. You remember? Told you he worked for the Labour Party.'

Hanley nodded.

'When I phoned him, he said he was devastated. He'd gone home from his office early. Said he liked her a lot. Would help us any way he could.'

'Well, get on to him again. We need to speak to him about this new info. Find out when he and Camilla went from being friends to spending the night together. Campbell, you were on family and friends with Thomas. What more do we know about these two blokes?'

'Dewlish was a city trader. Made plenty of money before the 2008 crash but seemed to disappear for a couple of years after. Married Camilla in 2014, divorced four years later and been in New York since then. Waiting for the East Coast to wake up to have a word with the NYPD to see if anything is known about him over there.'

'OK. That's better,' said Hanley. He calmed down and seemed to be beginning to realise that the time for bawling them out had passed.

'This Nancy Preston woman told Mason that Dewlish was at the flat a couple of days before Camilla was killed,' Hanley added. 'We need to know what brought him back over here. He looks as if he's got money so start with the big hotels first, Thomas. What about Wilson? What does he do with the Monster Raving Looney Party?'

'He's a Spad, guv,' said Deena.

'What's that when it's at home?'

'A special adviser.'

'Well thank you Laura Kuenssberg,' said Hanley, raising a laugh from Terry and Darren.

'He's pretty high up,' added Deena. 'He advises Saleem Singh, the shadow home secretary, on policy.'

'Ooh. Grown-up stuff,' said Hanley. 'If such a thing exists in that party. What about the mother? Where's she in all this?'

'Martha Bickler,' said Rachel. 'Divorced Carew ten years ago. Re-married a Swiss banker.'

'Is that rhyming slang?' Terry asked, laughing. Nobody else reacted, though there was a trace of a smile on Hanley's face.

'I rang her and Carew had phoned her with the news. She was naturally very upset and is flying in this afternoon.'

'That adds up now,' said Sanjay and everyone turned to him. 'You asked me to look into her finances? I went to Camilla's flat and had a root around. Found a letter from a solicitor in a drawer. About a new will that Camilla made only a month ago. Rang him and he sounded a bit flustered. Told me to contact the executor. One Martha Bickler. She has to agree to information being released if probate hasn't been granted yet. Gave me an email address.'

'Email the executor for permission? We're conducting a fucking murder inquiry here. Get back to him and tell him we need to know what's in that will. And get back to Mrs Bickler. Ask her to come see us at Hammersmith after she's landed. We need to find out why a thirty-eight-year-old woman would suddenly make a will.'

'Would it be best if I gave her a time for when Carew has left?' Sanjay asked.

'Anytime late afternoon will be fine. Carew's coming in early this afternoon and their paths shouldn't cross. Terry, you come into the Carew interview with me.'

Terry smiled. Then thought.

'But he's not a suspect, though guv? I mean, his own daughter?'

'No,' Hanley replied. 'But I want to know what Carew and Camilla talked about yesterday afternoon that led to this Preston woman saying he looked angry when he left. He would have known all these three blokes. He will have info that we need.'

'Do you think we should contact intelligence or counter-terrorism?' Deena asked. 'I mean, we've got two politicians here in Carew and Wilson. Or at the very least, both of them are close to the political scene.'

'On the fringes,' Hanley replied. 'One's an unelected politician and the other's some kind of researcher.'

'Bit more than that,' said Sanjay, 'Carew was a powerful voice in the country through Brexit and still has plenty of followers.

And some clout with the PM, who he campaigned with. According to the article in the paper, Wilson is quite an influence inside the Labour Party too.'

'Look,' said Hanley, his tone hardening again. 'I agree we need to speak to all of these people and build up our picture. But we need to be careful it doesn't lead us down rabbit holes. We continue with the search for Bexington, keeping on top of that. He's still got to be the prime suspect. Terry, contact his mates and known associates to see who might know where he could be. According to Mason, he knew all about Gavin Wilson and so had a motive.'

'If he was going to kill, wouldn't he have killed Wilson, guv?' Deena wondered. 'Why kill the woman he loved?'

'Jealousy. Heat of the moment. Them's the sort of things we need to find out, are they not?' Hanley replied. 'I want you,' he added, turning to Rachel, 'to go back round to Mrs Preston and see if there's any other things that she might remember. And get uniform to go door to door around the square again to see if anybody's memory has improved.

'I still smell this as a domestic. So we keep it within this department for now, all right? It's ours to solve. Not some smart-arse desk jockeys who've watched too many episodes of Spooks.'

The others nodded but Deena was unmoved, betraying nothing on her face. Hanley may not be thinking beyond a domestic, but it might just be worth an informal chat with Frank Phillips. After Regent's Park, there was a reservoir of respect between them, even if they hadn't seen much of each other since.

'So let's get to it,' said Hanley, pointing on the board to Bexington, Dewlish and Wilson. 'Something big. By tonight people, yes?'

15

THIS was a day to savour. A front page lead was always cause for satisfaction and walking that bit taller through the building. Jan arrived at around 10.30am, smiled at Pippa on reception and stood for a moment admiring the huge image of the paper, with her story in all its ten-feet high glory, projected on to the wall behind the front desk. She pressed her pass card down and the glass doors separated for her, a little bit more quickly and respectfully it seemed this morning. Voluntary redundancy? Back burner, today at least, thank you.

In the atrium, she ordered a double espresso from the coffee cart and made her way up to the newsroom. 'Nice work Jan,' said Damian from features as they entered the lift together. She thanked him. She was no threat to him in his cosy department, nor he to her, and he could afford to be magnanimous. It was just the odd news reporter, ambitious and envious of her, of whom she was wary.

She needn't have worried about Danny, at least. The youngest reporter on the news room floor said 'great story, Jan' to her and blushed a little. It was gratifying that he was in awe of her, a nice throwback to the days when she too had a huge respect for her seniors. She'd been like that when she did legwork for some of the Fleet Street greats, when the industry was still full of fire and selling big numbers of printed copies back in the 1990s. The press award had helped a lot, of course. In fact, it had so put the nose of Natalie Bridges out of joint that the up-and-coming blonde byline-bandit who thought she was about to replace Jan as the top dog reporter had decamped for a red top paper in search of seniority. Jan had seen off plenty these past twenty years.

She looked down the floor to see Vickers some thirty yards away having a rant at a kid working on the website. She couldn't quite hear what was being said, just the odd swear word, but could see a bollocking was being administered. The poor kid had his head bowed and wasn't answering back.

Jan wondered what that was all about, knowing that print and digital were pretty much separate these days, even if Vickers was nominally involved in both. They may have shared stories, more from the paper going to the website than the other way round, but by and large the two sets of staff had little to do with each other.

'Let's hope he's not just warming up for the day,' said Jan.

'Even if he is, you're all right,' Danny replied. 'You have carte blanche.'

'Ooh get you. All French. In this game you have to keep earning it, Danny,' she said. 'Still, it's nice to be back writing my own ticket without Vickers thinking he owns me. What's happening down there, by the way?'

With all the relish and relief of everyone in news rooms who enjoy someone other than them being bollocked, Danny proceeded to provide her with the juicy detail.

'Website did a story yesterday on bullying at work. Women tell their horror stories, all that kind of thing. Vickers liked the tales so much that he nicked it for the news pages this morning. Well buried but decent enough page lead for our readership. Seems the story actually started with that website kid though, posing as a Mum and posting a bullying story of his own on Mumsnet to get a thread going. Then he copied and pasted the replies.'

'That's what happens with all this "content" shit they expect on websites, rather than proper stories,' said Jan. 'People under pressure start making it up.'

'Oh, I don't think it was the ethics of it that bothered Ivan so much. He thought the stuff the kid had posted was about him and his reputation around the building.'

Jan laughed, a bit too long and loud so that Vickers could make out the tail end of her mirth as he marched back to his desk.

'Something fucking funny?' he asked.

'We were just having a laugh about the *Post* being so off the pace on our story,' Jan said. 'I mean, what's all that about, leading on snow being due next week and Camilla's murder just a basement story on the front? Anyway, good morning to you, Ivan.'

'What you got today?' he snarled in reply.

'Yes. Ours was a good front page. I thought so too.'

'Answer the question. Not the one you think I should ask and you want to give the answer to. You're not a fucking politician. And you need to keep on top of this story.'

'Patience, Ivan. Early doors.'

She wasn't going to tell him quite yet what she had. She would string him along for a bit longer before delivering. That way, he'd be more grateful when she did. and she would be controlling the dynamic. She had learned early on, from one of those legends she worked with and for, how to keep control of the dynamic with editors. One in particular had mentioned ringing his office "to tell my editor what he thinks."

She looked at her phone and decided to kill time by checking out the guy who had swiped right on her profile last night. Another couple of men had also swiped this morning but it was this one she liked the look of. Will Gaunt, fifty-one years old. Hmm. Actually, not a PR. He was more of a film and TV agent, the profile said. A quick Google check revealed him to be genuine. And not bad looking. Had some decent clients too. She needed to know more. Tania would have something.

'Yes, Jan. What you after?' If a voice, like eyes, could be bleary, this one was.

'Sorry. Have I woken the showbiz desk?'

'Late night at a premiere. Too much bubbly as per. What brings you my way? Some celeb been naughty?'

'Will Gaunt.'

'What's he done?'

'Nothing. That I know of. What's he like?'

'Got a few big actors. Very protective of them. Can get arsey but then that's his job. Doesn't hold grudges. Given me a few decent tales now and then.'

'Honest? Trustworthy?'

'As far as anyone connected with the media is, yes I suppose so.'

'Womaniser?'

'Not that I know of. Never hit on me or anyone I know. Considered a gent, in fact.'

'OK thanks.'

'Something I should know?'

'No. That'll do for now. Thanks Tania.'

Jan ended the call and looked at Will Gaunt one last time. His was a new profile on the app. What the hell, she thought. Maybe get in before someone else does... He would probably have swiped on a few to see who bit. She swiped right.

She got back to her laptop and began to trawl through the main news sites. Above the news desk, a TV was showing Sky News with a headline bar saying: *CAREW MURDER – POLICE TO INTERVIEW TWO MORE...* With a woman's eye on it, she'd hoped they would use Camilla's full name rather than just the family one, to humanise her and emphasise that this was a story about a woman being murdered rather than a well-known man being involved in the story. The professional in her had to accept it was more newsworthy, however.

On the hour, at 11am, the story was their lead and she watched a reporter appear on screen from near the police cordon in Charmouth Square. There was no more information given than in Jan's story but rolling news was a voracious beast, needing regular feeding, and the same words in a different order would do. Then the picture cut to another reporter, clearly briefed by the Met press office, who said that police were expecting to bring in Simon Dewlish and Gavin Wilson for questioning today.

Having got her feet under the table, checked her Twitter feed – ooh, look; she'd hit 100,000 followers this morning. Yay! – and consumed enough coffee, Jan decided it was time to move this story on, to put Vickers out of his misery and keep the paper leading the pack. She rose from her chair and ambled idly over to his desk.

He was himself trawling through websites until what she said stopped his scrolling finger.

'I think I might have something new we can put on the website and set the agenda for the day,' she said.

'OK. New. I like that word. Go on…'

'Well, the search for Bexington… We're all using pictures of him clean shaven. I have it from a very good source that he might well have facial hair now.'

'What source?'

'Come on Ivan, you know better than that. Let's just say it's better than somebody trawling and trolling on Mumsnet.'

'How do you know about that?'

'Oh, sources inside and outside the office.'

'Do fuck off Jan. You gonna write this story then?'

'Of course. And I suggest you get an artist working on an impression of what Bexington might look like with some kind of wispy, unkempt beard. My story will be ready in half an hour.'

Jan smiled at Vickers and opened a word document on her laptop.

She hadn't even begun when her mobile buzzed with a personal message from the dating app.

Will Gaunt here. Thank you for swiping on my profile Jan. Would you like to chat sometime today. Or maybe we could meet later for a drink? His phone number was included.

She thought about it. What was the point of a call really if she liked the look of him? Worth risking an hour early evening somewhere public for a proper conversation, see the whites of his eyes, surely? She realised that justifying the meeting to herself like this was a sure sign she wanted to go. She texted his mobile.

Sounds good. 6.30pm? She had noted his office was in Soho. *West End somewhere?*

Excellent, came the reply. He suggested a pub near Soho Square, the Seven Pillars of Hercules. She knew it. A nice old London pub.

Great. See you then, she texted back.

She was pleased with herself as she began to type and it took her only twenty minutes to finish the 500 words to go with the artist's drawing. It had to go through her "line manager" Vickers before it could go to the website but within half an hour it was online under the headline: **IS THIS THE CHELSEA CHOKER'S NEW LOOK?**

Within ten minutes, her mobile was ringing. She looked at the name on the screen and took the call. She had been expecting it, if not quite this quickly, and indeed was looking forward to it. She put him on speaker. She liked to put on a bit of show for the newsroom now and then.

'What the fuck do you think your game is?' yelled a man's voice.

Danny and Vickers looked up from what they were doing, as did a few other early reporters and sub-editors from a few banks of desks away.

'I did tell you, DCI Hanley, did I not? You'd be better off working with me than against me.'

'I could charge you with obstructing a police investigation.'

'How am I doing that?'

'Withholding information.'

'So which is it, obstruction or withholding? Not sure Jackie Donovan would take very kindly to you charging me, and thus turning off a potential tap of info. Not to mention you being distracted by me when there are rather more important things to be dealing with. Like catching a murderer. What do you reckon?'

There was a silence at the end of the phone.

'Me work with you? Over my fucking dead body.'

'Well, you'd better hope that I don't break another story that Jackie Donovan drags you into her office about, shall we?' said Jan.

There was a click on her speaker and then her phone went silent. She smiled to herself. She knew it was his loss. She enjoyed the smiles around her. Even Vickers was impressed.

She tweeted a link to her online story and the likes and retweets soon arrived. Next she went back to trawling websites, seeing that very soon others were running with the Bexington story. The reputable sites, newspapers and TV, had rung the syndication desk to use the artist's impression of him with a beard while some had an in-house artist hastily put their own version together. Others simply posted it without credit or payment. The internet could still resemble the wild west.

She hoped it wouldn't be long before there were genuine sightings of Bexington and she could get back to work on developments in the story. In the meantime, she began to delve further into the backgrounds of Dewlish and Wilson.

Dewlish, it seemed from bits dotted about in the New York papers, had become a bit of a face on the Manhattan scene after remarrying the daughter of a Congresswoman. There were stories, however, of a row between them outside a restaurant a few weeks ago. According to one witness, it had ended with her jumping in a taxi and shouting 'Enough, Simon.'

Wilson seemed like a smart cookie, though not your average Labour Party member. Born in Cheshire. Parents owned a clothing company. Posh Northern. Bright lad. He'd gone to Marlborough and Oxford, read politics and economics and become a researcher before his qualities had been spotted and he'd ended up as an advisor to the shadow home secretary. He was expected to stand as an MP himself in the near future and be given a winnable seat.

He figured in a piece in *The Guardian* about Labour's rising stars, with some nice old photos of him, playing Rugby, sitting astride a motorbike. She was interrupted by Gemma, the latest toothsome blonde-haired news desk intern no doubt related to somebody somewhere on the paper, or who might have won a work placement from some school or charity auction.

'Ms Mason,' Gemma said. 'Somebody on the phone for you.'

'OK,' said Jan, 'put them through.'

She picked up and said hello.

'Is that Jan Mason?'

'Yes,' she replied. 'Who is this?'

'My name is James Bexington,' said the voice on the other end.

16

HOW ABOUT, Frank suggested, somewhere around Regent's Park, for old time's sake? Not the cafe in the park, on Inner Circle, she said. She'd not been back since old Saul died there the day they caught the Mosque murderer. And it held poignant memories, too, of Rashid and their drifting apart due to his Manchester move that still hurt, the more so because she still had feelings for him. And so the coffee shop at Great Portland Street station it was.

Deena arrived first and ordered herself a green tea. The place was just right. Though it was on the Marylebone Road, a busy main London arterial on the edge of the congestion zone, the coffee bar itself was at the back of the station and out of sight. She picked a table away from the window where it was quiet, due to most people wanting to be in the beam of what few hours of daylight there were at this time of year. She didn't want them to be seen together in case anyone they knew might pass. Small world, big mouths.

She sat for ten minutes, checking her phone, wondering if Frank had found other, more important business. But then, what could be more important than a murder case? Actually, Deena thought, having a word with herself, something concerning national security. Camilla Carew may have been grand in her social standing but in the grander scheme of things, what would her death mean to the second in command at counter-terrorism?

And then he finally arrived, rushing noisily through the door. That was unusual for a start. He was normally understated in everything he did. Professionally and personally not wanting to draw attention to himself. Her memory of the man that day when they took down the Mosque murderer was of someone in complete control, trained and composed. Now he looked tired, even edgy. He hadn't shaved. The top button of his shirt was undone and his tie loosened. She hadn't been expecting this vision of him at all.

'Deena. Hi,' he said, spotting her as he came through the door and strode to her table. 'You look so well.'

Deena smiled.

'It's OK,' Frank said. 'You don't have to say it back. I know I look like shit. Got some stuff going on. You want another tea?'

'No thanks. You get what you want.'

He returned a couple of minutes later with a black coffee and stirred one lump of sugar into it.

'How have you been?' he asked.

'Yes. Good thanks.'

'You're doing well, I hear. What you reckon to Hanley?'

Deena smiled but didn't reply.

'Yeah, me too,' he said. 'Anyway, what can I do for you?'

'You know about this Chelsea choker case?'

'Chelsea choker? We're using Jan-speak now, are we?'

She looked a bit embarrassed.

'Fair point. This Chelsea murder then. You have heard about it?'

'I've sort of been following it, yes.'

'Well, is there anything we should know?'

Frank, she thought, replied a little too quickly and sharply for him to be only "sort of" following it.

'Like what?'

'Are any of those in the frame known to you…'

'Well naturally we keep tabs on politicians and those involved in political circles.'

'Like Carew and Wilson?'

'Yep.'

'So…?'

'Nothing I can really tell you Deena. Sorry. But there's no significant interest in them at the moment. Nothing out of the ordinary, let's put it that way.'

Significant. Hmm. Interesting use of the word, she thought. So there was some interest in them.

'But they're both of interest to us in a murder case.'

'A murder case. Exactly. Not linked to terrorism.'

'What about Dewlish? Hanley wants me to find him. We think he might still be in London.'

'Not known to us.'

'But can you help me?'

'Help you?'

'Find him.'

'Well, maybe. I could make a few inquiries in the department.'

'Thank you. I know you've got higher access to stuff than we have.'

There was a pause.

'Frank, is there something up?'

'No, why?'

Again, too quick for it to be the truth, Deena thought.

'You agreed to this meeting, and you must have known I'd want some help. But you're not giving me anything.'

There was a pause as Frank looked down into his empty coffee cup for a few moments.

'Deena. What you did on the Regent's Park case as a PC was amazing. And you've deserved your rise through the detective ranks. The least I can do is agree to a meeting. But I can't give you what I haven't got.'

Deena enjoyed the compliment and smiled. But she had learned enough not to be diverted by flattery. And enough to trust her instincts as well.

'Thanks Frank. But I'm guessing you also came because you think I might have something for you. You're more than "sort of" following this case. You're interested, even if it's just because of Carew's role in it. He's the sort who stirs everyone's interest. Right and left. Right or wrong. Politicians and public. A murder team and counter-terrorism.'

It was Frank's turn to smile, his first of the day. But it was a weak one. He admired the woman.

Deena persisted. 'What about James Bexington?'

Frank tried to suppress a flinch at the mention of the name. But Deena picked up on it instantly. Too quick once more.

'What about him?' he asked.

Now Deena was in no doubt about his defensiveness.

'You've seen Jan's latest story? About him maybe having some kind of beard now?'

He hadn't seen it yet but since he was the source of it, he could say, honestly, that he did know about it.

'So do you have anything at your end about his whereabouts?'

In Frank's response, Deena could see that he was choosing his words carefully and delivering them slowly. In contrast to his previous staccato answers.

'None. He's not somebody we've ever had to take an interest in… He's just a playboy as far as we're concerned… He and Camilla were just social, what, gadabouts. Living off her money, which came from Daddy. Until she stopped Bexington's supply.'

For somebody supposed to be of no interest to his department, Bexington still seemed to be a figure Frank had been scoping.

'Which makes him prime suspect,' Deena said.

'Yes, of course. Never underestimate the anger of someone who's seen his gravy train hit the buffers.'

'It's certainly a line of inquiry,' said Deena. 'Depends where you're coming from. Conspiracies or cock-ups. In your line, it's conspiracies. In mine, more often than not, it's cock-ups.'

'What do *you* know about Bexington?' Frank asked.

She'd known this moment would come.

'Ah, so you do want something from me?'

'Think he's capable of it?'

'I don't know. Nothing in his background suggests that he's a murderer. Bit wet by all accounts.'

'People can do the most frightening things though when they're not themselves.'

'What does that mean – not themselves?'

'You know. Torn apart by demons. Rage. Drugs...' He softened his voice and looked across the room to check if anyone was taking an interest in what he was saying before finishing his sentence. 'Or drink.'

There was another silence.

'Frank. Is there something you want to tell me here?'

Frank did indeed want to talk to somebody about this. Beyond telling his sponsor, that was. Somebody who wasn't a recovering alcoholic, and "normal", whoever or whatever that was. He was growing ashamed of himself, and shame was a dangerous emotion for an alcoholic, the driving force behind a relapse into drink. He had heard it so many times: a drink is not the beginning of a relapse, it's the end. The natural result of a series of events and feelings that can overwhelm if not halted. He wasn't exactly lying to people; his sins were more of omission than commission, but he was withholding, being evasive. He was not abiding by the code of honesty that his life since drink had embraced and which had kept him on the straight and narrow. Why not trust the girl? She had earned his trust through the integrity he could discern in her.

Before he could answer her question, however, Deena's mobile rang.

'Better take this,' she said, getting up and moving outside the cafe.

Frank checked his mobile while Deena was out but he had barely taken in the first email by the time she returned.

'Got to go,' she said. 'Another body's been found. Sounds like it could be linked to this.'

'Linked to this? How do you know?'

'Same MO,' Deena replied. 'A strangling.'

'Whereabouts?'

'Battersea. Not too far over the bridge from Charmouth Square. Hanley's already there.'

'Jesus,' said Frank. 'Got a name?'

'Young bloke. Name of Sean Malahide.'

Frank didn't know a Sean Malahide. But he did know a Sean.

17

THE 14.32 from Victoria slithered its way slowly through South London's snaking spaghetti of railway lines to East Croydon, before speeding up on the route to Gatwick, thence to Brighton. Jan tried to read her book – the bodies were piling up in *Betty Boo* now – but Jan was too nervous to concentrate. Nerves were good, though, she told herself. Just excitement by another name. She knew that what she was doing was dangerous – both professionally and personally – but she was just too intrigued to care right now. She'd taken care of herself for this long, hadn't she? And she'd deal with any disciplinary action, either from the paper for not informing them where she was going, or any media watchdog who might question her for meeting with a murder suspect. This was about one potentially amazing story.

Most of the passengers got off at the airport, leaving just a couple of dozen making the full journey to the coast. It was a rainy late-autumn midweek afternoon and darkness would be starting to fall by the time she got off the train. Even dirty weekends didn't begin this early and in such a passion-killer of a climate.

At the end of the line, she walked out of Brighton station to the taxi rank and hopped into one of the distinctive white and aquamarine liveried cars. The driver knew her destination. Everyone did; though quite why anyone would want to go there, especially on their own, on such a dank day, with the light fading fast, was anyone's guess. Each to their own. He drove down Queen's Road and then tacky North Road, with its stag-and-hen bars and nightclubs, to the sea front. There he turned left, passing the Brighton Centre and the cinema complex. The sign BRIGHTON PIER came into view and the taxi driver deposited her opposite. Out of season, with an East wind gusting, there were few people around. She wished she'd brought her cerise felt beret to keep her hair from blowing across her eyes.

Of course Bexington hadn't asked to meet her here. Much too obvious and even if it was quiet, they might be spotted and recognised by someone in a passing car who was abreast of the news. No, he'd instructed her to keep walking along the promenade, down Madeira Drive so that he could see her, and that she was on her own, when she approached.

She looked at her watch as she went. It was 4.15. Fifteen minutes to the meeting.

Her mobile rang, her brother's photo appearing on the screen. Anyone else, apart from the news desk or Frank or Deena, and she wouldn't have answered.

'Robert. Hi. Look, I'm going to ring the care home later. OK? Something's cropped up. Something vital.' Truth be told, she had forgotten. She could have done it on the train but her mind had been preoccupied with the delicious jeopardy of this job.

Once upon a time Robert might have responded with something like "for fuck's sake, Jan" but he was now just curt, business-like. And heard-it-all-before weary.

'She's taken a turn for the worse, Jan. They've told me it's not looking good.'

'What? She's broken her ankle. She'll be OK with a bit of rest, won't she?'

'Not that simple. It's disorientated her. She was agitated and in a lot of distress, they said, but now she's sleeping. When she wakes up they can only give her water.'

'Can't they give her vitamins intravenously, or some sort of nourishment?'

'Wish they could. Can't find a vein properly. Most have collapsed. And where they haven't, it's agony for her and her body won't absorb the liquid for some reason. You know how frail she is.'

'So what do you want me to do?

'Well, I'm going to drive there now.'

'That's great Rob. Brilliant. Well done.'

There was a silence on the other end of the phone.

'You think I should too?' Jan said, her embarrassment piqued by Robert's lack of response.

'Put it this way Jan, if you want to see your mother alive one last time, then I think you should get yourself up to Wakefield as soon as you can.'

Her mobile pinged with a notification. She was anxious to see what it was. She snapped. 'Don't guilt-trip me Robert. I'm up to my fucking neck in one of the biggest stories of my life. I'll get there if and when I can. She'll be fine.'

Jan shut down the call. Robert hadn't needed to guilt-trip her. She felt guilty enough about her mother as it was. Guilty, mainly, that she did not have as much feeling for her as she thought she should have. Anyway, Elsie had always pulled through in the past.

Jan checked what the ping on her mobile was. It was from her BBC Breaking News app.

Police discover strangled body of man, 28, in Battersea, South London. "Too early" to say if linked with Camilla Carew murder in nearby Chelsea. Full story to follow on BBC News website.

Thanks a bunch Deena, she thought. *You could have given me a quick heads-up, a bit of a beat.* Jan was tempted to ring her but she had more pressing business. Everyone had that story now. The smell of cooking fish wafted from the chippies on the pier. She had a bigger one to fry. She looked at her watch. Eight minutes to reach the meeting point.

Should she keep the appointment, though? Holy shit, there was a second body now. We were getting into the realms of serial killer. Two out of three… But then, police were saying it was too early to make a link. Had to be one, though, didn't there? Two strangled bodies a couple of miles apart in three days? Ah, to hell with it. She couldn't NOT keep the meeting. Curiosity may kill the cat but they had nine lives. She felt feline. She'd be fine. And there was a murderer to be caught, an exclusive to be nailed.

The rain had thankfully stopped and as her pulse raced, so did she along the promenade for a hundred yards, until she realised that the chill wind was penetrating even her Burberry's collar. She crossed over to the sanctuary of the arches behind the aqua-painted but rusting wrought iron stanchions underpinning the pavement of Marine Road above. It was spooky, though. There was no-one about. She felt panic-attack anxious suddenly, even claustrophobic despite being in the open air. Tried to keep the prospect of that exclusive uppermost in her mind to distract her from her agitation. Darkness had now descended. She remembered what a great name in her profession, Keith Waterhouse, had once written about Brighton: a town always helping the police with its inquiries.

Some twenty yards ahead, she could see steps that led up to the road. This was the designated meeting point but there was no sign of Bexington. Perhaps he wouldn't show. His voice had sounded nervy on the phone and it was more than likely that he'd got cold feet. She felt a moment of human relief at that thought before journalistic disappointment kicked in. She looked at her watch. 4.30pm. Time.

Her mobile rang and startled her. She took it from her bag. Another on the short list whose call must be taken.

'Yes Ivan?' she said.

'Seen this about another body?'

'Do we know it's linked yet?'

'Danny's phoned the press office. They're trying to work out if there's a connection. Same MO, obviously, but can't say yet. Strange one. Some Chelsea totty and a young bloke in a block of flats south of the river. May be nothing but thought you might want to get on to it. You want to do it from there? Wherever you are.'

'Maybe. I think my contact here may have gone to ground. We got a name on this body yet?'

'Danny told the press officer they'd have you to answer to if we didn't get one.'

'And?'

'Sean Malahide.'

She had no time to respond when a voice interrupted her conversation.

'Ms Mason?'

She turned and almost jumped out of her skin. A figure had emerged from the shadows under the arches by the steps.

'Fucking hell,' she shouted, though there was no-one near to hear her.

'Sorry, I didn't mean to alarm you,' said the figure.

'Well, you fucking well did,' she said. She could hear Vickers on the other end of her phone.

'Jan. Jan? You all right?' he was saying. She was at first touched by his concern then worked out he was probably more worried about getting some copy out of her today.

'I'm fine,' she replied not taking her eyes off the man standing about five yards from her. 'Get Danny to write it up for the website. I'll speak later. Got something on this end, yeah?'

She ended the call and stood staring at the man. Even in this light, with just a low wattage streetlamp some fifteen yards away punctuating the gloom, she could see that it was Bexington. Not the clean-shaven figure from the cuts, however, nor the bearded man from the artist's impression. This one had only a moustache.

'Did you find it OK?' Bexington asked.

'What? Yes. Obviously.'

'Of course you did,' he replied. 'We wouldn't be standing here together, would we, if not?' He gave a nervous laugh. Jan, of good Yorkshire flat vowels stock, had heard such well-spoken accents many times before since coming to London, but this was taking toffery to a new level.

'Look,' Jan said. 'Can we cut the small talk and just get straight to it. Why have you asked me here?'

He looked at her for a moment. 'I'm just trying to gauge if I can trust you,' he said. 'It's been a good start. I waited at the pier, saw you get out of the cab, and walked the top road watching you. I could see you were alone. You can't be too careful these days with journalists. Duplicitous lot to my mind.'

'Don't *you* fucking start…' Jan said. 'So why am I here?'

'You do swear a lot, don't you?' said Bexington.

'You're a fucking suspect in a murder inquiry and you think it's me needs to trust you? I'm taking my life in my hands just being here. Alone.'

What she didn't say was that she would never have shared where she was going with anyone else. She always had hated joint bylines.

'Well, when you put it like that…' he said.

'Anyway, you must trust me on some level to have asked me here. So I'll ask again. Why am I here?'

'I read your story this morning. About all of us who knew Camilla well,' he said.

'And?'

'I thought you might be a good person to tell my side of things.'

'Don't you think you should be telling it to the police?'

'Really? You'd pass up a scoop?'

Bexington smiled. Jan returned it. Perhaps he wasn't just some upper-class twit. He certainly knew what motivated her.

'I want it out there via you first,' he added, 'because I'll be able to get my version of events over rather than just being some posh boy under arrest. The public will judge me before they know anything about me.'

'Blimey, you should get a job in PR or crisis-management,' said Jan.

'Once it's in your paper, I'll give myself up to the police,' Bexington added.

'I've got plenty of questions,' said Jan. 'But before we sit down somewhere and do this properly, what are you doing in Brighton and why did you come here?'

'I came here with Camilla a couple of times. Stayed at a little Air B and B in Kemp Town. We liked it. Liked doing the daft things here and especially out of season…'

His voice trailed off. There was a wistful sadness to it.

'OK. And when did you come here?'

'I got a train here after rush hour last night. Why?'

'Do you know somebody called Sean Malahide?'

18

HANLEY attached two photos of the dead body onto the white-board. The first showed the smiling face of a young man, eyes wide with a future ahead of him. The other showed that face white and bloated, eyes staring and static, more grotesque than Camilla Carew's had been. He'd lain undiscovered for longer, on the living room floor of his top-floor flat of a four-storey block in the backstreets of Battersea. It was a district that the developers had not yet reached in their schemes to attract the overspill of money from across the Thames bridges of South West London.

'Sean Malahide,' said Hanley. 'Aged twenty-eight. Lived alone, worked as a barman and waiter at a gay club in Soho. The good news is we may well have our link between him, Camilla, and our killer. More on that in a minute.

'First off, and before we finally get over to Hammersmith to interview Carew and Wilson, I've asked uniform to do prelimi-nary interviews with Malahide's neighbours to see what else we can find out about his private life. Once those are in and up on the system, I'll go through them later and divvy up to see who speaks in detail to who, OK?'

Deena, Terry, Darren, Sanjay and Rachel all nodded.

'Sanj, you work with the researchers and find out all you can about him from other sources. Hit the internet. Social media, his Twitter, Facebook, Instagram. All that shit. I hate it but it's what they seem to teach at detective school these days. See what he's been saying and who to. One other thing that links this to Camilla. No phone found in the flat.

'I'll interview Wilson with Campbell. OK?' Hanley continued, looking at Deena. 'We'll talk privately about how we go about it, all right? Typical cunning politico. Got himself in here before we could pick him up. Knows it'll look better.'

'Him and his solicitor good and boiling according to the desk sergeant at Hammersmith,' said Terry. 'Been there since this morning.'

'Yeah, well. We have been a bit busy with a second body, have we not?' said Hanley. 'If he doesn't grasp that, then he won't be doing himself any favours, will he?'

Deena had been surprised and pleased to be asked to ride shotgun in the interview but then she realised why.

'Terry, you and Thomas interview Carew,' Hanley continued. 'But tread lightly. This is a bloke who's just lost his daughter. That's why I want you two to do it. Someone senior but not too senior, and someone who looks sympathetic. OK?'

They both nodded but neither seemed particularly pleased with their description, the subtext of which included their white faces. Deena had no stomach for a battle this morning, however. There was a war to be won.

'We're just looking for more info from him on these bees round the honeypot, and how they all relate to his daughter,' Hanley added.

He went to sit at a desk so he could contemplate the whiteboard and stretched his feet out on it, arms folded behind his head.

'Any further with Bexington?' he asked.

'Not yet guv,' said Terry. 'But all forces and transport hubs on highest level alert. Pictures out of him with a beard now. He's got to turn up soon. And we've found out he's got a best mate called Giles.'

'Well, he would have, wouldn't he?' Hanley replied.

'I can go and see him now, if Terry's doing the Peter Carew interview,' said Darren.

'Do it. And any more on Bexington's background?'

'Inherited a load of dosh when his father died five years ago. Owned the flat in Kensington, which is fifteen minutes' walk from Camilla's. Used the rest to set up the antiques shop. Doing badly. He wasn't often there to open up, according to couple of traders around him.'

'Anything on Dewlish?'

'Press office put the story out, guv and we got a call from a hotel in South Ken,' said Rachel. 'Stayed there Saturday, Sunday and Monday night but he checked out yesterday morning. We're hoping we get another sighting.'

'OK. Sanjay… What about the mother and the will?'

'Well, the solicitor seems to have done a disappearing act this morning. Not answering calls. Mrs Bickler says she'd rather not come in as she'll be tired from travelling but will see me at her hotel early evening. She's going to be at Claridges.'

'Claridges. Bloody hell,' said Hanley. 'OK. Keep me informed. What about the old biddy, Nancy Preston? Thomas?'

'Bit weird, guv,' said Rachel. 'Apologised for saying all those things to Jan Mason and not to us but did say she had rung in and left a message on reception wanting to speak to us.'

'From what I've seen, Mason fell for a line or two from an old woman grateful someone was taking an interest in her and taking her chance to get back in the limelight. Keep her in mind though. Might need to go back there.'

'Yes guv.'

'Right, let's get back at it,' said Hanley. 'Let's see what we get from Carew and Wilson. And then let's find Bexington and Dewlish.'

He took his feet off the table, got up from his chair and walked back over to the whiteboard for what would be his big moment this morning.

'At least we've got something now,' he said. 'Something that may link these two murders, as different as Camilla Carew and Sean Malahide are, coming from very different worlds.'

He picked up another 10 x 8 from a nearby table and stuck it on to the board. It was a picture of an orange cashmere scarf; an expensive one. And it bore two small initials in gold lettering in one corner – C.C.

'Found on a chair near Malahide's body. C.C. Camilla Carew.'

'Could stand for Coco Chanel,' said Terry.

'Ooh. Our fashion guru,' said Rachel.

'What?' said Hanley, who hadn't got the gag. 'No. It's got a Hermes label on it. I'm hoping forensics will be able to get some DNA off it.'

'I'm wondering,' said Deena, 'why it was left at the second murder and not the first?'

There was a silence in the room.

'That's something we need to find out, is it not? The killer could have been disturbed. Noises outside, something like that. Ran off and forgot it.'

'Or left it deliberately for us to find?' Deena added.

'That too. Whatever it is,' Hanley added. 'beyond any piece of material, there's got to be another link between these two corpses.'

He pointed to the pictures of the various men on the whiteboard.

'And a link between these two corpses and one of these jokers.'

19

BEXINGTON was jumpy and would not be seen anywhere in public in daylight, he said, even though he was now not quite as likely to be recognised, having just a moustache instead of a beard. A coffee bar was out of the question, as was a pub, and so Jan had to make do with a bench under these arches on Madeira Drive if she wanted the interview. The wind was coming off the sea and it was going to be cold. She turned the collar of her coat up before she started. It was all right for Bexington. He had a hoodie underneath his puffer jacket, though had pulled it down now. She could have done with a hit of caffeine but dared not leave him to fetch coffee in case he had second thoughts and made a run for it. His recent history suggested he would.

She took out her phone, set it on airplane mode so it wouldn't ring during the interview and found the voice memo app. She also took out a digital tape recorder from her bag. She was not about to abandon her belt-and-braces approach to taping interviews now, not on something this big. She pressed the record buttons on both devices and set them on the bench between the two of them.

'So, James,' she began. 'Confirm to me for the record what you've just told me about Sean Malahide.'

'I didn't tell you anything about him,' he replied. 'I don't know him. Didn't know him. Never heard of him.'

'OK. Fine. We'll park that for now.' She was keen to get into the meat of this. Normally, she would have danced around the subject with a few easy questions but he had summoned her here, so was presumably ready to sing. Besides, she wanted this done, and to get out of here with her prize.

'Let's start with your relationship with Camilla. How and when did you get together?'

'About a year and nine months ago. It was at the opening of an exhibition at a gallery in Fulham. Not far from my antiques place. Mate of mine's. We hit it off and that was that really.'

'Did you know whose daughter she was?'

'No. She told me a week or two later. Also told me she had been married to Simon Dewlish but hadn't seen him for a while.'

'So why did the two of you break up?'

'I relapsed.'

'You were ill?'

'No. I started drinking again. I'd been in rehab some time ago and was sober for quite a few months but started again after we met.'

'What caused that?'

'I don't know. Stopped going to AA meetings. Got a bit complacent. Camilla was a bit of a champagne girl who liked socialising. She called me boring a couple of times when we were out and I didn't drink. I really liked her. Didn't want her to dump me. Ironic really.'

'How so?'

'Well, given that she dumped me when I did start drinking again. I embarrassed her a couple of times in public, in front of her friends. At a party. It became clear I needed to go back to AA.'

'But you didn't?'

'No. I was ashamed really. And I didn't really want to stop drinking at that point. Couldn't. I was addicted again.'

'What was your drink?'

'Vodka mainly. But anything really, to be honest.'

'You said "at that point". So at which point did you want to stop drinking?'

'Well, after she benched me and took up with that arse Wilson.'

'You knew him?'

'Loosely. One of those prosecco socialists. Often at the same parties as Camilla and me. Saw a chance to carve out an easy career for himself in politics though I don't personally believe he had any real convictions. Then he hitched himself to Camilla and her money. It was odd, though. I know they were together but I phoned her once about him and Camilla told me he wanted to keep it under the radar. Make out they were just friends. She was going along with it, she said, but wasn't entirely happy.'

'You sound as if you know a lot about him rather than just loosely…'

Bexington hesitated.

'I asked around. I was at school at Winchester but had the odd mate who'd been at Marlborough where he was and had known him. Or known of him, as they were in years above him. He was pretty prominent around the school. Debating society and all that. Good Rugby player. A back. They're the clever ones. I was a forward. He was a devious shit, apparently. And a mate in politics reckoned he was ambitious and manipulative.'

'Standard qualifications for his job, I would have thought,' said Jan. 'Doesn't account for why you pestered him and Camilla.'

'I hardly pestered them. I did get a bit drunk one time and followed him to his flat in Camden. Confronted him. Told him not to hurt her. I wasn't at my best, I admit, and I'm not proud of it. Like now really. Not been shaving much in recent months, sorry to say. Oh, and I did go round to the flat to warn her about what she was getting into. I think he must have been there. She wouldn't let me in.'

'Sounds a little like pestering to me, if not stalking. What exactly was it you thought she was getting into?'

'He was a thief as well, according to one bloke at school. The sort who would nick stuff and hide it in his locker. Then deny it and pin it on others.'

'People say you weren't exactly honourable, James. Only with her for her money.'

'That's not true. I really fell for Camilla. It's true she helped me out, what with the business not doing so well.'

'She did? How much?'

'Well, she gave me 25K. Said it was an investment, rather than a gift, though. There would be another 25K but it never came because we broke up.'

'And did she want the first lump back?'

'She did. Yes. I didn't have it.'

There was a silence for a moment.

'You do know that doesn't look very good for you James.'

'I guess not. That's why I'm telling you all this. So you can tell people I would never kill Camilla. Not for £25,000. Not for anything.'

Jan stopped her questions for a moment and looked at him in the gloom, just a streetlight across Madeira Drive casting a pale beam. She wanted to see something in his face that she could believe. He helped by lighting a cigarette, the Zippo illuminating a careworn face.

'So fast forward me to two nights ago,' Jan continued. 'Nancy Preston said she saw you leaving the flat about 7.45pm.'

'Nice old stick, Nancy. Yes, I did.'

'But how did you get in there?'

'I rang the buzzer and somebody let me in.'

'Somebody? Not Camilla?'

Bexington paused and drew heavily on his cigarette, emptying his lungs with a sigh. He spoke slowly now, his voice growing emotional.

'Look, Camilla was dead when I got there. Lying on the living room floor. I was shocked and didn't quite believe what I was seeing at first. I let out a sort of yell as I recall. There was redness around her neck. I could see she'd been strangled. Despite what you may think, I was really cut up. I… I knelt over her. Gave her a little kiss on her cheek. A hug.'

He brushed a tear from his eyes. Jan reminded herself to maintain a professional scepticism.

'Let's assume you're telling me the truth. Who could have let you in and why didn't you look for them?'

'I wasn't thinking by now. I went into a sort of dazed state.'

'Any sign of what she might have been strangled with?'

'Same thing really. I didn't really think to look. There was nothing near her, anyway.'

'What were you doing there in the first place?'

'I got a text from her asking me to come round. I set off straight away. It was a fifteen-minute walk from my flat.'

'Show me the text.'

'I deleted it.'

'What? That's part of your story. Bloody hell. Why would you do that?'

'Once I came out of my dazed state, I started to get panicky thoughts. Knew it would connect me with her around the time of death.'

'But it will have been on her phone as well?'

'That's what I suddenly thought. So I tried to find her phone and delete it. She told me what her pin was once and I hoped she hadn't changed it. But I couldn't find the phone anywhere. Not by her body. Not in her handbag or coats. Not anywhere around the flat.'

'Christ, James. Had you been drinking?'

'Yes. I'd had a half a bottle or so, I guess. Been feeling a bit sorry for myself. I guess that was why I was making bad decisions.'

'So what did you do after looking for the phone and not finding it?'

'I sat there for a while. Not long. I walked around the flat. I cried. I took a swig or two from her voddie bottle. I knew where she kept the booze, of course.'

'You just said you wouldn't kill Camilla for anything.'

'That's right.'

'Not even when drunk. When not in your right mind?'

'No. Of course not.'

'So why didn't you just call the police?'

'Well, it had begun to dawn on me…'

'What did?'

'If anyone turned up and found me here, I was going to look as guilty as sin, wasn't I? I mean, you said it yourself. It doesn't look good, does it?'

'No. And you're on the CCTV in the hallway.'

'I knew I would be. I think I had my hood up coming and going and did think they wouldn't be able to identify me but again, I guess it points to me. That's why I want to explain all this.'

Jan looked him in the eye again, his hazel pair visible this time thanks to the glow from his cigarette as he took another draw. Her eyes moved up and down, to his black jeans and brown suede boots. She'd become caught up in his story but now a frisson of fear came over her and a proper realisation of the danger she'd put herself in. If he was a murderer, was lying, here she was, alone with him. Underneath arches with darkness now having descended and, with this road closed to cars, only the odd cyclist passing.

'And of course you're going to tell me you're not guilty.'

'Of course I'm not bloody guilty. You think I'd be telling you all this if I was? I'd have been long gone from here. Somewhere without an extradition treaty. Isn't that what murderers do?'

'OK,' Jan said. 'So where did you go once you left Camilla's flat?'

'Walked around for a while. Tried to clear my head. To be honest I was in a bit of a funk. Panicky. I was hellish sad. And angry at Wilson. For splitting us up. For getting his hooks into her. Leading to this.'

'And then?'

'I called an old pal. Went over to his place. Stayed there overnight.'

'Where?'

'Battersea.'

Jan's ears pricked up.

'So what time precisely did you come down last night?'

'Not sure. Walked from my friend's place to Victoria a while after it got dark. After the rush hour. Bought a sandwich. Got a train. Must have been in the B and B about 9.30pm maybe.'

Jan tried to piece it together quickly in her mind before asking her next question. Bexington had been to Camilla's flat – summoned by a text that no longer existed on his phone – and there found her dead, then went to a friend's house. This was a story Hanley was going to enjoy driving a big red double-decker bus through.

'Who was the friend?'

'An old school pal. Giles. I didn't tell him what had happened. Didn't want to drag him into it. Best he doesn't know anything. He didn't ask any questions, either. Giles is sound. Would always help me, no matter what. He always thought Wilson was a shit as well.'

'That doesn't necessarily make Wilson a murderer though.'

'Maybe not. But it's a basis.'

Jan decided it was time for some straight talking.

'James. You obviously know how this is going to appear to the police. You left the scene of a crime. You've gone on the run. You're looking very guilty.'

'That's why you're here. To show that I'm a bereaved man with feelings rather than a stereotype of an ex-boyfriend who must have done it. You're going to paint me as an innocent bystander, caught up in all this and who was just scared.'

'I am, am I? That's not how it works. I'm not your PR. And right now, if I write this and don't turn you in, I could be an accessory to murder.'

'You're a journalist, aren't you? You people like stories above anything else, don't you? Publish and be damned, that sort of thing.'

Bexington had nailed it. Found her sweet spot.

'OK. You went to your friend's. Give me a full name and address.'

Bexington did. She would get the office to check it out before she wrote up the interview.

'And you spent the night there before coming to Brighton last night?'

'That's it.'

'Did you go out on Monday night?'

'No. We stayed in and talked. I was in a state. Just told him I couldn't get over Camilla. He calmed me down.'

Jan could just see the whites of his eyes by the light of her phone that was recording and placed between the two of them on the bench.

'Sean Malahide was strangled in Battersea sometime yesterday.'

'Who?'

'The guy I asked you about earlier. The one you said you didn't know.'

'And I don't.'

Jan waited a moment. She spoke the next three words slowly.

'James... Battersea? Strangled?'

'And?'

And then he got it.

'Jesus,' Bexington exclaimed. He shook his head, puffed out his cheeks and stubbed out his cigarette.

'Well, it had nothing to do with me.'

Jan pressed on. 'Why didn't you just lay low at your friend's flat today? Ask me to come there?'

'I was worried the police would find out that Giles is a good mate and go round to his place by then. Anyway, I wanted to get out of London. When your story appeared today about me now having a beard, I guessed somebody might recognise me more easily. And so I shaved it off. Left the moustache. Don't think there are any pictures around of me with just a moustache.'

'Give me a moment to think,' Jan said. She paused the recordings and scooped up her phone and the digital device, just in case he was tempted to grab them while she took a little walk.

She got up, pulled up her collar against the cold again and sauntered across the road to the streetlight. She turned and stared at him. He was lighting another cigarette and she could tell he was not about to do a runner. He was in fact watching her intently.

All the ethical and practical questions competed for attention in her thought processes. The interviewing of a suspect – probably the prime suspect – in a murder case. The potential holes in his story. The likelihood she would be charged for contempt if she wrote the story without informing the police first. Above all, she might be letting the man who killed Camilla Carew, and maybe Sean Malahide too, walk away with no guarantee he'd be brought to justice.

Against that, she thought of how Hanley had treated her with disdain and refused to work with her at all. Even if Deena was doing her best. Perhaps she might tip off Deena that the story was going to come out. And she so badly wanted it to. She thought of the kudos of such an amazing exclusive, both in her profession and within the paper – and with a new Editor. It would guarantee her position, reassert her power over Vickers. As long as Bexington was telling the truth… She thought he was, sensed a love for Camilla, but he could still be playing her. And there were checks to be made. About this Giles, for example.

She walked back across the road and stood over him.

'Where are you staying tonight?' she asked.

'I've moved to a different B and B but just around the corner. Dear old Kemp Town again.'

She thought some more, this time for a much shorter pause.

'Right,' she said to Bexington after a pause. 'I'm going to tell your story, assuming a few things stack up.'

She could see in the light of the glow of his cigarette that he was pleased.

'But here's what you're going to do. And it's a two-part deal.'

'Go on…'

'First, you give me your mobile number and you answer it whenever my number comes up.'

'I bought a new burner phone today. Agreed.'

Jan handed him her notebook and he wrote it down. She called it there and then to check it was authentic. It rang in his pocket.

'Good. Now. You're going to go from here, go to the B and B and stay there. And you'll get the first train out of Brighton tomorrow. At Victoria, a police detective I know and trust by the name of Deena Campbell will be waiting to arrest you, probably with a colleague, and you will give yourself up to her. Deal?'

Bexington pondered it for a moment.

'How do I know that I can trust you to write the story first?'

'It's that word trust, James. You've trusted me this far. And you know how much I like a story like this.'

He thought about it.

'OK, deal.'

'It fucking well better be or I will write follow-up stuff that makes you look like the guiltiest man in England,' Jan said. 'One with nowhere to run and nowhere to hide. Got that?'

He said that he had.

20

THE digital video was already recording and now Hanley switched on the tape that was still a requirement. He noted the date and time for the tamperproof master tape that would be sealed, and the mandated two copies. Before he could proceed, however, the solicitor interrupted any attempt he was going to make to establish a quick upper hand, making it clear to all in the room, which included her client and Deena.

'For the purposes of the tape and for the record,' she said, 'I wish it to be recorded that my client Gavin Wilson made his own way this morning to your offices here at Jubilee House as soon as he was appraised of the fact that he was wanted for questioning in connection with the murder of Camilla Carew. On his behalf, I do not approve of him being kept waiting here at Hammersmith all day to volunteer his information. But I believe he does himself great credit for his patience. It shows he is willing to co-operate fully and has nothing to hide.'

Ruth Jenkins, regularly hired by the Labour Party and thus used to being placed in positions of conflict and staying cool, shot Hanley a cold stare.

'There you go, DCI Hanley. All yours.'

Hanley was not about to give her the satisfaction of a thank you. Instead he offered his trademark look of contempt.

'Right, Mr Wilson. You do understand why you're here? That we're investigating the murder of Camilla Carew, who you were in a relationship with. Yes?

'Yes indeed.'

'Good. So let's start at the beginning.'

'A very good place to start.' Wilson replied. His voice had a timbre between the North and the capital that had served Labour people well.

Deena watched as he began to smile before stopping himself as he caught her gaze.

'How long had you known Camilla Carew?' Hanley asked.

'Poor Camilla,' Wilson said. 'Lovely woman. This is all so tragic. It's really got to me.' He looked down at the table that separated them and shook his head.

'I'm sure it has,' said Hanley. 'And obviously we're very sorry about that.' His sympathy was not for Wilson, however. It was for Camilla. And for the benefit of the tape. This was more about the political correctness of modern policing and the need for empathy. That nicety over, he pressed on.

'Now perhaps you could answer the question?'

'Well, we met at a Party function back in, when, August. So three months ago.'

'Wouldn't have had her down as a Labour sympathiser.'

'She had hidden depths, did Camilla. She was a bright and funny woman. Very interested in the plight of those less fortunate than herself. As am I.'

'And your relationship with her began when?'

'Pretty soon afterwards. But we wanted to keep it low key. For political reasons.'

'Was she over Bexington?'

'She was. She'd dumped him. But he didn't seem to be over her. Was still being a nuisance. He couldn't accept that she was finished with him and he kept phoning her, apparently. Came round to the flat. She told me she was even thinking about taking out a restraining order.'

'And did he threaten you?'

Wilson paused. 'I got this tap on my shoulder as I was putting the key into my flat door one day after work. About six weeks ago. I think he may have followed me home. He knew where I worked. Wanted to make me aware he knew where I lived as well, I think. He tried to warn me off Camilla.'

'Did it become violent?'

'No. Though I was concerned. He stank of drink. He was a mess. Heavy stubble. Wearing a hoodie. He told me that Camilla still meant a lot to him and that I was bad for her. I asked him what he based that on and told him that Camilla was nobody's property and had made her own decision.'

'What happened then?'

'He just stood there and tried to look me in the eye, though he was unsteady on his feet. He was very angry. For a moment I thought he might hit me and I was ready to duck. I don't think he would have connected in his state, mind. Then he just turned on his heel and trudged off.'

'And your relationship with Ms Carew was sexual?'

'Really, detective,' said the solicitor, intervening. 'Do you have to ask that question?'

'No. But if you're as co-operative as you say you are, Mr. Wilson, you'll answer it. We know you stayed the night with her on Sunday.'

There was a pause as Wilson looked again at Ruth, who raised her eyebrows as guidance this time.

Wilson nodded.

'For the purposes of the tape, Mr Wilson has just nodded to indicate that he was in a sexual relationship with Ms Carew. Now, did you have any more run-ins with Mr. Bexington?'

'No. But Camilla did while I was there one night. Few weeks back.'

'What happened?'

'We'd had some supper and were just about to go to bed when the buzzer rang. Camilla went to answer and Bexington's face was on the internal video. He looked a mess again. Like he hadn't changed his clothes since that time he came round to me. She asked him what he wanted and he demanded to come in. She told him to go home. He got angry, started shouting and banging on the front door. Called her a slut who was sleeping with a loser. He sounded drunk again. She was tempted to let him in but I told her not to, to stay strong. Eventually he went away.'

'OK. So let's fast forward to two nights ago when Camilla was killed. Where were you?'

'I was in a strategy meeting at Labour HQ. We were discussing potential policy matters.'

'What time did it start?'

'At 5pm. It was a long one. Lots to discuss. Lot of dissent. Didn't get away till about midnight.'

'And people there will verify that?'

'Of course.'

'You won't mind us asking around at your workplace.'

'No.'

Hanley looked at Deena. He could see a suspect disappearing into the distance.

'We did take a break for a couple of hours. Maybe more.' Wilson suddenly added. Hanley perked up.

'Really? How come?'

'There was a significant debate and a vote in the Commons. New immigration bill. The MPs present had to leave.'

'What time was that?'

'About 6pm, I think. They got back around 9 pm.'

'And what did you do during that time?'

'I went to my office. Made some phone calls. Caught up with some emails. You wouldn't believe the number I get in my job. Went down to the canteen. Watched a bit of the Chelsea match on my laptop. They were doing all right in the first half.'

'So you would have had plenty of time to get to Camilla's flat and back during the break from the meeting?'

Wilson's solicitor interrupted. 'Are you seriously suggesting that my client murdered the woman he was in a relationship with, DCI Hanley?'

'I'm saying that there was a time window when he could have done.'

'And no evidence that he did.'

'I'm sure your client won't mind us taking his fingerprints while he's here today.'

Wilson looked across at his solicitor, whose face betrayed no reaction.

'Of course not. But naturally, they'll be everywhere in the flat.'

'Will they be on this, too?'

Hanley produced a polythene bag from a box file. It contained the orange cashmere scarf. He held it up.

'Seen this before Mr. Wilson?'

'Well, er, yes…'

'Where might that be?'

'It was Camilla's. She liked it. She said that Bexington had given it to her so she wouldn't wear it if it bothered me. I said it didn't.'

He paused for a moment as Hanley and Deena stared at him.

'My God. Is that what he used to…'

'We believe it might well have been used to kill Camilla, yes,' said Hanley.

Wilson leaned forward and put his head in his hands. He began to sob. Deena and Hanley swopped sceptical glances.

'Are we going to find your DNA on it as well? You won't mind supplying a DNA sample will you, Mr Wilson?'

'Can you please just back off a moment,' Ruth said. 'Can you not see that my client is distressed. Anyway, my client's DNA being on that scarf is entirely explicable given that he and Ms Carew were, as has been established, intimate.'

Hanley gave Wilson about fifteen seconds.

'You didn't answer my earlier question, Mr Wilson…'

Wilson looked up and rubbed his eyes. 'Which was?'

'About having time to get to Chelsea and back.'

'That was a question? I thought it was a statement.' Wilson looked pleased with himself. It was as much as Hanley could do to stop himself blurting out the words smart and arse.

'So did you go to Chelsea that night?'

'You released to the papers that Camilla was killed sometime around 7pm or just after. People from my office will have seen me in the canteen at 6.30pm. So how do I get from Victoria Street to Charmouth Square in thirty minutes? There was a football match on. How would I have got through all that traffic? The nearest tube to her flat is South Ken and that's fifteen minutes' walk. I'm sure you have ways of accessing cameras at tube stations anyway. I won't be on any of them.'

Hanley hated to think that Wilson had a point. He knew what match nights in the area were like.

'Anyway, the strategy meeting was a big deal. I couldn't have afforded to miss any of that. I didn't know when the MPs were going to be back so had to stay there. Plus I wanted to see the game.'

Deena noticed Wilson's solicitor give a little nod, while Hanley was looking down, to make a note.

'Shocking penalty miss,' Hanley said, staring up at him again.

'Shocking,' Wilson agreed.

There was a pause and Wilson quickly returned his face to a more appropriately sombre expression.

'I'm sure everyone is enjoying all this fascinating soccer chat detective, but is there anything else relevant to my client or are we done?' the solicitor said, rather than asked.

Hanley looked at Deena and nodded at her. She took a photo from a file and slid it in front of Wilson.

'Do you know this person?'

She watched him closely as Wilson studied the picture of Sean Malahide.

'No. Should I?'

'Found dead this morning at his Battersea flat. Strangled. Like Camilla. Sometime early evening yesterday.'

'That's very sad,' said Wilson. 'But what has this to do with me or Camilla?'

There was a pause, with Hanley and Campbell not wanting to defuse the tension, waiting for Wilson to break it instead. Finally, he did.

'Oh my God. You think there might be a serial killer about… who killed Camilla as well?'

'Let's hope we're not dealing with that,' said Hanley. 'You're sure that you've never seen this man?'

'Not that I remember.'

'You may have then?'

'Well, I meet a lot of people. I'm saying that I may have seen him but I do not know him.'

'Now you're fishing with a very long rod,' the solicitor followed up. 'My client is still in the early, stunned stages of grief but has been very helpful to you nevertheless. He really doesn't need you trying to involve him in some other murder you're looking to clear up in some two-for-one trawl.'

Deena looked across at Hanley.

'Now if there's nothing else,' the solicitor continued, motioning to gather up the legal pad on which she had been making notes.

'We found the orange scarf next to Sean's body,' said Hanley.

The solicitor replaced her pad on the table.

'Shit,' said Wilson. 'So they definitely are linked.'

'It would appear so,' said Hanley. 'So, anything more you'd like to tell me?'

'There is nothing I can,' said Wilson. 'But seems to me Bexington might.'

'DCI Hanley,' Ruth Jenkins intervened, having composed herself again. 'My client has answered all your questions in detail and told you there is nothing he can add. I'd like to remind you once again that Mr. Wilson came here of his own volition. It feels we have reached a natural conclusion and he and I would both now like to leave.'

Frustration descended on Hanley's face. 'You're free to go,' he said. 'For now.'

They got up and began to leave.

'But don't go too far will you?'

Once they were through the door, Hanley turned to Deena.

'Get his alibi checked out. See if people remember him staying within Labour HQ during those times.'

'Sure,' Deena replied.

'What did you think of him?'

'Not much,' said Deena. 'Happy to talk football with you two days after his girlfriend has been murdered.'

'Glad you noticed me getting him on that,' said Hanley.

There was a knock at the door and Terry and Rachel walked in.

'We've spoken to Carew guv,' said Terry.

'And?'

'Says he was at the flat in the afternoon as per the CCTV in the hall and had a row with Camilla. It was about her involvement with Wilson. He called him a pinko gold digger.'

'Colourful. What prompted that?'

'Carew says he was worried that Camilla was being conned into giving money to the Labour Party,' said Rachel. 'Camilla told him she would do what she wanted with her money but Carew pointed out it was really his money, in the shape of a large sum gifted to her a while back. The argument went on for about twenty-five minutes then he left.'

'OK. Anything from Darren on this bloke Giles, Bexington's mate?'

'Yes, guv,' said Terry. 'Said Bexington came to see him Monday night. Pissed and in a bit of a state. Wanted to stay the night. Left yesterday early evening.'

'He tell him anything about Camilla Carew or where he was going?'

'Only that he loved the girl. Got all sentimental on the Monday night. The bloke went to work at his art gallery in the morning. Bexington had gone by the time he got back around 6.30pm. Never said anything about where he was going.'

'We believe him?'

'Darren said he looked and sounded kosher. Was shocked to think his mate could have done it.'

Hanley's mobile rang. He listened for a minute to the voice at the other end.

'OK. OK. Not ideal but going to have to be tomorrow then, I guess. But early, yes?'

He ended the call and turned to the others.

'Sanjay. Camilla's mother just rang to put off their meeting. Fog in Geneva and plane delayed. She'll be too tired tonight. Poor woman. Doesn't want to talk about it on the phone. Sensitive and she's still sitting in departures. He's going to see her in the morning now.'

Deena's phone buzzed with a text. She looked down at the screen as Hanley gave her a dirty look.

'Guv, something on Dewlish,' she said.

'What is it?'

'He's been stopped at Heathrow. He's in the custody suite there. Carrying a bag with four grand in it.'

'Excellent. Get him sent here for questioning. Oh, and Campbell…

'Yes guv.'

'Who did that text come from?'

'Just an old mate down at Heathrow I was at Hendon with,' she said, swiftly putting her phone into a pocket.

21

JAN settled into a comfortable sofa in the corner of the large, airy foyer, took her phone and laptop out of her bag and placed them purposefully on the coffee table in front of her. She shivered as she took off her coat. It had been a cold walk back along Madeira Drive, past the pier and here to this chain hotel with its wide open reception area that was a welcome sanctuary. Fortunately, with just a few people dotted around at this time of day, the waiter wasn't long in bringing her large flat white and she gratefully wrapped her hands around the mug.

She checked her phone first. Two missed calls from Vickers. She would call him momentarily. Then a text from a number she didn't recognise.

If you're going to stand a guy up, at least tell him please! Will.

Shit. Will Gaunt. She was supposed to be with him now in a pub in Soho. She looked at her watch. Actually, with him in a pub in Soho forty-five minutes ago. She texted straight back.

Sorree! Something big came up at work.

A reply pinged straight back.

OK, you're forgiven this time. If you're nearly finished, we could still get together later?

She was surprised, perhaps pleasantly, but didn't want to get involved in phone ping pong right now. Couldn't afford to with a huge story to write.

Not in London. Not around tonight. Ring you later.

OK. Thanks, the reply came back.

She felt guilty. But not that guilty. Not as guilty as at the other message that came through from Robert.

At care home now. She's opened her eyes. Got a quick smile out of her but she's back sleeping now. They don't think it'll be too long. Please come Jan. For your sake, if not hers. Think you'll regret it if you don't.

'Fuck,' she muttered to herself. Was this for real? No, surely not. Elsie had had turns in the past. Robert was over-dramatising. Knowing she couldn't dwell on it further and needed her mind on something else, she pulled up Vickers's number. She could practically hear him salivating at the other end as she supplied him with the details of the Bexington interview.

'OK, Jan,' he said, his tone initially seeking to mask his admiration for what she had just done, before his excitement built. 'This is front page, with a turn inside to your big interview on page three. Big page one banner: **CHELSEA CHOKER: WE FIND PRIME SUSPECT**. Did you get a picture of him?'

'Ivan…'

'No, course you didn't.'

'He's not got the beard,' Jan said. 'But he has got a moustache.'

'Good, good. I'll get the artist on to that.'

'But listen. I don't want this becoming a freak show. He's given this interview on the basis that we tell his side of the story.'

'Yeah, yeah. Course. But this is massive Jan. We have this to ourselves. People are telling us print is irrelevant. We need to locate the biggest bloody trumpet we can and blow the fuck out of it. The new guy will love it. I'll go and tell him.'

She saw his point. Circulation had halved in three years. She still loved newspapers, realised that anything they could do to sell them needed to be done. But Vickers needed calming down, if only for a moment.

'Hold on, Ivan. Let me nail this down. How much for the front?'

'Don't worry about that. We'll write that here in the office. With your picture byline on it, of course.'

'No. If my name goes on it, I write it,' she snapped back, though she did ask Vickers to get young Danny to check out Bexington's mate Giles, address, background, all that. She also didn't want it being inferred that Bexington was guilty. He deserved, she thought, better than that – for now – having given her the interview. She'd asked the tough questions. Let his answers to them speak for themselves.

'OK. Six hundred for the front and the turn. Then whatever the interview makes. Let it run and don't worry about word count. We can put it over three pages, three, four and five. It'll have to go on the website tonight, of course, and one giant cat will be out of the bag, but even so. This is so big people will still want the paper tomorrow.'

'Good. OK. Let's get on with it then.'

Both wanted to get off the phone quickly, Vickers to go and bask in the editor's appreciation and Jan to dive into the comfort that words and stories brought her.

'Oh, one last thing, Jan…'

'What?'

'I need to give you the grown-up stuff in my capacity as news editor.'

'OK…'

'I'm assuming you've informed the police about this?'

'I'm about to. Just before we have this story running on the website. Legally, as you well know Ivan, it has to come out before any arrest is imminent.'

'Have you told Bexington he needs to give himself up? Otherwise, we're harbouring a criminal and perverting the course of justice.'

'Of course. Been done.'

'One last thing. You do realise that what you're doing could land you in a lot of trouble with the law and IPSO, don't you?'

'Yes.'

'Good. What are we waiting for then?'

They both shut off their phones and Jan got to work. She checked both tapes. Good. They had worked and she could hear the interview. She worked on the transcription, plugging her headphones into her phone, knowing where the good bits were, having placed asterisks and timings in her notebook when her ears pricked up at what Bexington was saying.

That done, she crafted the front page story first. That, clearly, was the most important of the two pieces – journalistically, if not for Bexington – and she wanted to get that intro right before writing up the interview and not duplicating.

Jan looked at her watch. 7pm. She had two hours. She was loving the buzz. She knew she had plenty of time but the excitement and adrenaline were carrying her so quickly that she had it all done inside ninety minutes. She was pleased with her front page intro:

THE SPURNED lover of strangled socialite Camilla Carew last night insisted that he was innocent of her murder as he poured his heart out to me in a dramatic, exclusive interview.

James Bexington claimed that he found the daughter of UK First party leader Peter Carew already dead at her Chelsea flat on Monday night and fled from London to Brighton in panic that he would be the prime suspect.

And, he insisted to me, he wants to set the record straight and tell of his enduring love for Camilla before giving himself up to the police to help them with their inquiries and find her real killer.

Bexington is also adamant that he does not know Sean Malahide, a 28-year-old Soho bar worker, who was also found strangled to death yesterday at his Battersea flat. Police are said to be keeping an open mind on possible links between the two murders.

It meant that she could then write a more featurey but dramatic intro inside on the interview itself.

JAMES BEXINGTON lights another cigarette, draws the smoke deeply into his lungs, and speaks of his love for murdered society girl Camilla Carew as a tear drips from his eye.

'Why would I kill her?' asks the 39-year-old antiques dealer who admits to having a problem with alcohol. 'I loved her. I just wish I hadn't started drinking again. If I'd stayed stopped, she might still have been alive.'

She was just getting into her stride with it when her phone rang. She cursed until she saw the name. ED. This was not any old Ed, hence the capital D. This was *the* Editor.

'George, hi,' she said.

'Ivan has told me what you've got, Jan. First thing I want to say is this is amazing work. Well done.'

'Thank you.'

'Second. I have a duty of care to my staff. That's what they call it these days. In the old days, it was just looking out for them. Are you OK?'

'One or two nervy moments but I judged it was safe. I'm all right thanks. Or will be when I've filed this.'

'About that…'

'What about it? It's great material. Sorry, content.'

'I don't doubt that, Jan. But if this backfires, it'll be me and thee going to jail. I have just one question…'

'Yes, George?'

'Is it worth going to jail for?'

'I will if you will.'

She heard a laugh down the other end of the phone.

'Ivan's told me that you've made best efforts to get Bexington to give himself up and you're liaising with the police, so that's fine then. See you in the dock.'

It was Jan's turn to laugh as the editor ended the call and she got back to her copy. She hated it when people talked of things writing themselves – did they not know what went into all this stuff? – but it certainly flowed, her beating of the keyboard interrupted only by a text from Danny that this Giles checked out.

She filed the copy with a triumphant press of the send button. Next, she ordered a taxi to take her to the station, where she bought a sandwich and another latte for the journey back to London. Just a few were heading back to town on the 21.04. She decided to phone Deena to tell her about picking up Bexington while the carriage was this quiet, before arrivals at Gatwick got on.

'OK. Listen up, my favourite copper,' Jan began.

She went through the call from Bexington, the trip to Brighton, the interview. The fact that it would be coming out at 10pm on her paper's website and she had half an hour to tell Hanley and piss him off. She heard the odd "bloody hell, Jan" coming from the other end.

She expected the warnings that duly came about dangling a red rag in front of Hanley, and the possibility of being charged with a bunch of crimes but she interrupted Deena with a shout of "STOP", which did have somebody up the carriage looking down towards her.

'I've laid it on the line for Bexington. He's to get the first train to Victoria in the morning and you're to meet him off it. He will give himself up for arrest.'

'Oh, and you expect him just to do that?'

'He gave me his word.'

'Jan. He might well be a murderer. And you're going to accept his word?'

'Yes. Because he knows if he doesn't turn up, I will be writing stuff that incriminates him, stuff that a jury will remember in a year's time, even if he doesn't. He called me. Wanted his story out there. And he knows that in this day and age he's going to get spotted and turned in sooner rather than later.'

Deena thought about it. It was an argument. She wasn't sure how powerful it was to her but had to admit it might sound so to Bexington.

'Where's he staying in Brighton?' Deena asked.

'Come on, Deena. My terms. You're not doing this tonight and ruining my story.'

Deena thought about it. Jan held the cards for now. 'OK,' she said. 'I'll get on to Hanley and prepare for a sleepless night and an early start. But if Bexington doesn't show, Jan. You are in very, very deep doo-doo.'

'When am I not?' Jan said, a smile playing on her lips.

Jan could hear Deena's "Hah!" on the other end and sensed her softening. If this came off, Deena too would be getting some herograms from her bosses. That sense soon became hard evidence.

'Listen Jan. If this works out, and on the back-scratching principle, I might have something for you in the morning. A development.'

'Yeah? Can you give me a sniff tonight?'

'Don't push your luck, eh?'

'OK. But just one quick question...'

'Go on...'

'Did you find Camilla's mobile in her flat?'

'Actually, we didn't. We think the murderer probably took it. Why?'

'No reason.'

Of course, there was. Deena knew there always was with her. While Jan had included in her copy all the stuff about Bexington having fled the scene after finding Camilla dead, she was holding back the incriminating detail of him having deleted a text on his own phone that he claimed was from Camilla. That was the follow-up story if he didn't show at Victoria tomorrow morning. Which she didn't want to contemplate.

Jan's mobile pinged with a text and she bade her farewells before Deena could press her further.

She's stable but they don't know how long for, the text said. *Will sit in the chair tonight with her.*

Jan looked out of the window but could see nothing in the darkness beyond. Just her reflection. She began to sob, silently, grateful that there was nobody near to witness it. In the cold and loneliness of a train carriage on a dark, chilly night that they didn't warn you would be part of the job. When you were just in love with all the potential glamour awaiting. But it had caught up with her, she guessed. What had she been thinking, exposing herself to the prime suspect in a murder case like that? A man who might have strangled a woman on her own? Was she getting too old for all this?

She shuddered, pulled her coat collar up again and sent Robert a text.

OK. I'll get a train up in the morning. Be there lunchtime.

Jan looked at her reflection again in the glass and pulled a tissue out of her bag to dab her wet eyes. With it came the redundancy document, falling into her lap. She looked at her signature and wondered. Maybe it was best to get out at the top, on the back of a banging story like this one. It would enhance her reputation all over again – and her freelance value. Once she'd seen the case and the full story through.

She was about to phone Vickers, to check her copy was all OK, when her mobile buzzed with a call. She recognised the number from earlier. And thought she owed the guy a fuller explanation.

'Will, look, so sorry.'

'No problem,' he said. 'Not the first time I've been stood up.'

'Work. You know…'

'Oh yes. Overtakes us all sometimes. How about we try again tomorrow? Lunch maybe?'

'No. I'm sorry. I have to go to Wakefield tomorrow. My mother is very ill in a care home and I need to see her.'

'Well, maybe I can help.'

'How?'

'I have a client in Leeds. Young actor. Was going to speak to him on Zoom tomorrow but I could go up and see him in person. I could drive you? We can talk, get to know each other.'

Jan was taken aback.

'What? That's very kind but no. I don't think so. I may have to do some work.'

'I have a nice, big comfortable Bentley and I can chauffeur you. You can even sit in the back if you like, to do your work. We can chat. Or not. I'll drop you in Wakefield, head over to see my guy, then come back and pick you up.'

Jan thought about it for a moment, weighing up the prospect of schlepping across London and on to a crowded train that may be delayed against stretching out in a luxury car. It was a stranger's car, though. But Tania had said he was considered a gent, hadn't she? And she'd just spent an hour alone with a murder suspect, for goodness sake. She could take care of herself. She had also treated Will a bit shabbily tonight. But it was a six-hour round trip in the company of a man she may not like. Ah, what the hell. She'd spent plenty more hours than that in the office around Vickers, a man she detested. If she could do that…

'I promise no funny business,' said Gaunt, as if hearing her mind whirring. 'Just a relaxed day. Well, as relaxed as it can be if your mother is not well.'

At the end of the day, Jan thought, it's just a free lift. That's all. 'OK,' she said. 'Let's give it a go.'

'Great,' said Gaunt. 'I'll pick you up on the corner of Maida Vale and Elgin Avenue at, what shall we say, 9.30am?'

Jan shifted a little uneasily on her train seat.

'How did you know I lived around there?'

'Tell me,' he replied. 'Did you speak to anyone about me after agreeing to hook up for a drink?'

'Er. I might have done,' said Jan.

'Goose and gander,' said Gaunt.

'Fair point,' said Jan. '9.30am is good.'

After ending the call, she stared out of the window again. She decided she needed some relaxation and put her earphones in to listen to her playlist. That song Frank mentioned, Don't Talk, came on the shuffle. Ironic, given that Bexington had just told her everything. Or at least she hoped he had. Yeah, good song. She liked it.

She could now could see growing larger in the distance the dotted red lights atop the tall buildings that marred the nightscape of Central London these days. And she realised that she may have asked Tania from showbiz about Will Gaunt but she hadn't asked where he lived.

22

EVER since the Six O'Clock News, Frank had been unable to settle in his own home, his own skin. He had known from Deena about the strangling of Sean but seeing it on the screen, tucked in about third or fourth item after apparently more pressing political stories, had brought it home. He was no longer the professional, detached, law enforcement officer. He was an agitated, unwilling participant in a murder case.

He had fetched himself a Coke from the fridge – taken to buying 12-packs now – and gulped it down gratefully, the sugar hit lifting his spirits, though only for a while. He had phoned Eddie and been through it all again with him, for an hour at least, looking at it from every angle. His sponsor too was alarmed at Sean's death but counselled caution, that they still didn't know for sure that his murder was related to what had happened in the AA meeting forty-eight hours ago now.

Frank knew better than that. How unlikely was it that two different killers would use basically the same modus operandum of strangulation? Within twenty-four hours of each other and just over a mile apart? And after a man walks into an AA room and says that he might have killed somebody, a murder nearby is on the news the next day… and a man at that same AA meeting is then also strangled.?

'Let's get real, Eddie,' Frank had said.

'Let the police do their job,' Eddie added and the irony was not lost on Frank. He realised, though, that Eddie didn't see him as a copper, just another drunk trying to stay sober. Frank hated that these two mainstays of his life were overlapping. He had always tried to keep them separate. In a Venn diagram, the word in the intersection between his sobriety and work would be fear.

After the call, he'd tried to calm himself. He fetched his book of daily meditations and read the subject to himself. It talked of faith. That all would be well. Normally he would have nodded and absorbed it. His mind was telling him now that it was bollocks though. He went into his bedroom, got down on his knees against the side of the bed, childlike, and prayed to the god of his understanding – a spiritual entity rather than a religious God – for the knowledge of what he should be doing in this situation. It was a ritual he had adopted in the early days, a sign of the humility he had needed to find if he was going to stay sober. Then he meditated for half an hour, eyes closed, lying still on his bed, waiting for answers to come.

When he received none, telling himself that it wasn't time for them yet, he tried to watch some TV, a soap, but the drama and raised voices didn't soothe. He went to the fridge and took out another Coke, having finished the first in short order. He hated himself for giving in to a sugar craving. He maybe had one or two of them a week, as a weekend reward perhaps for another week of sobriety and hard work. Now here he was, drinking two of them in an hour.

He rang Italian Bob from the Monday meeting. Yes, he had seen the news. Shit just got serious, he agreed, nervousness now in his voice. He, too was now more conflicted about what to do, about the dilemma of confidentiality versus citizen's duty. It was horrendous what had happened to Sean, he said. The poor bloke. Just when he had set about turning his life around.

Then something occurred to Frank.

'What if,' he said. 'The guy who came into the meeting is now targeting certain people who were there?'

'What? Hell. No…' said Bob.

'Think about it. He comes in and virtually confesses to a murder. Then regrets it, with the police on his trail, and decides he needs to cover his tracks.'

'But it was dark. A candlelit meeting. Surely he wouldn't have been able to see anyone.'

'Reckon he might still have picked some out.'

'Well, I'm not sure I'd be able to identify him. Not in that hoodie. Would you?'

Frank had to admit, however much he'd been poring over the picture of Bexington, trying to trigger some recognition, and despite observation being part of his training, that he probably couldn't. Which brought him back to one of the issues that had bothered him about reporting this at the very start.

'But we weren't wearing hoodies, were we? And think about it, Bob. He fits the bill for that Chelsea murder, doesn't he?'

'Frank, mate. You need to calm down. Your imagination is running riot right now. Get a good night's sleep and let's speak in the morning, eh?'

Frank agreed, though he doubted he would sleep. Being the news junkie that he was, he watched the Ten O'Clock News headlines, but there were no developments. What he couldn't see was the scrambling that was hurriedly going on behind the scenes in the BBC newsroom as they noticed what he was about to see on his phone as well.

BREAKING NEWS: CHELSEA CHOKER
– WE FIND PRIME SUSPECT

It came from Jan's paper. He subscribed to it and always received notifications of stories, wanting to know what she was writing.

He certainly wanted to read this one. And it needed more than a cursory glance on his phone. He went to his laptop, called up the website and saw the line between the various decks of headlines and subheads and the text: WORLD EXCLUSIVE by Chief Reporter at Large Jan Mason. He might have known. Frank scanned it quickly. The text was wrapped around a variety of pictures of Bexington, the first of them an artist's impression of him. The beard was gone, just a moustache now.

Frank was shocked. First by the detail in Jan's interview of what he was wearing – a hoodie, puffer jacket and black jeans. Then by the favourable coverage of Bexington. He guessed that was part of the deal for the interview. But whereas he might have once admired Jan for her sheer ballsiness, now he was angry with her for, as he saw it, falling for this.

It was a murder case and she was cosying up to a prime suspect just for a scoop. He had seen for himself Bexington showing up at an AA meeting, for he was growing sure it must have been him, and admitting what he might have done. And now an AA member was dead. The piece even showed a time-line that demonstrated Bexington could very well have gone to Brighton after Sean was murdered.

He found his phone and pulled up JAN on it. He got the "busy" tone. Clearly she was fielding all the calls following her story. He kept trying. Finally she answered.

'At fucking last,' Frank snapped. 'You ever not on that phone?'

'Hi Frank. You OK?'

'What the fuck is that shower of shit?' Frank replied.

'Well thank you. Yes, it is rather a good story, isn't it?'

'A good story? You are jeopardising a murder inquiry. Hanley will have you on a charge.'

'I'll live with it.'

'That's all you've got to say? This is so fucking irresponsible

Jan. And you've painted Bexington like a fucking hero instead of a potential killer. I thought you were better than that.'

'Now hold on. I've asked all the tough questions and just reported his answers. I've not offered any opinion on his innocence or guilt.'

'Come on Jan. We both know how these things work. You get a story out of someone in return for painting them in a good light. It's like deals your people do with celebs – you know they're snorting cociane, approach them with it and they agree to tell all about their heart-rending depression to shift the focus.'

Jan was quiet at the other end of the line. She couldn't argue with what Frank was saying. She regathered herself.

'Look, wind your neck in,' she barked back. 'I've phoned Deena, told her what happened and said that I've done a deal with Bexington. That he will give himself up first thing in the morning. She's going to meet him off a train from Brighton.'

'Fucking hell. You really think that's gonna happen?'

'I do actually, yes. Because he wants it to.'

'When did you get so naïve, for fuck's sake? Anyway, you were in serious danger.'

'Ah, I didn't know you still cared.'

Frank didn't respond.

'This isn't like you,' Jan said. 'You don't swear like this. Well, not since we were… since for years.'

There was no reply.

'Why has this got to you so much?' Jan continued. 'This isn't your case and you're not directly involved in it.'

There was a pause as something clicked with her that might explain him ringing out of the blue ten minutes after her story went online.

'Or are you?'

'Possibly,' he said, the anger disappearing, his voice quietening almost to a whisper. 'Or possibly not.'

'So which is it?'

'Forget it. It's nothing.'

Jan could sense his discomfort. Mostly their conversations were about him telling her what he shouldn't. This was different.

'Answer me this,' Frank said. 'I've read your description of what he was wearing. What shoes did he have on?'

'What? Why?

'Just tell me.'

'Um. Boots, I think. Yes, boots.'

'What kind?'

'Dark. Brown. Suede.'

There was another silence.

'What are you not telling me that maybe you should?' Jan demanded more firmly.

'Should? Should? You fucking journalists all have this sense of entitlement,' he said, growing angry again. 'As if only you deserve to be given information, or your version of the truth is the only one that counts.'

He shut off the phone and threw it across his bedroom. He lay on his bed and could feel himself sinking into the kind of darkness that had come to him in the early years of his sobriety but which he hadn't known for a long time. That alone, the fear of returning to a pain of the past, began to panic him.

He was embarrassed by the way he had berated Jan, instead of stopping to think. Restraint of tongue and pen, the programme of recovery taught, didn't it? How easy to forget in the heat of battle. It would be a long, sleepless night of soul-searching, self-doubt and disappearing self-esteem.

Above all, he was ashamed at not having gone forward with what he suspected about Bexington. And what that cover-up had meant for Sean Malahide.

THURSDAY

23

DEENA sipped on the piping hot coffee. She'd been grateful to see it was being served this early in the morning from a stand on the concourse of Brighton station. She looked up at the four-sided Victorian clock. Just ticking on to 5.30am. She gazed across at Sanjay, waiting over by the M&S shop at the entrance, and the two sizeable plain-clothed PCs borrowed from the Sussex constabulary and flanking her. Bexington was cutting it fine. The first London train departed in six minutes.

Hanley was simply not having it when she'd phoned him last night to tell him what Jan had agreed with Bexington. That he would be at Victoria by 7.30am and would stand by the entrance to the platform and await his arrest. The DCI had insisted she take a car down with Sanj and grab the bloke as soon as he showed up at his departure point rather than his arrival. Surprise him. 'Don't give him the opportunity to bottle it and run.' It was also Hanley's way of getting back on the front foot; doing unto others before they did unto you. And so Sanjay had picked Deena up at her Stockwell flat at 4am. She looked again at the photofit of Bexington with a moustache. It was now 5.32am. She sighed.

And then, all of a sudden, there he was, striding across the concourse, wearing a hoodie beneath a puffer jacket, the hoodie not covering his head today. Nothing left to hide. She moved swiftly and within seconds was standing in front of him, Sanjay and the two PCs at the other points of the compass surrounding him, like the four sides of the clock above.

'James Bexington?' said Deena.

'Yes….'

'I'm DC Deena Campbell of the Metropolitan Police,' she said and showed him her warrant card. 'I am arresting you on suspicion of the murders of Camilla Carew and Sean Malahide. You do not have to say anything, But it may harm your defence if you do not mention, when questioned something which you later rely on in court.'

'I don't know this Sean Malahide. Anyway, I was on the way to meet you at Victoria. Honestly.'

'Well, we're a little early and we've changed the meeting place. Perhaps you'd like to accompany us to a car…'

After Deena had read him his rights, Bexington nodded, though when Sanjay handcuffed him he insisted it wasn't necessary. Deena and Sanjay were not taking any chances, however – not with the spectre of Hanley ever on their shoulders. The two PCs took an arm each, bundled him into the unmarked BMW and sat on the back seat flanking him while Sanjay drove and Deena sat in the passenger seat.

Got him guv. Coming in, she texted to Hanley.

Just over an hour later, blues and twos on at the first sign of any traffic and barely a word exchanged on the journey, they were at Hammersmith police station, booking Bexington into a cell.

*

Hanley arrived at 8am, bright and breezy for a change. Wilson and Carew had been questioned. He could simply not be arsed last night, at the end of a long, draining day, to question Dewlish, apprehended at Heathrow and now in a cell at Hammersmith. He'd needed to think things over after Deena had phoned him telling her about Jan's story and Bexington. And to think about what he might need to ask Dewlish.

He also took pleasure in letting the bloke stew overnight, simply because he could. He was a suspect in a murder inquiry and he had forty-eight hours to question him. No rush. Now he had Bexington as well. Things were opening up, all the major players were in plain sight, and he was chipper. Even cocky.

'Looking forward to today,' he said to Deena and Sanjay, both gulping coffee after their excursion to Brighton and back, via Hammersmith. 'We might even crack this. Campbell, give Mason a ring, find out where she's going to be this morning and tell her we'll be sending a couple of our finest to arrest her.'

'On what grounds, sir?'

'I don't know yet. I'll find one to fit. Obstruction, contempt. Messing with me.' He smiled his smug smile.

Deena nodded but Hanley's eye had been caught by Jackie Donovan standing at the far end of the office. Donovan flashed a smile and beckoned for him to join her.

'Bit of a three-ringed circus going on this morning it would appear,' she said, gazing out of the window on to Putney Bridge, her back turned towards Hanley.

'Ma'am?' he said.

'Well, let's take stock, shall we… We have a second murder, Sean Malahide, with a very similar MO. We have Jan Mason finding our prime suspect James Bexington before we do and her persuading him to come in here.'

'I don't think it was quite like that ma'am. He was going to give himself up…'

'I'll tell you when it's your turn to speak Dave. OK?'

'Yes ma'am.'

'We also have Dewlish in custody and he has been in the cells overnight. Wilson, meanwhile, seems to have been able to tell us very little that we didn't know.'

There was a pause.

'Now it's your turn,' she said.

'Well. I think we've done pretty well so far. We have three suspects we're actively investigating and one of them has to be our murderer.'

'Has to be? I hope you're not leaving the net cast in the shallows, Dave?'

'Always keep an open mind, ma'am. You know me. But I'll bet one of those three is our man. I need to get at Bexington and Dewlish today and by close of play we'll know more about who killed Camilla Carew. Maybe even who *did* kill her.'

'And Sean Malahide.'

'And him, yes.'

'Here's the thing, Dave…' Donovan said, Hanley recognising the ominous tone. 'You know me. I'm light touch. I like my IO to be given plenty of latitude to run an investigation and a team by using their skill, judgement, experience and initiative. Right?'

'Right, ma'am.'

'I also have other cases going on. But I am the SIO for this and ultimately it's my head on the block. I've had the Commander on the phone. He would like to see progress. Rapid progress. You know why?'

'Why ma'am?'

'Because he has had the Commissioner on the phone. Who will have had the Home Secretary on the phone. All because Peter Carew's name is in the middle of this and most politicians these days would rather his name was not in the public eye any more. He brings bad memories for a lot of people. Carew, by the way, has refused a family liaison officer. Says he doesn't want people following him around and besides, he can cope. Did I tell you that?'

'No, ma'am.'

'Well, there we are. I don't like pressure filtering down, Dave but, well… you know how it is. I too would like to see rapid progress. Mainly because I want to see killers brought to justice.'

'Me too, ma'am.'

'Good. You need any more resources? I have some flexibility on this given its media prominence. More people on the team?'

'I prefer to run a tight ship,' said Hanley. 'Make the most then of all the support and techno people.'

'Make sure you do,' Donovan said, now staring at him. 'People tell me you're a bit stuck in your ways, Dave and like to solve things by instinct but I tell them good coppers can adapt to modern methods. So let's join the dots and have a good day, shall we? First we're going to need to establish a link here somehow between Camilla and Sean, beyond the scarf. And between the three men, Camilla and Sean.'

'Yes, ma'am.'

'We know all three men knew Camilla well. We need to find out what their motives for killing her might be. Crime of passion if it's Bexington.'

'That's my hunch.'

Donovan ignored him and carried on.

'Why was Dewlish back in this country?'

'I'm interrogating him this morning.'

'And Wilson's involvement with her?'

'Well, they were lovers.'

'Yes. Interesting one that. Somebody in politics rang me last night. Said he thought Wilson was gay.'

Hanley was, in a rare moment for him, surprised into silence, if only briefly.

'Really. So how come…'

'Quite, Dave. Quite. Get somebody to sniff around Labour Party HQ and find out more about that. On the quiet. Don't alert Wilson or the Shadow Home Sec.

'Yes, ma'am. I also need to get Mason pulled in and charged with contempt.'

'Yes, that's a good idea Dave. Let's arrest a reporter who broke a story. Let's incur the wrath of her proprietor and editor and turn them against us. And the whole of the bloody media, while we're at it. They may be at each other's throats most of the time but nothing unites a competing pack of freedom-of-the-press wolves quite like one of their own being muzzled does it?'

'But she…'

'She's a sideshow Dave. If we bring her in, we distract the focus of the investigation away from the murder and the suspects and open ourselves up to all manner of attention we don't need. Let her be. For now.'

Hanley was in no position to argue.

'And get digging on Sean Malahide too. How he might have known any of those men. I don't want him forgotten just because he's not posh and lives in a one-bedroom flat in Battersea. Solving his murder is just as key and he deserves justice too.'

'Right, ma'am. I'll make sure Deena Campbell gets on to it.'

'Good choice. She's talented that one. Keep her in the loop on everything, yes?'

Hanley couldn't bring himself to respond with anything other than a surly look. He had actually picked Deena the new girl because he wanted others for more important business.

'That it ma'am? If so, I've got two suspects in a murder case to interview.'

'Busy day Dave. But the sort we get up every morning for, eh?' She stared hard at him. 'I need you to stop my phone from ringing. Yes?'

24

WILL GAUNT'S Bentley was racing green with cream leather upholstery and a walnut dashboard. Not having much interest in cars, Jan only knew all that because as soon as she'd settled herself in the front passenger seat with her Costa latte and pile of newspapers, Gaunt gave her the verbal guided tour.

'You like the colour? Racing green?'

'Lovely,' said Jan, admiring the front page of her own newspaper with her byline on the **WE FIND PRIME SUSPECT** story. 'Same shade as the front door to my flat.'

'Cream leather seats,' he added.

'Hmm,' she replied, turning the page to look at the headline on her interview that began on page three. "**I would never kill my darling Camilla**" it read.

Gaunt pressed on as Jan took a sip of her coffee. 'Walnut dash,' he said, running his hand along it.

'No. Sometimes I have a caramel shot but today I had another shot of caffeine instead.'

It left Gaunt bemused. 'What?' he wondered.

'I'm winding you up. You're going to have to get used to it if we're going to spend the day together. Nice car. That what you want from me? Mind if I put some music on?'

'No, of course not.'

'She synched her phone with his sound system and her playlist began. She began reading her own paper.

'I like this one,' said Gaunt in the middle of one song. 'What's it called?'

'Don't Talk,' said Jan.

'Oh, right sorry.'

'No that's what it's called. But yes, no chat while I go through the papers. That OK?'

'Fine. Yes. Sorry again,' said Gaunt and pressed on up into the Kilburn High Road and thence to Cricklewood and the foot of the M1. Going against the remnants of the rush hour, the traffic was light.

By the time they got to the Watford junctions, Jan had seen enough of the half a dozen papers she had bought and Gaunt dared to speak.

'It really is a pleasure to meet you,' he said. 'You won't remember, but I was in a group of people at the Newspaper Awards those years back when you won. I was on a table with a couple of showbiz journos who'd been nominated.'

'Really? You're right I don't remember.'

'I really do admire your work. Not many I can say that of in the press these days. Looks like you've got another scoop today.'

'Right. Yes.'

Jan picked up her phone and texted her brother. *On the way up.*

'I never thought you'd swipe right on my profile and we'd end up on a date. I am flattered,' Gaunt said.

'A date? This doesn't feel much like a date to me,' Jan replied. 'You driving me to see my mother in a care home in Yorkshire?'

'OK. Not a date then. But maybe a chance to get to know each other a little bit. Maybe we'll have a proper date afterwards?'

'Maybe.'

She smiled. She felt she owed him a smile at least. He was well dressed and groomed and obviously liked her. That counted for a fair bit, she thought. And he was like some gangly puppy, so keen to please. Puzzling, but she'd go with it for now.

Her mobile pinged back with a text from Robert, looking forward to seeing her, then rang. It was Vickers.

'Look Will. I'm kind of sorry about this but also not. I'm not working today but I am. I'm in the middle of a big story and I really need to get this.'

'Sure, sure,' he replied and Jan took the call, listening to Vickers for a moment before interrupting.

'Ivan,' she said. 'It's 10.30am. Last night I delivered the website a massive exclusive that had everyone else running round in circles to catch up with. Today that massive exclusive will sell papers. Can you just give me a while to get my head together?'

She paused while he spoke but was not going to take too much more of it.

'Listen, I'm on my way to Yorkshire… What? Because I need to see my very ill mother, OK? What do you mean how ill? Fucking ill – that good enough for you? I am all across this and will do my best to supply something as a follow-up by lunchtime. Now, go and take out whatever it is that's pissing you off this morning on someone else, will you?'

She shut down the call and yelled a scream of frustration. She looked across at Gaunt. He was a mixture of admiration and fear.

'Wow,' he said. 'Very impressive.'

Jan did not reply. Instead, she burst into tears.

'Hey, hey,' said Gaunt, shifting in his seat.

'It's all right,' said Jan. 'Sometimes I just get so… so frustrated.'

'That's OK.'

'This isn't me, really,' Jan added. 'I'm much stronger than this, of course. At least in public.'

She took a tissue from her bag, blew her nose and looked across at Gaunt. He smiled at her. She managed a weak smile in return.

'Newport Pagnell services, one mile,' she said. 'OK if we stop to pick up coffee?'

'You not had enough yet?' he said pointing to the cup in its holder by the automatic gear stick.

'No such thing as enough coffee,' Jan said and Gaunt did what was asked.

Once refuelled, Jan was ready for more of a conversation with him, one eye ever on her phone.

'Tell me a bit about you then, Will.'

'Well, you know what I do and I'm guessing you might have googled my clients.'

'Might have, yes.'

'I'm not the sort to give you any juicy gossip, I'm afraid.'

'Really? This could be a long day then.'

He laughed. Jan let a moment pass.

'So what's Jason Hammett like?' she asked of a young actor he represented, one currently in a big drama on TV.

'Jason? Lovely young man.'

'Funny. Papers have him as a bit of an arse.'

'Well, yes, that too,' said Gaunt and Jan laughed. She was warming to him a little.

'He's a talented boy but a bit too fond of the Colombian marching powder, sadly. Still, he'll grow up. Nothing twenty-eight days in rehab can't sort.'

'Will, I do believe I read you denying that.'

He took his hands off the steering wheel for a brief moment and held them up.

'Busted,' he said. 'Though that was off the record.'

Jan laughed a little longer.

'Don't worry,' she said. 'I've got enough posh playboys to be dealing with at the moment.'

'Bexington, you mean?'

'You read my interview?'

'I did, yes. Strange business. Rings you up for an interview when he's on the run.'

'You know him?'

'No. Why would I?'

'Metropolitan circles and all that. Might have met at a party or something.'

'No. No. You think he's innocent?'

'I just wrote up his story.'

'But you must have an opinion, having met him?'

'Keeping an open mind. But he was plausible, I have to say.

Jan was torn. She always liked discussing her stories with people who had read them, found it flattering and was grateful they were taking an interest. But this was all a bit raw and sensitive. She was still processing yesterday, and thinking about today – whether she had been taken in by Bexington, might have a follow-up story and what she might find when she got to her mother's care home. She was grateful for the buzz of a text.

It was from Deena. *Can you speak?* it said.

Give me two minutes, she replied. She noticed a sign for an exit.

'Will, I have to make a call,' she said. 'Can you come off the motorway here?'

'What? Really? I might not be able to find anywhere to park. You can speak in front of me, you know.'

'This needs to be private, I'm afraid. I'm sure there'll be somewhere we can stop.'

Gaunt was clearly irked but acceded again and within a few minutes had found a layby on a dual carriageway. He looked uncomfortable about being in such an isolated spot in his expensive car.

'Would you mind giving me five minutes?' Jan asked.

'You want me to get out of the car?'

'Please.'

'But I thought…'

This time he tutted but did as requested. Jan didn't always like a soft-touch man, not being used to them in journalism, but right now she didn't care. She rang Deena, who picked up straight away.

'Thank you for the text at 6am,' Jan said.

'I'm not going to apologise for picking him up at Brighton rather than Victoria, Jan. Hanley was right not to take any chances.'

'Fair enough. As long as Bexington doesn't blame me.'

'He seemed OK about it. What's an hour or two between journalist and murder suspect?'

Jan gazed out of the car watching Gaunt pace up and down, clearly disgruntled.

'So what's happening.'

'Hanley's pissed off with you.'

'No change there then.'

'He wanted to bring you in but Donovan's blocked it. Then she had a word with me on the quiet to keep you in the loop. She's grateful that you delivered Bexington to us.'

'Well done me.'

'So… We've established a link between Camilla Carew and Sean Malahide.'

'Go on…'

'We found an orange cashmere Hermes headscarf at the scene of Sean's death. Think both were strangled with it.'

'An orange headscarf? And?'

'With the initials C.C. on it. When we questioned Wilson, he told us that he recognised it. Camilla owned one. It was given to her by Bexington.'

Jan tried to take this in for a moment.

'But Bexington told me he doesn't know Malahide.'

'And you believed him?'

'Yes. At the time. Looking him in the eye…'

'Well, I thought I'd tell you. You can have that ahead of us releasing it at midday. Got to go now.'

Jan thanked Deena and ended the call. It was a good story, all right. But as she began to ponder it, she thought of more and more questions.

She could now see Gaunt shivering ten yards down the layby. He in turn could see she was no longer on the phone and waved at her. She gestured for him to come back. He ran and jumped in, slamming the door.

'Bloody brass monkeys out there. Everything all right?'

'I did warn you it might not exactly be like a date today. I'm going to need you to pull in at the next service station, I'm afraid,' Jan said. 'I have a story to write.'

25

FRANK ordered two coffees and sat in a corner of the Butcher's Arms waiting. It was that anticipatory time before the mid-morning caffeine-hit brigade and the lunch arrivals so the place was quiet. He would have no fear of a nearby table overhearing them. In fact, he made sure of it by picking the one furthest from any other customers, and the toilets.

He didn't have long to wait. Deena looked around the pub momentarily and picked him out quickly.

'Americano with cold milk, as per your text,' he said.

'Thanks,' she replied as she took a seat opposite him. 'Oh, and thanks as well for that tip off about Dewlish at Heathrow.'

'No problem. It would have been called in quickly enough but it gave you a bit of a head start and some credit with Hanley.'

'I'm not sure there's any such thing with him. He doesn't like people looking cleverer or quicker to the punch than him. Which is why he hates Jan.'

'Yes. Men's egos eh? What are we like?' He smiled and Deena returned it. 'He needs to spit out his pride a bit and accept help wherever it comes from. Makes us all look good in the end. All boats rise with the tide.'

They both took sips of their coffees and a silence fell. Deena sensed an awkwardness that she wanted to break down. There was the same unease to Frank as at their previous meeting.

'We've got Bexington,' she said.

'Yes, I heard.'

'Guessed you would have done. And guessing that's why you wanted to see me.'

There was another silence but this time she had no need to fill it. Frank took a deep breath and set off.

'OK, I'm going to give you some information about this case. It will be relevant, even vital. It can be used in your inquiries. But you are not to tell anyone where this information came from. Understood?'

'Frank, you know I can't give you a guarantee like that. What if Hanley and Donovan ask me where it came from?'

'You can tell them that the source did not wish to be identified. It's quite simple.'

'What if it comes to giving evidence?'

'It shouldn't. You should have plenty of other stuff by the time you crack this.'

'And if not?'

Frank shrugged. 'Deal or no deal?'

'But why? What's so sensitive?'

Frank sipped on his coffee. He buried his head in his hands momentarily before exhaling loudly.

'If what I am about to tell you about myself comes out, there are plenty around the Met, including Hanley, who will make trouble for me. They won't understand what it means. And that will make it difficult for me to do my job properly.'

Deena looked very little the wiser.

'So you promise?'

'Frank, I am going to be honest with you. I'm going to do my best not to divulge my source. But if push comes to shove in the end, I am going to have to say where it came from. I'm not going to make promises I can't keep.'

Frank looked Deena in the eye. She had a look he could trust and knew ultimately that he would be saying the same as her if the roles were reversed. After a pause, he nodded. He just had to say it.

'OK,' he said. 'I am an alcoholic. A recovering alcoholic. That means I used to drink. Used to drink a lot. But I don't drink any more, one day at a time. I have been sober for fifteen years now.'

'OK...' said Deena. She didn't really know how to react but tried not to sound judgmental. She tried to imagine Frank drunk and couldn't. She'd only known him as in control, capable, competent.

'Three nights ago, I was at a meeting of Alcoholics Anonymous in Chelsea when a figure walked in,' Frank said. 'A bloke. He had a sort of wispy and unkempt beard and hood pulled over his head. As the meeting was ending, he was asked he if wanted to say something and he said that he thought he might have killed someone in a blackout when he was drunk.'

'You believed him?'

'We were all a bit stunned. I mean, I've heard all sorts in AA. Plenty of fantasists, I can tell you. I just didn't know. But it bugged me. He bugged me.'

'Right. So, what are you telling me?'

Frank was suddenly startled by one of the bar staff laying the next table with cutlery and a reserved sign and clammed up. He waited for the guy to return behind the bar.

'It was a dimly lit meeting and I can't be sure but...'

'Yes?'

'I think it may well have been James Bexington.'

Deena was the daughter of two devout Pentecostal Christians but this was a rare occasion where the language of a murder team rubbed off on her instead.

'Fuck.' She said. 'You serious?'

Frank nodded slowly, looking down into his coffee.

'What makes you think that?' Deena pressed.

'Well, the bloke was well spoken. And that night, as we all learned the next day, Camilla Carew was found dead in her flat a few streets away.'

'And that's it?'

'What do you mean "and that's it?". That's got to be more than coincidence, hasn't it? I've been bloody agonising over telling you this.'

'Well it's interesting, Frank, but all very circumstantial. I mean, who goes to an AA meeting and confesses to a murder?'

'Somebody deep in shame. Who wants to unburden themselves. Somebody who wants other drunks – or ex-drunks – to understand them without judging and crucially without divulging that confession outside of the meeting.'

'Why would somebody not repeat hearing that confession outside there?'

'Because we have a rule that what is said in meetings is kept confidential.'

'Right. Even if it involved a murder?'

'Well, that's the dilemma isn't it?'

'It doesn't seem a dilemma to me. Somebody confesses to having killed someone and you hold it back?'

'That's what I'm saying. I've been torn. Having examined my conscience, I'm no longer holding it back.'

'But three days, Frank. You've waited three days.'

'Well, you were sceptical, weren't you? You said it sounded circumstantial.'

'OK. So what changed?'

Frank paused again and sipped his coffee. He wiped some milk off his lip before continuing.

'There was somebody at that meeting who was left even more uncomfortable than the rest of us with what this bloke shared. This bloke I now reckon was Bexington.'

'Go on…'

'After the meeting, four of us went to a cafe. One young guy who was only at his second meeting said he'd met people like that before. Angry drunks capable of violence. It's gone through my head a lot ever since I found out.'

'Found out what?'

'That he'd also been murdered. The young guy at the meeting, and who said that in the cafe, was Sean Malahide.'

Deena drew in her breath and a look of shock came across her face.

'Holy shit, Frank. Seriously?'

'Seriously.'

Deena started taking everything in. The good news was that she – they, the investigation – now had a link beyond the scarf between the two murders of two very different people from very different backgrounds. A person connected them. And a motive. The bad news was that this was information they could have done with long before now.

'Frank, this is amazing information and I thank you for it, but come on, why have you been sitting on it? If you'd told us this before, Sean might not have been murdered.'

'I've thought about that a lot Deena and trust me, I've been through the mill about this. I owe my life to AA and I have had to think long and hard about betraying its code.'

Deena grew angry. She moved her face closer to his across the table and almost spat out her words.

'That's a luxury in a murder investigation Frank, surely you can see that? You above all people would know about the need to catch criminals, terrorists, before they strike again.'

He did and buried his head in his hands. Knew this was also about how he and his job might be affected. Deena waited for an answer.

'OK Deena. Pin this on me if you want. I know Hanley would like any stick to beat me with. But it's not about me. Let's park that diversionary tactic and consider where you and your team, are with all this shall we?'

'What do you mean?'

'Well, you were nowhere near Bexington were you? You'd interviewed Wilson, who came voluntarily, but couldn't find Bexington. It took Jan to find him.'

'We have him in custody now. Jan may have bent the rules big time but she insisted he give himself up. He was ready to do it. I picked him up in Brighton this morning.'

'Fair enough. But still, that was really all Jan's work, wasn't it? Then I handed Dewlish to you. I could have given you the info earlier and you still wouldn't have been able to stop Sean's murder. You were nowhere near any of the three. Assuming the murders are by one of those guys?'

'Who else could it be?'

'I don't know, do I? That's your job. Even there, I've just given you a link between Bexington and Sean.'

'And it's a good one. But...'

'But what?'

'I'm sure you've read Jan's piece. Bexington insists he has no clue who Sean Malahide is.'

'That's before Hanley's got stuck into him, isn't it? Anybody besides me who can establish a link between the two of them?'

'Not yet. I've got a bit of business this morning but then I'm going down to Sean's flat in Battersea to ask around.'

Frank drained the dregs of his coffee and was contemplating a Coca-Cola.

'Well, I've given you a pretty good head start again, haven't I?'

'You have. But it still stinks of you justifying withholding information. Hanley wanted to put Jan on a charge and Donovan had to tell him to back off. He'd love to get you instead.'

'And that's another reason why you won't tell anybody, right?'

'I thought you recovering alcoholics had to be honest about everything?'

'I am being honest with you. And it took a bit of time but I am being honest with myself.'

Frank could see that Deena was unsure of the logic.

'There's a difference between honesty and foolish openness to people who wish you ill,' he added.

'Well I told you I'd do my best, and I will Frank. But this is a tough situation you've put me in.'

'Now you know what it's been like for me.'

'I'll talk to people. I'll go see Sean's neighbours. See what I find. See if we can get there without you.'

'Thank you Deena. I appreciate that.'

She shook her head slowly. She was not about to let him off the hook.

'I wouldn't be too premature in thanking me if I was you,' she said. 'Let's hope for your sake that Bexington was just using Jan to make him look better and wants to confess to us as well as to a bunch of drunks who struggle with their consciences before they do the right thing, shall we?'

26

JAN couldn't be doing with Gaunt sitting opposite her as she wrote her story. And so, while she tapped away at her laptop in the coffee shop near the entrance at Donington Services, he strolled around what shops there were, taking a sad interest in cheap wax jackets and jump leads. Soon he wandered back outside though, keeping an eye on the Bentley and typing into his phone, apparently dealing with his own work issues.

It took less than half an hour to file the piece for the website. She looked up a couple of times to see Gaunt strolling around outside but she was so engrossed in what she was writing that it barely registered when he looked particularly agitated talking on his mobile at one point. He then dashed across the car to confront a couple of kids, who it turned out weren't actually going to key his pride and joy, but were just in awe and wanting to press their noses to its windows.

The new information, the scarf linking Camilla and Sean – Jan was determined to keep using their given names, to remind readers that they were people, not just murder victims – was sensational enough to hold the story. After that, it was just a bit on Bexington being as good as his word and giving himself up, and then the background to the case. Done and dusted by 11.30am, all six hundred words of it. Within ten minutes it was up on the site, half an hour before a Met press officer was scheduled to put it out.

She tweeted the link from her phone and saw she'd now hit 125,000 followers after the Bexington exclusive. In another ten minutes, she had another couple of thousand, more than 500 retweets and 1,000 likes. As well as some more "vile rag" replies.

She looked at her watch. Better get on the road again. She texted Robert. *ETA nearer 2 than 1*, she said. *That early?* he texted back. They say sarcasm may not translate well to bare text, she thought, but she'd never had any trouble discerning Robert's.

She went to look for Gaunt but, the cold having got to him, he was back seated at the wheel of the car, his right hand dipping into a bag of something. He didn't notice her coming, still absorbed in his phone, and her knock at the window on the passenger side startled him. She would have just opened the door but he'd locked himself in. He pressed the unlock button.

'Bloody hell, you gave me a fright,' he said.

'You're jumpy,' she replied.

'Always get a bit twitchy this far North. Forgive me if I develop a nose bleed at some point.'

Jan had to admit he wasn't lying on his dating profile – rarely, for a bloke – when he declared himself as having a GSOH. Her smile, though, was soon interrupted.

'What the hell is that smell?'

'Confession time,' he said, holding up the bag he had just been eating from.

'Want one?'

'Pickled onion Monster Munch? Yuk.'

'Guilty pleasure,' he said. 'Something about service stations makes you buy junk food.'

Jan screwed up her face and looked disgusted.

'Clearly you're not trying to impress me much,' she said.

'Well, you did say that it wasn't a date so I thought I might as well. And I'm guessing we're not stopping for lunch somewhere decent. If that exists in these parts.'

'There are some very fine restaurants in Yorkshire, actually,' she said. 'Not that we're there yet. Which means we need to crack on. So drive on Parker, and don't spare the horsepower.'

'Yes milady,' said Gaunt and they both smiled.

She felt she owed him at least a conversation and so asked him about his work, his life, his situation. He enjoyed telling his tall tales of showbiz folk, and a few mutual media people they knew, about life in Soho. Lived there, he said, since his divorce ten years ago, having ceded her the house in Highgate. No kids.

'This beauty is the love of my life these days,' he said, tapping the walnut steering wheel. 'I keep her in a garage in Berwick Street. Under a tarpaulin, of course. Pete, the bloke at the pay desk, keeps an eye on her for me.'

'Fascinating,' said Jan, unfascinated. 'Please don't let me stop you wearing your nice leather driving gloves.'

'Oh no, I don't...'

He couldn't get to the end of the sentence though before Jan laughed out loud and he suddenly realised she was taking the piss out of him. Not for the first time. He started laughing too. She liked that.

As the car passed the Sheffield junctions, she couldn't help remembering her days as a junior reporter there on the long-since defunct *Morning Telegraph*. Good grounding. Happy days. She was a starlet then, with a news editor she loved, in old Benny. What was it he used to say: "If someone tells you it's raining, and someone else tells you it's not, don't just quote both of them, go outside and check."

She smiled to herself, looking out of the window on to the Meadowhall shopping complex, which wasn't there in her day. The Tinsley Viaduct cooling towers had been, though they were no longer. What else did Benny say? "And if it is raining, don't run back inside. Put up your umbrella and keep asking ques-tions." She'd told him it didn't make sense, and he'd laughed and told her: "No. But you'll remember it, won't you?" She smiled to herself. She had.

Something had been niggling her. The scarf. Why had it not been found at Camilla's flat but had been at Sean's? Why would the killer have remembered to take it after the first murder but not the second? Were they disturbed during the second and panicked? Or were there two murder weapons? Or two killers? The latter seemed unlikely. How would they have got the scarf? What bugged her particularly was what the link between the two people could be, with their worlds and social circles so far apart.

'Penny for your thoughts…' said Gaunt.

Jan snapped out of her reverie.

'What? Oh. I was just thinking how much Sheffield has changed since I was a young reporter here.'

'Go on then, tell me all about you. It's your turn.'

She talked about growing up in Wakefield, getting the job in Sheffield after school, losing her Dad in her twenties then going on to Fleet Street on the promises of shifts on night news desks. Sleeping in a friend's back bedroom, before being offered a job on the paper where she remained to this day. Never married. Never wanted kids.

She did her best but found herself rushing her explanations, holding back any detail. She was always more interested in other people's stories rather than her own.

'Look Will, I need to make another call.'

'OK…'

He glanced across at her and she looked back.

'Don't tell me you want me to pull over again and get out of the car? Come on Jan. It's starting to rain.'

She saw his wounded face.

'Fair enough,' she said. 'I don't think it'll make much sense to you anyway.'

She took some headphones from her bag, put the lead into her mobile and keyed in a number.

'Of course, my dear,' said Nancy in response to Jan's question whether she had time for a chat. 'How lovely to hear from you. Somebody came round from the police. Rachel, I think she said her name was. But I didn't really enjoy speaking to her. No rapport, or real sympathy and understanding there. Much rather speak to you. I've got a coffee and walnut cake in. Why don't you come over?'

Jan explained the circumstances and Nancy naturally understood. She was very sorry to hear about her mother being so ill. 'It's a wonderful thing a daughter being so thoughtful.' Jan didn't feel this was the time to go into depth about her relationship with her mother.

She heard a sniffle on the end of the phone.

'You OK, Nancy?'

'Oh yes dear. Just a bit sad to hear about your mother. And it brings up memories for me. Of my Roland. What with Camilla, too…. It's felt very quiet around here. Still a bobby outside but they seem to have finished their work in the building.'

Jan sympathised in turn but Nancy was quickly pulling herself together.

Nancy smiled. 'Come on, then. What can I help you with? Fire away dear.'

Jan danced around a little, asking more about Camilla. Nancy repeated that she should be seen as more than just some privileged debutante type. She was a bright young woman with a good brain.

'As I said, bad choice in men, sadly,' said Nancy. 'That was her downfall.'

Having gone over old ground by way of introduction, Jan decided to go for it. She glanced across at Gaunt, who glanced momentarily back, then pretended he was looking in the rear view mirror, before gazing ahead at the motorway again. She cupped her hand over her mouth and lowered her voice.

'You know about my interview with James Bexington, Nancy...'

'Indeed, dear. I do find it hard to believe it of him, though he is rather in the spotlight, isn't he?'

'You know all the men in this case. Who do *you* think really did it, Nancy?'

'Well, they all had reasons. They were all after her money and hated the fact that she couldn't shake off other men in her life. Wilson was the current keeper of her heart, as she was with him latterly, and he was the cat with the cream, so I suppose he had more to lose, rather than gain, by her death.'

Jan wrote down the word Wilson in her notebook on her lap.

'I'm not sure Simon is capable of murder, though men seem to be capable of many things when spurned, don't they? As for James, I know he and Camilla had some passionate arguments but still... It might well have been him coming out of the flat that night. And he is a man scorned.'

Jan wrote Dewlish and BEXINGTON in her notebook. She caught Gaunt's stolen glance.

'Oh dear. I'm not being very helpful, am I Jan? And I so want to help you. Perhaps if we spoke in person...'

Jan said they could, of course, as soon as she was back in London.

'Do you know someone called Sean Malahide, Nancy?'

'The poor young man murdered? I read about him. No, I don't. I can't think how Camilla might have known him.'

'Well, the police think he was strangled with a scarf that belonged to Camilla. An orange one.'

'The Hermes? Oh she liked that one. James gave it to her. Did I read by the way that this young man was gay?' Nancy asked.

'Indeed,' Jan replied. She'd read it in the morning papers.

Thankfully for theirs, Danny had checked Sean's social media, which revealed it.

'You know, I always thought that Wilson was more that way inclined. A lot of Roly's and my great friends down the years were gay, but in those days they mostly hid it in public, even if they let their guard down in the theatre where they felt safe. Always felt it might harm their careers if it were widely known. I know this may not be – what do they call it – politically correct but Wilson has that air, to me.'

This was not leading to a story, Jan began to realise, even if it was interesting background. She wouldn't underestimate anything Nancy told her but it was theory and gossip at best. She'd already come to realise that Nancy responded best, her memory activated, when somebody was sitting in front of her and paying her proper attention. She thanked her and ended the call, promising to catch up properly when she was back.

Jan underlined the word Wilson.

'Useful?' he asked.

'All good, thanks,' she replied.

'So, the sat nav is telling me around thirty minutes to Wakefield. Tell me some more about yourself and what you do. It all sounds so interesting.'

27

HANLEY sipped the brown contents of his polystyrene cup as he gazed through the tinted glass from the observation area into Hammersmith nick's interview room where sat Simon Dewlish and his solicitor. Hanley had enjoyed his morning of letting them stew, along with Bexington, but there was method to it also. He needed proper preparation time as this was going to test him. The brief alongside Dewlish was no duty solicitor, but some hotshot from a Mayfair address, all cashmere coat and velvet collar.

'Right, let's do this,' he said to Rachel and they moved through to the interview room. As he took his seat, Hanley shot a smile to Dewlish and the solicitor. He switched on the tape and went through the formalities of informing them that it was running.

Dewlish fiddled with a signet ring on his right hand. Hanley liked him looking nervous. He was in his early forties. An unshaven night in the cells had done little for his dry complexion. Dark shadows hung beneath his eyes. His red wavy hair was tousled.

'I hope you've been treated well, Mr Dewlish.'

'I bloody well haven't, actually. Banged up in a cell overnight and all morning being told the bare minimum. Rude men taking my fingerprints and DNA.'

'You will know why you are here. As you were informed when you were arrested at Heathrow yesterday evening, you are a suspect in a murder inquiry. The murder of your ex-wife. You understand the gravity of that?'

Dewlish didn't get a chance to speak.

'I wish it to be known,' the solicitor interrupted, keen to establish his authority in the room, 'That my client is co-operating on every level and vehemently denies any involvement in the death of Camilla Carew.'

Hanley paused a moment before responding.

'Mr....?'

'Jensen. Edward Jensen,' the solicitor replied.

'Mr Jensen. You have the look of a man with a thriving business, which suggests you know your trade. You will realise, therefore, how damaging it looks for your client to have been stopped as he was trying to leave the country. He must have been aware that he was wanted for questioning. How is that co-operating on every level?'

'Detective Chief Inspector, my client…

The solicitor didn't get far.

'Mr Jensen, I'd just as soon hear things from your client's mouth, if it's all the same to you. I'm not sure why you're denying something on Mr Dewlish's behalf, something that he may have been arrested in connection with but has not been charged with. Yet.'

He paused for effect to let the "yet" sink in. Jensen fell silent.

'But we'll let that ride for now,' Hanley added. He turned to Dewlish, who, after the relief of seeing his lawyer in control, tensed up again as Hanley made eye contact.

'Mr Dewlish, perhaps you could tell us why you were attempting to board a plane at Heathrow bound for Bahrain.'

'I had business there.'

'Who with?'

'I'm a venture capitalist, which means I secure money to help fund projects. I was going out to meet a contact who helps secure those funds.'

'No doubt you'll be able to supply us with the name and address of that contact? And what project the funds were for.'

'Well, I have a number of irons in very many fires. It was a tentative meeting to discuss what ideas might appeal to Middle Eastern interests.'

Dewlish smiled lamely.

'That all sounds a bit vague, if you don't mind me saying so.'

'My client can't be expected to remember all his business dealings,' Jensen piped up. 'But I'm sure we can find paperwork. If it's relevant to this investigation of course.'

'I'll look forward to that,' said Hanley. 'Only I'm wondering about Bahrain… You live in the United States now and in fact through your latest marriage have dual citizenship with this country, Mr Dewlish, yes?'

'Yes.'

'And it would seem that there is no extradition treaty between Bahrain and the US, or Great Britain for that matter.'

'Really? I don't think I knew that. What's that got to do with anything?'

'You tell me. You wouldn't have been trying to escape justice, would you?'

Jensen intervened again.

'There is absolutely no basis for that accusation.'

'I don't think it was an accusation,' said Hanley. 'Just a question. Let's turn to why you were in Britain in the first place…'

'A flying visit. Just to see some family and friends.'

'Like who?'

'My sister Virginia in Kent. She'll vouch for me.'

'And Camilla Carew?'

Dewlish hesitated. His voice lowered, along with his face as he looked down and fiddled with his ring again.

'I did see her yes. Last Saturday.'

'For what reason?'

'Just to catch up with her really. When we divorced, it was all very civilised. We stayed on reasonable terms.'

'Really? In my experience, these things are rarely civilised.' Hanley spat out the sentence with a bitterness that had Rachel turning her head to look at him.

'Didn't she catch you with another woman?' Hanley continued.

'That was reflected in our financial settlement.'

Hanley stared across the table at Dewlish, willing his eyes to bore into his adversary's soul, trying to read the contents of his brain.

'So how did the meeting with Camilla go?'

'We drank tea, chatted about the old days. I told her about my life in New York...'

'And how is your life in New York?'

'Very good thank you. Same with everyone in the financial sector... We've all been through some difficult days but life is on the turn now that we have a more business-friendly administration.'

'Did I not read that your latest wife had kicked you out?'

'That's a slight exaggeration. We have agreed a trial separation.'

'Hmm. And as you drank tea, did you ask Camilla for money.'

'I did remind her about how well she had done out of the settlement and asked her if she might advance me some money to tide me over.'

'Was that where the £4,000 came from?'

'She kept some cash in her bedroom and gave it to me on the basis that I would leave and not come back again. I said I wouldn't. It was actually £5,000 but I spent a thou on the hotel and the plane ticket.'

'Really? She didn't in fact refuse, and you went back on Monday, killed her and found the money in the flat?'

'No I did not. She gave it to me. End of story.'

'I think we'll be the judges of what is the end, thank you. We've had your fingerprints sent up to Scotland Yard. How do you account for them matching some on an orange scarf belonging to Camilla that we believe was used to murder her?'

'I really don't know.'

There was a pause and Dewlish shot a worried look at his solicitor.

'Unless… Yes. That's it. I hung up my coat on a hook in the hall at Camilla's and the scarf fell off a peg. I picked it up and replaced it.'

'How convenient,' said Hanley. The two men sat staring at each for a moment.

'How did she seem to you?' Hanley asked.

'Fine. She seemed happy enough. She'd dumped that wet blanket Bexington and was with a new man. Said she liked him.'

'You don't like Bexington?'

'A wastrel. Always on the scrounge from Camilla. Boozer. Was doing nothing with his life.'

'So he was a wet blanket, a wastrel and a boozer. Mr Dewlish, you'd just talked Camilla out of 5K. And for somebody who's been in New York a while now, you seem to know a lot about him.'

'I know people who know him.'

'What people?'

'You know. People in the antiques world. That sort of thing.'

'No, I don't know really. So what did Camilla say about her new man?'

'Gavin, she said his name was. A decent man, she insisted.'

'Insisted?'

'Well, I asked her if she was sure. I feel – felt – a bit protective about her still.'

'Protective or worried she might be spending her money on him?'

'What? No. Of course not. She reckoned he was in politics for all the right reasons. She said he wanted to make people's lives better. Also mentioned her father didn't think much of him, mind.'

'Why was that?'

'The fellow bats for the other side.'

'What does that mean?'

'He was left of centre, politically.'

'Ah. Got it.'

'As I said to Camilla, you can't be too careful with those Labour people.'

Hanley paused and looked across to Rachel and nodded. She slid a file across the desk and Hanley opened it. The solicitor looked interested. Dewlish looked concerned.

'The thing is, Mr Dewlish. We've been looking into your background. Quite apart from the separation, as you call it, from your wife, things haven't been going quite so well in New York for you, have they? You seem to owe a fair bit of money to a fair few people.'

'Nothing I couldn't handle. Just a cash-flow issue. Which was why I was going to Bahrain.'

'Correct me if I'm wrong, but didn't Camilla's father always think you a bit of a scrounger yourself? And given what you've told us about last Saturday, he may have had a point. You sure you're not transferring your own stuff on to Mr Bexington?'

'Of course not. Camilla and I were in love back in the day. I'd had a bad couple of years after the crash and while it's true she lent me money, I was devoted to her.'

'So devoted, she caught you in bed with another woman. And not just any woman. Our inquiries have revealed that she was the wife of an old friend in the City. Who had introduced you to Camilla.'

Dewlish hung his head in shame.

'Really, DCI Hanley,' Jensen interrupted. 'Is this relevant now, years on?'

'We're actually giving your client the opportunity to clear all this up. If he's innocent, as you say he is, he will surely want to tell us his version of events.'

Dewlish looked at Jensen. The solicitor nodded.

'Biggest mistake I ever made,' he said. 'Regretted it and have paid for it ever since.'

'You see, I think you came back to point out to Camilla that she'd got a good divorce settlement because of your indiscretion and your need to keep it quiet and you felt you were owed. Big time.'

'That's not entirely accurate. I didn't come back just to see Camilla. I've met financiers in the City while I've been here.'

'And how did that go?'

Dewlish did not reply. The solicitor came to his rescue.

'DCI Hanley, I've gone along with this, as has my client, but are you going anywhere with this or is this just bullying an innocent man?'

Hanley was riled but tried hard to hold it together.

'Can I ask who's paying for your services, sir, now that we've had to impound Mr Dewlish's cash?'

'How is that pertinent?'

There was a stand-off. Dewlish spoke.

'Somebody who I thought was a friend said he couldn't help me financially when I went to see him. Felt guilty apparently. Offered Mr. Jensen here.'

'Must have felt pretty guilty given you will be on, what, up to a grand an hour, Mr Jensen?'

The solicitor didn't answer. Now Hanley grew angrier.

'So listen, forget any bullying here. Your client is being questioned in the course of a murder inquiry. He met the victim a couple of days before she was strangled and is still not properly explaining why he saw her and what was said.'

Jensen was in no mood to be intimidated, however. 'I think the tape will show that my client has answered all your questions, detective.'

'So here's one more. Mr Dewlish, where were you three nights ago between the hours of six and eight?'

'I was in my hotel room, watching television.'

'Anyone corroborate that? Did you order room service, perhaps?'

'Well, no. I'd had a good lunch with an old broker friend of mine. Didn't feel I needed to eat again beyond a snack from the minibar. I wasn't aware I would need an alibi for the evening.'

'Do you know a Sean Malahide, Mr Dewlish?'

'No. Why?'

'He was murdered last night, also with the orange scarf. In Battersea. You didn't take a detour there on your way to Heathrow?'

'Never heard of the man. I took a taxi straight to the airport.'

Hanley stared across the table at him. He paused, leaving a gap for the solicitor to exploit and prevent him thinking of a follow-up question.

'So is that all?' Jensen asked.

'For now,' Hanley said and Dewlish and the solicitor both got up to leave.

'However,' Hanley added. 'You will not leave the country and you will surrender your passport to us.'

'You can't do that. Mr Dewlish has not been charged with anything,' the solicitor said. 'And I'm guessing that you have no evidence to take to the CPS to charge him.'

'I think you'll find we can keep him banged up for another twelve hours minimum as a suspect if we need to. Or even hold him for longer under new terrorism laws.'

'But my client is not a terrorist.'

'He could be, if we say he is. Links to the Middle East and all that.'

'Nonsense. I could contest that.'

'Fine. Please do. But do you want your client to go back to the cells while you do all that, or would he prefer to be free but within reach to assist us, as you insist he is willing to do?'

'But I've checked out of my hotel,' said Dewlish. 'And you're holding the money Camilla gave me.'

'Well, we can provide you with another night at your accommodation of last night…'

'OK, OK,' said Dewlish. 'I'll stay around London.'

'Good. I'm sure one of your guilty City mates will come through with a few quid to keep you in the style you've become accustomed to. As no doubt he has for Mr Jensen here.'

'Or I could stay with my sister, I suppose.'

'That's the spirit. Now you're getting the hang of this. See you very soon.'

28

DEENA would have liked to have sat in on the Dewlish interview but she understood why Hanley wanted her to take a break after her pre-dawn trip to Brighton. Anyway, it turned out well that the meeting with Frank had yielded some important information to take the investigation forward. In fact, Hanley was so delighted with it when she rang him, that he offered her a seat at the table later in the day for the interview with Bexington.

Hanley had not pressed when she told him that the info about the AA meeting had come from an anonymous source. He sounded too pleased just to have something with which to surprise Bexington, given that the bloke was unlikely to diverge much from what he'd already told Jan. Besides, Hanley may not be the most engaging of work colleagues or superiors, but he understood the need to protect informants. When he was in a good mood, that was.

Before Bexington, though, there was one more thing to be done. Even though she'd already gone straight from meeting Frank to interview Gavin Wilson's assistant, Mike Evershot, in a cafe at the back of Labour Party HQ. He hadn't wanted to speak in the building, not within earshot of his boss and Wilson occupied the next office. He was also meeting someone else there after her, he said. As it was an informal interview anyway, Deena agreed.

Even so, he was jittery. She hadn't realised quite how much until she was mulling it over now as she drove to Battersea. And also that she was sure she'd seen Peter Carew walking up the street with two other men accompanying him as she left. What could they be doing there?

Evershot had confirmed that Wilson was at the strategy meeting the night of Camilla's murder. Also verifying that he had indeed gone to his office when the meeting broke, for the MPs to go the House to vote, from what, 6pm until around 9.

'Did you see him in there?' Deena asked.

'Yes. He was on his laptop. I could see.'

'For the whole time?'

'Well, yes.'

'Really?'

'Put it this way, he was there when I left and there when I got back.'

'Got back? So you weren't around all the time?'

'I went to the canteen for a while, probably around quarter past six with a couple of the other guys. Gavin told us to get a meal as it could be a long night. Then he came down to say that he'd heard from the MPs the vote would be dragging on and we could go to the pub to watch the Chelsea game if we wanted to. He'd hold the fort here and message us again when we were going to reconvene.'

'And that's what happened?'

'Yes. We went to the pub about seven. I went just for an orange juice and the game. I'm teetotal and a Chelsea supporter. We headed back about five to nine when Gavin texted us.'

'So actually, you can't corroborate him being there at all.'

'Like I say, he was there when I left and there when I got back. I just assumed he'd stayed in his office. That's what he does. He virtually lives in that office.'

'I'm hoping CCTV will confirm this?'

'There's only CCTV in the reception area. The staff think it would be an infringement of civil liberties to have it anywhere else. We are the Labour Party, after all.'

He had looked worried, Deena recalled. As if he had put his foot in it and soon it would be both feet. The guy was clearly torn; between loyalty to, maybe even fear of, his boss, and wanting to talk.

'Did you know about his relationship with Camilla Carew?' Deena asked.

'No, we didn't. We knew he had dealings with her but not like that. In fact, since we heard, it's been the talk of the office. We've all been a bit stunned.'

'Because of who her father was?'

'No. We didn't realise he liked women.'

'You thought he was gay?'

'Yes. Well, sort of. A few of the guys thought he might be because, he never seemed to date or even mention women.

'Anything else you can tell me about him?'

'Well. he liked to mimic people. He did a great impression of the Prime Minister.'

'OK...That it?'

'Sorry. As I say, he didn't seem to have much of a life outside the office. You won't tell him I've said any of this, will you? To be honest, we wouldn't have known if he was gay as he never talked about men either. He always seemed.... sort of asexual. Is that the word?'

So, she mused as she drove along the Embankment, she had two potential pieces of significant information: Wilson could quite easily have left the building on the night Camilla was murdered. He'd certainly had time. And that he might be gay. Or bi-sexual. Nobody knew because nobody really knew him.

Her computations were interrupted by her arrival in Battersea. This wasn't the gentrified Battersea on the south side of the Thames by the park, the area that had grown posher as people ventured over the bridges in search of value back in the nineties.

After Kensington and Chelsea exploded in value thanks to Russians and Chinese with wads of cash.

At Sean's block of flats, kids on half-term played in the empty car park spaces. It was early afternoon but Deena suspected that the bays were empty not because people were at work, but because they couldn't afford cars. The lift, naturally enough, was out of order and so she was forced to use the steps in the middle of the building to the top floor of the four-storey block. Just one copper was still here on the landing guarding the door. Forensics had long been and gone but for now they still didn't want ghouls contaminating the scene.

'Morning,' she said, brandishing her ID. The uniform moved aside to let her in and she wandered the flat's narrow corridors and small rooms; a living room/diner, kitchen, bathroom and one bedroom. It was all neat and tidy. Basic. Nothing much to see here, mainly because Sean hadn't seemed to own much. They would have to hope forensics came up with something.

She sat on the worn sofa and surveyed the room. One photo in a frame. Looked like his mum and dad. They would have long since been informed and she hoped they were coping amid the devastating news. She got out her phone and accessed the report that had been pulled together, as well as the interviews conducted by uniform yesterday. Sean had been single. Rented the place three months ago off a landlord who'd bought it fifteen years ago when the prices were still reasonable and the council needed to sell some stock to offset cutbacks. She read through neighbours' statements.

But Deena liked to hear people's voices, rather than just read their words. To see the expressions on their faces. The authenticity in their eyes. She went back outside and knocked on the door to the right. No answer. She went to the one on the left. As she knocked, she could hear the loud crying of a young child. Soon a woman came to the door with the baby in her arms.

'What do you want?' she snapped.

'Are you Aesha Sanbhat?'

'Yes.'

'My name is DS Deena Campbell and I'd like to ask you some questions about Sean?'

There was something in Deena's tone which stopped the woman as she was about to utter the standard: "Look, I've already told your people all I know." Perhaps it was because Deena was a woman. Perhaps because she showed more openness and empathy in her friendly expression. Deena felt herself being eyed up and down.

'OK. Come in,' Aesha said. 'I've got this one to feed but I'll try to help you.'

'Can I make you a cup of tea?' Deena asked, endearing herself further to the woman. The offer was warmly welcomed and Deena went to the kitchen to sort a couple of mugs. Soon, thanks to a bit of cooing from Deena and some soft-voiced chat – "What's his name?"; "Harsha"; "Lovely name,"; "It means happiness in Sanskrit." – the baby had stopped crying and they could talk.

'You were the one who phoned us?' Deena asked.

'Yes. We sometimes went into each other's flats in the mornings for a coffee. I knocked on Sean's door yesterday but there was no answer. I looked through the letter box and I could see down the corridor and into the living room. He was lying on the floor.'

'Must have been a terrible shock.'

'It was, yes. I did talk to a police officer yesterday but he didn't really ask me much. It was all a bit routine. I'm glad a detective has come back. In fact, I was thinking about coming in to the police station. Sean deserves a proper investigation.'

Deena smiled at her and nodded. 'And he'll get that,' she said.

'Thank you for calling him Sean when you knocked on the door, rather than Mr Malahide. That makes him sound more like himself rather than a body. I want that for him at least.'

'You sound as if you knew him quite well. Tell me about him,' Deena said.

Aesha talked of how Sean had moved in a few months ago and they'd become friends. She saw a fair bit of him during the day, having coffee in each other's flats, but not so much in the evenings as he worked in a gay club in Soho.

'You knew he was gay himself?'

'Yes, he told me. He's from a small town in Shropshire. Said he came to London because he used to get hassled by certain people there. Including the police. He liked the people at the place he worked with now, and the clientele but it wasn't good for him,' Aesha seemed to regret saying it.

'You mean because of his drink problem?'

'You know about that? How come?'

'I'm investigating his murder, Aesha. I'm speaking to a lot of people. Was he drinking a lot lately?'

'No. He'd stopped. In fact…'

Aesha rocked the baby in her arms, now asleep and stared at Deena, thinking.

'Go on…'

'I guess it's not going to matter now, is it?' she said. 'He was going to AA.'

'He told you about it?'

Again, Aesha pondered, clearly wondering if she could trust Deena.

'He came with me. He used to have terrible hangovers in the mornings. The shakes and everything. I told him I knew what that was like and that there was this place I went.'

'OK…' said Deena, her tone gently encouraging her to go on.

'It's tough being a single mother. It's even tougher being a single mother and a recovering alcoholic. With a family who've disowned you.'

'I can imagine,' said Deena. She thought of her own parents and their strict codes of behaviour. She hoped that their love for her would never let it go so far as pushing her out completely though.

'My parents were disgusted by my drinking,' Aesha continued. 'Mainly because the neighbours seemed to be. One of them wrote an anonymous letter to my father saying I was a disgrace to the street and the community.'

'Sorry to hear that,' said Deena.

'When they kicked me out, I took up with this bloke just because he had his own flat and was a drinker as well. Then I got pregnant and he kicked me out too. That shocked me into getting sober.'

'Something good came out of all that then...'

'Yes. Luckily I got this place through the council, what with me about to become a single mum. It was one of a few in the block that they hadn't sold off. I stopped drinking during my pregnancy and started going to AA after the baby was born. It's not been easy but it's a lot better than it used to be.'

'You sound very brave, Aesha, getting your life back on track. And Sean?'

'I told him my story one day and about a month ago he said he'd like to come with me. I took him to a meeting in Chelsea, which I heard was small and quiet and might suit him. We got the bus together. We both liked it. Monday was only his second meeting. Weird one though.'

'How come?'

'A bloke walked in and sat silently the whole time. Then he suddenly shared with us that he thought he might have killed someone in an alcoholic blackout.'

'Did you believe him?' Deena felt her heart-rate rising at hearing this corroboration of what Frank had told her.

'I don't know. It freaked me out. Not as much as Sean though.'

'Did he say anything to you about it?'

'We went for coffee after the meeting with a couple of people and Sean said he'd known scary blokes like that in his time. Then he got up and left. I caught up with him and we caught the bus home. But he never said a word, hardly. Couldn't wait to get through his front door.'

'You do know there was a murder in Chelsea that night?'

'Yeah. I follow that Jan Mason woman on Twitter. She has all the lowdown.'

There was a silence while Deena let the penny drop.

'Shit. You think that bloke could've killed that woman?'

'We're looking at every angle. Did you not think about telling the police about what this bloke said at the AA meeting?'

'Well, no. There was the confidentiality angle, that we were reminded of. And anyway, who could be sure he was telling the truth? To be honest, when I got home, I was so preoccupied with sorting the babysitter and then with Harsha that I didn't think much more about it.'

Deena nodded. 'Yes, lot on your plate. I get that.'

'You think there might be a link with Sean?'

'We do. Yes.'

'Oh my God.' Aesha brought her hand to her mouth and her eyes were wide with shock.

'Do you think other people in that AA meeting are in danger?'

'Could be. Is there anywhere you can go to stay? With a friend maybe?'

'Um. Possibly. I'll need to make some calls. What about Harsha...' Her voice shook.

'I'll see if we can leave the officer outside Sean's until you sort something. Did you hear anything the night he died? Any raised voices? Scuffles, that sort of thing?'

'Oh... What... Tuesday? Nothing. The walls are thin here but I'd got Harsha to sleep and I think I must have crashed out myself in front of the TV, I was so tired. When I woke up, I took myself off to bed.'

'Did Sean have many friends? Anyone who came to the flat regularly?'

'He had people round sometimes. He was a member of the local Labour Party and was the LGBTQ Plus rep. Three or four would turn up for meetings now and then.'

'Any other visitors?'

'There was a guy I saw one night a while back on the landing walking past my kitchen window and I heard him knock on Sean's door. I remember it as the guy looked, what's the word, sort of distinguished. I peeked out my front door to get a better look but the lights were out on the landing. Broken. Usually are. It took Sean a while to answer the door.'

'Did this man have a beard?'

'No. Pretty sure he didn't. Dark hair. Actually, might have had a moustache? Did he? I don't know. Wore an overcoat. Had the lapels up.'

'Would you recognise him?'

'Not sure.'

'Did you ask Sean about him afterwards?'

'I did but he didn't want to talk about him. I think it might have been a boyfriend but one with complications.'

'Such as?'

'You know. Somebody who's maybe not out. Married man or something. Sean talked about them coming into his club.'

'Ah, OK.'

Deena took out pictures of Bexington, Wilson and Dewlish.

'Could it be any of these three?' she asked.

Aesha pored over them for a few moments.

'This one,' she said pointing at a picture. 'This one looks familiar.'

29

'YOU take a right here and it's fifty yards along on the left,' Jan said. She knew the satnav was active but she wanted to show, to herself as much as Gaunt, that she was not a terrible daughter and had been to visit her dementia-stricken mother before.

'OK,' Gaunt said, going along with her. 'Here we are, St Mark's care home.' He pulled the car through the brick pillars bearing the home's name and found a parking space.

'Right, well. Unless you need me for anything, I'll leave you to it and head for Leeds. Text me when you're finished and I'll come and pick you up.'

'It all depends on how she… I might have to get a hotel room for the night.'

'Sure. Well, just let me know, eh?' said Gaunt, smiling again.

Jan closed the car door and she watched him drive off. She stood for a moment gazing at the building before going in. There was a trepidation in her. It had been a while since her last visit and she always felt nervous entering the building, echoes of her adolescence and some fraught episodes with her mother queuing up in her memory bank.

Was there a template for these places, she wondered. Whenever she saw them on the news, they all looked the same: red brick, angular, functional. But modern and humane, at least; not some latter-day workhouse or grey hostel. It seemed to be the same standard décor inside. Soft, somnolent colours of grey carpets and beige coloured painted walls up to a handrail running along all the corridors, light green and violet striped wallpaper above that. It was all designed to be calming and reassuring.

That was why she and Robert had chosen it. It was costing £3,000 a month, paid for from the proceeds of Elsie's terraced house that had fetched £120,000. She had been here two years now, six months longer than the average that people lasted in such a home, apparently. There was less than eighteen months left in the kitty.

Having gained access via the security phone at the front, then signed in at reception, she made her way along the corridors to the stairs that led up through the three floors of the house. On the ground were those still young enough to be able to look after themselves, then those requiring help and full-time care. Elsie was on the top floor.

Jan passed the hairdressing salon and the small cinema before arriving at the security door that prevented unpermitted access to the lift and stairs. She had forgotten the access code and had to check in her trusty, battered Filofax, home to all her personal data and contacts. She took the lift. Two flights was one too many.

'Hello Jan, long time no see,' said the young care assistant Emma, when Jan stepped through the double doors having remembered the access code on the second floor. Emma's Yorkshire tones betrayed no metropolitan edge, and it was said without malice.

'Work. You know how it is,' Jan replied.

'Yes. She's always been always very proud of you. When she was lucid. You know. Pointing out your stories in the paper.' Jan felt a stab of scepticism, mixed in with her guilt.

'Thank you. Guessing she's still in the same room? How's she doing?'

Emma smiled and shrugged her shoulders. Jan nodded, knowing what she was saying without saying anything, and headed down to the end of the corridor. She and Robert had been fortunate that a room had come up, due to the death of its previous occupant, in a corner with two windows, rather than just one as others had on the side of the building.

She pushed open the door hesitantly and poked her head around. She saw first Robert sitting at Mum's bedside in an armchair then her mother prone, either asleep or unconscious, and finally a care assistant at the foot of the bed. Robert turned his head to see Jan's face. He looked at his watch.

'OK. OK. I got here as quickly as I could. No need to be like that.'

Robert looked only a little chastised but he realised the time for sarcasm had passed.

'You're here now. Thanks for coming.'

The care assistant smiled at her.

'Hello Ms Mason. My name's Becky. Really pleased to meet you. I've heard a lot about you. From Elsie and from the other staff. Most of the residents read your paper.'

It was true. On the occasions when Jan had been here before, one of the first things she'd noticed was copies of the paper folded over the top bars of walking frames in front of residents in armchairs.

'Thank you Becky. That's kind.' Jan smiled.

'MUM,' Robert said all of a sudden, loudly into Elsie's ear. 'Jan's here.' Elsie did not move. Her breath was shallow. Jan moved to her bedside.

'Hello Mum,' said Jan. 'How you doing?'

Elsie's mouth issued a long sigh. Jan, Robert and Becky exchanged looks. Jan pressed on.

'I'm here now.'

Elsie's eyes suddenly opened and Becky gasped. Robert and Jan looked at each other.

'Bloody hell Jan,' he said. 'Keep talking to her.'

Jan gripped Elsie's hand. She felt a tear forming in her eye.

'What are we going to do with you, eh Mum?' Jan said with a smile. Elsie turned her head a little and tried to focus on Jan. They could just make out what she said, each word taking a few seconds.

'She writes stories,' Elsie murmured and more tears came to Jan's eyes. She looked up at Robert, whose bottom lip was quivering. Jan kissed her mother on the forehead. The smell of moisturised skin, the scent of her childhood, rose to Jan's nostrils. Elsie's eyes closed again and a smile played on her lips.

Jan's phone rang in her bag. She dived in to locate it.

'JAN...' Robert barked.

It was Deena.

'I've really got to take this,' said Jan. Robert looked daggers at her. 'What?' she added. 'She's perked up. You just saw her. Anyway, you heard Mum. I write stories.'

She dashed from the room and hurried down the corridor.

'Hold on Deena. Just give me two minutes...'

She descended the two floors and paced the car park as she listened to Deena, who had just got back to the murder team's offices at Putney. Jan listened intently as Deena outlined first her visit to Labour Party HQ, and how Gavin Wilson's alibi had a big hole of more than two hours in it, with his deputy unable to be certain that Wilson was in the building at the time Camilla was killed.

'Interesting. Very interesting,' said Jan. 'So you're veering away from Bexington then?'

Deena didn't answer that. Instead she asked how Jan's day was going.

'Well, my mum seems a bit better since I arrived.'

'I'm glad to hear it Jan. I meant more whether you had anything new yet.'

'Nothing concrete...'

'Come on Jan. I've been told to keep you in the loop but I don't want this to be a one-sided relationship.'

'Well, it may be nothing…'

'The number of people who say that and it turns out to be something.'

'One of my contacts who knows Wilson thought that he might be gay.'

There was a pause before Deena replied.

'Who told you that?'

'Deena, you know I can't give up my sources. I'm sure you're not going to tell me everyone you've been speaking to and who told you what.'

'We've already been looking into a gay link between Wilson and Sean.'

'Interesting.'

'Sean was also a member of the Labour Party.'

'That's just gone from interesting to intriguing.'

'Yes. I thought we might be on to something, to add the gay link to the scarf.

'What do you mean, you "thought"?'

'I then spoke to a neighbour of Sean's.'

'And?'

'She saw a man come to visit him. When I showed her photos of the three suspects, she identified James Bexington.'

Jan was stunned.

'Could he have been in a relationship with Sean?' Deena asked. 'Perhaps bisexual?'

'Shit, Deena. I don't know. I wouldn't have thought so but it wasn't something I asked him. I had no reason to. You met him this morning. Spent some time in his company. What do you reckon?'

'I don't reckon anything Jan. Not yet. We're interviewing him later and I'll see what his reaction is.'

'Christ. That would be a bit of a shocker. What can I write?' She felt a new nervousness in her stomach at the prospect that she had done a PR job for a murderer.

'Just hang on for now Jan. Let's speak again later. And see if you can come up with something more, eh? I'd like a bit back, yes?'

'Deena, cut me some slack today, please. Don't turn into my fucking news editor. I am up in Yorkshire at my very ill mother's bedside.'

'OK, Jan. Noted. Take it easy.'

Jan ended the call angrily and paced the car park for a few minutes. On top of her worry that she might have trashed her own reputation with the Bexington interview, she hated not having any new information of her own. And she sensed that there was something Deena was holding back and wasn't going to spill until Jan gave her more. She had a quick scroll of Twitter to see if anything was happening but it was still all about the scarf. Her tweet linking to her web story had had more than 2,000 likes and 500 retweets and she'd picked up another bundle of followers. The press statement from the Met had simply confirmed her exclusive.

Deep in thought, wondering how much mileage the gay angle would have for a story later, she meandered back up to the second floor of the home, remembering the access code this time. She opened the door to her Mum's bedroom with a "Sorry about that," to be greeted by a scene of Robert at the bedside with his head in his hands, along with a sympathetic half-smile on Becky's face.

And her mother's now lifeless body on the bed.

30

HANLEY was deflated. Even though she'd only known him for a month, Deena could read his moods. And the fact that any emotion he was feeling, from stress to disappointment, simply came out as anger.

'These fucking posh boys,' he said. 'They lie for a living and end up believing their own lies.'

'You think he's holding back on us guv?' Terry asked.

'Course he fucking is. Got to be.'

Bexington had told him and Deena pretty much what he'd told Jan. Yes, he had confronted Wilson and been fearful for Camilla. Yes, he'd been at her flat that evening but had found her dead when he got there. The yell a neighbour heard was his, not Camilla's. There was the text from her that he had deleted in his funk – the one thing Jan had kept back from her article – but no, he hadn't found and disposed of her phone. Blind alley.

And of course he recognised the scarf. He had given it to Camilla after all, and naturally his fingerprints would probably still be on it. His DNA might well be on her clothes as he had given her one last hug. Sure, he would be willing to provide both fingerprints and DNA. After leaving Camilla's flat, he had gone to his friend Giles's place in Battersea. Giles had confirmed that. He insisted that he had no idea how the scarf had come to be in Sean Malahide's flat. And he didn't know Malahide. Had never met him. Never been to his flat.

'What about you going to a meeting of Alcoholics Anonymous in Chelsea on Monday night?' Deena had asked Bexington.

'What? No. I told you I went to Battersea to stay with Giles. I have been to AA in the past, a few times, but then I'm afraid I went back on the sauce after meeting Camilla. You know that.'

'Have you ever seen this woman?' Deena had asked, showing him a picture of Aesha Sanbhat.

'Not that I recall,' he had said. 'Why?'

'Only, she claims she's seen you before. And she was at that AA meeting in Chelsea, with Sean. She lives in the next door flat and thinks you might have been the man she saw knocking on his door.'

'Not me.'

'How do you explain her identifying you then?'

'I can't. Maybe she's seen me in Battersea. Like I say, I have a friend there I stay with now and then and did so on Monday night, and Tuesday through the day. Maybe she saw my picture on social media or the news? Maybe a website or in a paper? I don't know.'

Hanley and Deena had looked at each other at that point. They could not argue with that.

'One last thing, Mr Bexington,' Hanley had said. 'Are you gay, or bisexual maybe?'

His eyes had widened in what seemed to be genuine shock and bafflement.

'What? No. Of course not. I don't mean "of course not" because there's anything wrong with it. It's just that I'm not. Some of my best friends are, and all that. Giles, the friend I stayed with, is.'

'OK. We'll be sure to have another chat with Giles,' said Hanley, frustrated.

Now Hanley, having had his rant about posh boys, was calming down. His anger was less about public school privilege and more about not nailing this down tonight, as Jackie Donovan had been pressing him to do. He loved that feeling of confidence when he knew the CPS would agree to a charge, and thought that Deena's new leads, plus his own faith in himself to break somebody down, was going to lead to Bexington coughing.

He'd wanted to keep him in custody. To have another crack at him. But his gobby solicitor, David Toller, had persuaded Jackie Donovan that what they had was circumstantial and would never stand up. So Donovan had told Hanley to keep building the case, firming up the evidence. There was very little in the way of forensics from the Malahide case, the killer probably having worn gloves. Hanley tried to tell her that Bexington was a flight risk but she'd pointed out that he'd been prepared to give himself up to them. And so he'd had to let the bastard go. For now.

'So,' said Hanley against a backdrop of rush hour headlights heading south over Putney bridge as he and the team sat looking at the Operation Camilla whiteboard, now plastered with pictures of suspects and murder scenes, and lines leading from location to location on the large map. 'Let's review the day.'

He got up and walked up to the board, using a Sharpie as a pointer.

'Dewlish. Waste of space. Short of money. Everything he touches turns to ratshit. But does that make him a murderer?'

'No matter how thick he is, he's got motive,' said Rachel. 'And he was at the airport, doing a bunk with a wedge of cash on him. To a place with no extradition treaty.'

'Yes, agreed,' said Hanley. 'Nothing to connect him with Malahide, though.'

'Would he really kill Camilla for five grand?' Terry asked.

'You were with me, Thomas. He sounded desperate for dosh, didn't he?'

Rachel nodded.

'And his prints were on the scarf. But then so were the other two's. And they both had motive as well. Bexington admits to being angry at Camilla's relationship with Wilson…'

'But wouldn't he have killed Wilson and not her? Then he might win her back…' said Terry.

'Nah. She'd moved on from him and he knew it. Jealousy does strange things to men. If I can't have her, the next bloke's not going to and all that. He's admitted being at the scene. Given us some dodgy sob story about finding her. Then Malahide's neighbour, who was at an AA meeting an hour later, tells Deena she recognises Bexington from somewhere. Said he coughed to maybe having killed someone in an alcoholic blackout. And Bexington's admitted he'd been drinking and he has been to AA in the past.'

'Except he has a point when he says he was all over the media,' said Darren. 'That might have influenced her.'

Hanley was in full flow now though.

'And then he stays in Battersea, for fuck's sake. Where twenty-four hours later, a man was also strangled. A man who was at that AA meeting. Bexington says his mate Giles is gay. Is there a link there, and what could be between them? Then Lord Snooty pisses off to Brighton and hides out. No matter what he told Mason for her paper about wanting a fair shout, is that the action of an innocent man?'

Deena looked around. All were shaking their heads, except her.

'But then, Dewlish and Wilson aren't exactly acting like innocent men either, are they, guv?' Deena said.

'So how come neither of them appears on CCTV in the hallway, except for Dewlish on Saturday and Wilson on Sunday going in, and Monday morning going out?'

'That back entrance,' said Deena. 'Both know the place and could have gone down the alley and through the communal garden.'

'No footprints,' said Hanley.

'There's a path. They didn't have to go on the grass and it was raining. Would have washed away signs.'

'Possible, yes,' Hanley acknowledged. 'Keeping alive my theory that Dewlish could have gone back on the Monday, having been turned down for money on the Saturday, and killed her then, finding the cash somewhere in the flat.'

'And let's look at Wilson,' he continued, tapping the mugshot on the whiteboard with the Sharpie. 'Maybe there's a link between Wilson and Sean Malahide. Labour member. Some political connection possibly. And we've had word, including from Wilson's deputy at work, Mike Evershot, that a fair few people thought he might well be gay.'

'But he told us he was in the Labour HQ building when Camilla was killed,' said Rachel.

'That's what he told us, yes. But this Evershot told Campbell that he couldn't be sure Wilson didn't leave the building.'

'But why kill the golden goose?' Deena asked. 'She was valuable to him.'

There was a silence.

Suddenly the double doors burst open and in walked Sanjay.

'Nice of you to join us, Sanj,' said Hanley.

'Sorry guv. Traffic. Mrs Bickler's given me the runaround. Flight didn't get in till late last night and she slept late as well. She was reluctant to talk. Obviously upset as well.'

'OK. So what has she said?'

'Camilla wrote a new will about a month ago with a solicitor in the firm the family has always used. She named her mother as her executor.'

'Yes, we know that...'

'She said the same as the solicitor before. Mrs Bickler was reluctant to tell me what was in it. But I informed her this was a murder inquiry and she needed to co-operate if we were going to catch the murderer. She said OK, but she would only talk about the parts of the will that relate to the men in Camilla's life.'

'Yep. Get on with it.'

'Well, the estate is worth around £1.5 million. There was a lot more as Daddy gave her £3 million on her thirtieth birthday but the lifestyle has eaten into it. That may have been part of the argument between her and Peter Carew on Monday afternoon. Anyway, there was nothing in it for Dewlish. She must have some soft spot still for Bexington as there was 50K for him.'

'Wish all the women who've dumped me treated me that badly,' said Terry, and Darren and Hanley laughed.

'The biggest winner was the Labour Party, though. She was leaving them £250,000.'

Looks were exchanged. Breath taken in.

'Jeez,' said Darren.

'Hang on,' said Hanley. So if the contents of the will were known, Dewlish could have killed her out of anger at not being in it. Bexington could have killed her because he was in it. And fifty grand's a lot of dosh for him these days. But what about Wilson? He didn't stand to benefit.'

'Maybe not personally, guv,' said Deena. 'But he's an ambitious boy. Would look good with his bosses. Could persuade them into upgrading a potential winnable seat to a safe one.'

'One other thing,' said Sanjay. 'Mrs Bickler also told me that Camilla had confided in her that she'd already given £50,000 to Wilson personally. He'd said he could get her a role in the party, probably a safe seat at the next General Election herself. But it would have to be on the quiet and he'd put the money through another party donor, so it wouldn't look bad coming from her if she then became an MP.'

'Shit,' said Hanley.

'As you can imagine, Mrs Bickler was very – to use her word – uncomfortable about all this. She'd asked her daughter why she would make a will now, at her age, and she laughed. Said she would enjoy its contents annoying her father, whose politics she hated. Mrs Bickler was concerned about Camilla having been pressurised into it. She thought her ex-husband should know, even got the impression Camilla wanted him to know, so she told him.'

'Carew knew about the 50K and what was in the will?'

'Yep. He was, apparently, in her word again, incandescent.'

'Bloody hell. Good work Sanj,' said Hanley. He stood back from the whiteboard and paced.

'So what happens to the rest of the money?'

'Mrs Bickler wanted to keep that private but said it didn't have any relevance to this case,' said Sanjay.

'You want us to round them all up again tonight, guv?' Terry asked.

'No. I think we've all done enough today. Been a long day. Some of us had a very early start.'

Sanjay and Deena looked at each other and smiled.

'But let's start with Wilson in the morning. Sanj, Campbell. You're our early birds. You get round to the worm's flat in Camden at 9am and bring him in. After that, we'll pick up Dewlish and Bexington again. See what they knew about the will.'

'Think we should speak to Carew again, guv?' said Terry.

'Let's see what the three stooges have to say first,' said Hanley. 'OK. Take a bit of down time tonight but be ready. Tomorrow will be a big day. I want this sorted by Saturday. Got tickets for West Ham.'

They began to disperse, Terry asking if anyone fancied the pub. Deena was about to insist that it had to be a very quick one when Hanley asked her to stay on for a word. She immediately feared a bollocking.

'You did good work today, bringing in Bexington, getting that out of Wilson's assistant and finding out about Sean,' he said instead.

'Thank you guv. I appreciate that.'

'You're right. None of them are acting like innocent men. They're all guilty.'

'Beg pardon?' Deena replied, taken aback. 'You think this is some kind of Murder on the Orient Express case?'

Hanley laughed.

'It's the only way to approach a murder inquiry. Briefs, judges and juries have the luxury of using the "innocent until proved guilty" thing. We have to treat them all as if they're guilty. Be suspicious of all of them. Don't believe a word they tell us. Test everything they say. Be hard on them. That way we've got a chance. At the end, if we have to apologise for misjudging someone, we apologise. Except we don't. We let Jackie Donovan do that. Pushing suspects to the limit is what we do.'

Deena actually found herself impressed. She had been warned about Hanley; that he was dismissive, disrespectful and a misogynist. And she'd seen some of it in action. But what he had just told her was worth remembering. Maybe there was some wisdom to be learned.

'You went to Hendon…' Hanley continued.

'Yes, when inductions were proper. Long courses, not the thirteen weeks now.'

'And you've been on all sorts of detective courses, right?'

'Yes.'

'Well, they won't teach you what I just told you. They'll tell you all about procedure and the rights of the accused. How we have to do the job and how we have to be above board, follow protocol. And you know what?'

Deena did, she reckoned.

'They're right.'

He'd surprised her again. She didn't know what.

'We have to do things different these days. It ain't the Sweeney or Life on Mars. You can't go knocking people about to get confessions that won't stand up in court. And I'm glad. These days, when you get a good result, you've earned it. You've done it by good detective work. Not bullying. That doesn't mean you don't mistrust them, let them know you're about. You do it with words and action, legwork and brainpower. Much as you may want to thump them now and again.'

Deena smiled at him. She had been tempted to start writing this down, such was her training thus far in police work, but didn't want to interrupt and break the moment. She felt sure this would sink in.

'Look Deena… You OK me calling you that?'

'Of course, guv. In fact I was going to ask why you call the men by the given names and the women by their family names.'

'Yeah, look. Sorry about that. Old habits and all that. I'll try and do better.'

'Thank you guv. Maybe call DC Thomas Rachel as well?'

'Fair enough. Look, I'm telling you all this because I think you've got talent. You can be a very, very good detective.'

Deena smiled at him.

'Right enough of this shit,' Hanley said. 'You got a family? A partner or something?'

'I rent a flat in Stockwell with two other women,' she replied. 'I did have a boyfriend but he went to work at a Mosque in Manchester and it kind of fizzled out.' An image of Rashid's face came momentarily into Deena's mind but she quickly dismissed it.

Hanley looked vaguely intrigued but she was not in the mood to tell.

'Long story,' she said.

'Whoever you've got. Get back home to them, have a meal, get some rest.'

It had been a long and rewarding day but she hadn't expected this to round it off.

'Remember, though,' Hanley added, smiling. 'The book you do things by – it does have footnotes. Now get out of here. Nothing more's going to happen tonight.'

31

THERE was nothing more Jan could do. The doctor had been, and signed the death certificate, citing pneumonia as the cause. A big enough illness to find a way through the shot immune system of a frail octogenarian no longer mobile due to a fall. The undertakers had come to remove Elsie's body and would store it until she and Robert could arrange a funeral. Becky had removed Elsie's engagement and wedding rings and Jan took them when offered as Robert nodded. They were now in that vacuum of the day that followed the death of a loved one.

Robert agreed that he would stay on tonight, book a room at a Travelodge, so that he could register the death in the morning and then arrange a date for the funeral, before heading back to Edinburgh. He didn't feel like driving tonight anyway.

'No, you get back to London, Jan,' he said. 'I understand.'

Any anger or resentment he might have felt towards her for stepping out of the room when Elsie died was gone. There was just an emptiness and weariness to his tone now. Jan's guilt, by contrast, was going nowhere just yet, much as she wanted it to. She happily accepted his offer of tying up the loose ends so she could make good her escape.

'Anything you want?' Robert asked, gesturing around the room. 'I'll take all the clean clothes in the wardrobe to a charity shop in the morning. Bin the rest.'

'I'd like those pictures,' she said, pointing to two on a sideboard of their mother and father on their wedding day more than fifty years ago, as well as the four of them, Robert and Jan still junior schoolkids, on Scarborough beach.

Jan had a quick look through Elsie's sideboard drawers. Old letters, saved greetings cards. Then, in the bottom one, she found a pile of newspaper cuttings. She swept them up and sat down to read. Many were from her days in Sheffield; news reports, a few arts reviews when she was sent to the Crucible. And then a heap from her paper now. Pride of place, in a plastic folder, was the collection of stories from the Regent's Park mosque atrocity, along with a picture of her with her two awards.

A burst of tears finally erupted so unexpectedly from Jan that Robert flinched, shock flashing across his face. He sat on the arm of the chair and wrapped himself around her, kissing the top of her head.

'Hey, hey,' he said. 'She was very proud of you, you know. Even if she didn't always show it. And I am too. Even though I don't always show it.'

Jan laughed through the ugly crying and took a tissue from her bag.

'I've been a shit daughter, haven't I?' she said.

'We've both done the best we could, Jan. She was difficult, especially with you. She felt she had to compete with Dad for your attention because you were the apple of his eye. She resented it sometimes and you were in the firing line, especially after Dad died.'

Jan nodded, wiping the snot from her nose.

'But I wound her up, didn't I? Arguing back. I wished I hadn't said that Dad was the lucky one, being free of her.'

'It hurt her, I know, but she realised you didn't mean it. And she told me she regretted all her comments about your looks in your teens, and wanting to be a journalist, who would ruin people's lives.'

'Yes. That hurt me too.'

'But she loved you underneath it all. Those cuttings show it. And I know you loved her beneath all the conflict as well.'

Jan looked up and smiled at him.

'Bless you bruv.'

She got up and hugged him again.

'Now I'm going back to London. I can't stay here any longer than I have to.'

She texted Gaunt.

Can you come and pick me up please?

The reply came quickly.

In the car park. My meeting didn't last long.

She kissed Robert on the cheek, thanked him for staying on and letting her go, and asked him to keep her in touch about the funeral. They could decide between them who would deliver a eulogy, what form the service should take, and all that stuff.

'Let's get out of here, shall we?' Jan said to Gaunt as soon as she'd got in the car and he turned on the ignition.

'Everything all right?'

'If you deem my mother just dying then yes, everything is all right.'

'Oh, God. I'm very sorry Jan.' He paused and looked at her solemnly.

He'd switched the engine off, but was soon re-igniting.

'Just drive please. South,' she said. 'In silence.'

He nodded, and did just as she'd asked.

Soon she was checking her phone. Two missed calls, one from Vickers and one from Deena. It had to be Deena first. It was cold and dark now and she really couldn't ask Gaunt to stop the car and get out. He'd been kind to her anyway. Besides, he'd listened in last time and nothing bad had happened had it?

'Look,' she said, as he pulled on to the M1. 'I'm really sorry for snapping at you. I'm just feeling a bit… a bit emotional.'

'Understandable,' Gaunt replied. 'Don't worry about it. We can talk or not, up to you.'

Jan's weariness began to assail her, along with the emptiness of realising that she was now an orphan, strange as that sounded at her age. At such times as this, remembering back to the night her father had died and she and Robert treated Mum to a lovely meal out, she found comfort in good food and wine.

'I need to make a couple of calls but why don't we stop and have a meal,' she said. 'Talk properly?'

'What, eat up here?'

'The North does have good restaurants, you know. I know a very fine one just south of Sheffield. With a Michelin star, actually.'

'Really. Who'd have thought in the frozen Norf. Sounds good to me.'

She checked on her phone and they had a table free, which she booked. She then rang Deena.

'What's happening?' she asked.

Deena took her through the day's unproductive interviews with Dewlish and then Bexington, still keeping her meeting with Frank to herself. Dewlish was upper-class dodgy, she said; he'd been told to stay in the London area.

'Next you'll be telling me scorpions sting,' Jan said. She looked across at Gaunt and smiled. He smiled back and looked in the rear view mirror. Jan made a note that Dewlish had been instructed not to leave the country.

Bexington was sticking to his story, Deena said. Released without charge.

'Maybe that's the only story he's got,' said Jan, wanting to hang on to her gut feeling about him.

'It's interesting. I really thought that neighbour of Sean's was going to tell me it was Wilson she saw coming to his flat, not Bexington.'

'Wilson? Because of the gay angle?'

She glimpsed Gaunt shifting in his seat.

'Yes. So, anything for me Jan? Or are you still with your mum?'

'Listen, I'm going to have to owe you. My mum's just died actually.'

'Oh Jan… So sorry. Why didn't you say?'

'Thank you but it's OK.' After a brief, awkward pause, Jan said quickly: 'Tell me more about Wilson.'

Gaunt checked the rear view mirror as Jan made some more notes.

'Well, Sean was a Labour party activist. Plus no-one can actually confirm that Wilson was inside Party HQ at the time Camilla was murdered.'

'Shit. You bringing Wilson in then?'

'Tomorrow, first thing. Hanley's sending me to pick him up. Hanley seems to be warming to me a little, by the way.'

'Steady. Don't go on any dates you shouldn't.'

Jan looked across at Gaunt, who returned a "ha-ha" smile.

'So can I write that there might be a romantic relationship link between Sean and a man police are investigating?'

'You can. There's other stuff too. But this is all off the record. For now. OK?'

'OK…'

Deena told Jan about Dewlish and the £5,000 then ran through the will, who did and didn't get money. About Camilla giving money to Wilson for a safe Labour seat. Jan's shorthand worked overtime. She was taking it down, just in case…

'Jesus, Deena. This is dynamite,' she said. 'You've got to let me print this.'

'Jan, no. I've just told you. We respect what you've done so far and I've been told to keep you in the loop. I'm happy to, so you're ahead of it and will give us stuff back when we need it. But we don't want any of the suspects knowing what we've got on them.'

Jan knew when it was time to back off; to lose a battle to win a war. Besides, she had nothing to give back.

'But I can do the relationship angle, yes?' she said.

'Yes. That's the story we want out there tonight. But don't say directly that Wilson is gay. Just hint at it. We want to unnerve him but have something to surprise him with. All three of them, really.'

'Fair enough. And thank you, Deena. I'll try and do better tomorrow.'

'Listen, Jan. I understand. We're all human, you know.'

Jan ended the call.

'Chasing a story again, even today?' said Gaunt.

'Even more today,' said Jan. 'My Mum knew what I did and who I was.'

Jan rang Vickers straight away and told him what she had. Dewlish and Bexington released without charge but the police were looking at a gay relationship and/or political link to the murders, with Sean Malahide also being a Labour Party activist. She wasn't going to tell him about Wilson and Camilla and the money. Even as background. He'd only press her to write it and thus piss off Deena. More than that, jeopardise her source for when she might need her more.

'That it?' Vickers asked.

Jan's hackles rose instantly.

'OK. Ivan, don't fucking start,' she said. 'I've had the day from hell and that is where we are with the case, all right?'

Jan's tone worked. He said he would settle for that tonight. She told him she would file six hundred words.

'Well, it won't make the front. Lucky to be on page two,' he said.

'Can't win 'em all every night, Ivan,' she said and shut down her phone.

'OK,' Jan said to Gaunt. 'Thank you for your patience. I'm

226

going to write this story now. It won't take me long. You key in The Milestone at Ridgefield on your satnav, off junction thirty, and we'll try and salvage the day with some nice food, OK?'

'Excellent. That will be lovely. Thank you.'

Jan got her laptop out of her bag and tapped out her story, such as it was, padding it with background to the case. When she was finished, they were still a few junctions from Sheffield South and, exhausted, she closed her eyes. Before long, she was dozing and didn't hear the buzz of Gaunt's phone, which he had left in his cup holder by the gearstick.

Nor did she see the name of Wilson that appeared on the screen.

32

FRANK needed a meeting tonight. Sean's death, and his talk with Deena, had shown him that he needed to ground himself again, to find some respite from the turbulence of his emotions. The AA grapevine – and it always amused him that the organisation used that word as the title of its international journal – had been buzzing all afternoon with calls among members, particularly in South and West London. All were shocked by the recent events, most were frightened now.

When he arrived, there were more in the room at Blandford Road than normal for a Thursday. Maybe twenty, certainly almost three times the number as on the night when the guy had come in and shared what now seemed truth rather than fantasy. Fear had kept some away but there were still plenty who were curious, a few wanting to share their – short – memories of Sean. Most wanted to gauge from others whether they too might be in some sort of danger.

The customary few moments of silence at the beginning of the meeting to think about those still suffering outside the room was extended by a minute as a mark of respect to Sean. It preceded an hour of sharing that sadness for Sean mixed with apprehension about whether this could happen again, specifically to someone at that meeting. Frank found himself looking around the room to see if the person from Monday's meeting might even be here, but then he realised he was being paranoid.

When his copper's mind took over, he realised the guy would not be that stupid. It didn't stop him viewing a couple of newcomers with suspicion, though.

At the meeting's conclusion, Frank went to the kitchen to bin the empty Coke can from which he had been sipping during the meeting. People were in no mood to go for coffee tonight to the local cafe – word had got round that Sean had done just that – but they did want to stay and chat.

As a senior figure – an old timer – Frank was in demand. He had hoped Eddie might be here too so he could share with him but instead people were coming to him and asking what he thought about these murders. Most knew that he was a police-man, even if unsure about what branch of the police he was in. Some were clearly angling for a professional opinion as well as a personal conversation.

He had to be firm with a couple whose curiosity went too far, wanting info on any inquiry and whether he knew anything about it. They were young in recovery, still not entirely familiar with boundaries between what people did for a living and who they were. They would learn that lesson from his tongue tonight and hopefully not repeat the error.

He was not really in the mood to chat for long afterwards anyway. Despite the longevity of his sobriety, the edginess that had accompanied him for the last few days rendered him unable to concentrate on what people were asking and he withdrew into himself, no particular advice or wisdom to offer. It was as much as he could do to help himself. To just not reach for a drink right now.

He slipped out of the door quietly and quickly into the night, turning his coat collar against the cold for the walk up to Fulham Road and a bus back to Pimlico. Blandford Road was quiet, curtains drawn or still dark. Some of these were second homes and empty, their owners in warmer climes. Others contained people who would be up early for the City and didn't indulge in long evenings.

He was about fifty yards from the bus stop at the top of the street when it happened.

The houses in the road had small front gardens, just a couple of yards deep, and short paths that led into porches. It must have been from one of those porches, Frank decided later, that the figure emerged.

Whatever or whoever, he suddenly felt something around his throat and neck, on the inside of his upturned collar. And then he was being dragged backwards down a small alley between two of the houses. The cloth around his neck – it was a cloth, not a rope from the smooth feel of it – was being pulled tighter.

The figure had surprise on his side and Frank was initially stunned. This surprise was not backed by an overwhelming physical power, however, and soon Frank, survival instincts kicking in, along with memories of his training as a constable all those years ago, had clawed a few of his fingers between the cloth – a scarf probably – and the skin of his neck. He inched his fingers further into the breach, loosening what had been a tightening grip around his neck.

Frank was struggling to breathe now but as he clung on, he began to manoeuvre the body on his back upwards, denying him the advantage of feet planted on the ground for stability. It had to be a him. And Frank swore – later, if not now being so preoccupied with survival – that he could feel facial hair against the side of his face. Beard? Moustache? Both?

Gradually he felt that he was gaining the upper hand and the figure must have sensed it too. Suddenly the cloth loosened around his throat, was whisked away and the figure made off at speed towards South Kensington. Frank wanted to give chase but he was in no fit state. He made a token effort, starting to run but soon gave up, struggling for breath. He saw the figure reach Fulham Road, turn right in the direction of the tube station and that was that.

In films, they always seemed to yell stop. But Frank knew the real-life futility of that. As if the bloke was going to turn round and say, "Yes. Fair enough. I'll stop." All he could shout, at the top of his voice, was "Fuck". It was enough to bring someone to their front door, perhaps thinking there were hooligans or a drunk in the street, perhaps worried about their car parked outside. The sight of Frank bent over, gasping for breath, greeted them.

'You want to mind your language mate. You had my daughter scared about what was going on outside.' He pointed to an upstairs window where a little girl was looking down.

'Sorry about that. Mate,' Frank said pointedly. 'It's just that someone was trying to strangle me.'

'Yeah, well. Keep the noise down,' the guy replied and shut his front door.

Thanks pal, Frank thought, for your concern. He stayed there for another minute or so, regaining his breath, before walking slowly to the top of the road. His legs were carrying him only slowly but his mind was racing. He needed to sit down. He found a low wall and began to answer the questions swirling in his brain.

First among them were what had just happened, and what the hell was it all about?

The fog in his mind slowly cleared as his body recovered. This was surely no random mugger after his wallet. It had to be connected with the case. Camilla and Sean had been strangled after all. And someone had just tried to do the same to him.

It had to be Bexington, didn't it? He'd been at the previous AA meeting and all but confessed to killing Camilla. It had happened just streets away from here and this was an area he knew well. Now that he thought about it, Frank was sure he could recall smelling booze on the breath of his attacker. Vodka, probably. That had to be it. So was Bexington killing people who had heard that confession, who might recognise him? People who could testify against him?

He might have picked on Frank because he'd found out that he was a copper – maybe from Sean before he killed him – and in Bexington's eyes the person most likely to break the code of anonymity, and to share information with his colleagues. But Bexington had messed with the wrong marine if he thought he was going to kill Frank. Still, Frank was pissed off with himself. He should have got the bloke on the ground. Should have made an arrest. Ten years ago he might have done it. But he was getting flabby, tired. Too old for all this.

The never-relaxed grip of alcoholism did this to you, he knew. You could spend years sober, building up confidence and self-esteem, and in the aftermath of an episode that lasted no more than a minute, feel as though you should have done better than just stay alive; that you were, in fact, a useless piece of garbage. Over the hill.

Right now, he just needed to get home and he needed not to drink. He could do with some company, too. He found his phone and keyed in a number.

'Hi,' Jan said. 'You OK? Got something for me?'

'No. But I need something from you?'

'Go on…'

'Can you come over, or can I come over to your place?'

'I'm up in Yorkshire, Frank.'

'How come?'

'Long story. Tough day. I'm just having dinner with someone.'

'Ah right. It's OK. I'll catch up tomorrow. Don't worry. I'll be fine.'

'Fearful, insecure, neurotic and emotional. Didn't you once tell that me that's what fine stands for?'

Frank laughed.

'Something like that. Take care.'

He ended the call and headed for the bus stop and home. It was good hearing Jan's voice but he swiftly realised it was probably for the best that she wasn't immediately available. He thought back to the bad old days of needy night calls. Don't want to get back into all that old behaviour. He knew where it would lead.

He smiled to himself and suddenly felt a surge of energy, replacing the agitation, as a realisation dawned on him. Tomorrow, he needed to ditch the anonymity and get stuck properly into catching this bastard before he killed any more people in AA.

FRIDAY

33

USUALLY, Jan rested her night-owl body until 9am, getting up as soon as the Today programme on Radio 4 had finished, but today she was planning to enjoy a lie-in. After all, she'd only got in from Wakefield around midnight, taking the risk of letting Gaunt know her address by dropping her off outside her flat, at around midnight. The meal together had been pleasant enough and he seemed a decent guy.

She had been awake at five, though, mulling everything over, memories of her mother flashing through her mind, both good and bad. Tears followed smiles. Regret at argumentative episodes pierced fleeting warmth. After that, she snatched just the odd doze, news stories insinuating themselves inconveniently into her brain until she could have sworn that the Chancellor of the Exchequer was reading the Shipping Forecast and throwing in a line about some gay bloke in the Labour Party. Any chance of getting properly back off to sleep was rudely interrupted by her mobile ringing on her bedside table.

Of course she kept it by the bed and switched on, against all advice about health and sleeping, not just in case the office or a contact rang but also because if she woke, she could check Twitter to see what was happening; reaction to stories breaking, stuff going on in America.

And then she remembered. Today was the deadline for handing in that signed voluntary redundancy form...

Her mobile rang suddenly to rouse her and "No Caller ID" came up on her screen. It revealed the time to be 6.33am, but it didn't stop her answering. Stories came from anywhere, not just contacts. Anonymous tip-offs maybe, colleagues who had given her mobile number to their own contacts in a different area of the paper. Perhaps someone on the Westminster desk in the hope of getting a favour returned in the future.

'Jan Mason,' she said.

'What the fuck do you think you're doing?' came the voice.

'Hold on, who is this?'

'It's Gavin Wilson and I'll ask again. What the fuck do you think you're doing?'

'You sound angry, Mr Wilson.'

'It's a good job I couldn't get a number for you until this morning after seeing that shit of yours online last night. Then you would have known what angry was.'

Jan was waking up pretty quickly now. He had read her story then.

'Well, I'm doing what reporters do, Mr Wilson,' she replied. 'I'm reporting a development in a murder investigation from what my sources tell me.'

'With a headline about a gay link in these so-called choker murders.'

'I don't write the headlines, as you well know.'

'For fuck's sake. Who are these sources?'

'That's not even a good try.'

'Well, I'm going to sue.'

'You have that right,' Jan said. 'But I wouldn't recommend it. I mean, for a start, you're not actually labelled as being gay in the story.'

There was a silence on the other end of the phone.

'But you insinuate it.'

'I merely say that Sean Malahide was gay and a Labour Party member, hosting LGBTQ Plus meetings of his local constituency party.'

'But the next sentence is about me being a Labour Party official. I know how you people in the press work with your juxtapositions. And how other papers will lift this and spin it.'

'If you want to go to court and tell everybody you're not gay, that you weren't closely involved with Camilla Carew and that there was no link between you and Sean Malahide, a gay Labour Party activist in Battersea, then feel free.'

'You people,' he said. 'You and your fucking paper. You're full of right-wing shit you shovel out just to keep your poxy owners in the feather beds they've made for themselves. You stand up for people like Bexington and target people like me in a personal way to make my life difficult when all I want is to make this country a more socially just place.'

'Why would I have made it difficult? As should be the case, being gay really is no big deal these days. Or in your case, by the sound of it, bi. Especially in the Labour Party.'

Wilson's self-righteousness and sense of victimhood disappeared for a moment, along with the irate bluster. There came a more measured tone to his voice.

'I think you should know that I know where you live,' he said.

'Not very original,' Jan replied.

'And your flat in the block is the one with the green door.'

A chill went through Jan. Her heart began to pound. Jesus. How did he know that? Had he been in here? While she was in Wakefield yesterday? She looked around the flat, wondering, picturing.

'I tell you, Ms Mason' he said, stressing the Ms. 'When the time comes, people like you will be held to account.'

'Is that a threat Mr Wilson?'

'No. It's a fucking election promise. Trust me.'

Wilson didn't finish the sentiment. Jan heard a bump at the other end and then the call was over. She sensed he might have thrown the phone to the floor in anger. While she was happy with the way she had conducted the conversation, the waves of anxiety continued to be strong. She wandered around the flat to check for signs of violation. No, he couldn't have been in here. Just some kind of scare tactic. But it had worked. No matter how assured some thirty years of experience in journalism had made her, she was human and an angry white young male on the phone, one with some clout and standing, still had the capacity to unnerve her. Echoes of being a young reporter when she'd been bullied by a local councillor over a story about him having his fingers in the till, triggered more butterflies in her stomach.

She needed coffee and a distraction. She put on her waffle robe, went to the kitchen and made a cafetiere, then to the living room to turn on breakfast telly.

Her mobile went again with a text.

Sorry about last night. Too early to speak?

She rang Frank.

'No need to be sorry,' she said. 'In normal circumstances...'

'How do you mean?'

'Mum died yesterday.'

There was a pause at the other end.

'Jesus, Jan. I'm so sorry. Listen, forget it. I'll be OK.'

'No honestly. Happy to speak.'

Frank would not have rung for no reason last night, nor texted so early this morning, if there had not been something serious going on. And she wanted to know what it was.

'What's happening then? Are you all right?'

He wasn't. He still needed someone to talk to, he said. If she was sure. Off the record. She agreed. He told her about his run-in last night and that he had barely slept and was still shaking. He was interrupted by just a rapt Jan saying "Jesus" every now and then.

'Any idea who it was?'

'First things first,' he said.

And then he told her about the AA meeting and the man he believed to be Bexington coming in.

'What? Really? Are you sure? He told me he walked around for a while before going to his mate's in Battersea.'

'Well, he would, wouldn't he? He's not going to incriminate himself with you, is he? He needed to get you on his side, get his story out there then worry about that emerging later. For a Hooray Henry, he's not as stupid as he looks. This bloody golden boy you wrote about has probably killed two people, just tried to kill me and may try to kill again.'

'Shit,' said Jan.

'Shit indeed. And you're up a creek of it without a paddle. He's used you Jan. Like all these public school charmers do. They somehow wangle their way through life without putting in the effort that comprehensive kids like us have to.'

'I know what you mean but…'

'You do know you're facing being an accessory at this rate?'

'Come on Frank, that's way over the top. I persuaded him to give himself up. Anyway, by the sound of it, you've not exactly played this by the book.'

'What do you mean?'

'Well, you knew that Bexington could very well be a killer. You saw my story that morning. But you said nothing to anyone, let alone your police colleagues.'

'I had to abide by a code in AA that we keep things confidential.'

'What, you keep murders quiet? Like the Mafia? That's a good story.'

Put like that, Frank knew it sounded weak and unlikely, that he was facing serious problems with his own police force. But he wasn't about to admit that now. Besides, Jan could not understand how much AA had changed his life and how much he owed to its rules. How loyal he felt.

'Sod off Jan,' he said.

She'd hit a nerve as her drilling and grilling so often did. It was one reason, why their relationship, such as it had been, had gone nowhere all those years ago. He was ashamed of himself for being so angry, so foul-mouthed, though.

'I'm sorry,' he said. 'I'm normally more detached from these things. But this one I'm involved in and it's messed me up more than it should.'

'Apology accepted,' Jan said. 'What happens now?'

'Well, I spoke to Deena yesterday and told her to use the stuff about AA and Bexington without using my name, if she could. I'll have to make it formal now. Go in to speak to Hanley. Tell him what happened to me last night and everything I know.'

'Good luck with that. I don't think Hanley is the sympathetic type.'

'Maybe not. But he'll need me for now, so he won't want to jeopardise a source too much. And I've got stuff he hasn't. About Wilson, for example. Intelligence that Hanley won't hear if he puts me on a charge.'

'Wilson?' Jan blurted out. 'What about him?'

'Counter-terrorism's been monitoring him.'

'Why?'

Frank paused, obviously debating whether to bring Jan in on everything at this point. But she was valuable. He needed her mind on this too.

'He's been meeting with Palestinians,' he said.

'Is that illegal?'

'No, but he's been talking to them about donations to his party in return for certain favourable comments and publicity, and a change in government attitude, if his mates win the next election.'

'You've got to let me use that. For God's sake Frank…'

'Hang fire Jan. Please. Just for now. Let me go see Hanley and I'll speak to you later today. Yeah? If it works out, you can have it for tomorrow's paper.'

Jan agreed. After all, she normally had to give something to get something but she had nothing yet. Frank was in generous mood, or rather in an apologetic one, and had needed to spill.

'And I could do with a bit more leverage,' he added. 'So maybe you'll have something new for me today?'

She hadn't got off after all. 'You sound like my news editor,' she said, laughing. She caught a short "Ha!" from Frank.

'Look. I think I'm going to need a friendly face after talking to Hanley,' he said. 'Or at least a familiar one.'

Jan smiled to herself.

'Meet later?'

'Sure,' she replied and they fixed a time and place before the call ended.

She took another deep draw of coffee and thought about having a shower and heading for the office. A semblance of guilt crept through, that she was carrying on as normal the day after her mother had died. But then, Robert was sorting out all the immediate aftermath, and they had agreed to liaise later about the funeral arrangements. What could she do? It would have made Elsie proud, she reckoned, if she saw this story through. Help bring a murderer to justice. She could do that – maybe even today – and then sort out the redundancy.

Already this morning, she'd had two people wanting something from her, from information to a shoulder to cry on, but neither could be as demanding of her as she was of herself. With so many daubed marks on it from the last few days, today was not a blank canvas but it was by no means a finished one.

She was just on her way to her bathroom when the phone rang again and she cursed it. It was a number that seemed familiar but not one she recognised.

'Yes,' she snapped.

'Jan, it's Will Gaunt,' said the voice. She hadn't put the number into her list of contacts yet. Wasn't sure yet if she was going to. She certainly wouldn't if he was this bloody needy after eight hours since dropping her off at her front door.

'Listen, Will. Thank you for everything yesterday and all that,' Jan said. 'It was a huge help and I enjoyed some nice food last night. But I really need to get on and get into work, OK…'

'Did you get a call from Gavin Wilson this morning?'

Jan was stopped in her tracks as she headed for the shower. He had her attention.

'I did yes. How do you know about that?'

'Can we meet later, for brunch or something. There's a few things I need to tell you.'

34

HANLEY sat with his feet on a desk, hands resting behind his neck, contemplating the whiteboard and all the things he needed to ask Wilson. His links to both Camilla Carew and Sean Malahide – the scarf, the political connections. He still had Bexington down for the murders but, he had to admit, the information that was emerging about Wilson was giving him cause for thought. He was also in early as he was waiting for someone who'd called him just after daylight to ask for a meeting, luring him with: "I think you'll want to hear this."

When Frank arrived at Putney, Hanley went down to reception to meet him. He didn't want him seeing the whiteboard. For his part, Frank had insisted on a room with no cameras and no tapes and so they ended up in one with a panel of glass in the door and a key so that it could be locked from the inside.

The recreation room had a coffee machine in a corner and Hanley offered Frank a cup. He took it readily, gazing at the front pages of the papers in front of him as he waited. The red tops had lifted Jan's story from the website late last night and cranked it up. Wilson was a "gay red" whom cops wanted to question further. Nasty. They guessed Labour wouldn't dare sue. Couldn't afford it and anyway, it would just look like whingeing.

'So,' said Hanley. 'To what do I owe this pleasure?'

'Where to start?' Frank asked rhetorically. He looked across at Hanley, who shrugged his shoulders and sipped his coffee.

'Give it a go. I'm all ears,' said the detective.

'First, I want agreement that I won't be named in any of this.'

'Come on Phillips. You know better than that. You here as a private citizen or in an official capacity?'

'Private.'

'That means your boss doesn't know you're here. That could be tricky for you if this gets messy,' said Hanley, enjoying Frank's clear discomfort.

'I just want to be treated like any other background source.'

'That depends on what you've got to tell me. If you're directly involved in some way in any of this, then it's going to be hard to keep your name out of it. Tell you what, you tell me and I'll see where we go from there, shall we?'

Frank took a long sip of his coffee, mind racing again with competing thoughts and consequences. He probably couldn't trust Hanley not to blab about him being an alcoholic – the snake would probably omit the crucial word "recovering" – but he needed to see this through. He'd made that decision. That was why he was here. Deena and Jan already knew anyway. And hadn't he told himself to ditch the anonymity? Two people had died and this was about justice for them. And saving anyone else who might be in danger.

He took a deep breath and started with the fact he was a recovering alcoholic of fifteen years' sobriety, then went on to relate the AA meeting and the guy coming in and confessing to a murder. He told Hanley that Sean had been at that meeting and in fact had gone for coffee with him and a couple of other people afterwards.

Hanley sat impassive as Frank paused and looked at him for a reaction.

'Go on,' he said instead.

'Then there was last night…' Frank continued, launching into his account of being attacked after the AA meeting.

'The thing is,' he added. 'I reckon the guy had a moustache but not any kind of beard. Bexington shaved off his beard before going down to Brighton but kept the moustache. And I reckon, the more I've thought about it and having googled pictures of him clean-shaven, that I saw Bexington at an AA meeting some while back. Also…'

'There's more?' Hanley's eyes widened at the scale of Frank's revelations.

'I could smell alcohol on the bloke's breath. Maybe vodka.'

'I thought that didn't smell. That alkies drank it to cover up?'

'That's a myth,' Frank replied. 'It smells. And we alkies, as you call us, can tell.'

'OK. This all makes sense. So you think Bexington killed Sean because he could identify him from the AA meeting and that he was trying to rub you out for the same reason?'

'Yes. He might also have recognised me from a meeting he went to that while back and couldn't risk me remembering.'

'Maybe. But why Malahide first? Maybe they knew each other from somewhere else?'

'That I don't know. Yet. But we need to find out.'

'OK. Say I buy that about him taking no chances with you. How come he overpowered you? He's some playboy and you're a trained and experienced police officer?'

'He took me by surprise. And I'm not as young as I used to be.'

Frank looked across at Hanley again hoping for some empathy, if not sympathy, but there was no response for what felt like an age.

'So,' said Frank. 'What do you reckon?'

'What do I reckon?' Hanley at last responded. 'What do I fucking reckon? I reckon you've withheld information that was very valuable to a murder inquiry and you're in deep shit, Frank Phillips old son.'

'That may well be,' Frank replied. 'But you need to understand the circumstances of Alcoholics Anonymous. We get a lot of space cadets who haven't yet learned to be honest. I didn't know if the bloke was credible. And we have a strict code of confidentiality.'

'Which overrides preventing murder, does it? And you only finally fucking come in because it's you in the firing line.'

Frank looked down at his feet in shame again, but momentarily this time. He raised himself sharply from his chair. He was not going to take this. Not from this arse.

'Listen Hanley. You can have a pop at me as much as you like and for as long as you like. You won't be saying anything I haven't said, and worse, to myself. But it's not going to help any others who might be in danger, particularly my AA group. This is not about me. And you need to get on this, rather than enjoying me squirm.'

Hanley thought about this for a moment. Then he stood up, so that he could look down on Frank, and began jabbing an index finger in Frank's direction.

'Now you fucking care? And you've got the front to ask to be kept out of this? You're going over to an interview room at Hammersmith nick right now and all this is going on tape.'

Hanley went to leave the room but Frank blocked his path and the two stood eyeball to eyeball. Each was enveloped in the other's simmering rage, each desperately wanting to punch the other and it became of question of who might land the first one. Frank had learned down the years to count to 10 down, however, and that was how many seconds they stood confronting each other before Hanley's mobile rang.

He answered with a bark of "WHAT?", then listened to the voice at the other end. Frank backed away and watched as Hanley's face darkened. The voice was interrupted only by Hanley saying "No fucking way," and "Jesus Christ."

'Right. Bring Bexington and Dewlish in then. Pronto,' Hanley said and ended the call.

'What's happening?' Frank asked.

'That was Deena,' Hanley replied. 'I hope you're pleased with yourself. They've found Wilson dead at his flat. Strangled.'

35

JAN agreed to meet Gaunt at his club in Soho, one of those trendy establishments on three floors, all bare boards and velour banquettes with menus that charged 7,5 (£7.50 to the uninitiated) for a coffee. This mid-morning it was filling up with its usual crowd of media types – though not her types – along with B-list actors and TV people. Membership was a luxury she didn't want, even if she could afford it, with her old Dad's voice still in her ear about the price of things in London, but she usually accepted invitations here as she enjoyed the people-watching.

Gaunt was waiting at a table for two, in a discreet ante-room, and smiled nervously when she arrived in the threshold, shown to the nook by a long-haired young guy from the reception desk, dressed in white shirt and chinos. Gaunt rose as she reached the table.

'Jan. Thank you so much for coming. Still so sorry about your mother. Are you feeling any better today?' he said, a tense formality to him at odds with the mellowness of their drive back last night following a convivial meal. Jan had lost that mood too. Doubly.

'Forget all that. Start talking about Wilson and what you know about him calling me,' she replied, just as the mobile in her bag sounded. She reached for it and took the call. She had barely uttered the words "What's happening" when a young girl was across from the bar.

'I'm sorry, Madam. Mobile phones must be switched off in the club.'

Jan carried on momentarily.

'Look Deena, I'm going to have to call you back. Two minutes.'

She shut down the call and stared at Gaunt, telling him not to go anywhere. Just as she turned to go out into the street, she saw a look of frustration cross his face and he blew out his cheeks. Nervous or what? Good.

Out in Dean Street, Jan paced as she absorbed what Deena had to tell her. *Wilson dead, strangled... Jesus... What does that mean...? Bringing the other two back in...? Bexington prime suspect once again... How could I have got that so wrong?*

'Wilson rang me this morning,' Jan said.

'Really? What did he want?'

'To bollock me for the story you gave. Ended the call abruptly.'

Interesting. Let's talk later about it.'

She thanked Deena and pondered her next move. She phoned Vickers, told him that she would be filing five hundred words about Wilson being found dead, strangled, in the next half hour but would tweet it for now to show they had it first, as it would inevitably get out any time now, probably from some- one inside Labour HQ.

'So what are you waiting for?' he said before declaring that he had to dash in to tell the Editor.

Jan got her thumbs working and put out on her Twitter feed: **Chelsea choker case – Gavin Wilson found strangled to death. Detailed update on website soon.** She watched momen- tarily as the likes and retweets mounted. She looked again at the entrance to the club. As good a place to work as any. Coffee. A table. If they let you use a laptop, that is. She asked at recep- tion, offered a relieved thank you and headed back up to Gaunt. Wonder what he had to tell her. It would have to wait, even if she was intrigued. Everything had changed.

'Ah, there you are,' he said. 'Can I order you some coffee and perhaps we can talk.'

'Coffee yes, talk no,' said Jan. 'I really need to write a piece and file it. I am interested so don't go away. But your Gavin Wilson news can't be as big as my Gavin Wilson news.'

'What is it?'

'He's just been found dead.'

Jan began to rummage in her bag for her laptop but looked up to see how Gaunt took the news.

'Wh-h-at? How?' he stammered, clearly in disbelief.

'Strangled, of course. How else?'

'My God,' he said, leaning forward and putting his head in his hands.

Jan was in the process of opening her laptop to log on but stopped.

'Will?'

He didn't move. Just sat there with his head in his hands.

Jan repeated his name and he slowly looked up at her but said nothing.

'You look very shocked by this.'

'I am.'

'OK, so spill. My story can wait a few minutes.'

He called the waitress over and ordered a double espresso each. Along with a large whisky and soda for himself.

'Come on,' said Jan, her impatience growing. 'What is it about Wilson?'

'He was sort of blackmailing me.'

Jan looked at her watch. She was anxious about filing for the paper as quickly as she could, but this was significant. Anyway, the paper's feed had retweeted her swiftly so it was known inside the building and by rivals that they'd been first. She shut her half-opened laptop and sat back into the shabby chic armchair.

'Go on,' she said.

'OK. Summer last year, I got a call from Wilson about a young actor I have on the books. Toby Turner. Promising. Was in a rather good ITV drama earlier in the year, love triangle sort of thing, and was attracting some attention. Bit of Hollywood interest.'

'Yes. I've heard of him.'

'Toby is very fond of social media and is often to be found opining on the state of the nation. Came through a comprehensive school in Wolverhampton and fancied himself as a bit of a champion of the underdog and bane of the establishment. Then he got invited on Question Time. Very outspoken. Lot of applause from the audience. Caused quite a stir.'

'Yes, I remember it now,' said Jan. 'This is very interesting, by the way, Will, but my news editor would have been screaming at me by now to tell him what the intro to the story was.'

'Please bear with me. I don't quite have your storytelling skills. But this is all leading somewhere.'

Jan said "OK" but looked at her watch as encouragement to Gaunt.

'So, after that I get this call from Wilson. He wants Toby to appear at the Labour Party Conference in Blackpool. Sprinkle a bit of stardust. Grab a few headlines. There was a good sum of money involved.'

'So naturally you said yes.'

'It wasn't quite that simple. Despite what you may think, agents – or some of us at least – don't just think in financial terms. Anyway, I'd started counselling him against social media for a while and now and then he would take a short break when he got some vicious comments from what I think are called trolls.'

'I am familiar with them, yes,' said Jan.

'But he missed the interaction and the breaks just made him more determined to speak out on social issues and what do you know, or what do I know, he continued to build his profile. Or grow his followers, as he calls it. It has made him quite appealing to casting directors, who know they will get publicity for their show and many of his two million followers watching.

'I didn't want him to do Blackpool, because it's one thing talking about politics, another aligning yourself to a party. Turns off swathes of the potential audience for his acting. In the end, he insisted on doing it though. And he liked the pocket money.'

'Coming back to me now. But where's this going?'

'While at Blackpool, I am afraid Toby committed an indiscretion. And this is off the record and not to be shared with Tania on your showbiz desk.'

'Go on...'

'He slept with a shadow minister. And she was married.'

'And I'm guessing that Wilson got to hear about it.'

'You would be guessing correctly. Finger on every bloody pulse that one. Assured me he wouldn't tell anyone or leak it to the press. As long as Toby was available to do more work for the party at a reduced rate.'

'But would it really be damaging for Toby if it came out?'

'Ordinarily, not a lot. Though obviously he felt bad for the woman concerned and didn't want to see her or her family or career damaged. But Toby had just taken up with a young woman that he liked very much. The Blackpool thing was just a one-off. He got caught up in the sea air and the cheap red wine of a faded hotel. But this young woman... well, they're talking about getting married. If it doesn't mean he loses all his female Twitter followers, that is.'

'Really? That matters that much?'

'I'm joking. It's not quite the golden age of Tinseltown and keeping stars single. But anyway, he didn't want her to find out. In addition, the offer came in from Hollywood. Millions.'

'I thought you said some agents didn't just think in financial terms.'

'This wasn't politics-money peanuts. This was huge. Would set both of us up for life. The movie was a family flick and the contract was specific about no scandal coming out of the woodwork, however.'

'Right. So…'

'So fast forward to Tuesday night just gone. Wilson phones me late. Says he needs a favour. He has just read your story online with that neighbour of Camilla Carew's. Wants me to try and get close to you to find out what you knew and stay one step ahead.'

'So you joined the dating site and swiped on my profile.'

Gaunt looked sheepish.

'Yes.'

'But how did you or he know that I would swipe right on yours?'

'We didn't. But I'm pretty sure I'm not the only one you might like that he had something on and was calling in a favour from…'

'Ah. That would account for me getting a flurry of interest on Wednesday morning.'

'Possibly so, yes.'

Suddenly, Jan grew angry.

'Well thank you very fucking much. So yesterday was simply about you getting anything out of me you could to relay back to Wilson?'

Gaunt looked apologetic.

'You didn't have a business meeting in Leeds, did you?'

He shook his head and looked embarrassed.

'I went to the Yorkshire Sculpture Park.'

'Good taste at least.'

'Thank you.'

And then Jan remembered she was angry.

'Jesus, why am I so tough with people in my job but cut them so much slack in my private life?' she said.

She grabbed her laptop and put it in her bag and was about to get up when the waitress arrived with the double espressos and Gaunt's whisky. She needed the coffee hit before she made her statement exit.

'Just hang on Jan. Two more minutes and you'll have the full story.'

As furious as she was with herself, and him, he'd certainly said the right thing there. She loved the smell of the words full and story in the morning.

'Anyway, he kept texting or ringing me and I had to keep my mobile out of sight in your presence yesterday so you didn't see it.'

'So what did you tell him?'

'Nothing, I promise. Nothing much anyway. He did ask me where you lived and I did tell him. I might also have told him about you mentioning your flat door was green.'

'That explains that...'

'I mean, I could tell from the calls you were getting and you making notes in your notebook that some serious stuff was happening but I didn't know much anyway. It was bloody freezing in that layby, by the way.'

'I'm glad I made you get out of the car now. Should have done the other times as well.'

'Thing is Jan. I found I rather liked you. You were bright and funny. I like a woman with spirit.'

Jan shook her head and cringed.

'Oh shit. One of those. You ever watch Fawlty Towers?'

'Yes. Why?'

'The one with the cowboy builder? Who tells Sybil he likes a woman with spirit. She proceeds to grab an umbrella and beat him with it. Now if only there was an umbrella handy...'

'Joking apart...'

'You think I'm joking? Yesterday wasn't enough to find that out?'

'Look. Wilson kept pressing me about what you knew but I said nothing. Even when I heard you in the car getting all that stuff about him being gay.'

'Is he? Was he?'

'Yes. I think he is. Was. But bi, I think. I mean, I heard. Anyway, he tried to phone me in the car coming home last night. Must have thought I'd already be back. You were dozing. I ignored his call. He sent me a furious text. Saying he would out Toby's fling with the Labour woman. I tried to call his bluff by replying it was old news now but he said he knew a Sunday paper that would love it no matter how old it was. I turned off my phone after that, spending a sleepless night worrying about a huge movie deal going up in smoke. But he rang me early this morning as soon as I turned it on, ranting about your story that all the other papers had picked up. I was still trying to appease him and I'm afraid I gave him your number. I'm sorry about that. I then went out to get the papers to see what all the fuss was about.'

Jan's brain whirred. She was less concerned now about Wilson's call.

'So you had a motive to kill him then as well?' she said. 'I have a duty now to tell my police contacts about you and Wilson and his death.'

'What? I didn't know about it until you just told me.'

'That might have been an act. You may have picked up some tips from your clients, for all I know.'

'Jan, for God's sake. Take ten minutes off from your job, will you? I am trying to apologise for spending the day with you under false pretences. And to say that I like you and your company very much. Is that so very hard for you to hear?'

36

BEXINGTON asked for black coffee and plenty of it. The murky liquid that emerged from a machine in the corridor of Hammersmith police station was not the expensive Americano that the hungover figure now sitting opposite Deena and Hanley with a lawyer at his side was craving, however. He clearly had the shakes as he raised the plastic cup towards his blotchy face, surrounded by dishevelled hair, and thence to a dry mouth.

He'd been asleep when Deena and Sanjay arrived at his mate Giles's flat, having had no answer at his Kensington address, at around 10.30am to take the pair of them in. After a minute or two of hammering on the front door, the mate opened up and admitted, that yes, James was here – "or at least I think he is," – and he went to fetch him.

'What do you lot want now,' he'd said, appearing in just a dressing gown five minutes later. Deena simply told him that his presence was required at the station. Here, an hour later, his solicitor David Toller alongside him again, he was about to have his own questions answered through a series of questions he was expected to answer.

Tape on, formalities completed, Hanley asked Bexington his whereabouts the previous evening and early this morning.

'Well, I started having a few drinks with some mates at a place in Chelsea at around six pm,' Bexington replied.

'And those mates will vouch for that?'

'Yes. Dicky and Jake were there. Oh, and Giles, of course.'

He gulped the black liquid before him and winced with disgust.

'What was the name of this place in Chelsea, then?' Hanley asked. 'The Bullingdon Club?'

'To tell you the truth…'

'That's what we're after,' said Hanley.

'I really don't remember an awful lot from last night.'

'What were you drinking?'

'Um. We started out on lager. Then I remember… I think we went up the West End to some club that Giles knew. I remember drinking vodka.'

'After that?'

'All a bit of a blur, I'm afraid.'

'You didn't go via Camden at any point?'

'Camden? God no. At least I don't think so.'

'How did you get home?'

'I have absolutely no idea. I'm guessing Giles took me home in a taxi and put me to bed in his spare room. He's good like that is Giles.'

'Seems you public schoolboys are good at covering for each other.'

'Taking care of friends is one of the things you learn when you live in that sort of environment,' said Bexington.

The solicitor intervened.

'Are you here to make snide remarks about the English educational system detective inspector, or do you have anything else beyond all the questions my client answered yesterday?'

Hanley stared at the solicitor.

'Can I ask about you, sir? Were you a schoolfriend of Mr Bexington and this Giles?'

'As it happens officer, we were acquainted, yes.'

'I see. Jobs for the boys and all that, Mr Toller.'

'Can we keep this professional please?' Bexington said. 'Anyway, what is this all about?'

Hanley went into his best procedural monotone.

'At around nine am this morning, my officers went to the flat of Gavin Wilson in Camden Town. We wanted to question him about his connections with both Camilla Carew and Sean Malahide. When there was no answer, my officers entered the premises. There, they found Mr Wilson dead. He had been strangled not too long before they arrived. Forensics are there now and they should be able to tell us more soon.'

'Holy shit,' said Bexington.

'That's one way of putting it,' Hanley replied.

'You don't think that I…?'

Hanley was aware that the tape was running and so refrained from swearing, given that this interview may well one day go public. He was desperate, as compensation, to indulge in some sarcasm, though, to release his frustration at what he saw as Bexington's complete lack of self-awareness and apparent ignorance of how serious the situation was he was in. And how deep it was.

Instead, forced to forgo the fun of a good expletive-littered rant, and despite being desperate to take the piss out of Bexington, he simply laid it all out.

'Mr Bexington,' he said slowly, unwilling to let go of the contempt he felt for the bloke right now, even if he knew he had to keep it civil for this to be usable.

'Four days ago, Camilla Carew was found dead. Strangled. Two days ago, Sean Malahide was found dead. Strangled. With an orange scarf that you had given to Camilla and on which we found your fingerprints.'

'I've told you, I didn't know the man.'

'We'll come back to that. Then this morning, Gavin Wilson is found dead. Strangled. Now, clearly you knew Camilla, and intimately. You were upset with her about her liaison with Wilson. We also have a witness who puts you at an AA meeting that Sean Malahide was at.

'That's just not true.'

'Well, let's examine the facts. You've told me that you can't remember where you were last night.'

'I've told you to check with my friends.'

'And we are doing that. Though, to be honest, given this honour amongst old Fallopians, or whatever you call yourselves, I'm not sure I'm going to believe them anyway.'

'That's unfair.'

'OK, moving on… At this AA meeting, you apparently tell the group that you might have killed someone in blackout.'

'What? That's ridiculous. Impossible.'

'Apparently not. I'm told it has happened. Really. People who don't remember what they've done until they sober up or are confronted with evidence of it.'

'Well, I've sobered up now and I have absolutely no memory of it.'

'Do you have evidence DCI Hanley for these wild accusations?' said the solicitor.

'I'm just laying out facts and scenarios. Bear with me,' Hanley replied. 'Is it possible that last night, in blackout, you attacked somebody outside the very AA meeting venue you went to the other night? After all, you were drinking in the vicinity.'

'What? Why would I go anywhere near an AA meeting if I was pissed?'

'Maybe precisely because you were pissed. Like the other night. And last night, you went back to try and kill somebody who you think recognised you from the previous one. Just as you did with Sean too. You waited outside for them and tried to strangle them.'

'This is bollocks.'

'The mind can do that, apparently. Find its way to places even when it's drunk. Like a homing pigeon. Which of us hasn't known that, eh? Just as you did with Gavin Wilson's place in Camden, where you have admitted you went to confront him a while back. You knew the location. Having failed to kill that person outside the AA room last night, you had the taste and then thought you'd kill Wilson instead.'

'No. Absolutely not. No.'

'But how would you know? You can't tell me what you did do. So how can you possibly know what you didn't do?'

Bexington looked across at his solicitor who raised his eyebrows.

'Look, officer, I freely admit I was at Camilla's on Monday evening. I also admit I'd been drinking, as well. But I didn't kill her.'

'Did you know that she'd left you £50,000 in her will. Which she only rewrote a month ago?'

Bexington's mouth opened wide.

'No. I didn't know that,' he said. 'Gosh, that was generous of her. But I wouldn't kill her for fifty thou, would I?'

'You're not exactly flush, Mr Bexington are you?'

'As for any AA meeting, I just didn't go there. I went to Giles's flat. We had a few more drinks and I went to bed.'

'Went to bed, or put to bed by your mate?'

'Look. Let me tell you again. I knew when I found her body that this looked bad for me. Then when I got myself together the next day, and read online about Camilla's death, I realised just how bad. I got panicky. When it got dark, I headed for Brighton, where we shared some happy times together. Giles rang me to advise me to speak to this journalist, Jan Mason, who was all over the story. He's smart like that. And so I did.

'I may have still been in Battersea when this man Malahide was killed but I didn't know him. As for Wilson, if I was going to go to jail for anyone it would be him but...'

Bexington stopped as his solicitor tapped his arm to attract his attention, shaking his head to aid the process of shutting up his client.

'Now that is interesting, Mr Bexington. You'd go to prison for killing Wilson?'

Bexington looked at Toller, who nodded, knowing that this was a chance to put the record straight.

'It was a figure of speech. I've told you before that I detest the man. Detested. I'm not going to deny that.'

Now the solicitor saw an opening.

'DCI Hanley. I can see how you might assemble this theory of yours. But is there any actual evidence or forensics to back any of this up?'

'We have the scarf with your client's prints all over it.'

'As I understand, so are those of Wilson.'

'Yes. But he's dead now. Unless you believe he strangled himself.'

'Do you have a murder weapon in his case?'

'Not yet. We are still working at the murder scene.'

'So you believe all three murders to be the work of one person?'

'We've no reason to believe otherwise.'

'And what about Simon Dewlish? Have you brought him in to ask him where he was last night and what he was up to?'

'That's our business, Mr Toller. But perhaps you'd like to tell me why Dewlish would kill Wilson?'

'You're asking me to do your job for you now, detective.'

'And Dewlish had no links with Sean Malahide.'

'Nor did my client.'

'We have a neighbour who has identified him as a visitor to Mr Malahide's flat.'

'What?' said Bexington. 'I told you before. That's drivel.'

The solicitor decided he needed a distraction.

'You mentioned that my client stood to benefit from Ms Carew's will, detective. I'm guessing so did other people.'

Of course, Wilson was the main beneficiary, Hanley knew. But he was dead. And Hanley was growing tired of Bexington's lying as well as the manoeuvring of his solicitor. He stared intently at Bexington.

'Look. You've got motive for all three murders. We've got you at Camilla's flat and you stood to benefit from her death. We've got somebody who saw you at an AA meeting virtually confessing, and a witness who ties you to Malahide, who was at that meeting. And at whose flat we found a scarf you gave Camilla. You've also just told me you would happily have killed Wilson.'

'We're back to where we started inspector,' said the solicitor. 'All theory. All circumstantial.'

'Well, it stacks up pretty good to me,' Hanley snapped. 'Mr Bexington, I think you've killed three people and you are a danger to even more so I don't have any choice.'

'What do you mean?'

Hanley leaned forward, looked Bexington in the eye and announced slowly and with relish: 'I'm sending everything I've got on you to a CPS lawyer. And I'm very confident you will be charged with the murders of Camilla Carew, Sean Malahide and Gavin Wilson.'

37

JAN'S mobile beeped with a text. She was relieved. She'd had enough of Frank's condolences about her mother and wanted to move the conversation on. She wanted to know the outcome of his meeting with Hanley and whether he'd told him more than he'd already told her.

'That was Deena,' she said. She wasn't going to tell Frank about her phone call with Deena suggesting that Gaunt might be a suspect in Wilson's murder or Deena's reply now confirming that he was seen buying newspapers in a newsagent's in Soho at around the time of death, so it couldn't be him. She did tell Frank about Deena's revelation of a major development, though.

'They've sent the file on Bexington to the CPS,' she said.

'Good,' Frank replied. 'About fucking time.'

The language took Jan by surprise. She had been too tired, bound up in the conflicting emotions around the death of her mother, to hear his anxiety properly last night. Today, though, she could not fail to detect the strain in his voice when he phoned to ask to meet her. Still, she wasn't expecting to find him in this state of agitation when she encountered him in the cafe by Blackfriars Bridge that was halfway between her office on the Thames by Tower Bridge and his at the Met building on the Embankment.

'You're going to have to give me a minute,' she said and went outside to phone Vickers to tell him of the development and update the intro to her earlier story about Wilson being found murdered. She tweeted the exclusive of Bexington being pulled in for questioning again, though wary about legal rules now a charge was imminent, to her now 140,000 followers.

She stood for a moment gazing up towards the London Eye and Westminster Bridge, deep in thought. Her instincts had always been good, she thought. Not this time, it seemed. Maybe her time was up. The new Editor might well be pissed off with her for what had appeared to be an amazing exclusive with Bexington but now seemed to be a heap of garbage that would bring ridicule upon her and the paper. And she could yet be facing charges for aiding and abetting a murderer.

'I must be losing my touch,' Jan said on her return into the cafe after taking a deep pull of coffee on her return.

'How come?' Frank asked.

'Well, I could have sworn Bexington was telling me the truth. I'm going to look like an arse now.'

'I always thought he was a wrong 'un,' Frank replied. 'Feckless sort who saw his toy being taken away from him. Spoilt kid who'd rather break it. Then started trying to kill people who might have sussed him. Wilson probably had something to prove it, as he knew Sean through the Labour Party, so your story said. So Bexington killed him too. You know, it was something you said that made me certain that it was Bexington who's done all this,' he added.

'What was that?'

'I asked you about what he was wearing when you interviewed him. It tallied with the AA meeting. Especially the brown suede boots. I noticed those same Chelsea boots on the man who sat in that room.'

Jan puffed out her cheeks before taking another long gulp of coffee.

'I've never told anyone what you once told me about you and AA, Frank. Looking back to... well, us... I can see it now with the drinking. But some stuff still doesn't add up. Killing in blackout is one thing. That is a thing, is it, by the way?'

'Yes. It's been known. Happened last year. Woman in Los Angeles claimed it as her defence. Got a much shorter sentence than she would have done for first degree murder.'

'But killing in cold blood? As he did with Sean, just because he might have recognised him from an AA meeting? And then Wilson?'

'Desperate man. And booze does crazy things to people Jan. The panics set in once people come off a bender. Some sober up and wise up when something traumatic happens. It sets others out on even worse boozing until they're ready to quit. Most never reach that point, sadly. Bexington seemed to know he had a drink problem but didn't really want to do anything about it. An alcoholic in denial is very dangerous and capable of scary things. Maybe he's even using this blackout thing as a possible defence if he gets caught.'

'You don't seem to have any sympathy for him.'

'I have empathy with him. Different thing. Sympathy keeps alcoholics sick. It's being told the truth and facing up to what they've done that they need. Taking responsibility.'

'That's a bit harsh Frank.'

'Never heard of tough love?'

'Yes, but I thought you people supported each other.'

'We carry the message, not the alcoholic. Anyway, who are you accusing of being harsh? Not looked at yourself?'

'What's that supposed to mean?'

Frank stayed silent, as if wondering whether to go on. He looked out on to Blackfriars Bridge, where people were beginning to scurry home for an early start to the weekend. He was clearly in a mood to be honest, though.

'You had Wilson on your front page this morning, as did the red tops.'

'And?'

'Well, you talked about him being gay and his connection with two murders. Now he's dead.'

'Are you saying I'm responsible for that?'

'Well, you haven't helped, have you?'

'Frank, I didn't kill Gavin Wilson, for fuck's sake. Some evil bastard did. I just wrote a story.'

'Which put him in the frame and thus made him vulnerable. To anyone who knew either Camilla Carew and Sean and who wanted him dead too. In this case, Bexington. How could you have fallen for everything he told you so easily? Does he have some kind of hold over you?'

'For God's sake Frank. Don't be ridiculous.'

'That's the trouble with your profession. You have power without responsibility and you revel in it. You don't feel in the least bit guilty.'

The thing was, Jan did. She looked down and stared at her empty coffee cup and a silence passed between them. She began to shed a tear and took a tissue from her bag.

'Frank, you know nothing about what I feel. Nothing about my guilt. Personal or professional. It's a myth that journalists only care about the story and not the people involved in them. I am competitive, I admit, and I like the thrill of the chase but I came into this job because I *have* humanity. Not because I *don't*. Because I care about people. I went for that Regent's Park story not to win awards, though I admit I loved winning them, but because I get my kicks from righting wrongs on behalf of those who have been abused or who don't have voices.'

Frank was staring intently at her.

'I hate what's happened to my profession and the way it's seen these days. Hate the way some elements of the media have gone along with those who've sowed division for their own political purposes. Half the country hates the other half. Politically.

Geographically. Everything's polarised, binary. And our press has reflected it. We used to have grey areas, nuances. Life wasn't simple, we understood that. Now everyone wants it simplified and we've been guilty of pandering to it. Short attention spans. Fast food. Everyone's got opinions to burn. Social media's full of cranks and trolls, but that's where people get their news and information from now and we feel we have to compete.

'People are torn, Frank. You should know that, after what you've been through this week. Torn between doing the right thing or taking an easy way out. Torn between principles and money in these hard times. Between their tiredness at all the information coming at them and what the really important issues are. Between work and family. As a nation, we're torn between those who care that we're being lied to and those who shrug their shoulders, weary of the information overload and tired of caring.

'But the one thing everyone seems to agree on is that journalists are a disgrace, when it should be those giving out all the messages, not the messengers, who should be in the dock.

'Me? I'm just trying to tread a path between modern ways and traditional virtues. Trying to stay in a job by using the internet as servant not master, and by sticking to old-fashioned virtues of legwork, using contacts, checking sources. Proper journalism, not knee-jerk crap. Trying to be on the right side of history with those who still care. I know we make big mistakes and my paper does some shocking things but I stay on the inside trying to put it right, rather than criticise from the outside. It's hard, Frank. Fucking hard.'

Frank looked at her.

'Great speech,' he said. 'So what did you check with Bexington?'

'We checked his alibi.'

'With his mate. Wow.'

'I asked him all the tough questions.'

'And got lies for answers. And now Wilson's dead.'

Jan grew angry now.

'Look, I was just trying to flush somebody out. Wilson maybe. And while I may have found Bexington believable, my interview with him never said he was innocent. I wrote it straight.'

'But you gave him credibility.'

Jan stared out of the window of the cafe and more tears came.

'I didn't want this to happen.'

'But it did.'

Jan dabbed her eyes again with the tissue. A silence between them descended. Frank broke it.

'I'm even more convinced now that it was Bexington who tried to strangle me last night. Bloke had a moustache and smelled of booze.'

'Not sure that would count in picking him out of a line-up or go down well in court.'

'You're doubting the word of a copper?'

'It wouldn't be the first time…'

'Jan. Christ. I may be many things but you know me better than that.'

'Now you know what I'm up against. What you've just said about my profession. Listen. I'm not accusing you of lying. I just think… You shouldn't be holier-than-thou about your own judgement lately.'

Frank looked down at his coffee. Pain came across his face. He spoke slowly, a tremor in his voice.

'I'm so used to being dispassionate about crime and terrorism,' he said. 'About thinking logically and without feeling for those involved. You talk about grey areas. For me it is black and white. There's bad guys and I've got to nail them before they nail us.'

He looked at Jan for reassurance. She smiled, if weakly.

'But this. This has knocked me sideways Jan. I'm involved and it's just made me question myself. Today I told Hanley what I should have said three days ago. And now I'm worried that he's going to go straight to my boss and tell him that he has an alkie for a deputy. Even though I'm usually a clear-headed, competent, sober alkie, rather than the drinking, all-over-the-place alkie of fifteen years ago.'

'Will he do that?'

'I don't know. Maybe he'd rather keep it for now. Have something over me for later use. I'm just trying to compose myself to go in and tell my superior myself. Take Hanley's power away. But I'm too much of a mess right now to do it. Somebody I knew, somebody I was having coffee with a few nights ago, was strangled to death. And last night, I could have been killed. Any peace of mind I had in my life has been shattered. Can't see the wood from the trees.'

Tears began to trickle down his cheeks. Jan reached across the table and took his hand in hers.

'Not you as well,' she said. 'What a pair.'

They both laughed.

'I do feel bad,' said Jan. 'You were right.'

'Bloody hell Jan, that's a first.'

'What, me saying I feel bad?'

'No. You admitting I was right.'

They both laughed again, him through a mixture of tears and snot, and he took out a handkerchief and wiped his nose.

'Now come on,' Jan said. 'We need to pull ourselves together. Get back to that buzz we both love. The buzz of seeing a story, a case, through. Don't tell me you don't love that too? Regent's Park?'

'Yep,' he agreed. 'We got the guy then. That felt good.'

'But we know that for all the ups, there has to be downs. That's the rhythm of life. A cardiograph is full of them. It shows we're alive. If it flatlines, we're dead.'

Frank nodded at the analogy.

'Am I to blame for Wilson's death? No. I didn't do the killing but I accept there is a connection. Same with you Frank. You've done nothing wrong. You're just feeling some survivor's guilt. And I'm feeling a journalist's guilt.'

'I guess so,' said Frank.

'That song you mentioned… Don't Talk. About alcoholism.'

'Best one ever written about it.'

'Love that line "take your poison silently." Well, I'm glad you've stopped taking your poison. And I'm glad you've dropped the silently bit too.'

'Listen,' Frank said. 'I think I'm going to go to an AA meeting. There's one in the City at lunchtime, not far from here.'

'You know what?' Jan said. 'Is it an open meeting? I think I might like to tag along.'

38

HANLEY was growing impatient but to show it to Donovan would have been to invite her contempt. He could take a certain degree of criticism from colleagues, and even superiors, but contempt from her was genuinely withering, especially here in front of the team. Ego, male and professional pride, meant that he would not be risking that. And so he nodded and smiled in the right places at this woman's observations.

'OK. I get that Bexington had motive for Camilla Carew's killing,' Donovan said from her position to one side of the whiteboard, Hanley on the other and the team sitting in a semi-circle around them. 'Maybe a crime of passion, committed in a drunken rage. Maybe he did find out, from her perhaps, that he was in her will. But does it all stack up? CCTV street footage? Forensics? On that and the other two?'

'Well, ma'am. There's nothing of him around Chelsea, as it's backstreets. The analysts did pick him up on a Battersea Bridge camera on foot around nine on Monday night and at Victoria Station just after seven on Tuesday night. No footage around Sean Malahide's block of flats. Cameras smashed. But we do have the fingerprints and DNA of him from Camilla Carew's flat and on her clothing, as well as on the scarf belonging to her that was used to strangle Sean Malahide.'

'What about Wilson?'

'Nothing left in the flat that we can find yet but forensics still there with a brief to call me if they do. And there are no CCTV cameras near Wilson's flat but we're looking at others in Camden Town.'

'I see,' said Donovan.

'What we do have,' Hanley quickly went on, 'is new information from a credible informant that Bexington was at an AA meeting confessing to a murder in a drunken blackout on Monday night and that he also has motive for killing Malahide, who was at that meeting.'

'Credible informant?'

'Yes, ma'am.'

'OK. I may need to know who at some point.'

Hanley nodded and pressed on.

'In addition, Bexington was on a bender last night and has very little memory of where he went and what happened. We're verifying that he was out with friends, getting drunk, but it could be that once he'd sobered up, he went round to Wilson's this morning.'

'Any sign of forced entry?'

'No ma'am.'

'So why would Wilson let him in the flat?'

There was a silence.

'Maybe Bexington knew something about the will that Wilson wanted to hear. Ma'am, James Bexington is the link between all three murders.'

'I thought his friend backed up his account of being at his flat?'

'He does. But we're not sure how truthful he is or whether he would even know, if he was still sleeping it off.'

Donovan looked at Hanley, then across to Deena. They could see the doubt on her face.

'I'm not sure I like the "it could be" he went round to Wilson's flat bit.'

'Look ma'am, I agree that we need to nail one or two things down but I've had a prelim call from the CPS lawyer and he likes what he's seeing so far.'

Another silence passed between the three of them.

'I don't know. Still feels a bit thin to me. A half-decent brief's going to drive a hole through all of that and Bexington will have a good one given his network. No real forensics on him from Malahide's place or Wilson's, for example.'

'We're not finished yet, ma'am. For now, I want him in custody. I don't want anyone else getting killed. He could be targeting other people who were in that AA meeting. We have enough to go to court for a committal and get bail refused as we believe he could kill again. While he's on remand, we keep working on him and build the case for the CPS. Who knows, he might even cough.'

Donovan turned her gaze to Deena.

'What do you think, DS Campbell?'

Deena could feel Hanley's gaze lasering into her face. She hesitated.

'Come on, Deena. The Met doesn't pay you to keep quiet. It pays you to have theories and hunches, and then find the evidence to back those up. So?'

'Well,' Deena began slowly, aware that Donovan would have known of her sanctioned contacts with the well-informed Jan Mason. 'I know everything points to Bexington and I think there are plenty of reasons to charge him.'

'But?' said Donovan.

'No buts really,' said Deena. 'I think it's a good idea. As DCI Hanley says, we need to stop these killings. And if it isn't him, then whoever it is might become complacent. Do or say something to break cover.'

'Tell me more about the "whoever it is"?'

'Well, there's still Dewlish…'

'Nothing like the same links to all this as Bexington,' said Hanley. 'No connection with Malahide. Only knew about Wilson from Camilla. We've let him go.'

'Maybe there's somebody else we're still not thinking about, something or someone we're missing,' said Deena.

'Go on,' said Donovan.

'Well, Bexington could have killed Camilla. Could even have killed Sean to shut him up, having been recognised at the AA meeting. He's more physical than both of those. Wilson is as strong as him, though. Researchers' profile says Wilson still plays – or was still playing – Rugby. Bexington played as well, I know, but a long time ago and it's hard to see him overpowering Wilson now.'

'Element of surprise. Soon as Wilson opened the door. Very powerful,' said Hanley interrupting, starting to get annoyed at his DS taking over this briefing with their boss.

'Yes, of course,' Deena said. 'And I'm sure that counted in the case of, um, another person from the AA meeting being attacked last night.'

'Another person? Who?' Donovan asked.

Deena looked across at Hanley, whose expression darkened. Hanley had told her about his interview with Frank before the briefing but told her to keep quiet about it for now. She knew, however, that if she held something back from Donovan, and it all kicked off later because the boss wasn't in full possession of all the facts, then they would be in trouble. Besides, while she didn't want to be the one who broke Frank's anonymity, she suspected that Hanley was keeping it back for his own purposes. Better out now. She owed it to the inquiry.

'Frank Phillips,' Hanley blurted out.

'Frank Phillips?' Donovan said. 'The one in counter-terrorism? What's he got to do with this?'

Hanley explained about Frank and AA, about last night's assailant and how Frank escaped.

'Bloody hell. I knew Frank years ago when we were DIs together. I knew he liked a drink but I didn't realise he was in AA.'

'I don't think he advertises it, ma'am,' Hanley said.

'Good for him,' said Donovan. Hanley looked annoyed.

'Thing is,' Deena said, 'why would Bexington go for Frank?'

'Because he recognised him from the AA meeting too,' said Hanley. 'Bexington was working his way through any of them he thought might connect him.'

'Yeah, I see that,' said Deena. 'But again, why try to strangle a bloke who was his physical equal? Why not do it another way? Hit him over the head or something? Same with Wilson. How did he overpower him?'

'Surprise element, as I've said. And it's Bexington's MO. Maybe he's getting good at it. More confident. It worked for him with Camilla and Sean. Stick with what you know.'

'Maybe. I just think he might have gone for someone smaller if he was going to do it that way, or found another way of doing it. Also, I think whoever it was, went for Frank deliberately rather than any of the others left who were in that AA meeting.'

"Whoever it was.' There's that idea of yours again,' Donovan said. 'Come on. Spit it out. Who do you reckon might be involved?'

'I'm not sure. But I think there may be a wider element to this. I have a source who thinks we should maybe check officially with other agencies about the monitoring of Gavin Wilson.'

'Really?'

Hanley butted in. 'I'm really not sure this is relevant, ma'am.'

'Let DS Campbell speak.'

'My information is that Wilson was meeting with Palestinian organisations with a view to them contributing to his party.'

There was a pause.

'So you're suggesting Wilson attacked Frank for some political reason?' Donovan asked. 'Knew he's in counter-terrorism and been watching him? Sometime before he was killed? And why last night?'

'Maybe he'd only just found out about it. Maybe got angry. Maybe he's the impulsive type.'

'We'd need a bit more than that,' said Donovan. 'Sounds a bit of a stretch.'

'Anyway,' Hanley piped up. 'The description Phillips has supplied sounds more like Bexington. Says his attacker had a moustache and smelled of vodka.'

'I just think we should keep an open mind,' said Deena.

'I don't know. I tend to agree with DCI Hanley,' said Donovan. 'This feels like a side issue.'

Hanley permitted himself a smile and a "thank you ma'am." His satisfaction was fleeting, however.

'But you're right, DS Campbell,' Donovan said. 'We need to keep an open mind. What else, or who else, are we considering?'

'With respect ma'am,' said Hanley attempting not to insult his boss but who knew that the phrase was about to introduce some disrespect. 'The simple fact is that Bexington is in the frame for all three murders, as well as the attack on Phillips, and I think we ought to concentrate on building the case against him. This is about people, not their politics.'

'OK. We'll hold Bexington for now,' Donovan replied. 'Let's split this. Dave, you work on nailing down the case against Bexington and you, Deena, see if there's any other loose ends. Working to DCI Hanley of course. All good?'

'All good ma'am,' Hanley replied through gritted teeth. Deena nodded. Donovan turned and left. When she'd disappeared back to her office. Hanley turned to Deena wanting "a word". He took her over to a corner, rather than out into the stairwell. He wanted the team to see him speaking to her, if not quite hearing it.

'What the fuck was all that about then?'

'Guv?'

'Fucking me over like that?'

'That wasn't my intention. The Chief Super asked me for my thoughts and opinions and I offered them.'

'And undermined me in the process.'

'I don't think I did. She agreed to you holding Bexington. I just offered other strands to the enquiry that need to be looked at.'

'Why didn't you tell me about the Wilson-Palestinian thing?'

'I didn't know if it was relevant. Even Donovan thought it was a side issue.'

'I thought we understood each other when we talked yesterday,' Hanley said just before his mobile rang. He barked a "Yes" into it then listened for a moment before replying, sarcasm in his voice: "Hang on. Let me ask someone who seems to know a bit better than I do. I'll ring you straight back."

He turned to Deena. 'Simon Dewlish's brief is downstairs. Says we forgot to let his client have his passport back in the agreed time. Reckons he needs it now and should be allowed to have it back. Since you're in charge of "loose ends", what do you reckon?'

Hanley's mobile rang again. 'Listen. I told you I'd ring you back. Oh, right…. Sorry.'

Hanley listened intently to the voice on the other end, Deena trying to hear but unable to. The call was soon over.

'Scene of crime. They've found a couple of things of interest at Wilson's. A gold cuff link with the initials SD on it.'

'Simon Dewlish?'

'Could well be, couldn't it?'

'And Wilson's phone. Text on it to Dewlish.'

'Saying?'

Enough Dewlish. I'm going to the police about what you've done.

Deena looked baffled.

Hanley made another call.

'Tell him no, his client can't have his fucking passport back. And what's more, tell him if Dewlish is not back in here in five minutes, we'll be coming to arrest him.'

He ended the call and turned to Deena. 'Jesus. I still think this is Bexington's work but this muddies the waters.'

39

THERE must have been about a dozen of them and they were all perfectly pleasant and welcoming to her but still Jan felt uncomfortable. She'd been offered coffee at the counter that separated the kitchen from the community room abutting the small church that would once have been the centrepiece of the district but was now dwarfed by office blocks. And she appreciated it, even if it was instant granules. She just wasn't used to people being friendly and open. They were more often trying to keep something from her.

'I'm Harry,' one said, seeing her standing on her own. 'Been coming for long?'

Jan thought that in other circumstances it might have been a chat-up line but the old guy was clearly trying to put her at ease.

'My first meeting,' she said. 'I'm here for a friend.'

She got a knowing look.

'Yes, I came for my wife at first,' he replied. 'She was going to leave me because of my drinking and I didn't want to lose her. But I ended up staying for myself.'

'Oh No. It's not like that. I'm genuinely here with a friend. To support him. He's having a tough time. Over there.' She pointed across to Frank, who was in conversation with a young woman.

'Ah, OK,' said the man and smiled at her, though there was scepticism in his voice.

Did she really look like an alcoholic who needed help? She liked a drink, for sure, a few glasses of wine after a tough day, but no more than that. Maybe a whole bottle if it was a really bad day. Or a day off on a weekend. Yes, she and Frank had sought company and solace together back in the days before hangovers bit so hard but they were long gone. No. She didn't need to be here, she told herself.

The meeting began with somebody, a man in his forties, reading from a book and then talking about it. It seemed to be about guilt and shame, the difference between them, and how to deal with both, without needing a drink to blot out the feelings. The book was then passed around for everybody to digest the passage for themselves while the speaker "shared" for around ten minutes.

He talked about how he was feeling today and how his life was different in the nine months since he had quit drinking, about how guilt and shame had informed his life before. The first one, his "sponsor" had told him, concerned feeling bad about an action, the other feeling bad about who you were as a person. He had spent, he added, so much time and energy covering up mad, bad and sad things he had done but no longer needed to keep secrets and cover up. His life, he said, was an open book because he sought to live it according to the principles of Alcoholics Anonymous.

There was widespread nodding around the room at his talk among the dozen or so people, and Jan looked across a couple of times at Frank to see him smiling, relaxing a little. Good. She was pleased about that. Otherwise, she began to drift off a little. And welcomed it. The peace in the room calmed her. Gave her time and space to think. She went back over the events of the last few days. And details began to dawn on her, pieces fitted together. Yes. That could well be it. She just needed to ask Deena – and Nancy as well – a couple of questions. Well, more than a couple.

She gazed around the room, assessing people. They were a diverse crew, mainly older, in their fifties upwards but there were a few in their twenties and thirties too. She felt sorry for those younger ones, denied years of drinking, until one of them, once the speaker had finished and the meeting was opened up for others to talk, shared how grateful she was for having stopped drinking this early in life, so that she could enjoy so many years free of booze. An older member shared back that he envied her, which raised a few laughs.

These were mainly professional people; office workers, one or two traders who had grown out of the champagne-fuelled life-style or been brought to their knees and their senses by recession. There was also a guy dressed in leathers, with a helmet on his lap. A motorcycle courier. Hmm.

Her musings on what people did, building a picture of what their lives might be like, what stories lay beneath the veneer of how well they looked today, were interrupted by a familiar voice that filled a silence after a few minutes of sharing by the courier.

'Hi' it said. 'My name is Frank and I am an alcoholic.'

Jan sat up in her chair.

'Hi Frank,' said the chorus.

'I don't know why I'm surprised,' he continued, 'but it always seems that when I come in pain to an AA meeting, in need of something to cling on to, the subject turns out to be just what I am going through.

'Many of you will have heard about the meeting in Chelsea on Monday night when somebody confessed to a murder and the fact that somebody from that meeting was found dead two days ago.'

The meeting hung on Frank's every word.

'Well, it seems the two are linked and I feel a terrible guilt that I was in that meeting and said nothing to the authorities. Confidentiality is central to our fellowship, I know that, but it shouldn't override our duties as citizens of the wider community and it took me too long to realise that. I've been telling myself over the last twenty-four hours that if I had realised sooner, Sean might have been alive today. There's guilt over an action, and also guilt over a lack of action. My guilt turned into a shame for who I am – somebody who didn't have the moral courage to take action. Somebody who was weak.

'Now, as I sit here thinking about that, and having said it out loud, I know it not to be true. On my good days, I know I am a decent, dignified human being who has turned his life around in sobriety and seeks to do the right thing.

'I thought I was doing the right thing in respecting the anonymity and confidentiality of this fellowship, to which I owe everything, but the reality was that I was using that to justify my fear of my own anonymity being exploited by people who wished me ill. I thought about myself instead of others. I am sure the founders of this fellowship, Bill W and Dr Bob, did not intend that murderers should find a sanctuary of silence in here.

'Some of you will disagree with me. You might say that we need to think about the guy suffering from the drink problem and needing help for it. Well, my answer to that – after much soul-searching – is that reporting the crime, making a person take responsibility for what they have done, is a huge part of getting sober. Once people own their stuff, and make amends for it, only then does true recovery and peace of mind begin.

'One of the reasons I have stayed sober for so long is that I have always come along to these meetings and been honest and true to myself. I wasn't true to myself the other night. It is why I have been feeling out of… out of alignment with myself. Restless, irritable and discontent.

'A murderer escaped to kill again. I will live with that, though as I get some balance and perspective on myself, I know it wasn't my fault and I didn't commit the crime. All I can do now is make some kind of amends, do what little I can to bring the murderer to justice. I thank you all for listening.'

A hush fell on the meeting. The power of Frank's sharing had moved everybody into considering their own potential reaction to the events of the other night. In addition, nobody wanted to follow that, worried that whatever they had to say might be feeble by comparison.

Jan was impressed. Mightily. She was even tempted to applaud, though it clearly wasn't the done thing. Frank shot a glance at her, vulnerability on his face. This was not the professional copper she thought she knew. This was someone with more depths than the man she had first met almost twenty years ago now. She smiled at him as reassurance.

A young man broke the silence. 'Thank you Frank for sharing that,' he said. 'My name is Mike and I am an alcoholic and I hope as I go on in recovery, one day at a time, I will find the same courage and honesty within myself that you have just shown.

'I needed a meeting after some news this morning and this is the nearest lunchtime one to where I work. I heard that somebody I work for was found dead in his flat. It's a terrible thing. But I have to be honest in here. He was not well liked, not that he deserved what happened to him. I've heard it said in rooms like this that secrets keep us sick. So I have something to confess...'

Jan began to feel that she should come to these meetings more often. She had heard tell that film producers and actors came here because there were contacts to be forged, good deals to be done, and maybe she might learn some things. That was, she quickly recognised, the natural storyteller in her, though. As both person and journalist, she knew that she couldn't use directly anything these people were saying. It would simply be unethical. She hadn't needed a workshop for "senior" journalists at the paper on new post-Leveson rules and regulations to understand that. She now had a glimmer of understanding of Frank's dilemma.

'I was interviewed at work by police about a person, my boss, a couple of days ago and I was a little, shall we say, economical with the truth,' Mike continued. 'I was scared of the guy. I didn't lie, exactly, but I didn't really tell the woman about my doubts and concerns about this man. He knew I came to AA and even used to ask me questions about it but I always felt that there was something untrustworthy about him.

'I also met yesterday with somebody wanting to offer me a job for a lot of money. They asked me about my boss as well and I told them a few things about him. Maybe I was a bit too frank, told them things I should have been telling the police. I regret it now. I feel compromised. And yes, some shame. Anyway, I thought I should share that among friends in a safe place. I'm going to have to think now about what I do with all this.'

The meeting chorused "Thanks Mike" and after some more sharing, the secretary brought the meeting to a close, save for the final formalities, including a mug being passed around the room for people to make contributions towards the costs of the meeting.

'Well, thanks everyone,' the secretary said. 'Some amazing sharing in here today that has certainly helped keep me sober, just for today. Now I know we've been discussing it today, and there will be different interpretations given what we've heard, but can I just remind everyone of the importance of the yellow card.'

And he held up the card that had caused Frank so much stress and which Jan was seeing for the first time today, before reading it in a loud voice.

WHO YOU SEE HERE
WHAT YOU HEAR HERE
WHEN YOU LEAVE HERE
LET IT STAY HERE

The meeting then ended with the whole group standing and holding hands – to Jan's further discomfort – to say the Serenity Prayer together, a framed copy of it in the middle of the table: "God grant me the serenity to accept the things I cannot change, the courage to change the things I can, and the wisdom to know the difference."

Jan suddenly found a new way to be torn – between wanting to join in, having shared an emotional tie with these people this past hour, and not wishing to feel too much a part of it. She mouthed the prayer, rather than said it out loud. As the meeting broke up, she got up and walked over to Frank, to give him a hug, but his eye was on the figure leaving the room quickly, without talking to anybody.

'Look,' he said, pointing, and Jan turned to see the person disappear through the door.

'You're thinking what I'm thinking, aren't you?' she said.

'Yep,' he said. 'Let's go.'

Fortunately, they caught up with Mike twenty yards down the busy lunchtime street, abuzz with people going back to work or heading off for a weekend away. And even more fortunately, the words of Frank's sharing about duty over confidentiality still in his ears, Mike was willing to talk to them.

40

ARMED with Mike's information, Jan headed for the office. She had calls to make. And she had a front page lead and backgrounders for inside the paper to write this afternoon. They would be needed. If she was right, and all went to plan, they would take as much copy from her as they could get.

Vickers, naturally, could not resist it when she arrived at her desk.

'So your blue-eyed boy's bang to rights then?' he said, making sure most on the news desk could hear too.

She, equally, was not going to let the prospect of a bit of a barney go. She started quietly, then raised her voice a couple of levels from his, sarcasm rather than anger infusing it, making sure most of the floor could hear.

'Maybe,' she replied. 'But I didn't notice you the other night when I had the exclusive telling me you didn't want it because he might be the guilty party.'

As usual, he ignored the logic of that and his role in events and instead deflected things back on to Jan. By now, every eye and ear on the news desk was on them, alerted by the "fight, fight, fight" tone of rising voices. Good, Jan thought. She wanted all to see Vickers in his true colours. As chief reporter, she felt she had a duty to the younger ones sometimes to stand up to him publicly.

'We ran it because it was news, Jan. Who wouldn't? But you wrote it sympathetically, like he was some bloke wronged rather than a suspect in a murder inquiry.'

'That's how we got the exclusive, arsehole,' she shouted. She could hear somebody in the background, in a stage whisper, saying: "Harsh but fair." 'He gave it to us on the basis that we would present his side of things. Everybody would have done that. It was a great "get" so don't you dare diss that. And don't you dare insinuate I wasn't tough with my questions.'

Vickers knew any reporter and news editor would have done the same thing, but he was not about to let go of a moment when he had a rare chance to embarrass Jan in front of her colleagues.

'Who you calling arsehole?' he said, the language and tactics of the playground still imprinted on his soul. 'Listen. You were fucking finished on this paper. Then you got lucky with that Regent's Park story when a killer landed in your lap, and since then you've Queen Bee'd it around the news desk.'

'I think you'll find I made my own luck by ignoring your instructions and actually going out of the office to find a story,' she replied.

'Well the old man's gone now and us looking daft by giving the front and three pages over to a murderer ain't gonna look good once social media and TV and sodding radio phone-ins start on us is it? Something the new Editor's not going to be able to ignore.'

Jan, hackles rising, could do no better now than 'Fuck off Ivan.'

She sat down at her desk and fired up her laptop. Vickers smirked. Neanderthal he may have been but, with some reason, he gave off the air of the one who felt he'd won the exchange. He strutted back to his own desk and watched as others got back to what they were doing.

Some were Jan fans, some wanted her job, some envied her special status. She could sense a mood around her that most thought that she had indeed been taken down a peg or two.

She stared at her blank screen for a few moments. She was trying not to let her anger show. Even less, her embarrassment. She felt again like a little girl told off at school, felt like sobbing as she did then, but she wasn't going to give Vickers that pleasure.

She composed herself by checking a few websites: BBC, The Guardian, Huffington Post, Buzzfeed. Life was already moving on. Wilson's murder and Bexington's file being sent to the CPS were still high on the news lists but other stories were getting priority now. Jobless figures, a footballer who'd cheated on his wife, fall-out from the new immigration bill...

She thought back to the AA meeting, with its theme about guilt and shame, and she understood the sentiment that some had shared about feeling small and not good enough. Imposter syndrome, somebody called it. Like them, she was a small-town girl achieving highly in the capital. They had solved it by drinking to blot out the feelings and the sorrows, they said. Somebody else shared back a Frida Kahlo quote, "I drank to drown my sorrows but the damned things learned how to swim."

It was not what Jan did. She was certain of that. She didn't feel she needed to drink to cover up things like that. Her drinking was confined to times when it was appropriate and wasn't going to damage her work. God help her, she thought, if she didn't have her work. But work here? With Vickers for years more? She didn't handle humiliation like she used to. Even if she wanted to show the bastard one last time...

Jan thought again about what Mike had told her and Frank in a thirty-minute chat in a coffee bar off Threadneedle Street. She then did a Google search and pulled up a couple of faces, lining them up side by side. She checked some older photos. She got up from her desk and walked away from the newsroom. Vickers gave another smile of satisfaction, figuring she was going to the ladies for a cry. Others watched her go.

Once in the stairwell, Jan got out her phone, only to be interrupted by Sarah, who had followed her from the newsroom floor.

'Look Jan,' said Sarah. 'I'm sorry. I didn't know what to do. Whether to intervene or let it go when he gets withering like that.'

'That was withering?' Jan replied. 'You've not been here long enough to see me and him have proper ding-dong have you?' She laughed and so did Sarah.

'I was trying to pay you the compliment of letting you handle it your own way, as I know you're big enough and old enough.'

'Less of the old, thank you,' said Jan with a smile.

'And I'm all for the sisterhood but sometimes we've got to handle these things solo, eh?'

'Too right,' said Jan, smiling.

'You sure you're OK? You decided about redundancy?'

'Yes, I have. Now sod off. I've got work to do.'

Sarah departed with a smile, not seeing Jan wipe a tear from her eye, only turning at the call of her name.

'And Sarah… Make sure you're on top of your game tonight. I think something big may be about to happen.'

Sarah smiled, more broadly this time, and gave a double thumbs-up.

Jan pressed a number on her phone. Her call was answered quickly and she replied in kind to the inquiry as to how she was.

'Your favourite journalist is doing OK, thank you. And you?'

'Well,' said Nancy, 'I want you to write my obituary in your newspaper please dear and as it's not in there today, I suppose I am doing reasonably well.'

'You've heard about Wilson being found dead, and James Bexington likely to be charged?'

'Picked it up on the lunchtime news. Doesn't quite look like a duck or walk like a duck to me.'

'Hmm.' Jan replied. 'Listen Nancy, I think I may know a few things, and may have worked out a few more. Some things that have been going around in my head since our first lunch.

Can I run them by you, as the person who's met or knows all the people caught up in this?"

Nancy agreed and Jan sat down in the stairwell. She outlined what she had learned earlier today, along with her theories and suppositions. Nancy listened, and did not interrupt. At the end, she merely said: "Well, aren't you a clever girl?"

Jan smiled. Nancy had become a friend, a confidante and an ally. Jan thought that her mother would have liked her, that she and Elsie, though having little in common in their backgrounds, would have liked each other. Different worlds but shared historical experiences and mutual respect.

She then asked Nancy if she would help her with the next stage of her plan. It was a lot to ask, Jan said, but she needed her. Nancy said she would do her best, that she thought it should be possible.

'You can pop round later to get the key when you've confirmed everything,' Nancy said.

Her next call was also answered quickly.

'You reckon Bexington did it?' Jan asked.

'Looks that way,' said Deena. 'We're holding him but there's new stuff on Dewlish.'

'Want to tell me?'

'You got anything to give back?'

'Plenty.'

Deena told her about Dewlish's cuff link and the text from Wilson to Dewlish.

'Hmm. That's curious. OK. Well, I've got a few thoughts myself and also rather a lot of new information. I need you and the charming DCI Hanley to trust me on this and meet me later.'

'I'm going to need more than that if I'm going to persuade him to have anything to do with you.'

'Listen, I've been ahead on this story so far, haven't I?'

'Ahead but wrong. Certainly on Bexington. That's all Hanley's seeing. So what new information?'

Jan outlined what she knew and what she thought she knew from all her conversations and enquiries. What she wanted Deena and Hanley to do next, where to go, and where then to meet her and at what time.

'You think you can do that?' Jan asked.

'Well, after what you've just told me, I think I might be able to stir his interest. We'll check if what you're saying is true. If it is, I'm sure we'll play ball. I'll text you to confirm.'

'By the way, I have terms and conditions.'

'Go on…'

Jan outlined them. Deena said that if this came off as she had outlined, even Hanley would agree to them.

And then Jan texted Frank.

She went back to her desk, all eyes on her, silence enveloping everyone, and took a signed piece of paper out from her handbag before going over to Sarah and giving her a hug. Sarah was stunned as Jan now made her way down the office floor to Human Resources.

After that, she headed for the ladies, where she checked her face in the mirror. The red eyes were gone. A relief had come over her. 'Good work my girl,' she told herself. 'Now for your big finish.'

She practised her rarely used conciliatory face one last time – not bad; something from that AA meeting must have rubbed off – and headed back to the newsroom, ready to write a pile of copy. Ostentatiously, she headed straight for Vickers's desk, making sure that all could see and hear. She could see him bracing himself for round two and as she approached, he rose from his seat to his full height. She guessed that he was determined, literally, not to be talked down to and was going to try to dominate her.

'Ivan,' she said. 'About earlier. I'm very sorry. I shouldn't have mouthed off at you like that. Apologies.'

'Oh… right,' he replied, disarmed.

'I've also got to apologise that I have nothing else for you tonight beyond the Wilson death and the Bexington murder charge but may well have something very decent tomorrow as a follow-up.'

'But it's a Saturday. I don't work weekends.'

'I know. But I think it would be worth your while to switch your shifts and take Monday off instead. Sarah can hold the fort while it's quiet. So how about you go home early now, have a Friday night with your feet up, and get yourself ready for the big one tomorrow?'

41

THE TEXT from Deena confirming that it was all arranged had arrived as Jan hoped and expected it would, and now Jan and Frank were waiting in a shelter in the gardens in the centre of Charmouth Square. From there, they had a clear view of Lyme Mansions.

'There's something else you should know about him,' said Frank.

'Go on.'

'I checked again with my people. He's been up to some very shady things. Meeting with some very bad people. Things they were storing up in a file ready to confront him with and things which could affect perceptions of him very seriously.'

'OK,' said Jan. 'You going to dish the dirt…'

Before Frank could reply, however, suddenly Peter Carew hove into view as expected, striding confidently up the street and ringing the chosen buzzer of the flats. The intercom was answered, the door opened and in he went.

Nancy had relished luring and intriguing Carew with promises of hearing something to his advantage and clearly she still knew how to entice an audience. Jan had worked out that Carew was a slave to the idea that information was power – anything that gave him the edge over people.

Jan and Frank waited a couple of minutes and then, using the keys supplied by Nancy, made their way through the front door of the building. As they did so, having been seen entering the hallway on the CCTV, out of Camilla's flat came two figures who were going to be needed for their shock value.

The entry of the four of them into Nancy's flat stunned Carew, as was the intention. He got up from his armchair, looked across at them entering the lounge, then at Nancy.

'What's going on here?' he asked, anger rising. 'Bexington, Dewlish. What are you doing here? How did they let you out? And who are these other people, Nancy?'

Nancy simply smiled in that way that had led so many people to underestimate her down the years, not least Carew.

Jan spoke out. 'I'm Jan Mason,' she said.

'That bloody journalist,' he said. 'I'm not having this.'

He made for the front door of the flat, surprised that Frank did not try to stop him. He soon discovered why. Jan had locked it from the inside behind her. He turned back to see Jan holding up a mortice key and smiling at him.

'I think you should come and sit down,' Frank said.

'And who the hell are you?' he asked.

'Me? Nobody special. Just another copper. Well, I work in counter-terrorism.'

Carew looked uneasy.

'And how is that relevant in any way to anything?'

'Well, you probably won't be surprised to learn you're on our watch list but my part is, how shall we describe it, rather more accidental and personal. Please…' he added, pointing to an armchair.

Carew slunk towards it and flopped himself into it. Bexington and Dewlish continued to stand, while Nancy and Jan took the sofa and Frank, as security guard, remained by the door.

Jan, her own heart racing but trying to look and sound in control and composed, was impressed. This was the professional, commanding Frank again.

'Right,' she said. 'You want to tell us what happened, Mr. Carew? What Camilla really meant to Nancy?'

Jan took her phone from her handbag, along with a digital recorder, placed them on a coffee table and soon the red lights were on.

'I don't know what you're talking about,' Carew replied. 'May I remind you that I have just lost my daughter.'

'And I'm very sorry about that. We all are.' Jan turned to Nancy. 'And I repeat my condolences to you as well Nancy.'

'What does that mean?' Dewlish asked.

'You want to tell everyone, Mr Carew?'

He looked around the room, stunned. Nancy stared at him.

'It was a long time ago,' he said. 'We were in love.'

'No we bloody weren't,' Nancy said. 'It was an affair that lasted a few months. I always loved my husband. But Roly was away on a theatre tour in the provinces for months while I was in something in the West End. It was a horrible mistake that I regretted of course. But you were charming back in those days Peter. Waiting at the stage door that night with flowers. And you seemed to have some principles then. I didn't know you were going to turn into the fascist you are, with thugs for friends.'

'That's nonsense Nancy.'

'It's not Peter. You became a nasty piece of work. I've never been able to say it until now. Not until there were people around who might protect me from your filthy temper.'

'Hold on,' Dewlish said. 'So Nancy is Camilla's mother?'

'That's right,' Jan said. 'And thank you for trusting me with that information Nancy.'

'God bless you dear,' said Nancy. 'It's about time the truth came out.'

Frank shook his head. 'Bloody hell Jan,' he said. 'You want a job interviewing suspects in counter-terrorism?'

'We're only just getting started here, aren't we Mr. Carew?' said Jan.

He looked at her angrily and appeared ready to get up out of his chair but the sight of Frank moving a pace towards him stopped him.

'The only good thing to come out of this,' Nancy said, 'was him letting Camilla have the flat across the hall so that I could finally get to know my daughter in the last few years. To talk to her and have her confide in me. I carried her and bore her, after all. Roland eventually forgave me, thankfully. But he didn't want this baby girl who wasn't his in our lives. It was too painful after losing darling Daisy. And so I agreed to give Camilla up soon after she was born, to be brought up by her father. His wife knew about us but she too was desperate for a child so went along with it all. It seemed the best solution all round and I believed I was doing the best for my girl.

'He and Martha named her Camilla and raised her as theirs. I was always waiting for the right moment to tell her she was really mine but it never came. I didn't want to upset her, you see. To turn her life upside down. And now the right moment never will come. I was too frightened anyway, if I'm honest. He had power over me…'

Her voice faltered, with the weight of what could have been stopping her. She looked at Carew with contempt.

'Shut up Nancy,' he said. Enough.'

'You've said that too many times and I've been cowed by it too many times,' she replied. 'I'm not listening anymore.'

'That's right. Tell your truth Nancy,' said Jan.

'He owns this whole block of flats. Roly and I, and then just me after he died, were allowed to live here rent-free on the basis we kept our mouths shut.'

'Thank you Nancy,' said Jan, smiling sympathetically at her. Nancy returned the smile, dabbing a tear from her eye.

'OK. So you know all this now but so what?' said Carew. 'None of this makes me a criminal. Aren't you more interested in my daughter's killer than any of my domestic arrangements?'

'Of course,' said Jan. 'But we need to establish a chain...'

The buzzer sounded. Jan looked at her watch. 'Bang on time,' she said and Frank answered the intercom, never taking his eyes off Carew. Mike from the AA meeting entered the room.

'For God's sake,' Carew exclaimed, 'What's he doing here?'

'Oh, we'll get to Mike in a moment,' Jan said. Mike went and sat at the table. Carew watched him with a worried face.

'You didn't really care much for your daughter's boyfriends, did you Mr Carew?'

Jan had found Carew's weak spot and he couldn't stop himself. 'All a bunch of time-wasters, if you ask me.'

'Steady on,' said Dewlish.

'Him chief among them,' Carew said with venom. 'I think Camilla only married him because she knew I thought that. I made a fortune in the City. He lost one. Failed in London, then failed in New York. Came back here with your tail between your legs, trying to get money out of her again. Yes, she told me.'

Dewlish looked insulted, and was meant to be, but he had no riposte.

'I actually loved Camilla,' said Bexington. 'If I just hadn't started drinking again...'

'Maybe you did care for her,' said Carew. 'But you looked to me like you also cared for her money and her social circle rather too much. I grant you were trying to make an honest living out of that antiques shop, but you were just so hopeless in business, for God's sake man. My daughter seemed to have a thing for lame ducks but I hated seeing her squandering the money I gave her on you. Any of you.'

'Well, I didn't kill her.'

296

'Clearly the police think you did. And from what I hear, Nancy saw you coming out of here after... afterwards. Didn't you?'

Nancy could only nod.

'What about Wilson?' Jan asked.

'Camilla was charmed by him and found him even more attractive when it sank in with her that his politics were so the opposite of mine. Nominally anyway. I think he was actually just an opportunist. She was rebellious like that. She knew it would upset me and she liked that idea.'

'Was that what the row was about between you and her on the day of her death?'

Carew looked down at his expensive brogues.

'I will regret to my dying day that that was the last conversation I ever had with her,' he said, slowly, pain infusing his voice. 'All about that nasty piece of work Wilson and him getting money out of her for his wretched political party. My ex-wife had told me about this will of hers. Camilla said to leave her alone. She was dealing with it and would make her own decisions about her own money.'

Jan pressed on.

'When and how did you find out who killed Camilla?'

'What? Well, after they spoke to Bexington again earlier today, of course. DCI Hanley rang me. How has he been released?'

'OK. So not when you went to see Mike Evershot, Gavin Wilson's assistant, yesterday?' She pointed at Mike, who smiled weakly.

'What? This gentleman? No, I went to see him with a couple of my associates to offer him a job. We had heard a lot of good things about the work he was doing with the Labour Party. Good political strategists are hard to find these days. We thought he was wasted and offered him a senior position.'

'That would be while pumping him for information about his boss, would it?' Jan asked.

'I just asked him a few questions about Wilson, that was all.'

'Like his movements on the night Camilla died?'

'Well, yes. But he was sympathising with me about my loss. He simply confided in me that the gossip was that Wilson was bisexual. Stuff that was implied in your newspaper article anyway.'

Mike piped up. 'You caught me at a bad moment. I was beginning to believe that Gavin might well have slipped out of the office that night, having been interviewed by that detective about it. And he looked red-faced when I came back from the pub. Like he'd been doing something active. His hair was tousled, too.

'I was worried at the time that if I said all this to the detective, Gavin would make my life hell. Well, another level of hell. Now I don't have to do that anymore. And I also knew, following our conversation yesterday, that I had to do the right thing and tell the police. I was never going to be interested in your scuzzy politics, however tempting the money you were offering me was. I pretty soon worked out what you wanted.'

'So are you going to tell us what happened this morning, Mr. Carew?' Jan said.

He got up.

'I think I need a lawyer at this point,' he said. 'You're keeping me here against my will. If you please, I'd like to leave.'

'I don't think so,' said Frank. 'We've come too far to stop now, haven't we?'

There was a stand-off, interrupted by Jan.

'Can I have a look at your phone please, Mr Carew?'

'What? No you can't.' He began to reach for the inside of his jacket.

Frank was across in a second, pinning him to the chair and retrieving his phone from the jacket.

'Give that back,' he shouted but it was forlorn.

'Pin number,' Frank instructed.

'Certainly not,' Carew replied.

'Shall we try Camilla's date of birth?'

Nancy supplied it. The phone opened.

'Nice one Nancy,' said Frank.

'I'd like to speak to a lawyer,' said Carew.

'How about speaking to the police?' Jan said. She raised her voice. 'DCI HANLEY. DEENA,' she shouted. Within fifteen seconds, both were inside Nancy's living room. Frank handed over the phone to Hanley.

'Where have you come from?' Carew answered.

'We've been watching you and listening from Camilla's flat,' Hanley said. 'Cameras and microphones set up in the paintings on the wall. We've got all the background we need. And I think this phone will give us all the foreground we need as well.'

He found the video recordings on the phone and sure enough there it was. He looked across at Jan and nodded his respect. A half-smile came to his face. Jan nodded back.

Carew turned and looked at Jan, the colour rising in his face, which grew contorted with anger.

'They all deserve to pay for Camilla's murder, you know,' he spat out, pointing to Dewlish and Bexington. 'That snivelling runt, that loser. And that poisonous snake Wilson.'

42

HANLEY and Deena sat with Carew and his powerless, expensive solicitor in the interview room, a laptop between them.

'OK, Terry,' said Hanley. 'Play it.'

From behind the glass panel separating the observation room, Terry, surrounded by the other murder team members Darren, Rachel and Sanjay, with Jackie Donovan standing behind them, pressed a play button and Carew's mobile phone footage appeared on the laptop's screen.

There, in the middle of what looked like his living room, Gavin Wilson was sitting in a carver chair, his hands tied to the wooden arms with plastic cable. At his right shoulder stood a sizeable man with a moustache. Carew's voice could be heard asking if they were recording and another voice from behind the camera answered yes. Carew took a seat a few feet opposite a clearly terrified Wilson.

CAREW: *Right, Wilson. Let's get down to business, shall we?*
WILSON: *I don't know what you want from me.*
CAREW: *I want answers about the death of my daughter. And you're going to give them to me.*
WILSON: *But I don't know anything about it. It's Bexington you need to be speaking to.*
CAREW: *You see, I think you know everything about it. And you're going to tell me. Vincent here will show you why.*

WILSON: *Shit. What are you planning with those?*

CAREW: *Vincent is very adept with pliers. And slow. He likes removing fingers one by one. As your fingers disappear, you will give me every detail. But if you are honest with me, I might just spare you a painful death to compound an excruciatingly painful final hour or so. What do you say?*

WILSON: *OK. OK. What do you want to know?*

CAREW: *Let's start with the money. My ex-wife rang me to say that Camilla had written a will. I understand why she gave you money for a safe seat and to spite me, but didn't you realise that as soon as the police found out about the legacy to your party you'd persuaded her into they would come for you?*

They all watched as Wilson squirmed, seeming to fight his mixed feelings of anger and terror, not wanting to say anything. But as Vincent moved forward, he wriggled on the chair and started talking.

WILSON: *All right, all right… I did talk to her about making a will. Just so that I could tell my party treasurer and get a pat on the back. Nothing more. We were all encouraged to get people to do it. But it came to a point where I was forced into… into it. I remembered that she'd told me she still felt sorry for Bexington and had included him in the will as well, while she was at it. She told me he was a drinker, had been to AA on and off. I realised I could use him.*

CAREW: *You say you were forced into it. Into what exactly?*

WILSON: *I was trying to impress Camilla about how important I was in the Party. I thought getting money in would impress my bosses. And I did get plenty of kudos when I told them. But they told me guaranteeing her a safe seat was out of the question. The press would have a field day if they found out. I could have unpicked it all, I guess. But that would have humiliated me inside the party. Might well have damaged my own chances of climbing the ladder. And...*

CAREW: *And, what?*

WILSON: *I let it slip one night that I'd met on the quiet with some Palestinian people I had sympathy for. Told Camilla that I'd be campaigning for strategy change within the party in return for them contributing funds. She was shocked, got angry. Said it could jeopardise serious peace negotiations, could cost lives. Threatened to make trouble for me and said she wanted her money back. I began to realise the implications in it for me. Couldn't risk it. Could see my career going up in smoke. As she got angrier, she told me she wouldn't be leaving money to the party any more. I saw an opportunity to solve several problems in one fell swoop...*

CAREW: *So you hatched a plan to kill her. Go on...*

WILSON: *Look, really. They've got Bexington for it. Why don't you just let things be? I can come and work for you. I'm a smart operator. I know politics.*

CAREW: *Let's discuss that later. Once I've heard what really happened. Don't make me lose my patience. I want every detail.*

WILSON: *All right. OK. So, I remembered speaking to my assistant at work, Mike Evershot. I'd noticed he'd stopped drinking. When I pressed him, he told me he went to AA. An idea started forming in my brain. I asked him about meetings, like they might be what I needed, and he told me what happened at them. Gave me a website address. I noticed one in Chelsea not far from Camilla's that was candlelit. Then I remembered a story I'd read about somebody in America confessing to having committed a murder in blackout. So Bexington came into my mind. The ducks all lined up then when a Commons vote was scheduled for that Monday night of our strategy meeting and I saw my chance to do it and have an alibi.*

CAREW: *Ah. yes. The immigration bill. Good to see plans coming together. Except in your case. So how exactly did you take your chance? Make everything clear and detailed for the camera, please…*

They watched the tape as a silence descended again, Wilson looking terrified anew. Carew leant forward, growing angrier.

CAREW: Talk, damn you, unless you'd rather deal with Vincent.

WILSON: When the MPs went off to Westminster, I told the others in the meeting to go over to the pub. I went to my locker in the basement of the building and put on a hoodie and puffer jacket and the kind of suede boots Bexington wore. I'd seen him dressed like that myself recently when he came to my flat, and to Camilla's. I had a motorbike out the back of the building and slipped out.

CAREW: And you rode over there and killed her.

WILSON: That's the long and the short of it.

CAREW: That may be the short of it. I want the long version.

WILSON: Honestly. I've given you the whys. I really don't think…

CAREW: Well, I do. Keep going. If you want even a glimmer of surviving this ordeal.

WILSON: So, I got there. She wondered why I looked so scruffy. Even joked that I looked a bit like Bexington. I didn't say anything. I just grabbed the scarf that I knew would be on the clothes pegs and when she turned her back to me, I… did it.

CAREW: Did she put up a struggle?

WILSON: Yes. She did.

CAREW: She was always brave. Unlike the bastards she went out with. Then what?

WILSON: I texted Bexington from Camilla's phone. Told him to come round. I knew he would if Camilla asked him. And he'd be on the hallway CCTV. When he buzzed, I let him in and I went and hid in the kitchen. I kept the door ajar and could see him. Checked he was wearing what he usually did. Once

I'd seen him, I didn't hang around in case he started looking around the flat. I made my way out of the back door in the kitchen, through the garden and into the alley where I'd left my motorbike. Then I went to that AA meeting a few streets away. I put on some expensive fake facial hair I'd bought on the internet, rubbed some vodka on it, and I told them I thought I might have killed someone in my drunken state. I did think about using the name James in the meeting but decided that might be too obvious. I mean, a murderer wouldn't, would they? But I figured that once it came out in the papers that Bexington was a suspect, someone at the meeting would put two and two together and go the police and identify him. The clothes. The voice. I put on a posh accent. It's easy for me. I heard enough of them at school and university. But there was a problem.

CAREW: *Which was?*

WILSON: *I recognised someone in the meeting and I thought he'd recognised me.*

CAREW: *Who was he?*

WILSON: *Labour Party activist. Sean Malahide. I'd met him at a club in Soho where I was a member and he worked and we'd had a bit of a thing for a while.*

CAREW: *So it's true you're bisexual. And this was the young man found strangled the next night in Battersea?*

WILSON: *Yes. After I left the AA meeting, I went back to Victoria Street, put the clothes back in my locker there along with Camilla's mobile. Been meaning to dispose of it all but haven't found a quiet moment yet. Police been around the place. I couldn't have the scarf being found at the scene by Bexington as he would have got rid of it knowing he was going to be a suspect. When I got to thinking the next day, I realised I needed to go and see Sean and I took the scarf, knowing it might be useful if I needed to take some action. I persuaded Sean to let me in to his flat by telling him that I needed his help for a drink problem. Compassionate bloke that he is, he did. But he was agitated and it was obvious he'd recognised me from the night before and said he'd been thinking of going to the police. I couldn't have that. I then left the scarf at Sean's place to implicate Bexington for that as well. I knew his DNA would be on it. I used gloves so there would be no trace of me in the flat. Took Sean's phone too.*

CAREW: You complete and utter bastard. You're not getting away with this.

WILSON: But you said that if I told you everything and was honest, we could discuss me coming to work for you. I can get you inside information...

CAREW: You honestly think I'm going to work with my daughter's murderer? Vince. Turn this thing off. I said turn the bloody thing off.

The recording ended. The laptop's screen went black. A silence descended on the room. On the other side of the glass, Terry and Darren, Rachel and Sanjay, high-fived. Donovan smiled.

'Peter Carew,' Hanley began in measured tones. 'Pending the agreement of the CPS, which I believe will be a formality, you will be charged with the murder of Gavin Wilson.'

The solicitor intervened.

'Hold it right there, DCI Hanley. You may have your confession from Wilson about the first two murders but you have absolutely no evidence that my client killed him. There is no footage of that.'

'Wilson was strangled with a scarf,' said Hanley.

'Which is where?'

'I suspect it's been disposed of by now.'

'Well then,' said the solicitor shrugging his shoulders.

The door to the interview room burst open and in walked Jackie Donovan.

'Turn off the tape please, DCI Hanley.'

He did as he was bidden.

'I did wonder if some hotshot lawyer might raise that,' said Donovan. 'Fortunately we have some insurance.'

Donovan nodded to Deena, who handed her a file. Carew and the lawyer looked worried.

'The man in Mrs Preston's flat this afternoon, Frank Phillips,' said Donovan. 'Were you at all involved with an assault on him two nights ago?'

'No. Of course not.'

'Only, as you now know, he works in counter-terrorism and this file they have supplied us with tells a very sordid story of some rather nasty, even shocking, things that you and your political party have been involved in.'

'Such as?'

'Let's just say, that if the contents of this file get out, your reputation would be compromised pretty much for ever. You would be disgraced as a man and your career as a politician would certainly be over. Murdering the man who killed your daughter is one thing. You might get a few less years in prison due to a judge and jury's sympathy. What you and your mates in UK First have been plotting is quite another and would get you sent down for a very long time.'

'This is outrageous, Chief Superintendent,' said the solicitor.

'If, on the other hand, you felt able to confess, then the file might just go back to counter-terrorism for them to put in a cabinet.'

'This is blackmail.'

'Leave it Nigel. I want to speak.'

'Good,' said Donovan. 'Turn the tape back on DCI Hanley.' She left the room.

'Can I ask you if you were involved in an assault against one Frank Phillips two nights ago, Mr Carew?'

'I knew of him but didn't know what he looked like. I got word that his people had been taking an interest, so I had one of my associates follow him. Vincent. Just told him to rough Phillips up. First step really in fighting back against them. Let them know we knew.'

'But he didn't know the real reason why he was being roughed up. He thought it was Bexington who had assaulted him.'

'A felicitous by-product. I think once it was all over, he might have put two and two together.'

'Perhaps you'd like to tell us about Gavin Wilson's final moments and how you expected to get away with it.'

'Fine, OK. I did it, yes. I strangled Wilson with Vincent's scarf after the recording stopped. When I got to Wilson's, my aim was to get the confession out of him on film and keep it back for if it was needed, should Bexington get off. I could have edited the final part. With things as they stood, Bexington would be tried for the murder of Camilla, and hopefully be found guilty, as well as that of Malahide. And Wilson would also have been punished. By paying the ultimate price. His life.'

'But if you'd given us that footage had Bexington got off, we'd have asked you why you held it back.'

'And I'd have come clean. That I wanted Bexington to pay. I would have been charged with perverting the course of justice, I know, but it would have been worth it. Grieving father. Public understanding. Minimum punishment. And I would have made sure somebody was convicted for Camilla's murder. I could have found another way to punish Bexington later.'

'Nice,' said Hanley, exchanging looks with Deena. 'But that footage does suggest you killed Wilson.'

'Suggests, perhaps. Can be explained as the act of a desperate man seeking justice. I could say I left and Dewlish had come over, roused by Wilson's text, and done the dirty deed. I dropped one of his cuff links under a chair at Wilson's place. It had the initials SD on it. He'd left them at Camilla's flat a while back after the divorce and I saw them on a dressing table. She'd kept them for sentimental reasons. I knew your people would find it sooner or later.'

'And the text, from Wilson's phone to Dewlish?' Hanley asked.

'I found his phone and got Wilson to send it as soon as we arrived at his place. So his fingerprints only would be on his phone. I thought the time on it would show up as being before he was dead, so that Dewlish would have time to get over there and kill him.'

'But he didn't know Wilson?'

'That's what he would have claimed. But the text suggested that Dewlish had killed Camilla, Wilson knew and would be going to the police. Motive enough for Dewlish to go over there and murder him.'

'We did indeed see the text on Dewlish's phone when we interviewed him again. But there were no others, nor any phone calls. He said he didn't recognise the number and was baffled by it.'

'Could have been lying. Could all have been conducted on burner phones that Dewlish disposed of after he killed Wilson. You know that. Wilson might have been breaking cover as he wanted a record on his main phone. Anyway, I was also going to provide some witnesses who saw Dewlish going into Wilson's flat that morning.'

'We might have bought it, I suppose,' said Hanley.

'Look, I just wanted all three of those scum to get the punishment they deserved,' said Carew. 'They didn't deserve my girl and ruined her life.'

He paused. Hanley picked up the file that was on the desk and clasped it to his chest and Carew continued.

'I now want it to be known that I killed the killer of my daughter. It was one last thing I could do for her, to ensure justice rather than risk any fancy lawyers getting any one of these three bastards off. No disrespect Nigel.'

The solicitor could only shrug his shoulders and shake his head.

'So there you have it. My confession. I hope a jury will understand a father's love and desire for justice for his daughter, however misguided, and that I will be treated with some understanding and leniency when I am tried and sentenced. I hope, too, that one day when I have completed my punishment, I may be able to return to society and play an active role once more.'

'Don't you dare use love as a justification for what you did,' said Hanley. 'Or expect us to understand why you took the law into your own hands.' This time, Carew's lawyer had nothing with which to interrupt Hanley as he spoke of a murder charge.

Deena got up, walked out of the room and dialled Jan's mobile.

'Go ahead,' she said after it had rung just once at the other end, 'He sang. Just like you said he would. You can print every bit of it as per your terms and conditions.'

SATURDAY

43

SHE had always managed to keep weekends off as part of her deal, despite the daily and Sunday papers being merged nowadays, but Jan thought she'd show her face in the office for an hour before her lunch date. She always liked going in after a triumphant scoop that not only had other journalistic colleagues and outlets envious and admiring, but had got the nation talking. Besides, as a satisfying cherry on this rich mix of a cake, she'd persuaded Vickers to change his shifts so he'd be in, forced to feel like an outsider at a party where everybody else knew each other intimately.

As she came through the reception area, this morning's front page projected on to the big screen greeted her. At the top were pictures of Wilson and Carew with a white-on-black strapline of:

Political duo in murder mayhem

And underneath the banner:

**WE NAIL CHOKER –
AND *HIS* KILLER**

Then came **Exclusive by Jan Mason** above four tight paragraphs containing the bones of last night's events, expertly condensed. This then turned inside to the rest of the story, before a double-page spread on Jan's role in cracking the crime. After that came two more pages of backgrounders on the main characters, along with a story, written by Danny the duty reporter, of quotes by Jackie Donovan praising Jan and acknowledging the role the press could still play in helping the police despite stricter regulations these days. Further into the paper, all the politicos got in on the act, too, chronicling the downfall of a significant national figure.

She'd loved seeing it online last night, of course she had, and watching the big News at Ten bulletins leading on it while she luxuriated in her robe after a long bubble bath, drinking Champagne and eating Kettle chips. She'd also been pleased to have a text exchange with Bexington.

Can't thank you enough. So relieved somebody believed me.

Touch and go at times. But the truth will out.

All got a bit hairy and scary.

Yes. But hopefully it will all have taught us both something. Adversity does have a habit of introducing people to themselves.

Good thought. Thanks to you again Jan.

It was gratifying to watch her Twitter following rattle up towards 200,000 too, but there was nothing like seeing it all in print – going to the paper shop first thing this Saturday morning (she'd not been able to find a newsagent who would deliver for years now) and having it staring everyone in the face. There on a newsstand. Except that it was one cutting that her mother wouldn't be able to add to her collection in the bottom drawer of her St Mark's care home in Wakefield. Jan had given a sigh at this thought as she handed over her money to Pietr behind the till.

People buzzing about the building were quick to give her a smile and a "great work Jan" as she waited for a flat white at the coffee cart. So too were her colleagues when she arrived on the newsroom floor. Well, almost all of them.

She'd barely taken off her coat before, predictably, he piped up.

'What you got for a follow-up then?' Vickers asked.

'Not a lot Ivan. There's not a lot else is there? Wilson's dead. Carew's been charged. End of story.'

'Something with Bexington maybe?'

'What, after you slagged me off for writing his interview the other night?'

'You can't just quit on this story.'

'That, Ivan,' she said loudly, so pretty much the whole newsroom would hear her, 'is a bit rich coming from you, is it not? You chose to have an early cut last night on the biggest human interest news night of the year for this paper. I don't think I'll be taking any lectures from an absentee news editor.'

There were sniggers all across the floor. Sarah, who had put it all together the night before, made an excellent job of suppressing her delight.

Vickers started to blurt out that Jan had told him last night that she had nothing and that it was a good idea for him to go home early but he didn't get far, before the Editor had appeared on the news room floor.

'Ah, Jan,' he said, 'You should be having a day off.'

'Just thought I'd come in and see if you needed me here?' She winked at Vickers.

'No, no. You deserve some time for yourself after all that amazing content last night. Bloody amazing. I'm glad you're here though as it saves me a call. Just wanted to thank you for giving me the same quality of big story that you gave my predecessor.'

'Thank you George. If it's OK, I'm going to have a nice lunch now with some contacts who helped me bring it all together.'

'Well, make sure it's lavish, involves bubbles and posh nosh, and send the bill to me.' He smiled. Jan could only smile at Vickers, red thunder in his face.

'Could I just have a word in private, too?' the Editor asked.

Jan nodded and they walked out on to the terrace overlooking the Thames. They had it to themselves.

'So what's with taking the voluntary redundancy?' he said.

'Oh, I don't know. Just feels like time for a change. Thinking of going freelance. Get a bit of my life back.'

'This is your life, Jan,' he replied. 'And I'm not going to accept it. This redundancy round is for dead wood, not the likes of you. I need you bringing in more stories like this. I might get the sack myself if the proprietor sees I can't hold on to an asset like you.'

Jan smiled. 'Sorry about that,' she said.

'Look,' he said. 'Go and have lunch with your people. Think it over at the weekend. Then let's talk again on Monday, yes? At least do that for me? I've got this idea about you focusing on special human interest investigations...'

'OK,' she said. She didn't want to say any more lest she found herself committing to something she hadn't thought through.

'Thank you.'

As he turned and went back inside. Jan's phone rang. It was Robert.

'Hey you,' he said. 'Congratulations on your exclusive.'

'Look...'

'No. It's not a dig. Honestly. Great work. You've done something good there Jan. Helped secure justice for people.'

'Thanks. I appreciate that.'

'Sorry I didn't ring last night. Was shattered when I got back from Wakefield. I registered the death, sorted some sadmin.'

'I'm really grateful for you taking that on, bruv.'

'I'm fixing up the funeral for Thursday 26th. That work for you? I can't really legislate for a big story...'

'No. I'll be there. Definitely. Big story or not.'

'Great. And Jan... Mum would have been proud. She would have cut it all out for her file.'

*

The red from crying in Jan's eyes had thankfully gone when she arrived at Le Gavroche. Deena, Frank and Nancy were all waiting. Hugs and kisses were followed by lobster and lashings of fizz, except for Frank who was more than happy with elderflower cordial and sparkling water.

'To my friends,' said Jan in her toast.

'I'm glad to hear we're more than contacts,' said Deena.

'Well, contacts primarily today so I can claim the astronomical cost of this lunch back.'

'It may breach guidelines about common sense hospitality between journalists and police officers,' said Frank.

'Stop being so common and start talking sense,' said Jan. 'I think given the result everyone has had, it'll be acceptable to Jackie Donovan and your boss.'

'What's the difference then between friends and contacts, dear?' Nancy asked.

'Well,' Jan said. 'You ring contacts. Friends ring you.'

'You feel like more than a friend now... what with everything,' Nancy said.

Jan reached across the table and took her hand.

'Remind me not to ring you any more,' Frank said and Jan smiled.

'Of course technically, Nancy,' Deena said. 'You did initially pervert the course of justice by not telling us that Camilla was your daughter.'

'Oh, lighten up,' Jan said. 'Or you'll be paying for this yourself.'

'OK,' said Deena. 'Busted. But tell me Nancy, what made you tell Jan?'

'I don't know,' Nancy began. 'When you get to my age, mostly people ignore you. Those who do speak to you usually want something from you. They often listen only to what's in their interests. Jan took me and my story seriously.'

'It's kind of our job to do that,' said Deena.

'Maybe,' said Nancy. 'But there's ways of speaking to somebody beyond being purely professional, like your Tommy Handley.'

'Dave. But point taken,' said Deena.

'Jan here, she was interested in me. In my life, my husband, my story.' And Nancy smiled at Jan.

'Thank you Nancy. It's part of my job too, but yes, I am interested in you and your story and I very quickly got to like you. Sit long enough with people and everyone has a story. And they usually want to tell it.'

'It's true,' said Nancy. 'I'd kept Camilla a secret for so long. I really did want to talk about her to someone. Still do. There was so much more to her than has been portrayed.'

'Right, I'll be round for tea tomorrow to hear all about her,' Jan said. 'You have been brilliant you know. So brave in the circumstances.'

'Thank you dear,' Nancy replied.

'Can I ask you Jan,' said Deena. 'When you rang me to tell me all that about Wilson, to persuade me to get Hanley to play ball and come to Nancy's flat, how had you worked it all out?'

'Well, it started to come together when I was sitting in Frank's AA meeting yesterday. I had some space to think. James Bexington told me that Wilson had been a Rugby player, so he had physical presence to be able to overcome people. Then when I spoke to Mike Evershot yesterday, he told me a few things that added up.

'Wilson liked mimicking posh people, he was good at it he said, which meant he could have impersonated James at the AA meeting. Comparing pictures of the two, with facial hair and wearing a hoodie, I realised Wilson could definitely pass for him. And Mike had his doubts about Wilson staying at Labour HQ for those two hours and more. There was a motorcycle courier at the AA meeting yesterday, which jogged my memory about seeing an old picture online of Wilson astride a motorbike. I asked Mike and he said, yes, he did have a bike. Kept it out the back sometimes.'

'Mike also told me that the only CCTV was at the front of the building,' said Deena.

'Yes, and Nancy, you took me into the back door of Lyme Mansions down an alley. It occurred to me that Camilla had probably given Wilson a key and he'd come in that way. Which was why he wasn't on the hall CCTV.'

'And finding all his gear in his locker at work?' asked Deena, 'Which was what persuaded Hanley to go along with your scheme…'

'Again, James. He said people at school who knew Wilson said he was a thief who used to hide his stash in his locker. I was worried he might have got rid of it all somewhere else but I reckoned all the anxiety about Sean being at the meeting could have thrown his plans out and he didn't get round to it in time.'

'Well it was some stash all right,' said Deena. 'Motorcycle helmet. Two phones, Camilla's and Sean's. Fake facial hair, which frankly looked ridiculous on its own but seemed to look real enough on to fool an AA meeting.'

Frank shrugged his shoulders. 'It was candlelit,' he said. 'What can I tell you?'

'And of course hoodie, puffer jacket, black jeans. Plus brown suede Chelsea boots.'

'It didn't really register with me when you told me the man at the AA meeting was wearing Chelsea boots, Frank,' said Jan. 'But then I remembered that Bexington was wearing laced-up suede boots when I interviewed him. That's what gave me new belief that he didn't do it.'

'Damn,' said Frank. 'When you first said suede boots to me after interviewing Bexington, I just assumed the Chelsea boots that I saw in the meeting. That'll teach me.'

'I wouldn't beat yourself up,' said Jan. 'Having been to that meeting yesterday, I can see why you were so torn about all this and not seeing things straight.'

'Thank you,' said Frank.

'And what about the footage of Wilson on Carew's phone? How did you know he would have that?' Deena asked.

'Something Mike said,' Jan replied, 'He said Carew had told him he would be recording their talk on his phone as he did with all important contacts, especially those in politics. He never knew when he might need it later to remind people of their agreements. I couldn't be sure what was on there, but I was certain there would be some kind of evidence of his encounter with Wilson – that he might have been trying to use him in some way before killing him.'

'It's odd, you know,' said Deena. 'I saw Carew in the street with his goons after I came out from seeing Mike Evershot on Wednesday. Didn't think any more about it really. His party's office is not far from there.'

'No reason you should have connected them,' said Jan. 'Though didn't you tell me that I'd be surprised at what was relevant?'

'Touché,' said Deena, smiling.

Jan continued: 'Once he'd twigged Wilson, via Mike confirming his suspicions, it made sense that Carew would want the dirt recorded knowing that the Bexington case could fall apart.'

'What about you, Frank?' Deena asked.

'How do you mean?'

'Well, we had Wilson admitting to the two murders but as Carew had stopped the recording before he killed him there's no evidence, as such. What exactly was it that you told Donovan that made him want to sing?'

'Can't tell you in detail,' Frank said. 'But let's put it this way. His whole life and career built on being a patriot would have been over. There was a scheme to blame an Islamist group for an atrocity his party were plotting but thankfully it was only in the planning stages. We'll round up those involved and still have it on him when he gets out of jail if he goes back to his old thuggish ways.'

'And don't forget what Jan said earlier,' said Nancy. 'I think Peter wanted to talk. He was sad and angry about Camilla's death. He wanted justice to be done, and he wanted vindication for taking the law into his own hands. He's also a politician. He likes to justify his behaviour, no matter how unacceptable. People get tired of keeping secrets.'

They all nodded.

'Wish we had more people like you in counter-terrorism, Jan,' said Frank. 'Someone who can ask the right questions the right way, who understands what makes people tick and gets them to talk.'

'What's happening with James?' Nancy asked.

'A free if sad man,' Deena said.

'I think he needs a goal in life,' Nancy added. 'Apparently, Camilla has left me some money. For being a lovely neighbour, the solicitor said. Quite a lot actually.'

'That might explain why Camilla's mother didn't want to talk to us about what other things might be in the will,' said Deena. 'Didn't want us looking into you.'

'I'm sad to be receiving this money in many ways, naturally,' said Nancy. 'It's particularly poignant because the will apparently said that if I died before she did, which was of course likely, it was to go instead to any children she might have.'

A silence came over the gathering.

'I think it should be used for a young person's benefit. I wonder if James could administer a scholarship fund for a drama student? He has a little bit of money of his own from Camilla now but we need to find something for him to do to stop him spending it.'

'You're far too compassionate,' said Jan.

'I can afford to be,' said Nancy. 'And at my age, I need a bit of credit with Him upstairs.' She pointed skywards and they laughed.

'Frank. Perhaps you could help him a bit as well?' said Jan.

'Maybe. If he's willing to come to a meeting.'

'What about Simon Dewlish?' Nancy asked.

'Can be summed up quickly,' said Deena. 'Got his passport back, immediately headed for Heathrow. He seems to be hoping that there's still just about enough British prestige left to persuade some Middle East potentate to invest in some more of his snake oil.'

'And how's DCI Hanley?' Jan asked. Deena smiled.

'Well, he's got his result. Didn't much like Donovan coming over to him in front of everyone and saying how well you and I had done in sorting all this, though. Or her quotes in the paper praising you and saying how the press and police still need to work together.'

'Tough on Tommy and the causes of Tommy,' said Frank.

'Don't be too hard on him,' said Deena. 'He gave me some good advice about playing things by the book but being willing to look at the footnotes in the book too.'

'Meaning?' Jan asked.

'Something you might well understand. To not be afraid to do things that might seem left field. Which was another reason he gave you your head on staging that scenario last night. And he did pay you a compliment when I spoke to him this morning.'

'Really. What did he say?'

'Said he was off to West Ham and he hoped they played half as well as you have this week.'

'Wow,' said Jan. 'There's a first time for everything.'

They laughed and complimented the waiter on the lobster when he came to clear away the plates.

'So Jan. I'm guessing you're not taking the redundancy,' said Deena.

'What's all this?' Frank asked.

'You're guessing wrong, Deena,' said Jan. 'Going out at the top. Going to get Mum's funeral out of the way then maybe travel. Do a bit of freelancing. Maybe get a column somewhere.'

'Wow,' said Frank. 'I can't believe that,' said Deena. 'Goodness,' said Nancy.

'But you love newspapers, Jan,' said Deena.

'Being a freelance, working from home. Is that really for you?' asked Frank.

'I did love them. But it's not the same. The old sights and smells and sounds are gone. All a bit antiseptic now.'

'Everything changes,' said Nancy. 'And we all have to change too. You've done it so far. But people stay the same. Full of flaws that make stories. And newspapers, I would think, still contain people with flaws themselves who want to tell those stories.'

Jan paused to take it in.

'You're right Nancy. There's still memories, history in the walls. The sounds of clacking keyboards. TVs tuned to the news channels. Gallows humour. Only journalists in groups see the world in such a warped and wonderful way…'

'There you are dear,' said Nancy.

Frank and Deena were listening intently. Jan flashed them a quick smile.

'Anyway,' she said, changing the subject 'How are things at your office Frank, now everyone knows your background? You OK talking about it with us?'

'Sure,' he replied. 'I trust everyone here. To be honest, I'm glad it's all out in the open. I've heard it said around AA rooms that honesty is our only way of life and I've believed it, but never put it into practice in my job. I guess I thought it would count against me. But I feel good today. Back on track.'

'Good stuff,' said Jan, taking another glug of Champagne.

'Want me to keep a chair free for you at a meeting?' Frank asked.

'Save it for somebody who needs it,' Jan replied. She noticed that Deena seemed to be day-dreaming.

'All OK, Deena? This is a good day, no? Want to tell your face?'

'Oh, yes. Of course. Was just thinking about your news. I'm shocked Jan. And I was also thinking that it would be nice to share a day like today with someone, you know, special.'

'I'm long past that,' Jan said. 'Sisters before misters and all that.'

'Yeah, but, you know. Just now and then, when you've got something to celebrate.'

'I know what you mean,' said Jan and they giggled. 'Sounding like you might not be over Rashid. Spoken to him lately?'

'No. He hasn't rung.'

'Well, ring him then, for God's sake. Don't let life pass you by.'

'Relationship advice from you?'

They both laughed. Deena picked up her mobile and began texting.

Jan's mobile buzzed with a text. *Can we speak?* Will Gaunt was asking.

She took no notice. Deena and Frank began talking shop and Nancy took her opportunity.

'A young man texting you?' she asked Jan.

'Well, a man.'

'And someone you like, by the look on your face.'

'I do. Or maybe did. He tried to use me, though, Nancy. Though to be fair, he did come clean and apologise. Said he'd got to like me.'

'Well, that sounds promising. If my Roland could forgive me for what I'd done...'

Jan texted Gaunt back. *Perhaps you'd like to take me to a funeral in Wakefield on the 26th?*

Your driver awaits milady, came the reply just ahead of her phone ringing.

'Sorry,' she said to Nancy, Frank and Deena, getting up to go and find privacy. 'Got to take this. It's the office.'

'Yes, Ivan,' she said once outside. Pacing the Mayfair street, she listened with growing concern, then anger, as the *Schadenfreude* in her vengeful news editor's voice rose with each sentence. 'Shit, shit, shit,' she shouted, alarming passers-by.

She brought a face as dark as the November afternoon back into the restaurant to interrupt the revelry.

'Problem dear?' Nancy asked.

'You could say that,' Jan replied. 'They're letting Carew go.'

'What? Surely not…' said Nancy, a fear growing in her voice.

'You mean not contesting bail?' Frank asked.

'Go, go. As in dropping the charges,' said Jan.

Deena's phone beeped. 'Bloody hell, you're right. I've got a message on the team What's App.'

'How the hell is that even possible?' Frank wondered. 'We had him coughing to it all.'

'Seems his lawyer persuaded the CPS that the confession was invalid due to Jackie Donovan putting the pressure on with your file, Frank,' said Deena. 'If she denies it, she knows she's lying and that will leak out. And, as we know, that footage with Wilson stops short of the actual killing. Hanley's fuming on the What's App. Says Carew reckons that him telling Wilson on the footage that he wouldn't be getting away with it just meant he was going to turn him in if Wilson didn't give himself up. It was all just threats, he says. Now saying Carew left with Wilson alive. Suggests we look at the evidence against Dewlish again. Yeah, right.'

'But it's already been in the paper, Jan,' said Frank. 'His reputation's in tatters anyway.'

'Lawyer saying they will be suing us for printing details of a false confession made under duress, news of which should never have been released, according to my bastard of a news editor,' said Jan,

'That means he'll be trying to get us as well for wrongful arrest,' said Deena. 'Jeepers, we're going to get such grief, from Donovan down.'

'Plus,' added Jan, 'Carew's got friends in high places.'

'What does that mean?' Frank asked.

'The CPS has had a call on the quiet from the Home Sec, according to our Westminster crew. Apparently, Carew has dirt on a load of the government. Now they have dirt on him, they're holding the cards and can shut him up. And they reckon they might get Carew to defect to their party.'

'Why would they want him? He's scum,' said Frank.

'Useful and popular scum,' said Jan. 'If he goes over to them, he takes a lot of voters with him and they get to silence a loose cannon forever on TV stirring up Middle England about their policies being too liberal.'

The table descended into stunned silence.

'This is too cruel,' said Nancy, reaching for a tissue to dab the tears beginning to fall. 'What will happen to me? He owns my flat.'

'Don't you worry,' said Jan. 'We won't let him get near you, will we Frank?'

'Of course not. We still have that file.'

'Stinking people,' said Jan. They and their dodgy mates just think they can get away with anything these days, don't they? Literally even murder.'

She got out her mobile and called up ED. He answered immediately.

'I want to withdraw my application for voluntary redundancy, George,' she said.

Deena, Frank and Nancy all smiled at her as they listened in. Nancy gave a thumbs-up.

'I'm not having Carew getting off and suing us. He's guilty and dangerous. We've got to fight it George. I want to stay on it and go after him.'

'Agreed Jan,' he replied. 'We can't take this lying down. This is great news. See you Monday and we'll talk about a pay rise. I've also got another great story I want to put you on. Disappearance of a 1960s Miss World down on the South Coast. Needs the Jan Mason touch.'

'Sounds good. I can work on both stories. You know about women and multi-tasking...'

Jan ended the call and accepted the congratulations of Frank, Deena and Nancy.

'Thank you all,' she said. 'But enough of that. We've got work to do. Tell me Frank, those files of yours, ones like Carew's... they've been known to end up on trains or park benches by mistake, haven't they?'

NOTES AND ACKNOWLEDGEMENTS

I didn't think I would write another novel after my debut OUTER CIRCLE appeared in January 2018. In fact, bereft, I didn't think I would write anything again after my wife Vikki Orvice died in February 2019, aged just 56.

It was Vikki, an English Literature graduate and avid reader, who had encouraged me to fulfil my ambition to write fiction after a career of writing sports books and being a football correspondent for national newspapers. She was my muse, in so many ways indeed, with the character Jan Mason based on her, V having herself been a news reporter before becoming a sports writer.

A few months after Vikki died, I saw something on Twitter about the celebrated crime and thriller author Sophie Hannah hosting a writing workshop, with one place left. Vikki had booked and interviewed Sophie for our local book festival and I thought it was something that would at least get me out of the house. At the event, Sophie said she had become course director for a new part-time Master of Studies degree in Crime and Thriller Writing at Cambridge University. She suggested I apply.

That day, though not an easy one with my grief still raw, marked the first stirring in me of thoughts about writing again, and I would go on over the next year to pen a memoir about Vikki, and watching cricket to deal with my grief, entitled *The Breath of Sadness*. It also got me thinking about applying for Sophie's course. After considering it for a month, I did and was awarded a place.

I went to Cambridge with the germ of an idea – a premise – for another novel. What would be the consequences if somebody walked into an AA meeting and shared that they might have killed their partner in a drunken blackout? From there, over the next two years of our Covid-interrupted course, DON'T TALK took shape.

Thus am I grateful first to Sophie for helping set me back on my writing path, then her expertise in imparting the intricacies of plot, structure, hooks and twists that have gone into this book and helped progress the original idea. I am also grateful for the support and knowledge of Midge Gillies and Elly Griffiths at Cambridge, along with my supervisors Emily Winslow and Jon Appleton. The feedback and fellowship from my fellow students, notably Tracey Ann Morton and Matt Williams, have been a huge help through a tough time.

In that regard, I don't think I would coped without the support and practical help of my loving and loved children, Alex and Jack. Alex has also helped me set up and run V Books. I am immensely proud of, and grateful for, two wonderful human beings.

For personal and pastoral help, my thanks go to Tony Adams, Jimmy Mulville, Ian Chapman, Steve Claridge, Seth Burkett, Mike McMonagle, Rev Tom Sander, Shekhar Bhatia, Emma and Richard Visick, Moira Thoubboron, Serena Bird, Janet King, Jane Purdon, Amanda Smith, Amanda Newbery, Sacha Sachag, Daniela Sieff, Jackie Brock-Doyle, Liz Sparke and Rosemary Clough.

Thanks also to my skilful and perceptive editor Claire Baldwin, brilliant cover designer Steve Leard, and to three very different but all superb writers in Rev. Richard Coles, Candy Denman and Stephen Leather – Vikki's great mate from her days as a news reporter on the *Daily Mail* – for reading this book and contributing cover quotes. Special thanks to "Monaco" Mick O'Mahony, retired Metropolitan Police Flying

Squad detective for generously sharing his expertise and advising me on police procedures.

I will also be forever in the debt of Bill W and Bruce Lloyd, who both continue to save my life on a daily basis, and have done so for 34 and 30 years respectively.

That life was enhanced for 23 of those years by my Vikki, for whom my love and gratitude will never die. It dawned on me at Cambridge that Jan Mason, the character I most enjoyed writing in OUTER CIRCLE probably because she was so Vikki, could now become the protagonist of a series of books. That way, I could take her wherever I wanted to go and she could still be with me whenever I wrote. I hope something in the resourceful and resilient Jan inspires you the way V continues to do with me.

Ian Ridley
St Albans,
September 2022

ALSO IN THIS SERIES

OUTER CIRCLE
A Jan Mason Story – Book 1

"An outstanding debut novel – storytelling at its finest."
STEPHEN LEATHER

"This exceptional thriller is one of the best books I've read all year."
NATASHA HARDING, THE SUN

ALSO BY IAN RIDLEY

The Breath of Sadness:
On love, grief and cricket

"Ian Ridley's beautifully crafted memoir shows there is no right or wrong way to grieve, and yet grieve we must. A moving insight."
JULIA SAMUEL, author of Sunday Times bestsellers Grief Works and This Too Shall Pass.

"A fine meditation on life, love, death and grief forged during a gentle summer of county cricket."
MICHAEL ATHERTON, former England cricket captain.